"This book should be in every home." —**Myrlene Tippetts**, Lindon, Utah

"A page-turning debut from an author whose writing is filled not only with excitement, but also with true patriotism and principle in a time when both are sorely needed. This book will not only thrill you, it will inspire and educate you too!"—**Darren Andrews**, Owner of ldsfreedomportal.net, Hertfordshire, England

"Donny's ability to convey the complex yet fundamental principles of economics, freedom, and the Constitution is uncanny. The story of *Hanging by The Thread* draws you into an intense action plot while educating the reader. The story keeps a quick pace that is well thought out and has you guessing till the end. This entertaining book is a must read for anyone seeking to better understand the founding principles and the present and future state of the noble nation of America and Freedom.

"I cannot tell you how many times I have tried to regurgitate the lessons from *Hanging by The Thread* in classes, in assignments, and to friends. These principles are true and so poorly understood, and Donny's teaching method is exactly what is needed. These are things that my generation is screaming to be taught but we know not where to find them." —**Paul Garner**, Graduate Student, University of Hawaii/ Taber, Alberta, Canada

"It's not very often that one finds a book that is both grippingly entertaining and applicably educational. *Hanging by The Thread* is both. In this, his first published book, Donald Anderson wastes no time in showing his ability to tell an intricate, well thought-out, suspense-filled, action-packed story. Interwoven throughout the book, Anderson is able to teach clear principles of truth in a way that makes them widely applicable to economic and political situations we see all around us today.

"When you pick up this book, be prepared to devote some time to it; you won't want to put it down. As a bonus, you won't want to miss the lecture series in the appendix. It provides a powerful framework for better understanding connections between economic freedom and human happiness. Donald powerfully illustrates these connections through the economic and political lenses our Founders used to set up this great natio[n]

“You will be left with a greater understanding and appreciation for the Constitution and the liberty that it delivers, and will be able to better recognize the forces that are seeking to quietly and carefully cut the very threads that hold it up." —**Tyler Griffin**, PhD, Educational Technologist, Providence, Utah

“There is a deep and growing concern that our basic freedoms are slowly eroding as government increasingly seeks to provide all its citizens with a better life. Yet in so doing, we lose elements of individual freedom that, when practiced virtuously, have led to growth and prosperity. We risk becoming increasingly dependent on government for our prosperity; and in so doing, we willingly--yet unwittingly--progressively give up our individual freedoms. As this happens, the virtues of a hard working, industrious society also begin to erode as we increasingly rely on the government to provide for every man that all might be equal.

“The diminishing of individual freedom is the premise of Donald Anderson's first book, *Hanging by The Thread.* Packed with action, adventure, intrigue, danger and surprise at every turn, this book is a page-turner that highlights the potential threats to our individual freedoms, and does so in a masterful way that grips the reader and provides keen insights and principles underlying the basic freedoms. Donny also brings out the power of influence that concerned and active citizens can have in the protection of those same freedoms.” —**Reed Anderson**, Brussels, Belgium

“Considering that I am not remotely interested in politics or economics, it speaks highly of the author and this gripping story that though I hesitantly picked it up, I didn't put it down until I had read every single word. Donald Anderson has created an engaging story that is as entertaining as it is educational, and will be so to all audiences. It is fantastic!” —**Brook Mora**, Cancun, Mexico

"Only Donny could make economics and politics this exciting and understandable! This is a lot more than just a great story." —**Brian Smith**, Wellsville, Utah

"What an intriguing way to learn more about economics and the potential plagues that face our country. *Hanging by The Thread* is entertaining as well as enlightening. A very fun read!" —**Laura Johnson**, Farmington, Utah

HANGING BY THE THREAD

DONALD B. ANDERSON

Although *Hanging By The Thread* refers to historical and /or current events, the work as a whole is a work of fiction, and the dialogue and characterizations of individuals reflect the author's interpretations.

Published & Distributed by:

Stone Haven Publishing
1579 Monroe Dr, Suite F
Atlanta, GA 30324
Toll Free 1-800-827-0089

Cover Design By: Jolene Johnson
Page Layout and Design By: Michelle L. Elias

ISBN: 978-1-59936-056-0
Library of Congress Control Number: 2010925771
First Printing May 2010
10 9 8 7 6 5 4 3 2 1
Printed in the United States of America

ACKNOWLEDGEMENTS

An editor on television recently warned that you should not give your manuscript to friends or family because they will not be honest with you. I offer my gratitude to the many friends and family who definitely lacked that problem. They were refreshingly brutal with their honesty, and this book is so much better than what I could have produced without them.

Thanks to Gordon Ryan and Darren Andrews for taking time out of their busy lives to offer timely eyes to a manuscript in need; Teresa Jones and Lorie Humpherys for patient editing; my marketing team (Jolene Johnson, Woody Johnson, and Logan Johnson) for countless donated hours and skills in creating covers, websites, and trailers; and the team at Stone Haven Publishing who have been a delight to work with and who grasped a vision of the timely message of this book.

I also express gratitude for the great minds whose teachings about economic freedom have influenced me greatly. Those minds include Ezra Taft Benson, Marion G. Romney, J. Reuben Clark, Milton Freidman, Friedrich August Hayek, Thomas Sowell, Walter Williams, and many others. I recommend their works to all who have an interest in liberty.

Thanks to the influence of kind parents, who even liked the first draft—though it was terrible. Thanks especially to a perfect wife who raises wonderful children and has been such a level headed balance and support throughout the whole process. And finally, thanks to my little ones, whose persistent prayers that Dad's book would get published outpaced my own pleas, and for whose faith I as an author will be forever indebted.

HANGING BY THE THREAD

DONALD B. ANDERSON

CHAPTER 1

EARLY SUMMER
WASHINGTON, D.C.

The President looked at a sea of wealthy faces. The applause, though formal and meaningless, was all very natural to him. He felt at ease. The people encircled tables spangled with plates. The President considered the vast amount of money he would take from this one evening. Two thousand dollars a plate for anyone who wished to attend. Over five hundred participants filled the dining hall. Not bad.

The President had waited until the end to boast about his popular reforms. He cleared his throat and concluded his speech: "Let us move the improved America forward. We are a more compassionate and responsible country than we have ever been. We are now a nation that refuses to allow anyone to go unhoused, unfed, or uncared for medically. We are cutting off the power of the greedy few and giving it to the people. Social solidarity is replacing individual selfishness. We have done so much good. But we can still improve…" he paused a moment, entertained by the applause and joy with which the wealthy in the room loved his attack on the wealthy. Ironic.

"We will move forward and meet our obligations to social justice. Let us use our power to do good. Let us abandon—more than we have in the past—the roots of corruption that dominated us as a nation for so long: greed and selfishness." As he rolled into his final punch, the crowd was boiling with energy.

"Let us hold as our motives of public service the elevation of mankind and not the elevation of self. Let us establish the equality that would make us ideal!"

The mass was now on their feet, filled with adulation for the President. He smiled, breathed deeply, and relished the moment. His countenance was awash with flashes of light that strobed him from the cameras across the room. The smile came easily now.

With the pressure of presenting now passed, the President grinned and waved for a few moments before dismounting the stage. He plunged into the crowd. He greeted each person with charisma. In the thrill of the moment, he paid little attention to the drink a distinguished-looking server handed him—a drink he gladly accepted.

He moved from person to person, shaking hands with one hand and sipping from the glass in the other.

After a few minutes of mingling, another server offered a second drink to replace the one he had just finished. He accepted this new drink, but would never finish it. He began to feel drained. The skin across much of his body became cold and clammy. His head began hurting, and the rest came on fast. He remembered having heat exhaustion a few years back, and thought it felt similar—but he knew it wasn't that.

Within just a few minutes, he knew he needed to leave and get some rest. The conversation he had enthusiastically begun just minutes earlier had now become drudgery—he wanted to lie down somewhere. He tried to excuse himself, but his efforts were lethargic and came across as nonchalant. He motioned to the security personnel around him and stumbled toward an exit. He never made it.

He collapsed—in the middle of the pressing crowd—onto the ground, striking a table with his face as he fell. Unable to raise his arms to catch himself, he hit the ground hard. The crowd gasped and a sense of panic filled the entire dining hall. Screams followed. The crowd pushed back in a well-formed circle around the President.

The security entourage engulfed him. A doctor was at his side in seconds. After a moment of assessment, the doctor looked up at those gathered closest and said with blank surprise, "He's dead."

After a long bout of CPR in the dining hall and while en route to the hospital, multiple doctors officially declared the President dead eleven minutes after the President's arrival.

The country mourned the sudden loss of a popular president. Speculation that the President had been poisoned swirled around the nation and across the world. However, the autopsy report concluded the President had suffered a heart attack from natural causes. Except for the few conspiracy theorists, the suspicions ceased.

For The Thread, it had all been very easy.

CHAPTER 2

THREE MONTHS LATER
UTAH STATE CAPITOL BUILDING
SALT LAKE CITY
3:05 P.M.

The Utah State Senator had nearly finished making the copies he needed. He usually sent someone from his staff to do menial tasks like this. He was a large man, whose physical presence dominated any room and any gathering. His rise to power in Utah had been quite sudden. In fact, he had been so successful in accumulating power in this state that he was now poised to try his hand in national politics, if that had been his plan. But it was not his plan. In public, he was charming and authoritative. In private, he was gruff, manipulative, and short fused.

He was nearly finished making copies when his phone rang. It was his private secretary.

"Frank, you have a call. I would've taken a message, but the caller insisted on waiting."

"Who is it?" asked Frank.

"Well, that's just it. The name is Judy." She paused. "But Judy is a man." Frank first felt a twinge of fear, then smiled and chuckled to himself at the audacity of the caller. He knew who it was, and was surprised the man would call him at such a critical time.

"Tell him I'll be right there."

"Will do."

Frank grabbed the satchel—gripping the handle to remind his consciousness he was not forgetting his critical cargo. Frank had decided to keep the satchel with him at all times for these last twenty-four hours prior to the transaction. What he did not know was that this precaution to secure *Key* #3—the most important document he had ever possessed—would prove disastrous.

Distracted by the call, he failed to close the satchel. Frank turned to leave the room. He had not seen the small, older lady enter the room. The two collided—hard enough that Frank dropped his precious load. As his satchel hit the ground, its contents spilled under the copy room table. Folders and papers from the satchel spread out across the floor much like a deck of cards.

Frank's heart sank. Ironically, his first thought was not about the document in his satchel. Rather, because of the woman's presence, his first thought was about the magazine that had fallen out and was now in plain sight. He bent and confiscated it, quickly placing it back into the satchel.

He jabbered quick and profuse apologies to the lady, trying to perceive whether she had noticed the magazine. He was satisfied she had not, and that brought him great relief. Someone spotting him with a magazine like that would have been political poison—not to mention the career-ending fallout that would happen if the people of this state were to discover that he, Frank Tomlinson, was its principle financier.

In his relief, he failed to notice the document that had scattered the farthest. In fact, it was well under the table and out of sight. He gathered what he supposed were the entire contents of his satchel from under the table, finished packing, and apologized again to the lady. In the most careless act of his life, Frank Tomlinson left the room.

Less than ten minutes after Frank Tomlinson left the copy room, Colton Wiser walked in. He made the copies he, as an aid, was often required to make. As he stood near the copy machine, he noticed—in his peripheral vision—a tan colored document far under the table. He walked over and picked it up.

From the instant he held it, he felt a bit like an intruder. He recalled being much younger; hiding in a tree, listening to his older brothers and their friends meet in their club—a club that kept secrets from him. As he began to scan this document, he felt much the same way. Colton was holding something that was strange—to the point of being fascinating. This was not an ordinary document.

The paper was so thick it almost seemed like a tan fabric. It had a leathery feel to it. He now could see that there were three pages stapled together. Yet, the pages were thick enough the document looked and felt to have more pages than three.

It had the feel of something private. He felt a sense of duty—he wanted to identify the owner and return it.

The title was odd: *Master Plan for the Rising of The Thread.* He began skimming the document, looking for clues as to what it was or who its owner might be. The headings on the first page held no meaning for Colton—just an outline.

The outline spoke of a series of transactions. The points under each heading were elusive, even childish gibberish at times.

He analyzed the second page, which made more sense than the first page. The second page was mostly economic jargon—much of which he could at least identify: the Fed, price controls, universalized medicine, and so on. Most of these things had been in the news recently.

He had had a small dose of economics at Brigham Young University, where he had excelled, and had graduated with a bachelor's degree just a few months prior. His degree was in political science, and he had landed a job as an aid to a state senator. It was an ideal entry job. Colton loved politics.

He looked at the inside of the final page, which was blank.

And then, for the first time, he looked at the back of the document. His heart quickened as a shot of adrenaline coursed through his body. Across the center of the back page, from left to right, was a long, thin, outlined rectangle. A raised red blotch filled the inside of the rectangle. It was a smear of blood. The page bore the title: *Key #3*. Below the blood was an ominous, almost silly warning: "This key must be secured until transaction. Great trust has been placed in the holder. Ample reward will follow its proper use. If this key is lost or misused, the life of the key holder must recompense."

CHAPTER 3

UTAH STATE CAPITOL BUILDING
3:15 P.M.

Colton marveled at what a strange document he had found. It was a combination of technical economic jargon, coded phrases that sounded ridiculous, and a death threat. Was it real? He doubted it. Yet, so much about it seemed real. He began walking back to the office to deliver the copies he had made and return to his cubicle. But he could not focus on anything other than the document. If this were a death threat on the back, the owner would want it badly.

Here was a dilemma. How do you find the owner of a confidential packet that is either silly or dangerous in the extreme? Just as he got back to his cubicle, inspiration struck. His roommate and best friend, Jeff Palmer, had worked at the Capitol Building for almost three years. Jeff worked security. Surely he would have some ideas.

As Colton made his way to the security office, he concealed—for some reason he could not explain—the mysterious papers by hiding them in a folder.

He found Jeff in the security office as he had hoped. To Colton's relief, Jeff was at a secluded work station.

Jeff had an appearance that was similar enough to Colton's that the two were often mistaken for brothers. Both had brown hair that they kept short. Colton's hair was a little more inclined to stand up and poof out, while Jeff's hair was softer and rested on his head. Jeff was a bit taller and more athletic, but both were good athletes and loved to compete with and against each other.

"Well, well. It's the 'cool' aid," greeted Jeff. Colton usually matched Jeff's lighthearted wit; but not this time. Instead, Colton was serious and focused on what was in the folder. Jeff sensed Colton's mood. He adjusted and asked, "What's up?"

"I found a crazy document. I'm not sure if it's legitimate, or part of some sort of game."

"Where did you find it?"

"In the copy room about ten minutes ago. It was on the floor under the table."

"Well then," said Jeff, "I'll bet it's sensational. All great documents are discovered under the tables in copy rooms." Colton again gave no response to the jesting. Without otherwise reacting, he removed the document from the folder and tossed it in front of Jeff. Jeff looked at the title.

"'*Master Plan for the Rising of The Thread*,'" read Jeff. Looking up at Colton he whispered, "So you've gone and joined Utah's secret sewing club."

Jeff picked it up and scanned the first page, then turned to the second page. As he perused it, he made little mumbling noises—mocking the way one might read it with great sophistication. He glanced at the blank third page. Assuming he had seen the entire document, he tossed it on the desk in front of him.

"Well," concluded Jeff, "we should call some very important people and have them deal with this amazingly boring treasure you unearthed in the great copy room of the Utah State Capitol Building."

Colton knew Jeff well. Had he not known his heart so well, Jeff's jovial reaction might have been offensive. Colton, absorbing Jeff's humor, reached, took the document, turned it over, and once again set it in front of Jeff. The back of the document was facing up.

"That's sick!" said Jeff upon seeing the blood stain. He read the warning. The mood change was complete and his curiosity peaked. "You think this is just some kind of joke, don't you?" Jeff asked, hoping for an affirmative answer.

"That's what I'm wondering. But there's too much serious stuff in this for me to pass it off as a joke or a game."

"And you have no idea whose it is?" Jeff was fully inquiring now.

"That's why I brought it to you. I would have taken it to Senator Nelson, but I thought you could help me find out whose it is."

"Yeah!" Jeff said as a plan unfolded in his mind. "Come here." He led Colton across the room to a computer. "Were you in the copy room on the south side of the building?"

"Yes. About ten to fifteen minutes ago is all."

Jeff sat down at a console of computers and multiple screens and went to work, punching information on a keyboard. In just a few moments, Jeff had an image of the copy room pulled up on the monitor. In the top right corner of the screen was a large series of numbers that made no sense to Colton. In the upper left was the time of the recording. Standing near a copy machine was Colton, examining the document. The footage was too recent.

Jeff began rolling the image back in time. Both men watched as Colton seemed to awkwardly bend to put the document under the table, back up to the copy machine, wait, turn around, and back out of the room. After a little while, an older lady seemed to back into the room and wait at the copy machine.

"Okay," said Jeff, "let's watch her closely."

Not long after her entrance, the older lady seemed to back most of the way out of the room before a large man seemed to back in and around her.

"Here's another one to watch," said Colton.

The hefty man squatted down and rummaged around the floor. After he popped up, there was what appeared in reverse footage to be a visible collision between the two people.

"Bingo," said Jeff, "that must be it right there."

"That's where the document was," said Colton, pointing at the screen, "under the table."

They continued watching as the large man backed into the room and put his hand to his ear—apparently talking on his cell phone. The older lady had already backed out. Satisfied he had found the source of the strange document, Jeff froze the image and began tinkering with it. He honed in on the face of the large man until it filled most of the screen. Even before Jeff had the image made sharper, Colton identified the face.

"Frank Tomlinson."

"Are you sure?" asked Jeff. "I see these people all the time, but I only know faces. I don't know many of their names."

"I'm sure," said Colton. "Anyone involved in the workings of this state will soon get to know Frank Tomlinson. He's sort of an in-your-face kind of a guy. He gets his way a lot, but he burns a lot of political bridges. He does have quite an influence in the Senate; but he's a thorn in Senator Nelson's side and opposes him on most major issues."

"So," said Jeff, "we think we know who the document belongs to and when it was lost. Should we just take it to his office and hand it to him and say, 'Here Senator, we found your death threat document. Did we save your life? Maybe you could see that we get a raise.'"

"You know, if this thing *is* part of a joke or game, he'd be embarrassed to know we saw it. If it's *real*, he'd be mad. We have to find a way to return it without him knowing we've had it."

"True," said Jeff. "But if it's serious, this thing is sinister to the tenth degree, and there's no way this document should ever get back into his hands. Maybe these transactions are some sort of drug deal, or fraud."

Jeff thought of something important and continued. "You know, Colton, if this is a raw deal going on, and this document is important in a bad way, that man could use this same footage to learn that you were the discoverer—that you know about his paper. This video record puts you at risk."

"You're right!" said Colton. "What should we do?"

Jeff did not answer. He inserted a device into the computer, continued working, and then pulled the device out of the computer.

"Done."

"What did you do?" asked Colton.

"Solved your problem."

"Are you allowed to do that?"

"No," said Jeff honestly. "Now, what do we do with this document?"

"How can we find out if this thing is legit?" asked Colton.

Jeff sprang up. He grabbed Colton's shoulders and looked him in the eyes. "Hey, do you trust me?" It was a strange question at a strange time. Colton looked at Jeff quizzically. "Do you trust me?" repeated Jeff with a large smile.

"Sure," said Colton untrustingly.

"I've got a plan. You just wait here and watch." Jeff, with his hands on Colton's shoulders, sat Colton down in the chair. "I'll be back in a few." And he left.

Jeff returned eight long minutes later, brimming with energy.

"Check this out." Jeff sat again at a computer and pulled up the current image of the copy room. The room was empty.

"What did you do?" asked Colton.

"Okay," said Jeff, using his hands as he talked, "Tomlinson's secretary is receiving a message about an important document Frank left in the copy room."

"You're crazy. That could be traced right back to you."

"Yeah, you're right," said Jeff, "but I think we're about to find out if we need to run and hide, or if it's safe to play." Jeff chuckled to himself.

"How?"

"Just watch. My guess is that it won't take long. We should find out if it's bogus once he gets back to that room."

"How?" said Colton again.

"You see that white thing on the table right there?" asked Jeff.

"Sure."

"That, my friend, is the golden ticket."

"What do you mean?"

"Just watch."

It did not take long. In walked Tomlinson. He seemed frazzled—almost in a panic. Jeff honed in to where he was standing and focused the image. Tomlinson bent and looked under the table. He jerked up in distress. He noticed the white envelope on the table. Tomlinson tore the envelope open and removed a small piece of paper from within the envelope. His face turned ashen, as if someone had just punched him in the gut. With panicked eyes, he raced out of the room.

"Whoa!" said Jeff. "I wasn't expecting that."

Jeff pushed buttons and the monitor now showed the large, open rotunda and foyer through a different camera's perspective. Tomlinson was running, as best he could, across the great open space of the Capitol Building. He was swiveling his head in paranoia. He ran for the doors that led out of the building and toward the covered parking garage. Soon he was gone. Jeff switched to a parking garage camera. Both young men watched, stunned, as this large man continued to run in a panic to his car. The car sped away, out of the Capitol.

Both roommates looked at each other in shock.

"How 'bout that..." It was all Jeff could say. Colton was silent. After a while he looked at Jeff.

"What in the world was in that envelope?"

Jeff shrugged. “The envelope said, ‘For Frank Tomlinson.’”

“The paper, Jeff, what was on the paper?” asked Colton.

“I just wrote a little note. All it said was… ‘Frank, you were warned.’”

CHAPTER 4

UTAH STATE CAPITOL BUILDING
3:52 P.M.

"Wow," said Jeff, "if this document is just a joke, our friend Frank deserves an award for playing along so well."

Colton continued to play in his mind Tomlinson's panicked flight. He wanted to laugh hysterically. But such a funny performance by Frank Tomlinson was a sinister portent for what this document may be. The loss of it seemed to ruin Frank Tomlinson's whole day. What was Frank into? Jeff was wondering the same thing. Jeff, however, kept letting out bursts of laughter and fits of snickering as he replayed, repeatedly on his computer, Frank Tomlinson's dramatic exodus.

"Don't you feel bad about what you just did to that man?" asked Colton. Jeff straightened in his seat and snapped his face around to look at Colton.

"No," said Jeff. "No way. That man has some serious rats in his cellar."

"Rats in his cellar?"

"It's something C.S. Lewis said."

"C.S. *Lewis*?" asked Colton.

"Yes. C.S. Lewis talked about how you can go to some cellar doors and throw them open, and rats go scurrying. You throwing the door open does nothing to cause the rats to be there—it just exposes them. For our friend Frank Tomlinson, we threw the cellar door open. He's involved in something that caused the reaction. Do I feel bad about making him confront whatever this is? No. I'd do it again. I would just hope it would be as entertaining next time." He grinned and began laughing again as he replayed the event.

Colton shook his head. Jeff was the last person he'd expect to read serious stuff. It was strange to hear Jeff talk about C.S. Lewis.

Jeff gained temporary composure again and looked at Colton. "Where do you think he went?"

"How should I know?" said Colton. "One thing I'd bet on is that he won't be coming back today. I wonder if he'll ever come back here at all. This is crazy. What could he be involved in?"

"You know what I'm going to do?" said Jeff. "I'm going to wait 'til his secretary leaves and go and see what he left behind in his office."

"You're a lunatic."

"If this man is into some serious corruption, the bad people he is in cahoots with are likely to come and go through his stuff once they realize Frankie here is gone. I just want to have a shot at seeing what's there before they run off with it."

"If this is some significant crime Tomlinson is involved with, you would be tampering with evidence your own self."

"True," said Jeff, "but if we find anything important, we could save it as evidence—maybe we'll do some good by it."

"You'll get busted," said Colton.

"Okay. So who do we give this document to anyway? Do we take it to the police?"

"I say the Attorney General's office. They'll know what to do with it." Colton was relieved that Jeff had dropped the idea of searching Tomlinson's office.

"Let's take it now," said Jeff.

"You know what? Their office is closing in just a few minutes," said Colton. "Let's just take it tomorrow, first thing in the morning. I want to let Pete look this over. He has a much better grasp of economics than I do." Peter Wright was their other roommate. The three shared an apartment.

"Colton, are you sure you don't want to take this over to the Attorney General's office tonight? I bet there will still be plenty of people in there even if it is after closing time."

"I don't want to let it go yet. Maybe that's stupid, but I want to figure out what kind of transactions Tomlinson is into. We'll turn it over tomorrow morning. I want Pete to give his feedback. You're almost done here, right?"

"Yes, in five minutes."

"I need to wrap up some things, but I'll meet you back here in a few minutes."

Fifteen minutes later they met and were ready to go. As they turned to leave, Jeff froze. He seemed to debate something in his mind. He walked over to the computer and punched a few buttons. The monitor displayed an office foyer. Colton discerned what Jeff was doing.

"Jeff, don't do it. Leave it alone."

"No, Colton. I don't feel great about leaving his office free for anyone to tamper with. I'd rather be first. *You* are not willing to let go of that document until you learn more about it. *I* am not willing to let go of what Frank might have left behind. You can stay here, meet me at the car, or go with me. But I'm going to Tomlinson's office."

"You'll be on camera in his office," said Colton as a last ditch effort to thwart his impetuous roommate.

"Oh, you're right." Colton thought he had persuaded Jeff not to do it. Instead, Jeff walked back to the computer console, punched buttons for a few moments, and headed for the door again. He looked at Colton. "Camera's turned off." Jeff smiled and walked out of the security office.

Colton was just a few steps behind Jeff. The past hour left Colton feeling detached from reality. He knew that he was being foolish and irrational; but he found himself going along.

Without a secretary present in Tomlinson's office, they walked right to his door. It was slightly ajar and the lights were on—not a surprise. A note from the secretary was on the door letting Tomlinson know that she had gone home. Jeff paused at the open door, peered around it and scanned the room. It was empty.

Tomlinson's office was not messy, nor was it particularly tidy. There were a few folders on his desk, and a stack of papers.

"Let me see the document again," requested Jeff. Colton handed it to him. "'Master Plan for the Rising of The Thread...' We want to find anything that has to do with that title or the transactions it talks about."

"Jeff, don't go digging deep. We're already being idiots."

But Jeff did not have to dig deep. Three folders, in plain sight on the desk top, bore some reference to *The Thread.* Each also had the phrase *social network analysis* on the title tabs, along with reference to a particular Utah region. Jeff waved Colton over to see the folders.

"Do you have any idea what 'social network analysis' is?" inquired Jeff.

"I think it's when people analyze social networks," said Colton, smiling. Jeff returned a sarcastic grin.

Jeff continued to snoop around the desk, even opening the desk drawers. Colton scanned through the folders. They were full of charts and graphs and statistical information. Nothing stood out as understandable or sinister. Colton looked at Jeff.

"These are obviously related to this Thread stuff. But they don't make any sense."

"We have a safe in the security office. I'm going to put the folders there just in case. We'll turn them over to the Attorney General with the *Master Plan* tomorrow."

The two left Tomlinson's office and returned to the security office. Jeff put the three folders into the safe. Colton secured the *Master Plan* in his brief case, and the two headed for their apartment.

CHAPTER 5

HOLLADAY, UT
4:55 P.M.

"This is poppy-cock," said Pete as he looked over the first page of the *Master Plan*. "This doesn't make any sense to me at all." Colton had explained the document saga to Pete and had high expectations of Pete's ability to interpret the document.

"Well, Pete, what we were hoping," said Colton, "is that you could help us out with the economics stuff on page two. Page one doesn't make sense to us either. I can recognize a lot of the stuff on page two, but I don't pretend to know as much about economics as you."

"I didn't have *that* much economics," said Pete.

"Well, you seem to do well in economics and like it," said Colton. "Just do what you can."

Pete turned to page two and recognized most of what he saw.

Jeff seemed bored and filled the time by pacing the apartment. He began fidgeting with the doorknob. "How many times have we told the landlord about this hunk of junk?" inquired Jeff out of annoyance. "He's under some serious liability if we get stuff stolen."

"No kidding," said Colton. "It's been more than three weeks. Mr. Buttars never fixes *anything*. This place is falling apart now. We should just find another place. But most of my friends say their landlords don't keep their places up either.

Landlords are a bunch of crooks if you ask me. They insist on getting their rent, but they're so slow to keep things up." Then Colton added as an afterthought, "At least it's cheaper than it was before the new rent laws last year."

"Okay," said Pete, who had given the document enough attention to comment on it. "I know what the Fed is, but I don't know what it means by *saturate* the Fed."

Jeff asked what the Fed did. Pete explained that the Fed was the Federal Reserve and how it sets interest rates to stimulate economic growth and control inflation. Then he moved on with his review.

"It says in the heading above all these economics things: 'Successful action items in the past ten years.' So, whoever these people are, this seems to be a brag session of what they've accomplished. Things like the universal medicine that started last year, entitlements, minimum wages, price controls, and protectionism.

"But you know what?" Peter seemed to have reached a frustrating conclusion. "I know a bit about most of this stuff, and I could explain a couple of these things really well..." he continued to pore over the document as he surrendered, "but the wording on most of this stuff is over my head."

Peter was done. He looked up from the document at his two roommates. But they just stared at him in a way that made him feel awkward enough that he began to think of a solution.

"All right, if I had to figure out all this stuff, what I'd do is take it to Harold Isaacson. He's the best professor I've had in economics—he even makes economics seem fun. Anyway, he's about as smart and clear on these things as anyone you'll find."

Pete was close to graduating from Brigham Young University with a Master's degree in accounting and had had a few economics classes along the way. Though he had not yet graduated, Pete had landed a wonderful job with an accounting firm in Salt Lake City and had chosen to live closer to work than school. He made the forty-five minute commute to Provo three days a week.

Pete had mentioned the idea of talking to his professor without any intentions of acting on it. But Colton and Jeff continued staring at him. Colton broke the silence with a simple, direct mandate.

"Call him."

"Are you serious?" asked Pete.

"Absolutely. We're turning this thing in tomorrow. We have tonight to figure it out. Call him." Pete was slow to act, but he soon sought for a directory on a book shelf. He found the professor's information and dialed the number.

"Professor Isaacson, you're in your office." Pete looked down at his watch, saw it was 5:00 P.M., and was pleased to have reached the professor. Colton and Jeff both began snickering at the way Pete had begun the conversation. Peter was far quieter and much more gullible than Jeff and Colton, but he had a pleasantness and innocence that made him good company.

"Well listen, this is Peter Wright," said Pete, talking loudly into the phone, "I've had you for two different courses... yes... intro and managerial... Anyway, my roommates found a document at the State Capitol Building. They think there's some sort of fraud, or corruption, associated with the document. It's loaded with economics stuff. We're wondering if you wouldn't mind looking it over for us."

The two roommates watched Pete as he listened to Dr. Isaacson's response. "Well, that's just it. They want to turn it into the Attorney General's office in the morning and were wondering if they could bring it by tonight." Something Peter said had caught the attention of Dr. Isaacson. There was another pause. Pete kept pacing and ran his hand through his red hair. "About forty-five minutes if my roommate drives... Yes, I know it's getting late... Great! We'll be there soon! Thanks, Dr. Isaacson!" He hung up the phone grinning.

On the drive to Provo, Pete insisted on holding the document so he could study it further. Colton agreed so long as Pete read and studied aloud. Jeff was behind the wheel and

Pete was in the back seat. All three munched on snacks they had grabbed on the way out of the apartment, knowing they would not have time to stop for anything on the way.

"Okay, '*Master Plan for the Rising of The Thread,*'" Pete started into the document, broadcasting his voice to his two roommates in the front of the vehicle.

"There are four major headings: *Pre-Transaction Goals*, *Foundations*, *Transactions*, and *Post Transaction Objectives*," said Pete. His voice had to be sufficient to overcome the effects of the wind funneling into the car through both windows in the front and Pete's window in the back. Pete's hair was dancing around wildly. But the evening was so pleasant that the men chose the annoyance of the wind over having to roll up their windows.

Everyone focused on the words and meaning of the document. "Now, under the first heading, *Pre-Transaction Goals*, there are five goals listed. The first goal is to 'Neutralize traditional institutions.' Second goal: 'Continue to concentrate power to the Center.' Third goal: 'Remove the Rooster so The Hen can rule the coop.' Fourth goal: 'Create desperation.' Fifth goal: 'Use desperation to facilitate reform, create dependency, and rise to power.'"

"Okay," said Jeff, "all these points sound complex and sinister, but that third point sounds like something from *Animal Farm*. It just seems lame."

Without responding to Jeff, Pete read on. "Under the heading *Foundations*, there are the following unnumbered subheadings: *The Hen is in the Coop*, *The Fed is saturated*, *Both branches are bearing fruit*, *Pre-transaction goals proceeding as planned*, and *The goods are ready for transaction*."

Colton broke in, "This stuff seems coded. But what seems obvious is that the transactions—whatever is being exchanged—seem to involve the transfer of actual, physical merchandise."

"The third heading," Peter continued, "is *Transactions*. Under this heading, there are three entries. The first two transaction entries suggest they will happen on Day One. The first is to happen in the morning, and the second entry says it will be in the afternoon of Day One. The third entry is to occur on Day Two." Pete looked up and summarized: "So, the transactions happen over two days, and the first day has stuff in both the morning and in the afternoon."

Colton was having a hard time sorting things out as Pete read them, but his curiosity was moving faster than Pete's reading.

"So what's supposed to be happening on these days? What does it say about the transactions?" asked Colton.

"Well," responded Pete, "it's just a bunch of letters. But it looks to me like the letters signify the location of the transactions."

"What are the letters?" asked Jeff as he eased through traffic. Jeff was not traveling at an insane speed, but he was making his trademark headway—which was faster than both of his roommates were comfortable driving themselves. The evening sun still showed some willingness to influence the day as it floated above the mountains, flooding the car with a light that illuminated the right side of the three passengers and the vehicle.

"Okay," Pete was careful to sound out where the commas and periods were as he read the letters as they appeared in the transaction entries. "After the first entry, which is the morning of Day One, it says, 'NY, U.N. S, S.N.'"

Pete paused, but nobody commented, so he proceeded. "After the Day One afternoon entry it says, 'SLC, C.B.'"

"That's gotta be Salt Lake City… and something about a place that is C.B," said Jeff in response.

Colton turned his head toward Pete in the back. "Read the letters for the first one again." Pete did so. Then Pete, looking at the paper and having the best chance of seeing it, said, "I think the Day One morning thing is two locations. Listen to it again." Then, for a third time, Pete read the letters that went with the morning of Day One.

"I think you're right," Colton agreed. "And the first location must be New York, at some place referred to as the *U.N.*" Colton said it, knowing it would be obvious to everyone in the car what the letters meant. But the two others still went after it as if it were a great discovery on their part.

"United Nations!" said Jeff and Pete in unison.

"So, what is meant by the 'C.B.' listed for the Salt Lake transaction?" asked Pete.

"Capitol Building," said Colton.

"Good job!" said Pete. He pressed ahead with the document. "And the Day Two stuff—under the third entry—says, 'LA, LAX. Chgo, S.T.'"

"So the Day Two stuff seems to be in Los Angeles and Chicago," explained Colton, who was clearly the most talented at this activity. "LAX is the international airport in Los Angeles. Does anyone know what is meant by 'S.T.' as it has to do with Chicago?"

"Sears Tower!" said Pete.

"Good job," said Colton. "I bet that's right."

There was a moment of verbal silence, the sounds of the wind and highway being the only backdrop to their thinking. Then Pete spoke, offering yet another mystery.

"Okay, but look," he said, "after the New York listing—in the first entry, for the morning of Day One—there are the letters that say 'S, S.N.' I have no idea what that refers to. If it's consistent with the Day Three bullet, then 'S, S.N.' is some other location for another transaction." There was a spell of silence again. "Does anyone have a clue where that might be?"

As everyone seemed to be drawing a blank on that one, Pete proceeded with reading the document.

"Okay, it gives some instructions for the transactions: 'Couriers are to deliver the goods to the transaction site. No transaction can be completed without the scanning of a legitimate *Key*. Couriers are to then scan document. Couriers will then initiate the full transaction. Couriers are to have no contact with anyone for the three days prior to the scan until the moment of scan. Only the key-bearers are to interact with the couriers at that point—at the moment of scan.'"

"That sounds weird," said Jeff.

"Hey!" said Colton, "I'll bet that's what Frank Tomlinson has to do with this. I'll bet he's involved in the Salt Lake City transaction for this Thread group!" It sounded plausible, but there was no way to know that for sure, so the conversation moved on.

The three continued—without any new discoveries—to hash out the Transactions section of the *Master Plan* until they parked at the athletic facility on the west end of Brigham Young University. They walked around the north side of the building, up the long steps that scaled the sharp hill that formed the brow overlooking the valley. As they neared the top of the steps, the small building that hosted some of the offices for the economics department came in sight. It was more like an old house than a standard office building.

As they approached the door to the office building, Colton requested that they move past the transactions and look over the last heading's subtopics before they meet with Dr. Isaacson. They had not yet looked at this section as a group. Colton wanted to be as familiar with the document as he could before the professor began looking at it.

Pete, still holding the document, resumed reading it aloud as they stood outside the small building. But the other two were now free to look at it as Pete read the items listed as Post Transaction Objectives:

1. Enact 'temporary' high security levels and martial law
2. Sustain reports of escalating threats to sustain control
3. Assume command control of economy
4. Launch full military and economic security programs
5. Initiate final regime change—the rising of The Thread

"Whoa! Martial law? Regime change?" For the first time, that phrase sunk in, and Colton began to understand a little of what he had been reading and listening to. He took the document from Pete and stared at it. The weight of it all began to hit him.

"These are not typical financial transactions…." Colton said to the others, holding the document up as they stood outside the office building. "These transactions sound like they're designed to pull down some country's government."

CHAPTER 6

PROVO, UT
5:55 P.M.

The longer Colton had possession of this *Master Plan*, the more the document seemed to morph into a greater phenomenon. It had begun as a strange looking joke. It was now the source of one man's apparent mortal fear as well as their own deepening curiosity. Was it true that this document revealed an attempt to bring about regime change in an entire nation? Was this plan as evil as it seemed, or could there be some good behind it—like the overthrow of some evil dictator, or something of that sort?

They entered the small office building. Peter had been to Dr. Isaacson's office a couple of times and knew right where it was. It was the fourth office on the left.

Pete knocked. A voice beckoned them. As they walked in, they saw two men in the room—a younger man behind a desk and an older man sitting in a chair against the wall. The older man stood up as the three men came in. He had a dignified look. Yet the man behind the desk did not look much like what Colton had imagined a talented Economics professor to look like. Dr. Harold Isaacson was a 38-year-old man who could pass for a man in his mid twenties. He could blend in with many of those he taught. He had dark hair and a youthful face.

"I think I'm going to go home now," said the older man to Dr. Isaacson.

"Well, good night, Tim," said Dr. Isaacson. "Tell Sarah hello. Thanks for chatting."

"Good night, Harry." The older man excused himself, not seeming to notice that the three even existed until he passed Colton. Colton had already removed the *Master Plan* from his brief case and uncovered it from the folder protecting it. The older man noticed it, paused, took a good look at it, and made a grunting sound showing interest in the document's unique appearance. The man seemed to consider inquiring, but decided against it and slipped out of the office.

"Dr. Isaacson, I'm sure you don't remember—"

"Peter. How're you doing?" he asked, leaning over his desk and extending his hand.

"Good memory! There must have been around two hundred students in both classes I took from you," said Peter as he shook Dr. Isaacson's hand with boyish gusto.

"Remembering students' names is much easier when they've just told it to me on the phone within the past hour," said Dr. Isaacson.

"Oh… Yeah…" stammered Pete. He pointed to his roommates.

"Dr. Isaacson, these are my roommates: Jeff Palmer, who graduated two years ago from the University of Utah with a bachelor's degree in criminal studies, and Colton Wiser, who just graduated a couple of months ago from here at BYU with a degree in political science. Colton is the one who found the document we want to show you."

"So," inquired Dr. Isaacson with a wink as he shook Jeff's hand, "coming from the school up north, do you feel like you're in enemy territory this evening?"

"I have no worries, professor. My shields are up," said Jeff. "I plan on still being single when we head back to Salt Lake tonight." Both men laughed. Jeff had often teased Colton for the fact that he had graduated from BYU without getting married.

Professor Isaacson turned to Colton to shake hands. "Having gone to school here, I don't suppose you have to put your shields on."

"Oh, no. My shields are down. I'm vulnerable and hoping for attack. In fact, if you have any daughters you wish to arrange a date with, I'm game."

"I've got three daughters. You can pick. But you'll have to wait about as long as Jacob waited for Rachel. My oldest daughter's now eleven." All four men in the room laughed. Colton was surprised not only with Dr. Isaacson's youth, but also his approachability and natural disposition to build instant rapport with people.

"Well," said Dr. Isaacson, "it's already late. Where's this document you want me to see?" Although kind, Dr. Isaacson was also direct. Smiles tapered and lightheartedness gave way to weightier business. Colton presented the *Master Plan* to Dr. Isaacson by handing it to him face down.

After reaching for the document, Dr. Isaacson pulled his hand back in reaction to the blood mark.

"I know…" said Colton. He held it out until Dr. Isaacson again reached for it—this time taking it. Before Colton allowed Dr. Isaacson to examine the document, he pointed out the warning on the back and relayed the events of the day, including the document's discovery and the dramatic Frank Tomlinson episode.

Following the explanation, Colton sat in a chair against the wall—next to where the other two had already seated themselves when the business had begun. The friends waited while the professor delved into the contents of the *Master Plan*. Colton noticed that Dr. Isaacson had pictures of his wife and children throughout the office. Colton counted six little children—and they all looked like they were about the same age. The pictures alone told Colton a lot about the man who was now scrutinizing the document. Other than family, Dr. Isaacson had on display three large paintings in the office that took up the rest of the wall space. The first painting was a religious scene.

The other two were portraits of George Washington, and another man Colton did not recognize.

"Who's that?" asked Colton, interrupting Dr. Isaacson.

Dr. Isaacson took a moment to pull away from the document, and another moment to register Colton's question.

"Oh," said Dr. Isaacson. "That's Adam Smith, the father of economics."

"Oh," said Colton.

Dr. Isaacson pointed to the paintings as he spoke, "The gospel, America, and economics. After you consider my family, those three topics pretty much sum up my life."

"That's cool," said Jeff. Then the room went silent again as Dr. Isaacson immersed himself in the document.

Colton turned his attention to the professor. Dr. Isaacson was expressionless most of the time with the exception of occasional raised eye brows and brief, subtle displays of interest. When it seemed he had perused most of the first page, Colton interrupted Dr. Isaacson's investigation.

"The second page is the page that's loaded with economics. We were hoping you might have some insights into that stuff. The first page is kind of crazy—coded and elusive, as you can see. The nearest we can figure is that this *Master Plan* is based on some series of financial transactions in America that are designed to help some country undergo a regime change. Maybe this 'Thread' is the group poised to take over whatever country is involved. That is, assuming the document is legitimate."

"Or," offered Pete to supplement Colton's theory, "perhaps this 'Thread' group is going to fund the regime change and then benefit financially from the results."

"Hmm." Dr. Isaacson looked back down to the *Master Plan* without much reaction. He finished studying the first page then flipped to the second page. He seemed focused, but almost bored with the obscure contents of the document. The boredom did not last.

The heading at the top of the second page read: 'Action items accomplished in the past ten years.' These items were all issues dealing with the economy, and as soon as he began reading the bulleted subheadings, Dr. Isaacson's eyes widened. His head lowered closer to the document and his mouth opened as he continued to read.

"Remarkable..." was all he said for a while. He began shaking his head at intervals. The intensity of his demeanor was escalating. Colton, Jeff, and Pete were ready to hear an explanation of what the professor found so engaging about the economics material they had found so boring and enigmatic. Dr. Isaacson finally looked up.

"This is phenomenal." He looked back down, and the three thought they may have to continue to wait, but Dr. Isaacson began to explain as he looked at the document. "This document lists most of the major changes in economic policy in America over the past five or so years. These have not been good changes, in my opinion."

"Like what changes?" asked Jeff.

"Well, that's just it," said Dr. Isaacson. "Like everything on page two of this document. We now have a near-universalized health-care system. We have major price controls compared to fifteen years ago. We have had massive growth in entitlement programs—more than at any period except perhaps the Great Depression."

"Entitlements?" asked Jeff. "Like welfare stuff, right? Government hand-out stuff?"

"Yes. This document talks about licensing and regulation, minimum wages, etcetera—all of them are policies that have been enacted or gotten lots of recent attention."

"Not to be rude, Professor," Jeff said, "but what's so special about this economics list? It seems to me like it's not that big of a deal, but you seem like you are suffering some kind of heart condition over it."

"Your name is Jeff, right?"

"Yes."

"Jeff, all these policy changes have moved us further from economic freedom—which is the heart of freedom. I have supposed that these were all just bad policies that came about from normal political influences. This document, however, suggests there's an organized effort to bring about the overall result of these policies."

"Like a conspiracy," said Colton. It was not a question.

"Yes. Of course, every time there's a terrorist attack, it seems as if every terrorist group under the sun tries to claim credit for it. Maybe this is just some group wanting to look more powerful than it really is by claiming credit for normal economic changes."

"Wait a minute. Here's what I don't get," said Pete. "What would all these economic policies in *America* have to do with crazy and powerful changes in some other nation?"

"Good question," said Dr. Isaacson.

"You know what?" attempted Colton. "There's such a strong link between economies nowadays that economic activities here may have huge repercussions in some other nation."

There was thoughtful silence for a time.

"Dr. Isaacson," said Colton, "you said these things all have something in common; that they were all policies that—in your opinion—remove what you call *economic* freedom. You also said that economic freedom is the heart of freedom. I think I know what that is, but tell us what you mean by economic freedom?"

"Okay," said Dr. Isaacson, "when people imagine a country that becomes free, they often imagine a country where the people can choose their leaders. This is *political* freedom. Political freedom is an important part of total freedom. If I'm politically free, I can pick who governs me.

"*Economic* freedom, on the other hand, means I'm free to make choices, so long as in doing so I do not infringe the rights of others. If I am economically free, I can freely buy and sell, produce and exchange, own and trade. I can choose where I live and where I go. I am entitled to enjoy the fruit of my labors and responsible to bear the burden of my poor choices.

"Economic freedom is to have the right to private property and is what the Founders meant by the 'pursuit of happiness.' Many early constitutions in various states in America talked about the pursuit of *property* as being an unalienable right. What we do with our resources is at the very heart of our efforts to be happy. That is what I mean by *economic* freedom.

"Now, many countries are quite free politically, and are free therefore to choose their leaders and governors, but have let go—usually in small steps—of economic freedoms. To be able to fully pursue happiness, people must be economically free along with being politically free."

"All right," said Jeff, "whatever all this stuff about economic freedom means, what in the world does U.S. economic policy of the past ten years have to do with this regime change transaction stuff?"

"Right," agreed Dr. Isaacson. Then he turned to Colton, holding the document up. "Colton, you mentioned that you're turning this into the state Attorney General's office in the morning, right?"

"Yes."

Dr. Isaacson flipped back to the first page.

And then it happened. He saw it.

"Un-be-lievable! How did I miss this?" Tension filled the room. "The Rooster…" was all Dr. Isaacson said. The three waited.

"The Rooster…" repeated Dr. Isaacson with more intensity and conclusion.

Jeff cut into the awkwardness, "Rooster… rooster…" then after a pause: "Goose!" Colton smacked Jeff on the chest—this was not a time for silliness.

Dr. Isaacson once again pulled out of his own private world of discovery back to interaction with the others. He looked at the three.

"The *Rooster*." This time the word rooster started high and ended lower—said as if it should be obvious to everyone.

"Doc, I think you've said that much already," said Jeff.

And then Dr. Isaacson quoted the *Master Plan*. "'Remove the Rooster so The Hen can rule the coop.'"

To Dr. Isaacson's surprise, it still was not clear to the other three. Dr. Isaacson offered a hint. "Think about what happened about three months ago."

And then Colton understood. "The President is the Rooster! The 'Rooster' had to be removed so the 'Hen' could rule the coop!"

"That's it!" confirmed Dr. Isaacson.

"No way!" said Pete. The impact of what this might mean in even its smallest proportions began to settle on the four gathered men.

"Man," said Jeff, "our friend Frank Tomlinson has handed us a document that may prove that the death of the President of the United States was no accident."

"So, is the President—the former Vice President—in on this?" said Colton.

"This is huge," said Pete.

"But it's more than just the death of the President," said Dr. Isaacson. "I think this *Master Plan* is a plan to remove economic freedom to facilitate regime change *in our own country*."

Colton marveled. "If the Rooster is the President, this document must be about an attempt to overthrow freedom itself and the very Constitution of the United States of America."

"Yes, Colton," said Dr. Isaacson. "That's exactly what this would mean."

CHAPTER 7

6:07 P.M.

Still holding the document, Dr. Isaacson walked around his desk and spoke to Colton. "You can't wait until tomorrow morning. This document has got to get into the hands of the proper authorities *immediately*."

"I agree." Colton knew he could no longer hold onto the document out of curiosity.

"But it's too late to get it to the Attorney General's office tonight," said Jeff.

"Oh, I think this goes far beyond the State Attorney General's office. This is a federal security issue. We've got to get this into the hands of the FBI," said Dr. Isaacson.

"Excellent!" exclaimed Colton. "My uncle works for the FBI right here in Utah Valley."

"That's right!" said Jeff. "What was it that he does for the FBI?"

"He is a field agent. He works with white collar crime. I'll give him a call and find out what we should do."

"Sure," said Dr. Isaacson. "And I think we should make a couple copies of this *Master Plan*. Colton, would you be kind enough to go to the first office you passed in this hallway? There's a copy machine there."

"No problem," said Colton. "I'll make the copies, call my uncle, and be right back."

"Remember, Colton," said Dr. Isaacson. "We've got to treat that document like fragile gold until it is out of our hands."

"Right." Colton excused himself and walked to the first office in the building. After starting the copies, he pulled out his cell phone, scrolled to find his uncle's number, and dialed. James Berry answered on the second ring.

"Hello, this is Jim."

"Uncle Jim. This is Colton."

"Hey Colton. What's up?"

"Jim, I found this document earlier today, and we think it's a plan behind a plot to take over the country." After he said it, he realized in the silence how silly it sounded. He felt like rescuing himself.

"Jim," he broke into the silence, "I know this sounds crazy. I found the document in the State Capitol Building this afternoon. We tracked down the man who had lost it, and when he realized he had lost it, he totally panicked, ran out of the Capitol Building, and drove off. Anyway, I'm now on the campus at BYU. We brought it here to show an economics professor—we wanted him to look at it because it's loaded with economics stuff."

"Okay, Colton, I've been smiling because I know your sense of humor. But you're sounding serious about this. Let me tell you right now, I'm not in the mood for a practical joke about national security. If you're serious, then you can keep talking to me."

"I'm completely and deadly serious, Uncle Jim."

"Okay, tell me more about this document."

"It's by some group that calls themselves 'The Thread.' Have you heard of them?"

"I haven't. Doesn't sound too threatening though," Jim chuckled. "So, what makes you think this is a plan to take over the country?"

"Well, we brought it to a professor, Harold Isaacson, to interpret some of the economics. He did so, but he also noticed a phrase in the document that now seems obvious. It's a reference, we believe, to the death of the President. Uncle Jim, I don't think the President's death was an accident."

Colton now had Jim's full attention.

"Let me make sure I understand what you're saying," said Jim. "You're telling me that you've found a document that reveals that the President of the United States did *not* die naturally but was *killed*?"

"Yes," said Colton.

"And you also think this document talks about *taking over* America?"

"Yes, through some series of economic policies and financial transactions."

"That doesn't make much sense, Colton," said Jim.

"We've been very curious about this thing from the moment we found it, and it seems like the longer we have it, the crazier it gets."

"All right, Colton. I'm in Payson right now. Tell me where you are at BYU, and I'll meet you there as soon as I can. It'll be about twenty minutes."

"Thanks Jim." Colton gave directions and hung up the phone, grateful his uncle had not passed it off as a practical joke. He finished making two copies, stapled them, and returned to Dr. Isaacson's office.

Dr. Isaacson was in charge now. With more copies of the document in their possession, the four gathered and read over the *Master Plan* while waiting for Jim. Discovering the meaning of the rooster phrase was like a key that opened up a much larger range of the document's meaning. They now figured the "branches" the document referred to as bearing fruit were the bicameral branches of Congress—suggesting The Thread had infiltrated Congress. The Fed was "saturated," indicating the money supply was also under the power of The Thread. These revelations implied The Thread was already a tremendously powerful organization. However, they still could not decipher what the 'transactions' were all about.

"What I find shocking," said Dr. Isaacson, "is that The Thread could become so powerful and intertwined with our government and yet remain a secret. Usually, as a group like this grows, things happen that reveal its identity. But this group seems to have remained hidden."

It had been about twenty minutes, and Colton was expecting Jim any minute. The front door to the small office building burst open. Colton's mind told him it was Jim, but the burst was too abrupt, too harsh.

All four men rose to their feet. They then heard what sounded like the door to the first office—the one in which Colton had called his uncle and made the copies—burst open too. Something was terribly wrong. Without any exchange of words, they all knew it was not Jim.

They heard frantic rummaging in the front office, followed by the next office door bursting open. They did not wait to hear the rummaging in that office before they acted.

"Professor, is there a way to get out other than the front door?" asked Jeff.

"Yes. The back door of my office is by the rear exit."

Jeff poked his head out the back door of Dr. Isaacson's office. The way to the exit was clear. He motioned for the other three to follow. They did so. Dr. Isaacson yanked a briefcase off his desk as they took off. As they opened the rear door and filed out of the building, they made too much noise. Jeff was the last to leave. As he bolted, he could see a man turn the main corner of the hallway. He saw a gun in the man's hand and Jeff's heart exploded with adrenaline.

"MOVE!! Run as fast as you can!" cried Jeff as he slammed the door shut behind him. The four raced for the steps that led down the hill a short distance away. The rear door of the building burst open. Jeff looked back to see two men racing toward them. The four scrambled around a hedge and out of sight. Never had any of the four men scaled stairs as fast as they were doing now. They reached the bottom of the long, straight flights of stairs as the two men chasing them reached the top.

Colton realized that their flight required them to run around the athletic building, which would put them in open view of their pursuers for too long. But they had no choice. Colton wished the gun-toting men behind them would not open fire. Reality shattered that wish.

They heard two loud pops. With the first shot, Colton heard a thud off the brick of the building, followed by an object that came skidding to a halt right in Colton's path. He knew it would slow him down a pace, but he bent in full stride and picked it up. It was a cross between a bullet and a miniature dart. He jammed it into his pocket as he ran.

The second pop preceded a ripping sound through the air. Pete's hand flew to his head as a reaction to pain. As it passed, the bullet had torn through Pete's hair, and the outside edge of the projectile had scraped a swath of flesh across Pete's scalp, near the top of his head. The small wound began to bleed. Colton's heart sank when he noticed the dark red blood coming from under Pete's hand. But Peter never slowed. He kept running at full speed.

Dr. Isaacson was in great physical shape, but he had to lag enough to let the younger ones lead the way. He didn't know where they were going, and the professor chose to race with them to wherever their car was.

The four rounded the corner of the athletic building and closed in on the car. The pursuers fired two more shots. Both went thudding or skidding off the ground and peripheral objects. To their relief, the car was unlocked. They all plunged in. Jeff had the car started in miracle speed. As he sped away, the other three looked back to see the two men turn and race back around the building where they had just come from.

CHAPTER 8

6:27 P.M.

Jeff pulled hard out of the parking lot and headed toward Bulldog Avenue.

"Pete! They shot you in the head!" exclaimed Colton.

"I think they just nicked me good," said Pete. "It's a long gash, and it's bleeding like the dickens. But I think it is just a good graze. I don't think it's very deep. At least, I can hardly feel it." On close examination, the bleeding seemed to have slowed.

Colton pulled the bullet/dart out of his pocket. "Jeff, what do you make of this?" Jeff was ready to fight. He was driving with a similar facial contortion someone might have had they been sucker punched by someone and were now looking for a chance to punch back. But in response to Colton, Jeff took his eyes off the road long enough to take the small object from Colton's hand. He examined it in the evening daylight, dividing his time between the dart and traffic. He had never seen anything like it before.

Dr. Isaacson took out his cell phone and dialed campus police. Just seconds later, Dr. Isaacson reported the incident to a dispatcher. The shocked dispatcher began asking a series of questions. After a few moments of recounting, Dr. Isaacson—contrary to the plea of the dispatcher—closed the connection. He was livid and nearly in a state of shock.

Jeff took an erratic course through the streets of Provo. He kept looking in his mirrors and at surrounding traffic for any signs of danger. They seemed to be in the clear.

"What was that all about?" Dr. Isaacson scanned the other three passengers, as if they might have answers.

"I suppose it was all about this document," said Colton, "but how would anyone know where we were?"

Then Colton realized that Jim should be arriving at that office at any time. He ripped out his cell phone and called Jim. It rang three times. Jim answered.

"This is Jim."

"Jim! Where are you?"

"Colton, I'm almost there. Why the panic?"

"Jim, we were just attacked! …at least two men with guns! We ran from the building after they barged into it. They shot Pete—grazed his head—but he's okay."

"Colton, *who* attacked you?"

"I don't know. I've never seen them before. Jim, the bullets they're using look like some sort of a dart. I have one. Jeff, my roommate, works security, and he has no idea what they are. They look like a cross between a long bullet and a tiny dart."

"How strange. Is everyone okay?"

"Yes. We think they were after the document. That seems obvious, but it doesn't make sense. How would they know where we were?"

"Let's think. If it's the document they're after, it may be bugged. You've got to check for any kind of a tracking device on that document—it could be tiny. If that thing is bugged, you're in great danger as long as you have it with you."

Colton turned in his seat and addressed Pete and Dr. Isaacson in the back seat. "See if you can find any bugs or electronic tracking devices on this thing." He handed them the document.

Jim kept instructing. "Colton, if the document isn't bugged, they must have some other way to track you—but that doesn't make sense. Can you think of any way they could know where you were? Is there anything else—any objects—that came with that document? Is there anyone else who knows you have that document or where you were taking it?"

"No... wait! There was a man who was already in Dr. Isaacson's office. He took a quick look at the document, but then he left right after we got there."

"All right Colton, find out who that man is. Anything or anyone else?"

"No." Colton shook his head. *How could they find us*?

Dr. Isaacson and Pete both announced their conclusion that if there were some sort of tracking device on the document, it was too small to identify. Colton again pulled the phone away from his face. "Dr. Isaacson, Jim was wondering who might have known about the document. The only person other than us four who has seen this document today is the man who was in your office when we arrived. Who is he?"

Dr. Isaacson smiled and shook his head. "That was Tim Brough. He's the head of the Economics Department at BYU. I don't know a better man. I wouldn't be worried about him at all."

Colton resumed the conversation with Jim. "Dr. Isaacson said he wouldn't worry about the man in his office. He's Tim Brough, head of the Economics Department at BYU. And we can't find anything on the document..." and then he thought of something. "Hey, maybe there's some device under the blood mark."

Jim suggested holding the document up to a light to see if they could see anything under the mark. Colton had the two in the back seat do that, but this too turned up nothing.

"Nope," said Colton. "No sign of anything under the blood."

"This isn't good, Colton. The only other thing I can think of is that, somehow, whoever's after that document has compromised your phone. If that's the case, your conversation with me revealed your location. I don't see how they could have done that, though. That would take some major access to technology. But if it *is* your phone, they could be tracking you wherever you are right now. Do you know where the field office is—my headquarters?"

"Yes," confirmed Colton.

"This could turn out to be a race that puts you all in great danger, but meet me there. I'll have plenty of security in place to try to keep you safe upon your arrival, but we need to get that document out of your hands and into safe keeping. Do you follow?"

"Yes. I think we can be there pretty fast."

"Good, I'll meet you there." And then he cautioned, "Colton, don't answer your phone unless it's me. I'll call you back as soon as I call the office and make arrangements. Good luck."

"Thanks, Jim. Talk to you in a minute."

Jim had just hung up the call to Colton and was about to call his dispatcher when he noticed there had been three missed calls from the office. Jim hated call waiting, so he had to be in the habit of checking to see if he had missed any calls. It had only been a few minutes, and to have three missed calls was strange—especially at this time of the day when things should be slow. He dialed the office. His Branch Director answered.

"Jim, it is about time! What's going on?"

The confrontation confused Jim. "What are you talking about, Joe?"

"Jim, we've got a real situation on our hands, and it sounds like you're right in the middle of it. So what's going on?"

"Joe, I'm calling to let you know of an emergency. I just got off the phone with my nephew. He's in a mess and needs our help. When I went to call the office, I noticed three missed calls. So what do *you* mean 'what's going on?'"

"Jim, I got a very interesting call at my home about fifteen minutes ago. It was from Federal Headquarters—Jim, it was the *Executive Director of Field Operations*! He informed me that there was a document in the hands of yourself or one Colton Wiser—I suppose this is your nephew's name?"

"Yes," confirmed a very confused Jim.

"He ordered that that document—and any documents associated with it—be given immediately to a special agent who is in route from Denver. Maybe I shouldn't be saying all this. Anyway, any copies of that document must get here to the office; and I'm to hold them until this agent arrives. Am I clear, Jim? You must get that document here. You and this Colton Wiser—and anyone involved with this document—must remain here for questioning by this special agent from Denver."

This was so shocking to Jim, and so terribly wrong that his mind was sluggish—slow at putting things together. But then he began to see it.

"Joe, this is not right."

"What do you mean, Jim?"

"Joseph, listen. My nephew finds a document this afternoon in the State Capitol Building. He takes it to a professor at BYU to help interpret it. They figure it's some national plot and call me to check it out. Just a short time later, and before I even get there, someone *attacks* and shoots at them. I hear this, go to call you, and *you already know about it.* Sure sounds bizarre to me. It sounds to me like whoever this agent is, he may be tied to whoever attacked my nephew."

"Jim! I don't care if there's a link. If so, we'll sort it out. But right now, I'm under direct orders by the *Executive Director of Field Operations* to hold you, your nephew, anyone involved, and that document, until this agent arrives from Denver. I plan to obey those orders. And I now order you, Jim, to obey those orders too! Do you understand me?"

Jim held firm. "Joe, you say you don't care if there's a link. These men shot my nephew's friend! They didn't show up with a warrant, didn't follow any local or federal law enforcement protocol. If it's friendly, then it's covert and harsh. But this isn't right. I don't feel good about handing this document to the agent who's coming in from Denver. Get the whole department involved, whatever. But I'm not turning it over to this guy."

"Jim, your tail is in the fire here! Don't do this. You bring that document in right now, and we'll get this sorted out."

"Sorry, Joe. I can't do that. I'll keep in touch when I can figure out how to protect my nephew and this document that he's found."

"Jim—" but Jim broke the connection.

CHAPTER 9

6:37 P.M.

Jim called Colton back.

"Colton, where are you now?"

Colton sensed the haste and responded in like manner, "About three minutes from your office. There must have been some event at the stadium. Traffic was thick, but we're past it now."

"Colton, you can*not* go to my office. Do you understand? There's been a change of plans. Something's wrong. I think whoever attacked you may have compromised the FBI. They knew about the document before I even called. Don't tell me where you are right now—we may have others listening in to our conversation. Just don't go to my office. You got it?"

Colton passed on instructions to Jeff to change course. "Got it. Jim, how did they know about the document?" asked Colton.

"That's what I can't figure out. But there's a man in the FBI, coming from Denver, who's to receive the document. My fear is that he's linked to whoever attacked you. If that's the case, the integrity of this document is threatened if it gets into his hands. Perhaps whoever killed the President has infiltrated the FBI—assuming your conclusion about this document is correct."

Colton marveled at the dark and intricate situation. Jim went on after a pause.

"Colton, we're in a lot of danger. First, we need to know for sure whether that document is bugged. Second, we need to protect not only that document but also ourselves. We also need to figure out, as best as we can, what's going on and in whose hands to get this document."

"Okay." It was a sign from Colton he was listening.

"Colton, you shot a squirrel when you were little, and your mother gave you a severe lecture about only shooting what you will use. Do you remember that lecture?"

"I don't think any normal human being would ever forget a lecture like that. Of course."

"Okay," said Jim, "don't repeat the location on the phone. But meet me as soon as you can at the place where you got that lecture."

"I understand," said Colton.

"We've got to learn," said Jim, "whether that document is bugged with a tracking device. You cannot take it with you to the place we just agreed upon, nor can we let it out of our grasp." Jim paused to think. Then inspiration struck.

"Colton, did you already make a copy of the document?"

"We did, back at Dr. Isaacson's office."

"Great! Now listen carefully and only respond as much as you have to. Your family's vehicle broke down one year on a vacation. While you waited for a tow truck, you and your brothers played on a small slope. Your younger brother rolled down that slope and got skinned up a little. Do you remember the exact slope I'm talking about?" asked Jim.

"I do." Colton resisted the temptation to prove it.

"Good! Place the original document on that very slope—about halfway up. In fact, place it more toward the western side of that slope. Maybe secure it with a rock or something. Don't cover it up. Are you crystal clear on that?"

This request was bizarre to Colton, but nothing made much sense now. Why would Jim say they needed to protect this document and then order him to put it in plain sight right by a major roadway? This was not the time to ask, however. He simply let Jim know he understood the instructions.

"Yes, Jim."

"You may be in terrible danger until you put that document there—that is, if it's bugged. Be careful!"

"We'll be careful," assured Colton.

"One last thing before I meet you there, Colton."

"Go ahead, Uncle Jim."

"Your phone may be compromised. Dump it. Just to be sure, have everyone else dump theirs, too. Got it?"

"Got it."

"Tell me again Dr. Isaacson's name."

"Harold Isaacson," answered Colton.

"Tell Dr. Isaacson and anyone else with you to call their families before they dump their phones. Tell their families to make themselves unavailable for a couple of days. Their families should use cash and shouldn't use their phones unless they have to."

"Okay, I'll tell them."

"One last thing."

"Yeah Jim, I think this is the third last thing. Go ahead."

"Until we know how they found you, you must realize you could be captured at any moment. You're at a constant risk. Do you realize this?"

"Well, Jim, after what happened today, I think it'll be a while before I feel anything like cozy."

Jim chuckled a bit. "You're a good man, Colton Wiser. God bless you."

"You too, Uncle Jim."

As Dr. Isaacson concluded the last call he would ever make on this cell phone, he felt terrible knowing the fear he had just caused in his wife. He had to pass on too much overwhelming information in such a brief moment. He tried to reassure his bride, but that did not work. And he had no idea how long it would be before he could speak to her again. For a while as they drove, Harold Isaacson could think of nothing other than his wife and six little children.

Colton dialed a 1-800 phone number he had memorized from a commercial. Jeff sped the car alongside a truck. Colton had just begun talking to the operator before he launched the phone into the bed of the truck. He offered a silent prayer that this act would not bring any harm to the driver of the vehicle.

Colton did not hear a clang, and supposed there was something in the back of the truck that softened the phone's landing. He was grateful for that. The truck headed up toward Provo Canyon. Those who still had phones called their homes and gave serious and awkward warnings to their families. Then they threw their phones out the window off to the side of the road.

Colton had given Jeff instructions on where to head, and Jeff turned away from Provo Canyon and set a course for the Salt Lake Valley.

The mountains on the east side of Utah Valley were breathtaking as the day's final rays of sunlight lit them up before the sun retired for the day. It would soon be dark, and they had about an hour before they would arrive at the agreed upon location.

The group in the car got quiet. Dr. Isaacson—who was never one to waste precious time—opened and turned on his lap top and went to work studying the *Master Plan.*

Within ten minutes of the phone dump, four dark vehicles surrounded the truck. The black SUVs put on their emergency lights at the same time and slowed in unison, forcing the truck over to the side of the canyon highway. A very scared and angry driver received questions from a few men about someone named Colton Wiser. They discovered a phone in the back of his truck. The men went on their way. The driver felt perturbed, but was relieved that the harassment had ended as quickly as it had begun.

As soon as Jim hung up with Colton, he called his own home. To his tremendous relief, his wife, Sarah, answered. She had had a long day with the little ones. They had seven children, and although the oldest was in college, three were still very little. His wife was an amazing wife and mother. He understood that her employment—spending the day with the children—was far more rigorous than even his FBI career. She inquired when he was going to be home. He did not respond. Instead, he made what sounded like a strange, random request.

"Honey," said Jim. "Why don't you and the children go out for some pizza without me?" Jim struggled to give her no sign of the emotions he felt. Not now. She would need all the assurance he could muster.

She answered his request at first with silence. During the silence, he recalled the day he had agreed with her about this request as a code phrase. It had been an emotional day sixteen years ago. She was not so sure she wanted her little family to be presided over by an FBI dad. She wanted him to have a career that would be less dangerous. He assured her they would be fine, and the sixteen years since had been quite pleasant. He loved his work and was able to be with the family enough to be a great husband and father.

But they had agreed that day that if he ever used the code phrase, she should pack up the children within just a few minutes, get cash for spending, and head out of town for safety. He had supposed he would never have to use the code. But he knew that dealing with such a sophisticated group could mean his family may be in danger too. He was grateful for the planning he and his wife had done. Were anyone listening to this conversation, they would have little sense of the meaning being exchanged.

Sarah understood. Her long-held fears that Jim and perhaps their family would be in danger were now realized. She too struggled to keep her emotions contained and to sound tough.

She was eager to know what was going on, but could not ask—could only know he was in danger and she may be too. Jim broke the silence.

"Also, Sarah," he said, "maybe, *once you've already left,* you could pass on a similar message to the family and friends of my oldest sister's oldest son."

She now knew that whatever was going on involved Colton, too. Not inquiring became nearly unbearable, but she somehow managed. She agreed, and told him she loved him. He returned the expression, and they both hung up. She was out of the house with a loaded vehicle within a phenomenal thirteen minutes. Jim had no idea where she was heading. He set a course that would take him to a cabin in the mountains east of Salt Lake City.

CHAPTER 10

7:15 P.M.

Jeff had passed from Utah Valley into the Salt Lake Valley. He had headed—per instructions from Colton—toward the east bench. But before leaving Salt Lake, Jeff exited off the highway and pulled into a gas station. To the frustration of the group, a long line of cars waited at each pump—nearly into the street. But Jeff did not have much choice. His tank was just about empty.

"I'm getting sick of lines at gas stations!"

Another car pulled in behind Jeff's car. Waiting at this gas station, in a line of cars, made everyone in the car feel vulnerable. All four occupants were regularly scanning the scene, watching for any signs of danger. With his computer and the *Master Plan* on his lap, Dr. Isaacson looked up .

"Jeff?" said Dr. Isaacson.

"Yes, sir?"

"Do you realize that the reason we're in this line may be because of this secret group that attacked us?"

The strange comment from the professor had the effect of sending Jeff into a near panic. He began looking around and prepared to flee the gas station.

"No, no!" said Dr. Isaacson. "We don't seem to be in danger at the moment. Don't worry."

Dr. Isaacson held up the *Master Plan* and shook it as he spoke. "What I am saying is that one of the economic policies this

Thread group has pushed for, and succeeded with—according to the economics page of the document—is price controls in every area they can get. About a year ago, America passed price controls on gasoline. And gasoline price controls explains this line."

"So, why would The Thread push for price controls?" asked Colton.

"Good question," noted Dr. Isaacson before speaking with surprising intensity, "*The concept of price is at the heart of economic freedom*. If you want to destroy economic freedom, you have to mess with prices." Dr. Isaacson paused to gauge whether the three others understood what he was saying. "Does that make sense?"

"No," confessed Jeff.

Dr. Isaacson proceeded to give a simplified, yet thorough explanation of prices, how they affect an economy, how they deal with economic freedom, and why The Thread might benefit from controlling them. As he taught, Jeff would edge the car forward as the line intermittently moved toward the pump.

Jeff pulled back onto the highway again and drove his two roommates and the professor up Parley's Canyon—the home of I-80. It was the connecting roadway between Salt Lake City and Park City. About four minutes before they would have reached Park City, Colton instructed Jeff to exit. At the bottom of the exit ramp, Colton told Jeff to pull over under the highway. Jeff did so. And then Colton did something that seemed psychotic to the others.

They watched Colton as he worked under the brightness of a highway streetlight. Colton took the document—grateful to have arrived here safely with it—and walked halfway up the cement slope under the overpass. Once there, Colton put the document down and placed a rock—large enough to secure it in moderate wind—on top of it.

When Colton got back into the car, the others were staring at him, waiting for an explanation.

Colton shrugged. "That's what Uncle Jim told me to do. I have no idea why. But he's the FBI guy, and if he tells me to do it, I do it. Now, let's head to the cabin."

"So, we're supposed to protect this thing, and the way we protect it is to stuff it under some overpass on I-80?" asked Jeff. "Why do you think Jim wants you to do that?"

"I think," said Colton, "that it's Jim's way to see if the document is bugged."

Although the others were still confused, they realized they had reached the edge of Colton's ability to shed light on the reason behind what he had just done.

"How far away is this cabin?" asked Dr. Isaacson. It was the first thing he had said since the gas station. He had been working feverishly on his laptop.

"We're within about ten minutes," answered Colton.

They took the next exit to head to the cabin. Colton knew that this convenience was likely part of Jim's plan.

The cabin had been built when Colton was just three years old, and had been a major part of his extended family's lives ever since. Colton's parents had sold it many years previous to some close friends, but they still had full access to it. The cabin was far enough into the mountains that it was stunning, and felt secluded. Yet it was also within fifteen minutes of major stores and shopping centers. It was ideal. It had full power, running water, plumbing, and even had full media access.

The private driveway to the cabin wound through the woods for about a quarter of a mile. The driveway eased into a large open meadow with the spacious cabin at the back end of the meadow. In the hovering twilight, the cabin was spectacular. The surrounding trees and slopes made for a gorgeous backdrop. Near the cabin was a large shed that was similar in style to the cabin.

Jeff drove up to the cabin itself. The men unloaded and proceeded to walk around the cabin not only to survey its impressiveness, but to also check for any signs of danger. They had not yet settled down from the previous hour's drama. Little noises from each other or from nature had an aftershock effect on their nerves.

Colton retrieved the hidden family key. The others marveled at how nice the cabin was. Every room had vaulted ceilings, and stairs from both ends of the cabin spiraled up to a spectacular second floor that overlooked the spacious first floor. The cabin seemed much larger on the inside than it had looked from the outside. The bulk of the first floor formed a large, spacious great room. The kitchen area was to the far right, and the dining area was a bit closer to the middle. The remainder of the main floor was a large gathering area that included many couches, a large television, and a huge fireplace—all dominating the area directly in front of the door and to the left wall.

As soon as the group entered the cabin and turned the lights on, attention fell on Pete. They moseyed into a bathroom and inspected the gash—which had since stopped bleeding.

"I don't think this is going to need stitches," said Colton.

"Good," said Pete.

"But you'd better get it cleaned up," said Dr. Isaacson. Pete did so as the others left the bathroom to explore the cabin, get to work, and find food.

Dr. Isaacson set up an office on the dining table, opening up his brief case, setting up his lap top, and digging in to work once again. The younger three headed for food. Colton showed them the pantry, which had enough canned foods to satisfy their now-raging appetites.

As they were making their selections, there was a thud. The door flew open. All four men dove for cover. The professor hid beneath the table, but felt exposed. The other three men ducked behind the large island in the kitchen. They each scanned for possible weapons and options of escape. All this happened in a moment.

A deep-voiced chuckle filled the cabin.

To the shock of the other three, Colton removed a large, plastic bowl from the cupboard under the island, stood up, and flung it at the source of the voice. "You don't do that after what has happened!" But he was smiling.

The others emerged from their places of safety. They now understood they had heard the voice of Jim. He was laughing for the first time in a while and had to recompose himself.

"I'm sorry..." He was still laughing. "I wasn't trying to scare you. I didn't have full use of my hands, so I had to let my back do most of the work, and I accidentally sent the door flying open. I should've knocked first, but the damage had already been done. You all scattered faster than a bunch of cockroaches when the light goes on." Bags of groceries filled his arms. Jim set the groceries down on the island counter and loosened his tie. He tossed his suit coat onto a kitchen chair and sized up the four men he had summoned to the cabin.

"I stopped by a grocery store," he said. "I wanted to see if I was being followed. Then I thought we could use some sustenance while we tried to sort this thing out." With fresh food present, Jeff and Pete both abandoned the canned food. They plunged right into meal preparation.

"You must be Pete," perceived Jim upon seeing Pete pressing a bandage to his head. Pete used the bandage to assuage the new bleeding that cleaning the wound had initiated.

"You know about me?" he seemed surprised and honored.

"Colton mentioned you were the one who was hit."

Colton removed the bullet from his pocket and handed it to Jim. "This is what they shot at us." Jim took the object and began studying it. He had an urge to seclude himself and study it fully, but social sense pulled him back to the people he was meeting.

Colton finished making introductions, and everyone migrated toward the kitchen.

Jim addressed Dr. Isaacson after Colton introduced him. "So, how long have you taught at BYU?"

"I am heading toward my fourth year. I first taught two years at Purdue."

"You seem awfully young to be a professor."

"It's my shampoo."

Despite being such a corny statement, they all laughed. It was a sign of the stress they had been through as a group. Pete had laughed loudest, and for too long.

"Let's get a bite to eat then put our heads together on what we need to do here," said Jim. "And I want to see this document of yours."

As the group prepared and dove into their much-appreciated food, Colton asked Jim to explain what had happened earlier with his boss.

"Colton, you were attacked fifteen minutes after we talked, and at about that same time, my office was trying to track me down—before I even contacted them about the document. My commander informed me that some special agent from Denver was en route to receive any documents in the possession of Colton Wiser, myself, or others involved. I was also told that all involved would be questioned by this special agent."

"Wow," said Dr. Isaacson, "so you refused to obey the order to go to your office?"

"Yes. I've never disobeyed an order my entire career. But this was happening too fast and seemed all wrong. Everything about the situation suggested that this document is a big deal, and that sophisticated hands want it back. I decided that neither the document nor any of us involved with it at that point should end up in the hands of this agent. I concluded we needed to get away and protect it and each other until we could figure out who to get it to and how to best do it."

"Which is a challenge, because if the FBI is compromised, who else or what else may also be compromised?" said Colton.

"Exactly," said Jim.

"Yes," said Dr. Isaacson as he pointed to the document in Jim's hands, "based on what we've learned about this *Master Plan*, The Thread has infiltrated a portion of both the United States Senate and House of Representatives. They have also 'saturated' the Fed, so they control the money supply. The

President himself, through murder, is also an apparent member of this group. Every major part of our national government seems infiltrated with a portion of this group."

Jeff had assumed the role of an active observer. He usually dominated social environments, but he also had a frequent tendency to just observe and be ready to contribute. Jim and Dr. Isaacson—by sheer age and experience—assumed a dual leadership role in this new team. Colton, however, had no hesitancy to participate in any way. Pete was by far the quietest and least confident member of the group—as was the case with him in most any group. He was content to quietly follow other people's lead, although he was fascinated with what was going on and was a full mental member of the team who longed to belong and contribute.

"Uncle Jim," said Colton, "you say we'll soon know whether the document is bugged or not. How?"

Jim thought for a moment. "Well, I could explain it, but it will be more fun to show you. I want to give it about another half hour. We'll find out then."

The conversation continued with everyone sitting and eating their meals.

"So what do we do now?" asked Jeff between bites.

"Well," answered Jim, "the most nagging thing on my mind is this: how did they get access to Colton's phone? I hope the fact that we're here, safe, confirms my assumption that they did not bug the document and that they somehow compromised Colton's phone. But how could they do that so quickly? There's technology out there for eavesdropping on cell phones, but to do what they did as fast as they did it is amazing. That takes a heap of technology and power. But we know from personal experience that this group is capable of pouncing in a hurry."

"Wait a minute!" said Colton. "Jeff, the security system at the Capitol Building!"

"Ooh, that would be easy if they had access to the security system. I deleted the footage of you finding the document in the copy room, and I turned off the camera in Tomlinson's office, but there's still plenty of footage in the system to nail us."

This conclusion sent a shock through Colton. He tossed his arms rubber-like into the air. "How could we be so stupid? I knew we were being risky, but now I feel like an idiot."

"Okay," said Jim, "So maybe whoever these people—"

"The Thread," clarified Dr. Isaacson.

"The Thread," said Jim. "So maybe The Thread noticed right away that their *Master Plan* was gone. Let's say they found you two on tape getting that document. I suppose they might then have the power and technical savvy to get access to your phone. Your conversation with me would have revealed your location at BYU. I guess if they moved fast that could explain it." Jim was nodding his head. "That makes sense."

"I would think a cell phone would be hard to pinpoint," said Colton to his uncle.

"Nope," answered Jim. "Colton, did you dump your phone already?"

"Yes. And so did everyone else."

"Good. I did too. In fact, by now, if any of us were to still have and use our cell phones, we may become sitting ducks. We have to assume that electronic communication devices could act as homing beacons. Nobody touches the cabin phones. Understand?" Everyone nodded. Jim paused, and for the first time in a while, even looked a little relieved. "But this also means we have a shot at being safe here—at least for a time."

CHAPTER 11

THE CABIN
8:05 P.M.

With the discovery of how The Thread had tracked down Colton and the document, Jim felt more at peace. He remembered the bullet Colton had given him earlier. He removed it and began scrutinizing it. Jim sat back further in his chair, his exhaustion overriding the adrenaline he had been living off the past hour and a half.

Dr. Isaacson, on the other hand, seemed as uptight as ever. He was not at ease being away from his family—especially the way things had unfolded. He was agonizing over the whereabouts of his little ones and the safety and emotional state of his wife. But along with the pressing concerns for his family was the weight of realizing what was happening to his country.

The professor had gathered himself enough after the shooting to settle down and go to work. He had become, in effect, a federal economics and political detective. He had torn apart the various segments of the plan and—in a period of less than two hours—had amassed a thorough understanding of what The Thread had done in the past few years and why they had done those things. He could now see a big picture coming together.

In fact, Dr. Harold Isaacson understood more at this moment about the overall workings of The Thread than did many members of The Thread itself. And Dr. Isaacson did not want to be the only one in the group who knew what he knew.

He resolved that he would help everyone in the group understand the plan of The Thread.

"It seems like every generation must deal with those among them who wish to destroy liberty." Dr. Isaacson let that settle into their minds before going on."And that is exactly what this Thread group is doing. And based on what I'm seeing in this plan, and what has happened in America the past few years, I believe we may be facing the greatest threat to America and our Constitution that America has yet faced. The Thread seems to not only understand liberty, but they also seem to know how to destroy it."

"But why would people want to destroy freedom?" asked Pete.

"Because, Pete," answered Dr. Isaacson, "people who are free are hard to control. If I wish to get power over you, your freedom is the first barrier to my power. Freedom, ironically, is the greatest protector we have against power-seeking tyrants who wish to rule and control us. And tyrants always seek for power in ways that diminish the freedom of others."

A large snapping sound caused everyone at the table to jump, especially Jim. His hands recoiled backward to behind his head with lightning speed at the sound, much like the way someone would pull back their hand after getting burned. The sound had come from the bullet Jim had been fidgeting with throughout the conversation. When the bullet made the snapping sound, Jim dropped it reflexively. Following Jim's reaction, the bullet came to rest on the table. He carefully picked it up again.

"Wow! That is fascinating!" said Jim.

"What happened?" said Jeff.

"I think I just figured out how our little missile here works. I'm lucky I wasn't injected."

"What do you mean, *injected*?" asked Colton.

"Well," said Jim, "I think this would be a lot safer to show you with a fork. Colton, would you get a fork, please."

"Sure." Colton was back in a moment. The projectile looked like a dart because it had tiny fins on the back. It also had a skinny shaft that came to a point in the front. It looked like a long bullet that had small fins on the back. Jim held the back of the bullet and pressed the point against the prongs of the fork. He pressed harder and harder until it happened. The same popping sound recurred.

"Did you see that?" asked Jim.

"I *heard* that," said Jeff, "but I didn't *see* anything."

"Watch really close this time. Keep your eyes on the front of the bullet." He again pressed the bullet against the fork, causing it to snap for the third time. This time they saw something. The front third of the bullet seemed to flare out. It was just for an instant, and then the bullet was back to normal again.

"What in the world was that?" asked an amazed Jeff.

"I think I know what it is," said Jim. He did it again. The flaring of the front of the bullet was even more evident now that they had already noticed it. "I'm pretty certain this must be some sort of a tranquilizer. Let me test my theory." Jim pressed the bullet—point down—against the rough wooden table surface. The bullet popped once again, but this time bounced back away from the table.

"Look," instructed Jim pointing to where he had just pressed the bullet against the table. There was a small hole. Everyone pulled their heads in a tight circle around the little hole as they analyzed the mark.

"Yes," said Jim, "when pressure is put on the tip of this dart—it is more of a dart than a bullet—the walls of the tip are flared out to keep the bullet from penetrating into whatever it hits. At—"

"Why would it do that?" interrupted Jeff.

"My guess is that whoever shoots this doesn't want it tearing though its target."

"Then why would they shoot?" asked Jeff.

"To tranquilize," said Jim. "The tip flares out, blocking it from going in. But at the same time, a needle of sorts seems to protrude the instant these sides flare out. That protruding needle explains the hole in the table. That needle will deliver whatever chemical this bullet is armed with."

"So you could tranquilize *or* kill," asked Colton, "depending on what you put in it?"

"Sure. I suppose," agreed Jim.

"Do you think they were trying to tranquilize or kill us when they shot at us earlier?" wondered Pete aloud.

"Tranquilize," said Jim. "You have information. They want to know what you know more than they want you dead."

Colton understood something very important. "So, the fact that they don't know what we know gives us some power?"

"Perhaps," said Dr. Isaacson, "but that is not an advantage I would bank on. A group this powerful could be determined to just eliminate us and clean up afterward, I would think."

FORT MEADE, MARYLAND
10:39 P.M. EASTERN (8:39 P.M. MOUNTAIN)

Four images were alive on the large screens on the wall. The equipment and computers across the room that were usually quiet were humming in full operation.

When the alarm had gone off on his computer, Dave Jeffries had looked at his watch. It was 8:10 P.M. And at that point, the other two who were on duty were not in the room. That was three hours ago. The room had since gone from a quiet, dark room to a crowded war room.

The Thread had tapped into the NSA's national communication network and was filtering communications for key words and phrases.

Catching this phone call had not been hard. The conversation between Colton and Jim had included almost every criterion for which The Thread was listening. The computer system set aside most items that trip the filters for later analysis; but the level of matches of this particular phone call had triggered the alarm. The computers transferred the call into text in real time and presented the words on Dave's monitor. Dave could not miss the flashing dialog on his screen. As he read the words between Colton and Jim, he knew The Thread was in trouble.

Dave was fantastic at what he did, and had the location of the phone call pinned down to the exact office on the campus of Brigham Young University. He had contacted two agents in the area—that's all there had been in Utah Valley at the time. The pickings were slim, but the two men responded and were on site within fifteen minutes. Unfortunately, the group had escaped.

On the eve of the transactions, The Thread was now in full fury and action. More than three hundred members of The Thread from the western United States were pouring into Utah. And Judas, for some reason, was vehemently determined that all transactions—including the Salt Lake Transaction—proceed as planned. For the first time in its ten-year history, The Thread was legitimately threatened.

CHAPTER 12

THE CABIN
8:45 P.M.

"I think we've given it enough time. We'd better find out whether our document is bugged," announced Jim.

Colton was thrilled. He wanted to know why Jim had asked him to put the *Master Plan* in such a strange location. Now he would find out.

"Dr. Isaacson," asked Jim, "I presume your laptop can go online?"

"It can. Does the cabin have media access?"

"Yes. But before we go online, I need to block your computer's identification. Otherwise The Thread could trace us to this very cabin."

"Go ahead," offered Dr. Isaacson, sliding the computer across the table over to Jim.

Jim punched away at the keys. A black screen came up with a flashing cursor. He entered various pieces of information. After a couple of minutes, he was ready. "That should do it," he announced. "Now, let's go online."

He opened up the internet browser and entered in an address. The others stood behind Jim and huddled around the computer screen as he worked. They could see he had gone to the website for the Utah Department of Transportation.

"UDOT?" asked Colton. "What are you doing, getting a traffic report?"

"You might say that," said Jim with a smile.

Jim clicked on a camera link. A map of the state appeared on the screen. Jim clicked on I-80, just east of Salt Lake City. A new map appeared with little blue marks along the highway on the map.

"This should be the one," said the FBI agent as he clicked on one of the blue marks.

"Wow, Jim," said Colton, "that was brilliant! I can't believe you thought of that so fast."

Pete looked at Colton. He thought Colton had seen something on the screen that he had not. "What was brilliant?"

"You'll see in just a moment," said Colton.

It did only take a moment. An image appeared. It was a streaming video. The scene was a highway at night, with moderate traffic. The camera was on the south side of the highway, facing west. The traffic was coming from the west, around the bend, and over the overpass. Before the cars finished crossing the overpass, they left the right side of the image. Peter now understood. Dr. Isaacson and Jeff also saw what Colton had figured out a moment earlier.

On the slope under the overpass—at the bottom of the image—was a small rectangle, easily visible under the direct light of the streetlamp. They were looking at a live video feed of the *Master Plan*. It was still there, just as Colton had left it.

"Well, it appears as if our friends in The Thread don't have a tracking device on that document."

Peter's head popped up from the screen, his eyes wide. "What if," he asked with sincere drama, "this is a trap?"

Jim tried to reassure him, "Well, Pete, it may be a trap. You're right that they may know it's there and are patiently waiting for us to go and get it. But we need that document. I think we take the risk and get it back into our possession."

Dr. Isaacson came alive with hope. "Jim! If you can cloak this computer, I can email my wife!" It was really a question.

"Too risky," said the FBI agent.

"Why? We just went online with my computer!"

"That's because I've told your computer to tell cyberspace that it's a different computer—some random computer. The Thread might be able to trace any email that you send to your wife directly to this cabin. As it appears, a random computer visited this web site. But if any of us use it to contact our families, we might reveal our location. It's just too risky."

The professor, exasperated, plopped into a love seat. "I have to talk to my wife somehow."

"Me too," said Jim. "But I don't know any safe way that it's going to happen tonight." Silence prevailed for some time as the thoughts of everyone in the cabin dwelt on their respective families. Jeff broke the silence.

"So, why do we need to have that thing with us?" questioned Jeff as he gestured toward the image on the screen. "Can't we just leave it there? I mean, we have copies."

"That's the most critical evidence we've got," replied Jim, also gesturing at the computer screen. "We need to get that document and protect it."

"So who goes?" asked Dr. Isaacson.

"Well," said Jim, "I doubt they bugged this document, and I doubt this is a trap. I don't think they know where it is. So I say we go together so the professor can continue teaching us what he sees in the *Master Plan*."

Dr. Isaacson was not sure if he agreed. But he deferred to the FBI agent's judgment in the matter. And although he would far rather have been with his family, he was eager to continue to teach the group what he understood about The Thread's plan.

"Okay, Jim," said Dr. Isaacson, "you're the boss here. We'll stay together."

Jim got the group moving. "Colton, get some of our food in case we can't come back here for any reason. Pete, is that head of yours okay for more travel?"

"Yes," said Pete as his hand moved reflexively to his head to fidget with his wound. "I don't think it's a problem at all."

"Good. It's only about a fifteen minute trip," noted Jim. Then he announced to the whole group, "Just in case, let's take with us one of the copies of the document, and hide the other copy here at the cabin. And lest we can't come back, be sure to bring with you anything you might need if we're forced to bolt."

In response, Jeff moved to the large screen TV and took hold of one side. Dr. Isaacson was closest. Jeff requested, "Doc, would you mind grabbing the other end?" The professor understood and laughed.

"What're you doing with it?" It was Pete. Innocent as always, he didn't get it. Jeff's humor and Pete's oblivion had formed an interesting combination for the roommates. Jeff had learned to be very cautious when it came to teasing Pete. Pete could sense that caution and had always appreciated it.

9:08 P.M.

As Jim drove out of the meadow, a sense of vulnerability overcame the group. Without voicing it, everyone was glad to be together. They were forming a unique cohesion from their shared experience and mission. Circumstances beyond their control had bound them together. None of them wished to be here at this time, but all felt a sense of responsibility to do all they could to bring to light the dark things they were discovering.

The full moon was now high enough that it lit the meadow. As they left the meadow and entered the winding trail, the foliage of the mountain forest broke the light of the moon. Shards and odd shapes of moonlight illuminated the scene. When they reached the main road, Colton got out of the vehicle and unlocked the gate. He was soon back in the vehicle.

Jim was driving; Dr. Isaacson was in the front passenger seat. The three roommates were in the back seat, with Pete in the middle. Jim headed south on the mountain road—a course that would have taken him straight to the highway. However, after a short distance, he turned right, heading west on a smaller road than the one they had just been on.

Then Jim did something unusual. He reached down and turned off the headlights of the car.

"What happened?" Pete panicked.

"No worries, Pete," said Jim, "I'm making it harder for anyone to track us."

"Wow!" it was Pete again. He was leaning forward, with his head between the two front seats, his eyes wide. He was amazed at how vivid the mountain road was in the moonlight. "That's awesome!"

The group was quiet while everyone in the car enjoyed the strangely spectacular moonlit mountain scene. The silence did not last long though. There were more questions to ask Dr. Isaacson.

Jim felt a special sense of compassion for the others in the group, knowing that they were in great danger and that he was partly responsible for their predicament. He could have gone to his office and yielded to the special agent from Denver. But he sensed disaster in that alternative. Jim knew he had better be wise and vigilant; else the blood of these good people he had pulled into hiding would be on his hands—and forever on his conscience.

Jim reached the intersection where the narrow road they were on met a wider road that would take them to the highway. He turned the car left and headed south. Jim turned the headlights back on and continued in the direction of the highway.

As the highway came into view, a pall settled over the car's occupants, and a spell of observant silence ensued.

Cautiously, Jim approached the overpass. He was driving slowly enough now to take in every sign of danger he could gather. However, he did not want to be so slow that he looked overly conspicuous. The underpass was dark, and that made Jim nervous.

They passed through the darkness of the underpass. As they emerged from the other side, the light of the street lamp on the overpass illuminated the scene. They all saw the *Master Plan* to the right, on the slope of the underpass. It seemed untouched, with the rock still in place. Jim pulled a u-turn and headed under the overpass again.

Jim slowed the car and came to a stop just inside the shadow of the overpass. He put the car in park and began to unbuckle. Colton snapped forward and placed his hand on Jim's shoulder. "Uncle Jim, I'll get it. You be ready to drive."

Colton had said it casually, but Jim and the others knew it was a subtle, yet fearless willingness on Colton's part. They all knew that if something went wrong, Colton would be in peril. The simple trip up that slope to retrieve that document could be a fatal trap. Jim agreed, made penetrating eye contact, and warned, "You be cautious, young man. Your mother would kill me if she knew that I let you do this."

"I'll be fine," and Colton meant it. His courage was displacing his fear. He did not wait for the fear to return. As he left, Colton felt an unanticipated jolt of adrenaline.

In the car, Jim realized how at risk they were. He had parked in the shadows, under the overpass, for cover. But he considered afresh how vulnerable they now were to a trap. As he watched his beloved nephew walk away from the car, Jim prayed silently.

Colton did not waste any time. He bounded across the street and up the slope. He had placed a corner of the rock on the first letter of the title. He could see that it was exactly where he had placed it. He also noticed that it was the genuine document. This gave him confidence. He removed the rock and picked up the document. He turned to scurry down the slope toward the safety of the car. Then his heart froze.

A car was coming off the highway down the exit ramp. This was a seldom-used exit, particularly at this time of night. Colton felt paralyzed. He was in plain sight and fully exposed. His initial impulse was to run—to bolt to the car. Another part of him sensed the need to act casual. That part prevailed.

Jim saw the car too, and lowered his window. His first inclination was to yell and order Colton back into the car. But he realized it was most likely a harmless driver, and he did not want to make Colton look any more suspicious than he already did. Jim just watched and waited, poised in the car with total readiness to move into major action. He removed his gun from its holster and held it.

As the car neared the bottom of the ramp, Colton stood, holding the document, acting as if he were standing casually on a street corner. It certainly was not natural, and he could see now that the driver was looking at him. His heart was pounding, and he could feel his chest twitch with every beat.

He was relieved to see only quizzical curiosity on the face of the driver as the man in the car came to a stop at the intersection. In an awkward move that made Colton feel like an idiot, Colton waved at the driver. He wanted to crawl into a hole. He willed the car to move on. Slowly, the car moved straight across the intersection and up the entrance ramp to get back onto the highway. Colton supposed the guy had taken the wrong exit.

Relieved, Colton bounded down the slope, crossed the street, and plunged into the waiting car. Jim did not waste time. He punched the gas and the car streaked out of the underpass and headed once again up the mountain road that would lead them back to the cabin.

CHAPTER 13

NEW THREAD HEADQUARTERS
SALT LAKE CITY, UTAH
9:45 P.M.

Nathan hung up the phone and placed it in his pocket. Good news was hard to come by this evening. He would much rather have learned about the success of the next day's transactions from the comfort of his casino in Las Vegas. But that wasn't to be. His lot was to lead a manhunt. Nathan scanned the entire office space, making a sweeping, visual inventory of the resources put in his charge.

Nathan's presence breathed a ruthless charisma. He did not have problems with people obeying him. Some would argue that Nathan was even more a symbol of authority in The Thread than was Judas. Nathan's hair was so blonde that it almost looked white. This gave him the appearance of seeming a lot older than he was.

The office's transformation was astonishing. Screens, projectors, computers, cords, and other trinkets of technology dominated the office space. The new Utah headquarters of The Thread would have a direct, encrypted link to the National Security Agency, extraordinary eavesdropping technology, unbelievable access to law enforcement and private surveillance systems throughout Utah, and a highly-trained, qualified staff to run it all.

Most of the men in the room had been in Utah for less than an hour. In fact, just two hours ago, this entire portion of the building had been an empty, quiet, unused office space. The owner had been shocked that someone wanted it so urgently—not to mention the fact that they had paid three months worth of advance rent in cash. But what the owner could not have known was that these renters would burn down the entire building within the next twenty-four hours.

THE CABIN
8:59 P.M

Jim was eager to see if their adventure had made it onto the evening news. When the time came, Jim succeeded in hushing the group. He raised the volume. Focusing on the television had a calming effect on the feelings of the group. But that calm feeling did not last long once the news broadcast began.

The standard introduction to the news crossed the screen with familiar faces and music. The music ebbed, and the camera honed in on the man and the woman sitting behind the news desk. The first anchor, the woman, began to speak. The small group in the cabin did not have to wait long to hear the report on their story. But it was not the version of their story they expected to hear.

"Our top story tonight involves a local FBI agent who is on the run from the law. James Berry, an agent who works in Provo, is wanted by the FBI for possible conspiracy to commit terrorism against the United States…"

The room exploded with gasps of surprise, Jim being the most vocal. "What?" But the uniform desire to not miss any details of the story quelled the outburst almost as quickly as it had started.

"…Colton Wiser, a twenty-five-year-old political adviser, who works at the Capitol Building, is wanted for questioning as well. Both men are on the run and have evaded law enforcement officers…" Pictures of Jim and Colton filled up the screen. "Anyone with information regarding the whereabouts of either of these two, please contact the FBI at…"

"You know," Jim announced, "I was really interested to see if the news depicted the BYU incident, and how they'd cover it if they did. But this is unreal!"

The news anchor continued with the story. "Also with the two is Jeff Palmer, Peter Wright, and Dr. Harold Isaacson, a professor of economics at Brigham Young University. We have not been informed whether these three are being held against their will or are with the other two of their own volition." And that was the extent of the report.

"I'm a hostage!" said Jeff, handling the stressful revelation with his usual humor. Colton found himself laughing. He kept laughing for longer than he wanted to. His laughter was an expression of his exasperation.

The second anchor had already begun discussing a shooting at a business in Salt Lake earlier in the day. Their story was over. The news at this point became a distraction. Jim got up and turned it off. For some reason, Jeff wanted the television back on. He turned it on, but then turned the volume down most of the way. He continued to look at the television screen, but was listening to what the others were saying about the skewed news broadcast.

"This has got to be the influence of that special agent from Denver," said a frazzled Jim. "I disobeyed a direct order from Joseph Hansen, the director of the Provo office. I've never done that before, and that's a serious issue. But Joe wouldn't allow what we just heard. This is a media release that comes from the work of The Thread, *not* the FBI."

Jim paced the cabin. He reasoned aloud as he did so. "There is nothing in what we did today that would suggest anything about terrorist activity—as far as I can see. There was no mention of the shooting at BYU, which means The Thread is doctoring the information going to the press. The news missed the real story entirely. A shooting at BYU is big news. The only explanation that makes sense is that The Thread has not only infiltrated the FBI, but also appears to have control over what makes it to the media and how it's depicted."

Pete spoke, concerned. "Agent Berry, if you and Colton are tied to this cabin, and the FBI is actively pursuing you, aren't we in great danger being here? Don't you think they'll find us?"

Jim had set that concern aside as a small enough risk. He now reevaluated it in light of the news broadcast, but came to the same conclusion he had come to earlier. "Pete, I think we're okay here. This cabin is no longer in the name of Colton's parents. Colton, explain the situation, would you?"

"My parents sold the cabin to some good friends. Those friends began coming up with us years ago. They loved the place so much that they kept coming up more and more. Eventually, they came to use this cabin more than any of our family did—including extended family. They felt bad about mooching so much off my parents that they offered to buy it. My parents agreed. That was more than ten years ago, but nothing else has changed. They give us full use of it, just like my parents gave them full use of it before they bought it. We still come up a few times every year—as often as we ever did when we owned it. It's turned out to be a good deal."

"That's weird," said Pete.

Jim ignored Pete and continued. "Well, when I considered where we should go, I had to decide right then. Since then, I've been going over and over our situation. Colton's family, my family—and the extended family as well—have many other properties in the state we own and use often. This property is low on the list of possibilities and would take a lot of research."

Dr. Isaacson warned, "Jim, this group is resourceful."

"True. But for The Thread to find us, they'd have to rely on financial records. But by the time you go back far enough to find this property, there are dozens of places in the state that are just as likely for Colton or myself to go. Yes, we're at risk, but I think that risk is minimal. Now that we're fugitives, most places will be more risky for us than this cabin is. I think we should stay. But we had better get an early start in the morning."

In all their surmising, they concluded that to get word out about The Thread they would have to pour out information to the media simultaneous to placing the document into the hands of authorities. They must blast the nation with information about The Thread. How much control did The Thread have with local and national media? The group concluded that The Thread probably had infiltrated the media, but the media potentials in America were too enormous to fully control. There would be outlets and a way to get word out. But when and how could they get word out without The Thread intercepting them? These would be concerns they would have to sort out, and they knew their safety at the cabin weakened as time passed.

Jeff had continued changing channels as the group talked. His eyes bulged when he got to a channel at which he never before had stopped. It was C-SPAN. On the screen was a man for whom Jeff would normally have had plenty of respect. The speech was a recording from earlier that day.

"Look everyone," announced Jeff as he turned the volume back up to a higher level, "there's the Hen!"

Jeff had made the announcement about the Hen in a sarcastic way, but the others responded with a genuine fascination as they once again gathered in front of the television. The group sat mesmerized, looking at a man on the large screen who was likely a key figure in what they knew may well be the worst assault on the Constitution in history.

Colton thought about how the President had placed his hand on the Bible and had sworn to protect the Constitution. As he watched the President speak, Colton recalled the depth to which the President had paid tribute to the former President, whose heart attack had shocked the nation. Colton had tremendous respect for any man holding that position. But with what he now knew, Colton found himself watching the President with disdain.

Just how much did the President know about the death of his forerunner? Did he know he was the 'Hen,' or was he just a puppet of others who were in power? Did he have a hand in the plot that brought him the highest office of public service in the world? Was he the leader of The Thread?

The volume was up very high now. The bottom of the screen indicated that the President had given the speech earlier that day to a labor union. Colton could not identify the particular union the hats and uniforms signified, but the crowd seemed enormous. The raucous cheering of the crowd indicated they loved the words and the man speaking to them.

The hand of the charismatic President was in a fist. "Gone are the days when America sends its jobs across the world. We will no longer sacrifice the jobs of the many to the greed of the few. What can a work staff in any nation do that American workers couldn't do as well, if not better? The International Job Displacement Elimination Act is having a mighty effect. Greedy executives who fatten themselves off the labor of their workforce now pay stiff taxes for abandoning their workers by exporting labor to other nations. Businesses who conduct all interactions in the United States of America enjoy a preferred corporate tax rate."

The crowd went wild.

"No longer will America shut out its workers by patronizing artificially cheap foreign products. Other nations may choose to allow greed to exploit labor and expect America to pay tribute. America cannot prevent other nations from producing cheap products at such high costs to human dignity. But we, as Americans, can choose to not patronize those products. We can choose to not subsidize international greed and unfair competition. We can choose to see that the price of their goods is penalized to the point that the playing field is leveled. We can be fair." The crowd again erupted in applause.

"And no more will America play the one-sided game of welcoming products from nations that do not welcome our products. Free trade is over. Fair trade is in!" The President waited smugly for yet another long pause during wild roaring.

"The unwillingness of employers to pay a livable wage has collided with our resolve. Minimum wage has been raised more percentage-wise these past three years than in any period since the minimum wage was enacted. And these increases won't fade away. We have finally indexed minimum wages to keep pace with inflation indefinitely."

And then the President spoke in dramatic conclusion: "More and more, the evil grasp of greed of the few who own nearly all of America's wealth is being weakened and is finally slipping. Public control of what has been private domination of wealth will soon empower the vast but economically weak middle class of America to finally enjoy the fruits of its labors."

"This is unbelievable," said Dr. Isaacson. The President's speech was having far less effect on the younger three than it was having on the professor—who was looking back and forth from the *Master Plan* in his hands to the television.

Dr. Isaacson stretched his hand out toward the screen. "That man is laying out the specifics of the economics portion of The Thread's *Master Plan*." And with that announcement, a wave of shock passed through the room. "Why don't you tell us, Mr. President, about the virtues of regulation and government control of industry?"

And the ongoing speech from the President made Dr. Isaacson look like a prophet. "...We are making great strides toward safety and stability in our markets. The trend of deregulation is over, and unrestrained and reckless pursuit of profit is now, more and more, checked by public oversight. And the vast resources of America are aligning with public interest. All these measures serve to limit the immense and unbending power of the few profiteers who have controlled so much of our lives."

And then the President said a few words to rally the crowd once again, and the speech was over.

"We just listened to the last half of the economics section of the *Master Plan*. I'm guessing that he covered the first half of this plan before we tuned in."

"I guess that puts to rest the question of how culpable that man is," said Jim.

"So what all did we miss?" asked Colton. Everyone crowded around the professor to look at the document.

"Well, most of the first half of the document deals with using federal power through legislation and grants to enact price controls of all kinds." Dr. Isaacson pointed out in the *Master Plan* the many price controls The Thread has sought for. Among the issues he pointed out were rent controls, universal medicine, executive wage caps, and price controls on many food staples.

"So Doc," said Jeff. "I know The Thread is not exactly an affiliate of the Boy Scouts of America—they're obviously evil. But you act like all these policies he's talking about are bad policies. I'll be frank. It sounds to me like a lot of these things are pretty good things for the President to push for."

"Jeff," said Dr. Isaacson, "some of these ideas are very popular, and a lot of good people believe in them. But the one thing all these policies have in common is that they all hurt or destroy economic freedom. And that makes all these policies foolish—evil or not. But politicians—especially demagogues who play off emotion to sway the public toward bad policies—are good at making bad ideas sound wonderful to the emotional masses. That's one reason why freedom is so fragile. The forces that oppose freedom can sound so appealing. And a public that is not educated on economic freedom is very vulnerable."

"Are you saying I'm stupid?" asked Jeff. It was in jest, but Jeff delivered it as if he were serious.

"Sorta," said Dr. Isaacson in mock candor that made everyone laugh.

Along with working through the realities of their situation, the group continued to barrage the professor with questions, and he continued to imbue them with a greater and deeper understanding of economic freedom and the opposing economics of The Thread. As the conversation wore on, Dr. Isaacson became deliriously tired. Through his insistence, everyone set up makeshift beds of blankets and pillows. All readied to sleep within close proximity to each other in the middle of the main living area.

As everyone went to bed, Colton and Jeff knelt to pray. Their example beckoned the others to do the same. Each prayed with a depth of sincerity people seldom achieve outside of crisis. For a while, Jim paced the cabin, standing watch and thinking about solutions. Conversation ended and silence filled the cabin. Other than the exhausted professor, their minds were too active for sleep at first. But eventually even Jim settled down and sleep engulfed the cabin.

As the night wore on, hundreds of people were arriving in Utah. Among the arrivals were some of the most talented and deadly members of The Thread. There would be no rest for The Thread this night. For their little document—what the group in the cabin referred to as the *Master Plan*, and what The Thread referred to as *Key #3*—was in enemy hands. All they had planned was in jeopardy. They were desperate. They knew they had but a short time.

CHAPTER 14

NEW YORK CITY
THE NEXT MORNING, 8:03 A.M. EASTERN
(6:03 A.M. MOUNTAIN)

Kaleed eased the armored vehicle into the place described in his instructions. They told him to park as closely to the United Nations building as he could. As ordered, he maneuvered the stout vehicle and parked it on the street facing away from the United Nations building. This, they told him, would signal to the purchasing party that the transaction was ready.

With the vehicle parked, Kaleed turned the engine off. And then he waited. He waited for a transaction as he had done many times each week these past months. Only, this time was different. He was nervous. Never before—in all the transactions for which he had served as the deliverer—had there been so much security. Never before had there been so many instructions. And never before had the commission been as high. He would make enough money in this transaction alone to bring the rest of his family to America. This job was proving to be a tremendous blessing.

They had told him this was his most important delivery yet. They stressed that he must follow, with exactness, every instruction they had given. If he failed, he would lose his commission—all of it. Yes, Kaleed was nervous.

In all the previous transactions, the documents he delivered were in a small case, or in plain sight. This time, however, there was no folder, no dossier, and no briefcase to his view—only a large, locked safe. They told him that this transaction would not only include documents, but also a large sum of money. They instructed that when the time came, he was to open the vault, wait for the clients, and to not—under any circumstances—inspect the money or the documents.

They had housed Kaleed the past three days in a nice hotel in New York City. He was forbidden to speak to anyone he knew for the three days leading up to this transaction. They instructed him to relax and lie low. He must do this transaction with great discretion. He was eager to hear the sound of his wife's voice again, and to be with his two small children. He would be back to them in New Jersey by late afternoon. He looked forward to that.

The strangest part of his instructions was what they referred to as *The Key*. As his mind reviewed what he was to do with *The Key*, he pulled out a scanner from a small bag. Kaleed thought the scanner looked like one of the scanning guns a grocery store might use to scan the larger objects in your cart. It had a trigger, with a large snout through which the scanning lasers would emit.

They told him that at transaction time, a key-bearer would arrive and present him with the key. The key was to be a document. On the back of the document, Kaleed was to scan the red mark. If the document was legitimate, the small screen on the top of the scanner would say "Confirmed: Key #1." If it was not legitimate, the screen would remain blank. The key-bearer, upon confirming the exchange, was to leave. Once Kaleed had allowed the key-bearer three complete minutes to leave, he was to slide a card—one that looked much like a credit card—through a slot on the safe.

Kaleed was then to return to his seat in the front of the vehicle. Within five minutes, the receivers of the transaction were to arrive and remove the documents and the money from the safe. They instructed him not to interfere. They also mandated that if the transaction receivers were not there within five minutes, he must reseal the safe by re-sliding his card through the scanner and then drive back to the warehouse from which he had obtained the vehicle. After reviewing the instructions in his mind, he felt calmer. Kaleed looked at his watch. He still had just over eight minutes before the key-bearer was to arrive. He was prepared. He breathed deeply and waited.

THE CABIN
6:07 A.M. MOUNTAIN

Colton's eyes cracked, surveying the scene. He could see through his squint that although the sky was dark still, it was beginning to glow with the coming dawn. It was not light that awoke him, it was his sense of smell. Colton opened his eyes and blinked a couple of times. He took in a deep breath through his nose and smiled. He loved the smell of bacon.

Colton rolled over and looked toward the kitchen. Jim was working by a small light above the stove. The sound of popping and sizzling was surprisingly loud. Colton sat up abruptly and stretched. As he did so, he saw movement in all the others. Whether it was the sound and smell of the bacon, or whether it was his own arising that caused them to stir, Colton did not know. But with others' eyes cracking open, Colton felt no obligation to be quiet.

"That smells great, Uncle Jim!"

"Bring back some memories?" asked the federal agent. The extended family revered Jim for being the big breakfast cooker. Colton smiled at the memory, but did not verbally respond to the question.

Colton got up and walked to the kitchen—letting his blanket fall to the ground—and sat at a bar stool at the island. Within a couple of minutes, his two roommates joined him, stretching as they arrived. Dr. Isaacson seemed the most reluctant to arise.

Jeff looked at his watch, saw what time it was, and let out a moan. "Why are you up so early, Mr. agent-man?"

"Because we've got to eat and get going," said Jim. The FBI agent was wearing the same white shirt and slacks he had worn the evening before and even slept in. "Our window of safety here is limited. So I think we have to get a great breakfast and head out. I still haven't sorted out how we're going to communicate what we know or get this document into the right hands. Until we have that figured out, we need to buy more time."

"So what's your plan?" asked Dr. Isaacson.

"Well," said Jim, "we have packs, tents, and four wheelers. I think we follow the back trails up to the peak of the mountain to the west. That mountain peak overlooks the Salt Lake Valley. From that point, we could use multiple trails and paths to get down the mountain in either direction. We have a portable two-meter Ham radio. If we were to use it, it could give us away. But at least we could communicate if we need to. If we take the car, we're too vulnerable. I'm sure both our vehicles as well as ourselves have APB's out on them."

"It's an awful day when a group who is trying to take over America can use the police as a tool to go after someone," said Jeff.

"You're right, Jeff," agreed Jim. "If we're caught by the police, I imagine we'd then be sitting ducks. We've got to stay free until we get word out about The Thread."

"Well," said Dr. Isaacson, "We covered so many things last night that if we have the right opportunity, any one of us could do a pretty good job explaining what The Thread is attempting."

It was true. Colton smiled with amazement as he considered how much he had learned from the professor the night before. He thought to himself how ironic it was that he had learned so much about freedom and economics on such a crazy day.

NEW YORK CITY
8:14 A.M. EASTERN (6:14 A.M. MOUNTAIN)

The key-bearer arrived a minute early. He knocked on the passenger-side window just like they told Kaleed it would happen. The key-bearer had dark hair, speckled with grey. Kaleed unlocked the door, and the man entered the armored carrier. The key-bearer was wearing an expensive business suit, and seemed to be in his late forties. The businessman did not say anything, but his look and demeanor disturbed Kaleed. There was an unusual intensity—as if the man were afraid of Kaleed. Perhaps it was the transaction. Maybe he, like Kaleed, was afraid of failing in his role during this vital transaction. But whatever the cause, Kaleed sensed fear. That fear did nothing for Kaleed's own nerves.

Kaleed turned the document upside-down so he could see the title on the back of the document. This was, indeed, the key. But Kaleed's attention fell to the mark. He felt a moment of revulsion. The mark made him feel as if he were handling something from the occult.

For some reason, he did not want the man to sense his disgust—Kaleed did not want to display any hesitancy. That could mean the end of this miracle job were he to be unprofessional in the presence of clients. So Kaleed moved with authority to scan the mark. The machine beeped, and the screen on the scanner confirmed that the mark was authentic.

Without any prompting from Kaleed, the key-bearer took the document back into his possession and left the vehicle. Kaleed breathed a large sigh of relief. The rest of the transaction would be much less stressful. Knowing all had gone well thus far, Kaleed relaxed for the first time in days.

After the three minutes had passed, Kaleed made his way to the safe. With an attitude that was almost casual, he removed the scanning card and placed it at the beginning point of the slot on the safe. With less drama than it should have taken, Kaleed pulled the card forward through the slide. With that seemingly inconsequential act, Kaleed Khavis took the last breath of his life.

CHAPTER 15

THE CABIN
6:19 A.M.

As the food became ready, Jim shoveled pancakes, bacon, and scrambled eggs onto everyone's plates. Waves of thanks and gratitude met Jim as he served the food. As they sat around the island in the cabin, the conversation merged back to their predicament and alternatives, and then to the *Master Plan* of The Thread. They essentially resumed the conversation from the previous night.

SEATTLE, WASHINGTON
5:45 A.M. PACIFIC (6:45 A.M. MOUNTAIN)

Heshi was eager to do this job and move on. This job seemed strange to him. He was not comfortable with it. If this particular assignment required so much security, why was he to perform it so publicly? He thought of his revulsion just three minutes ago when he saw *Key # 2.* His instructions were to scan the red mark. They did not tell him the mark would be a smear of blood.

Heshi looked down at the scanner on the floorboard. It was some sort of a blood scanner, for crying out loud! What kind of a transaction would require such bizarre security? And why would they stage such a secretive transaction in the open in downtown Seattle? They ordered him to be as close to the base of the Space Needle as he could get. They told him to park with the truck facing the Space Needle itself.

After the scanning, the key-bearer had departed with haste. Heshi was now alone, waiting for the time to pass before he opened the safe for the clients.

Heshi removed the credit card-like access key from its envelope. He studied it, but there was nothing strange about it—only a card with a scanning bar on the back. No writings were even on it. He looked at his watch. It was almost time.

His mind drifted, taking in how strange his life had been these past six months. Six months ago, he was in Pakistan. His life had been devoted to studying capitalism. He and his group had not been popular, but they had done some good, he thought. But everything changed once the American recruiters found them. Within six weeks of that first encounter, they were on their way to America. They had been promised—the five of them—lucrative jobs. These jobs would allow them to earn enough to bring their families back with them. He worried about his family—especially his wife and child. He spoke with them often, and relished those moments.

With a twinge of envy, Heshi thought about Kaleed and Abdul. Both men received permission two months ago to bring their families to America from Pakistan. They had to borrow money to do it, but both had gotten at least part of their families here and were now enjoying them. He knew he was close to getting authorization for his own family. That would be a great day. And this morning's job alone would pull in enough funds to bring his family.

Heshi knew that his brother was also doing a special transaction. Kaleed had let slip that he would not be able to talk with anyone for the next three days. How strange that Kaleed was doing something very similar, but so far away. Heshi took one final look around the Space Needle in front of him. He leaned forward in his seat so he could peer up the awe-inspiring tower.

Heshi checked his watch. He had not wished to unlock the safe too early. But he was now a minute late. His heart lurched. He must open the safe and return to his seat in the front before the clients arrived. He felt like a fool to let the moment pass so carelessly. He got up and walked between the two front seats of the van. In a rushed motion, Heshi placed his card in the scanning slit.

Heshi pulled the card forward, hoping to make it back to his seat quickly. His hasty scan did nothing in the moment to open the safe. He thought he must have scanned incorrectly the first time. He reached to scan again. And then it happened. His brain was in the process of recognizing something was wrong. But long before Heshi would have become conscious of that fact, everything went blank.

THE CABIN
6:56 A.M.

Not yet aware of dramatic events now cascading across the country, the small group in the cabin continued to discuss their situation.

"The news is coming on in just a couple of minutes," announced Jim, cutting into the group's discussion. "I want to see if there are any new updates. And we need to get ready to get out of here. We have three four-wheelers in the shed. That means one of us will ride alone, and everyone else will ride with a partner. We have to pack the four-wheelers with camping gear and food. I'd like to see us out of here within about twenty minutes." Then Jim spoke to his nephew. "Colton."

"Yeah," Colton was ready to work.

"You know the shed better than anyone. Why don't you and Pete pack the four-wheelers with camping gear?"

"Sure," said Colton, and he turned to leave the cabin. Jim stopped him for more instruction.

"Remember to pack plenty of things for sleeping and cooking. We have to be prepared to cook without a campfire." Colton nodded, and then resumed his trip to the door. Pete turned to follow him. Before they reached the door, Jim continued handing out assignments to the others.

"Dr. Isaacson, why don't you help me pack a couple of days' worth of food?"

"I'd be glad to."

"And me?" asked Jeff.

Jim thought for a moment. "Why don't you scan the news, Jeff? If you hear anything that has to do with us, holler. I want to hear it."

"That sounds like a job I could do," said Jeff with an air of mock confidence.

When Jeff turned on the television, he expected to see commercials because he was tuning in just prior to the hour. But what he saw was a reporter in a large city amidst smoke and commotion. The reporter's comments were interspersed by questions coming from the news anchors. Based on the news anchors, Jeff could tell that this was a national news story.

Although the feeling of breaking news permeated the report, Jeff nearly changed the channel to look for information about their story. But Jeff was soon fixated on the report with no desire to change the channel.

Jeff announced to Jim, "There's been a major explosion somewhere." Jim made a thoughtful, partially interested 'hmm' sound.

In just a couple of short minutes, Jeff gathered that a major explosion had rocked a downtown segment of a major city. Within another minute, it became apparent the city was New York. The focus of the blast was into the open—not at any particular building's foundation—and had cast shrapnel and caused damage over a large radius. But the explosion did not decimate any particular building.

The reporter surmised that the blast most likely emanated from a certain street location, and that the cause was unknown, but seems likely to have come from a vehicle. With that notice, Jeff sensed he was witnessing the outcome of something terrible.

"Jim, it looks like there might have been a major terrorist attack on New York City."

At this announcement, Jim dropped the food that he was in the process of loading into the cooler. He walked over to where he could see the television. Dr. Isaacson was right behind him. Jeff turned up the volume.

Colton and Pete had gathered the items they would need to pack and had placed them in a pile next to the four-wheelers. Colton was looking for the bungees and straps he would use to secure the gear when the door to the shed flew open.

"Colton! Pete!" Jeff's announcement charged Colton with a jolt of adrenaline. "There's been a major terrorist attack in New York City! Come check it out." As Jeff peeled and ran back toward the cabin, Colton's relief that there was no immediate danger at the cabin gave way to intense curiosity. He ran out of the shed and into the cabin, with Pete right at his heels.

CHAPTER 16

With the entire group in the cabin watching, the television now displayed the anchors at the national news desk.

"We now have a reporter in place and ready near the second blast site. The details that are coming in, though sketchy, make this blast sound similar to the New York blast. They seem to be part of a coordinated attack..." With that, the men in the cabin looked at each other, sharing the weighty seriousness of the situation. America was again under attack. All had been alive during September 11, 2001, but the three younger men were just little boys when that attack had occurred.

The anchor was finalizing the transfer to the on-site reporter. The screen now showed a reporter in a semi-chaotic blast zone, waiting to talk, with the microphone in front of his mouth. "We now go to Tom Alverson near the base of the Space Needle in Seattle. Tom?"

"Yes, Mary, I am about three blocks—almost a half mile—from the base of the Space Needle, and I am surrounded by effects from the blast. Shrapnel from the bomb has pock marked many buildings around me. Some small fires that may soon turn into large fires speckle a large area…"

"Tom, does the blast seem to have come from the Space Needle itself?"

"No, Mary. It seems the blast has emanated from the parking lot near the base of the Needle. I am told that that parking lot is now just a large, smoky crater. The Needle is damaged, but seems to be standing just fine. It appears that the blast sprayed debris mostly in one direction—much like a giant shot gun. In fact, the buildings in the direction away from the Needle seem hit worse than the Needle itself. And the buildings behind the Needle are harmed very little."

Jim, staring at the television, was lost in the situation, and spoke to the television as if he were speaking to the reporters. "You've got to get everyone away from that area!" Jim had said it with intensity, although it was not a yell.

"Why, Jim?" Dr. Isaacson attempted to step into Jim's thoughts. "Do you think there're going to be more attacks there?"

"No," Jim snapped out of his hypnotic gaze at the television and looked at the professor. "No, Professor, but those blasts—both of them—were in the open. It's apparent that whoever did this did not do it to destroy any structure."

"Well, that's good," said Dr. Isaacson positively.

"Maybe not," said Jim soberly. "A coordinated terrorist attack like this is designed to do as much damage as possible."

"But you just said these blasts don't seem to have succeeded at destroying anything." Dr. Isaacson remained positive, not seeing what the federal agent was seeing.

"Dr. Isaacson, those blasts were meant to destroy, but not buildings."

"What do you mean?"

"A blast like that seems most likely designed to scatter something, not to pull anything down." And as Dr. Isaacson understood, a turned pale.

"Jim, what would someone want to scatter?" asked Pete.

"Anything that can kill or destroy once it's scattered. Perhaps a chemical, or a biological agent, or something radioactive. Who knows? But whatever the purpose of that bomb, those areas have got to be evacuated and quarantined immediately—until we know for sure."

And then Colton made the discovery. "Jeff!"

"Yeah?" said Jeff with a casualness that did not match Colton's communication.

Before Colton resumed his inquiry, he arose and began darting from place to place in the main area of the cabin in staccato fashion. He was looking for the *Master Plan*. He saw it, finally, on the counter top, under a bag of potato chips. He grasped it. As he looked back up to a waiting Jeff, he asked, "Where in New York did they say the blast went off?"

Without hesitation, Jeff said, "Within a block or two of the United Nations building."

That confirmed it. Colton's grasp on the *Master Plan* turned into a death grip. He stared at the first line under the "Transactions" heading. So many puzzle pieces came together too quickly. His head was swimming with a sense that what he had just understood was too ethereal to be true. His behavior had diverted the attention of the entire group away from the television to himself. Jim came over to Colton and put an arm around him, looking at the *Master Plan* with his nephew.

Colton looked up at his uncle, then at the faces of the others. "This attack is not from some foreign terrorist group." The announcement hung as an incomplete message. Colton resumed. "This attack was from The Thread." With that, Dr. Isaacson burst across the room to look at the *Master Plan* with Colton and Jim. He had understood where Colton was heading with the announcement.

"How do you know, Colton?" demanded Jeff.

Colton motioned for Jeff and Pete to look at the document too. In just a moment, all were standing beside or behind Colton. He pointed to the lines just below the "Transactions" heading.

"The 'transactions' The Thread is planning to use to destroy the American government are not *financial* transactions. They're bombings." Jeff and Pete both understood.

"It all makes so much sense now," said Dr. Isaacson, lost in thought. "The Thread has gone after economic freedom to make America less resistant to the iron-fisted government control that they will use when they rise to power. And that rise begins today."

After waiting a moment to allow that thought to settle, Colton brought them back to the plan. "The first two transactions are to take place on 'Day 1,' in the morning. The third transaction is to occur that same day, in the afternoon. The last two transactions are scheduled for the next day."

Everyone was seeing what Colton was seeing. He concluded: "The first two transactions happen in New York and somewhere that is denoted as 'S'."

"Seattle!" vocalized Pete.

Colton pressed on. "After the New York transaction, it says, 'U.N.' and after the Seattle transaction, it says, 'S.N.'"

This time Jeff translated. "United Nations in New York, and Space Needle in Seattle."

"Now, look at what must happen this afternoon," said Colton. Jim had already left the group and was pacing around the room, having understood everything Colton was saying.

They could all see it now, but Colton still said it. "Sometime today, there's going to be a third bombing. And based on the *Master Plan,* we think this one's going to be at the Capitol Building in Salt Lake City."

As they pondered what it meant, the realization that these bombings intertwined with their current predicament was surreal.

With the knowledge of what the Salt Lake transaction meant, Colton felt concern for his coworkers at the Capitol. He glanced at Jeff and could sense the same thoughts from his roommate.

Jim took charge of the discussion. "There will apparently be an attack tomorrow in Los Angeles, at the LAX airport. There will also be another in Chicago, at what seems to be the Sears Tower." Jim paused, looking at the others. "The world is now watching America, because America is under attack. We may be the only people in the world outside of The Thread who know that America is under attack by fellow Americans."

"We've got to get word out about this right now!" declared Jeff who was as close to panic as Colton would have thought possible.

"That's right, Jeff," agreed an in-charge Jim. "We've got to communicate to authorities what we know. We have to do it now. But we have to do it in a way that breaks through or sneaks around the defenses of The Thread. The Thread is powerful, and they're after us. They know that we're probably their greatest threat."

"So, why don't we just get into the car right now, and drive down to the police station and tell them what we know?" wondered Jeff.

"No, Jeff," said Jim, "think like The Thread."

"What do you mean?"

"Well," said Jim, "if I were The Thread, I'd be prepared to catch us were we to go to FBI headquarters, the police station, media outlets, and perhaps a few other places. If they have the manpower here in Utah right now, they may be ready for us at any place we might want to go. We have to find a way to get word out without The Thread first apprehending us. We've got to have a great plan."

Jeff was about to explode. "Well, we can't just give up! We have to take a risk! There's going to be a bombing in Salt Lake City in just a matter of hours, for crying out loud!"

Colton stepped into the foray with a suggestion. "Why don't we go to a media outlet or FBI office outside of this area—like in Idaho, or something?"

But Jim shut that down, too. "No. For one, we don't have time. We have to not only be smart, but we have to be fast as well. We're within hours of a major attack in Salt Lake City. The Thread will no doubt have secured airports and law enforcement and media outlets throughout the western United States. Remember, as far as they know, we're in Montana by now. They must know we could have driven to anywhere in the west by now."

Colton had another idea: "What if we split up? I mean, we all understand their economic strategy enough that any one of us could explain what The Thread is trying to do. We could totally blitz news places."

"That's a great idea," said Jim, "and we may have to do just that; but I don't like the idea of us throwing ourselves individually into the hands of The Thread at this point. That may not be necessary."

After a very short pause, a plan took shape in Jim's mind. "Here's what we'll do. I'll go alone. I'll call headquarters from a pay phone that is near a major highway interchange. I'll talk specifically to my supervisor and inform him about the Salt Lake City attack and the attack's location. I will quickly tell him about The Thread and what is really going on. I can make the call brief and get right onto the highway. The highway interchange will give me the best chance of escape. In the meantime, you all stay here and finish preparations to head into the mountains. If I'm not back by a set time, you all bolt into the mountains without me."

Jeff had backed down from panic mode, but he was still riled. "This is crazy. It seems like we could just go to the highway, flag down a car, borrow their cell phone to make a call to the police or news, and voila." As he said voila, he threw his hands into the air, showing how simple his plan was in comparison to what Jim had suggested.

Colton jumped in. "Jeff, The Thread would expect something like that and is probably prepared to intercept any message to authorities. Maybe they've done it through the FBI. Maybe they have other resources. Who knows? But a group powerful enough to control U.S. economic policy, assassinate the President, and bomb five major cities has got to be powerful enough to protect itself from a small group like us."

"Don't you think there's got to be some easy way to warn people?" said Jeff.

"Easy, yes; but extremely risky," said Jim.

"But this group is bombing major cities! Don't you think it's worth the risk, even if we do get caught?"

Jim paused, feeling a huge appreciation for the courage of this passionate young man. Colton was smarter, and more grounded than Jeff, but Jeff's flare for doing gutsy things—

even if they were reckless—was impressive. Jim stepped over to Jeff, held his shoulders, looked him in the eyes, and spoke with finality. "Jeff, I'm going to go and make a call in the valley. That's the safest way that gives us the best chance—as far as I can see."

Jeff was too agitated to handle the awkwardness of the moment with humor. He just pulled away and walked to the window to stare outside.

CHAPTER 17

The men watched through the window as Jim's vehicle passed from the clearing to the narrow, winding road. Before he was out of sight, however, everyone resumed their assignments. They worked with determination, having a renewed level of purpose.

Colton and Pete both fired up the four-wheelers and parked them in front of the cabin. Colton had jammed an amazing amount of useful camping gear into a relatively small space.

Dr. Isaacson brought out the cooler that Jim had packed. He and Colton worked together getting the cooler snug amidst the camping gear on the back of one of the all-terrain vehicles.

With their assignments completed, they headed into the cabin to watch more of the news and wait for Jim. Jeff—content to get back to his own assignment—had already resumed watching the news.

"Anything new, Jeff?" asked Dr. Isaacson as he settled on the furniture around the television along with Pete and Colton.

"Yes. This keeps getting crazier. They've begun evacuating most of both cities, because—"

"They think there's going to be more attacks there?" interrupted Pete.

"No," corrected Jeff. "They now realize what Jim said earlier—these bombs may be dirty bombs."

"Maybe I'm the only dumb one here," said Pete, "but will someone please tell me why they call it dirty?"

"It is called dirty because it leaves a nasty, dangerous mess of radioactive debris to clean up," answered Dr. Isaacson.

"So the radioactive stuff inside the bomb won't necessarily make it kill more people?"

Jeff turned from the television to look at Pete. "Well, Pete, it might not kill people instantly, but a bunch of radioactive waste spread over part of a city can have some bad effects for a long time to come."

With Pete's nod, all attention went back to the television.

SALT LAKE CITY

Jim signaled and exited the highway near the heart of Salt Lake City. He chose to make his call near the interchange of I-15 and I-80. This would give him the opportunity to make a quick call, bolt, and be heading in any direction within minutes.

Upon exiting I-80, Jim turned right onto the road then turned left into a gas station on the west side of the road. Looking at his gas gauge, he was grateful to still have over three-quarters of a tank. His cash reserves were low and he knew his credit card was useless in his circumstance.

The parking stall in front of the pay phone was open. Rather than just pull into it, he maneuvered the car and backed into the stall. Jim knew his call might attract pursuers.

Jim knew he was just another person in a busy, public place until he made the call. But he still found himself scouting out the environment, looking for any signs of danger. He saw none. He did see that most of the people in the convenience store were huddled around a television.

Jim looked at the phone. He had rehearsed over and over what he must do in this phone call. It had to be brief. After a few moments, authorities and members of The Thread may know his location. His window of time to communicate and flee was agonizingly small.

He had to reveal to his superiors that there would be a bombing in Salt Lake City at the Capitol Building in just hours. That was his first priority. He also must apprise a superior that the document they had revealed much of the plan behind the bombings and the death of the President. Jim had to accomplish all this in moments. He had to be both concise and thorough.

Jim took one last surveillance look around him. He was ready. It was time.

Jim had determined to call the director of the Salt Lake office, Jesse Saunders. He had Jesse's cell phone number on a card in his wallet. He decided to call Jesse directly.

Jim inserted cash into the phone to make the call. He dialed and waited. After just one ring, Jesse Saunders answered.

"Jesse?" asked Jim.

"Yes."

"Jesse, this is Jim Berry."

There was a click of sorts. Jim paused and furrowed his eyebrows.

"Jesse?"

After a brief, silent pause, a voice unfamiliar to Jim spoke.

"Jim, where are you?" The voice carried a cold authority and a tone of sappiness, as if the speaker were trying to sound concerned when he was not.

"Who is this?" said Jim.

"Calm down, Jim," said the voice. The feigned concern was gone now, and only the cold authority remained. "You are in a pit of trouble that you had better climb out of fast, Jim. We are in the middle of terrorist attacks nation-wide and we have reason to bel—"

Jim realized that the man, whoever it was, was pushing the conversation into a stall—a delay so they could track Jim down. Jim cut the man off.

"If I don't hear Jesse Saunders's voice within two seconds, I'm gone!" demanded Jim.

Silence. After a pause, Jim expected to hear Jesse's voice. But it was the same man again.

"Jim?" it was said again with the mock kindness.

Rage welled up in Jim. He knew he was speaking with someone from The Thread. Jim hoped that perhaps others were listening who may not be part of The Thread.

"Jesse, or anyone listening," began Jim urgently, "the attacks and the assassination—" There was a click. Jim paused. "Hello?" Jim supposed someone cut the line.

"Jim, come to the office in Salt Lake…" It was the same man, the line was still connected. Jim cut the man off.

"A secret group known as The Thread is behind the President's assassination and today's terrorist attacks! There's going to be an attack in Salt Lake City sometime today!" They were yelling simultaneously. Jim was out of time and he knew it.

Frustrated, Jim slammed the phone down and ran to his car. He sped onto the road and entered the highway heading back east, toward the mountains.

THREAD HEADQUARTERS
SALT LAKE CITY

For the first time since he had come to Utah, Nathan felt happy. A technician had blurted that Jim Berry had called another FBI agent and was on the phone. The technician had diverted the call to the phone of Richard Williams—the agent who had taken over the FBI office. Everyone in The Thread's Salt Lake City headquarters heard the conversation over the speakers.

Amidst his thrill, Nathan set in motion the great machinery of technology The Thread had harnessed and channeled into this office. Within ten seconds, even before Jim had closed the connection, one technician yelled out the location of the call. Others were pinpointing the site on a map displayed on a large screen. The screen showed all resources and personnel of The Thread.

Meanwhile, other workers were tracking down the location with the satellite image. Before Jim even made it onto the highway, members of The Thread in both the national headquarters and the Salt Lake City headquarters were watching an aerial view of his car.

"Gotcha!" said Nathan with vicious glee. Then he ordered loudly, "I want every agent within reasonable proximity to close in. I don't want to overtake that man until he reaches his destination. We'll keep plenty of distance. We can watch him from the sky. But we pounce as soon as he arrives."

CHAPTER 18

I-80 WESTBOUND, SALT LAKE CITY
8:10 A.M.

To his relief, Jim could see no sign of anyone following him. He kept glancing in the rear-view mirror as he drove. He was now about to leave the valley via Parley's Canyon. He breathed a big sigh of relief as he entered the canyon, glad that he had made the call so close to a major highway interchange. He was also glad to see that the way into the canyon was still open. Had The Thread sealed the valley, they would have cut Jim off from the others. Jim desired to get to the cabin and head into the mountains. He felt such urgency that he had to work at keeping to the speed limit. The last thing Jim needed was attention from law enforcement.

But with the relief, Jim was also disgusted. The call had been so hasty that Jim was certain he had failed to communicate anything substantial about the impending bombing.

In retrospect, Jim was also frustrated with himself for not writing a note that he could hand to multiple people just prior to making his phone call. Although doing so would have put those he gave the notes to in danger, it would have been worth the risk considering what the city was facing within just hours.

As it now stood, he still had information that had to get out, but he felt powerless. He felt like a trapped mouse in a hole with someone ready to stomp as soon as it leaves its hole. It never occurred to Jim that he might fail as badly as he had.

THE CABIN
8:12 A.M.

For the group at the cabin, the information coming across the news was reaching a saturation point—not much was new anymore. The professor sought out a copy of the plan. He sat down at the dining room table.

Dr. Isaacson remembered a speech at a convention where the speaker discussed an experiment where researchers dropped sand, one grain at a time, to form piles. In studying those piles, they found that each pile would reach a "critical mass," at which point the next grain of sand would cause every single grain of sand in the pile to shift and resettle. He felt that he kept coming to understand the plan of The Thread quite well, only to have something new cause everything to resettle. And all the resettling had an unsettling effect on the professor. How far did the diabolical plan of this secret combination extend?

After a few minutes with the document, Dr. Isaacson was eager for the young men watching television to understand what he could now see. He called to the others, apologizing for the interruption, and requested that they come learn something else about the plan. Though they were all very familiar with the contents of the plan, they were still connecting the plan's words to their current reality.

Jeff lowered the volume on the news, but left it on loud enough that they would notice if anything new or critical were to emerge. The three roommates gathered around the table with Dr. Isaacson. He took a moment longer to study the plan and prepare his thoughts. The silence created awkwardness. Jeff, always ready to utilize such moments, broke the silence.

"Should I say the opening prayer?" The roommates smiled. Dr. Isaacson responded soberly.

"I think America needs prayers more than ever before." This statement matched the mood well. Without any further chit chat, the professor launched into his instruction mode that the others had now become quite accustomed to.

"It appears as if The Thread has learned a great lesson from history."

"What lesson?" asked Colton.

"I'm referring to how The Thread is using dependency and desperation to topple the nation. And here's why that is so ingenious. When people are dependent, the government is powerful. The greatest expansions of federal power in America have come when hard times or crisis have created a sense of desperation. For example, the Depression primed America for a huge increase in the size and role of the federal government. The attacks of 9-11, the financial credit crunch of 2008 and 2009, and many other examples from the past confirm this tendency."

"True," said Colton.

"At any rate, The Thread is using the same strategy. The difference here is that whereas American leaders during the Depression and other tough times took advantage of America's desperation to reform our country, The Thread is actually *creating* desperation to enable them to expand the federal government and destroy the Constitution."

"I get it!" said Pete. "The Thread wants America so freaked out that we turn to the government for massive protection, in a way that gives up freedom and allows the government to get rid of the Constitution."

"Yes. That seems to be the general idea. Death is not necessarily the design of dirty bombs, so much as to create panic among people. The panic created by these multiple attacks will allow The Thread to step in, dressed as our saviors, and remove our freedom."

After a pause, Dr. Isaacson went on. "Now that you understand this, looking back at the *Master Plan* makes this obvious. Let me read the section entitled 'Post Transaction Objectives.'

"Their first Post Transaction Objective is to enact 'temporary' high security levels and martial law. Do you know why they put *temporary* in quotation marks?"

"Because the restrictions aren't going to be temporary—they're going to be around for a long time," said Colton.

"Surely," said Dr. Isaacson. "Now listen to how they're going to keep them around for a while. The second Post Transaction Objective is to 'sustain reports of escalating threats to maintain control.'" Dr. Isaacson paused to look around. Nobody had a comment, so he proceeded. "From there, it gets real ugly, in my mind. The final three Post Transaction Objectives are to 'Assume command control of economy,' 'Launch full military and economic security programs,' and to 'Initiate final regime change—the rising of The Thread.'" There was again a brief silence. Colton broke it.

"That's flat out disturbing."

Jim turned off the highway onto the mountain road that would lead to the cabin. His mind was swirling in an attempt to formulate a better plan.

But something was eating at him. He felt uneasy—and it was more than the failed phone call and desperate situation. There was something he was missing… something right before him that he could not sort out. And it was something he needed to know now. It was like remembering a name that had just slipped his memory but was passing in and out of the edge of his consciousness. The closer he got to the cabin, the more unsettled he became.

"Calm down, Jim," he said aloud to himself. He took a deep breath. As he attempted to master control over emotions and distractions, he set his mind free, to see where it wanted to go. He found himself thinking about the night before. And then he began asking himself the right questions. How had they tracked the others so quickly to Dr. Isaacson's office based on his brief phone conversation with Colton? He had asked that question repeatedly last night. What technology had The Thread used?

And then the picture cleared a bit. The last time he had thought about what technology The Thread had used to track them, he had very little understanding, compared to now, what The Thread was like or how powerful it was.

As Jim approached the turn-in from the mountain road to the small dirt road that led to the cabin, his anxiety was at a crescendo.

Jim turned and drove through the gate—which he had left open. He stopped his car, walked to the gate, and closed it. As Jim returned to his car, he heard a vehicle off in the distance. People rarely used this mountain road, and Jim did not wish anyone to see him. He hurried back into his car. He still felt unsettled. There was something obvious he had not grasped, and he knew it.

Jim accelerated down the small dirt road into the woods, away from the mountain road. Then, it came to him all at once. It was an ugly revelation. He felt as if his heart had fallen through his body, onto the dirt road.

Yes, the FBI had tapped into massive federal technology to intercept the phone call he had just made. That was impressive, but not surprising. The FBI has resources to do that. But he understood, finally, how The Thread compromised his phone call with Colton the night before. The Thread had infiltrated a formidable resource: the National Security Agency!

Jim accelerated his car, realizing he was now in a race that could mean life or death.

If only he had realized this new fact even just seconds sooner, before he had turned onto the road leading the cabin! His anger and frustration with both the situation and his own foolishness exploded inside of him. His conversation with Colton about the *Master Plan* last night must have tripped some computer filter that listened for certain things about The Thread or their plans. With that, they would know Colton's location. The Thread would also know Colton was talking about The Thread to an FBI agent. Hence, they could get their agent from Denver to Utah under the direction of the Executive Director of Field Operations—who was apparently a member of The Thread. The Thread would overrun the FBI offices in Utah.

Knowing he had just compromised the entire group, Jim slammed the steering wheel out of frustration. The only hope would be to get into the mountains on the four wheelers before The Thread would have a chance to overtake them. Jim knew that his plan to make the call then get on the highway would probably have succeeded against standard law enforcement technology. But the NSA has powers he had not factored in. The instant his phone call was interrupted, his location would be pinpointed by satellites. Before he even hung up the phone, they could be watching him on some screen in full color. They would have easily tracked his car by satellite. And now that he was close to the cabin, he knew he had just exposed the group's location to The Thread.

CHAPTER 19

THE CABIN
8:35 A.M.

Jim floored his car and raced through the stretch of forest and burst into the cabin's clearing. The sound of his approach apprised the others that something was terribly wrong. Colton and the professor opened the front door and were standing in it. As he rounded the car and came to a sliding stop, Jim noticed that Pete and Jeff were standing in the main window.

"Get on the four-wheelers, now!" The mandate stirred the four others into a somewhat-panicked action. Jeff and Pete came bursting out of the house. Colton moved with haste to start all three four-wheelers. While the three younger men had surged out of the cabin, Dr. Isaacson had pushed his way in and was rummaging around. Jim called to him.

"Dr. Isaacson, we need to move, NOW!"

"We need the Plan, Jim. I am getting the copies of the *Master Plan*!"

Good thinking, thought Jim. "Great! Move it!"

Jim's horrors were confirmed. But he was not at all surprised. A vehicle was moving through the woods, approaching the clearing. Jeff jumped onto one of the four-wheelers. Pete jumped on the same four-wheeler as a passenger. Colton and Jim both mounted the other two four wheelers. Jim sped his four-wheeler right to the cabin door.

The pursuing vehicle burst into the clearing, quickly closing the gap to the cabin. Finally, Dr. Isaacson emerged with two documents in his hand—the original and one of the copies.

"Where is the other copy?" demanded Jim as Dr. Isaacson jumped on the back of the all-terrain vehicle.

"I hid it!" With Dr. Isaacson on board, even before he was completely settled, Jim took off. The lurch forward nearly threw Dr. Isaacson off the back, but Jim did not let up and the professor held on. Colton and Jeff both followed Jim by launching toward the woods to the north of the cabin, away from the oncoming vehicle. But it was too late.

Jim realized he should have waved Colton and Jeff on ahead. Jim and Dr. Isaacson, being in the lead, reached the safety of the woods. He looked back and saw that the pursuing vehicle had reached and cut off the other two ATVs before they could accelerate into the woods.

The vehicle was a van. It was not a recognizable law enforcement van, but it was capable of going off road. It was battle ready, much like a reinforced law enforcement van might be.

The instant the van rounded in front of Jeff's four-wheeler, his only alternative was to stop. Colton had room to go around Jeff and bolt for the woods to join Jim, but he hesitated. His mind was screaming at him, telling him to get away and join his uncle. But his heart would not let him leave Jeff and Pete.

Three gunmen rushed out of the van. Each of the three roommates had a gun pointed right at him. The guns were the same as the weapons used to shoot at them the previous evening—the high tech darts. The driver was still behind the steering wheel of the van. With the three roommates secured, the van accelerated once again, heading toward Jim and Dr. Isaacson at the edge of the woods. The van was eating up the distance of about forty yards in a hurry.

Jim acted swiftly. He rolled off the four-wheeler, taking his gun out of its holster with full intent for using it for the first time since encountering The Thread.

"Isaacson! Go now! Get those documents out of here!" Jim scurried to the largest tree near him and pointed the gun at the approaching van. The professor pressed the gas, but had seldom driven an all-terrain vehicle before now. The four-wheeler lurched, almost jerking out from underneath him. In an effort to get it under more control, Dr. Isaacson let up on the gas almost as instantly as he had gunned it. The four-wheeler came to a near-complete stop. As he moved to press the gas again, he turned back to see the van.

The van was not stopping. It was nearly to Dr. Isaacson and was still accelerating—despite the subtle uphill slope. To Jim's horror, he could see that the intention of the driver of the van was to ram the four-wheeler. Dr. Isaacson understood this too. Jim made a critical decision and opened fire, aiming directly at the driver. He fired a burst of three rounds. All three rounds were well aimed, and struck the windshield of the moving van within six inches of each other. But they had no effect. The windshield blocked all three bullets—bulletproof.

Out of sheer reaction, Dr. Isaacson lunged upward on the four-wheeler until his feet were on the seat. From there, he leaped sideways with all his strength.

Jim saw Dr. Isaacson jump, but did not know if he had made it in time, as the van—now going about thirty miles per hour—slammed into the four-wheeler. The four-wheeler crumpled partially under the impact and was wedged to the ground under the assaulting van—causing the van to come to a quick and complete stop.

Jim's shelter behind his selected tree was quite feeble now. The driver of the stopped van turned and focused on Jim. Jim heard two doors on the van open up—one that he could see was the driver's door. The other sounded like a sliding door on the far side of the van. Jim supposed that there was another gunman in the van and that he would be honing in on Dr. Isaacson.

"Put your hands behind your head!" said the unseen gunman. Jim felt a rush of relief, knowing that the gunman must be ordering a living professor around.

With extraordinary confidence, the driver walked out of his open door and around the front of the van, into the open, with his gun pointed at Jim. He assumed that Jim would not risk the others' lives by shooting him. Jim could not hide behind the tree—his back left side was exposed to the other gunmen who were with the three roommates down below. He was vulnerable.

"So… you must be James…" The gunmen said calmly, still walking slowly toward Jim.

Jim heard the other gunman speak authoritatively to Dr. Isaacson. "Now, get up and join your friends down below. If you do anything more or less than what I tell you, you will regret it. Now move!"

The man approaching Jim and his meager tree stopped, allowing Jim to observe the professor emerge from behind the van, limping down the slope to join the others, with a gunman following him closely.

"Okay, James… don't be an idiot. You and I both know you are not going to do anything that would risk your friends down there. Lower your gun and toss it aside."

Jim still aimed his weapon between the man's eyes. His mind was swirling, analyzing his options. He knew he really did not have many choices, but his mind kept exploring anyway. But it was fruitless. He lowered his weapon. With a sigh of hesitation and surrender, he threw it off to the side.

The man walked around to Jim's gun, keeping his own weapon pointed at Jim. The man calmly bent down, retrieved the gun, and waved his gun toward the others. "Now, get down to the others. You know what'll happen if you don't comply. And don't test me. You've already been alive too long in my estimation."

The gunmen had caused the three roommates to form a line—a line that Dr. Isaacson had since joined. The gunman instructed Jim to join them. He obeyed. The gunmen had spaced the group about four feet apart from each other. Having formed a line, the questioning began.

The interrogation started with a threat to Jim. The leader of the attackers, the man who had been driving, looked at Jim. "James, we know everything about you and your little group. Your job is to make sure everyone tells the truth. The youngest one in your group is Peter Wright. If you allow any mistruth to come out of this group, we will first kill Peter. Next, we'd kill your nephew. Next would be Palmer. Dr. Isaacson would go before you. So, you can either be our guarantee that your friends here tell us the truth, or you can have the privilege of observing their early death, one by one." The last three words were said with punctuated finality.

Jim felt immense rage, but managed his body so that almost none of it showed. His mind was still whirling. A very unpersuasive part of him believed there had to be something he could do, despite being outnumbered and seemingly helpless.

The leader looked now at Colton. "Colton Wiser… you started this whole mess, did you not? And did you not, one by one, involve everyone else too?"

Colton's rage was not as concealed as was Jim's. When he spoke, he maintained dignity, yet spoke through clenched teeth. "I did."

The man stepped forward, somewhat charismatically, like a dramatic attorney might do when questioning someone in court. His hand swung in gesture toward Colton. "And how did you ever come across this document?"

"I saw it under the table in one of the copy rooms at the State Capitol. When I found it, I wondered who had left it, so I went to Jeff here, and we looked it up on the security system."

"And how did Senator Tomlinson find out you had found his document?"

"We left a little note," said Colton, still speaking tersely.

"And what did that note say?"

"It told him that he had already been warned. We were just curious to see how he would react. We weren't expecting the reaction we got."

"I'll bet you weren't."

Then, abruptly, the leader turned to Pete, stepped toward him in an intimidating manner, and asked, "Peter… who is the Hen?"

Peter stiffened up. He thought that if these men knew that the group knew who the Hen was, the men would realize the group knew a lot. His hesitation brought an impatient shout.

"Just answer the question, NOW, Peter!"

Jeff jerked a bit in reflexive fury. His fists were clenching and unclenching. Multiple guns moved to point at him in warning. He maintained control, but it was difficult. Peter answered the question.

"The Hen is the current President of the United States." Peter said it with a calmness and confidence that surprised all four of the other hostages.

"That is right, Peter. I knew you knew that. Thank you for telling the truth. You have spared your life for a while longer." The leader spoke with manipulative adulation.

The man turned back toward Jim. "James, how many copies of *Key #3* do you have?"

Jim did not hesitate, and he spoke the truth. "As far as I know, we have the original, and two copies."

The man stared at Jim, and then scanned the others for any signs of untruth. The Thread evidently did not know the answer. Colton determined it was perhaps the most important question they wanted to ask this group. Satisfied he had gotten a straight answer, the man pointed to Dr. Isaacson.

"You, Dr. Harold Isaacson… do you know where all three copies of this Plan are?"

The kind professor was bold. "Yes, I do. Do you know where people like you go after they die?"

Jeff and Colton smiled broadly. The comment was foolish. But the silly jab from the professor had the surprising effect of filling both Jeff and Colton with confidence and perspective. With their smiles, their fears largely vanished.

Seemingly ignoring the jest, the gunman requested, "Harold, go get all three copies."

"Let me do it," requested Jim. "He's hurt. He can barely walk."

"Well, he won't try to run away, then, will he?" retorted the leader. Now the gunmen smiled.

Without further invitation, Dr. Isaacson began limping away. First he shuffled into the cabin. Then he headed up toward the four-wheeler and van, grunting as he went, with a gunman following. Dr. Isaacson was in agony, and labored with each step.

The short trip up the slope and back took Dr. Isaacson a long five minutes. The climbing sun had drenched the clearing and the woods with September warmth, and the blue sky was radiant. But the wait was uncomfortable, and given the circumstances, the crisp beauty of their surroundings created an odd irony.

When Dr. Isaacson was halfway down the slope, still holding the three documents, he collapsed with pain. The trip down the hill was more difficult than the trip up the hill had been. Dr. Isaacson grasped his knee, grunted and grimaced, then fought to stand up before hobbling along even more slowly.

Jeff broke rank. He was calm and slow at first. Guns snapped to his direction and bursts of angry yells came from the four gunmen standing in front of the line of hostages. Jeff disregarded this for a few paces. The warnings became frantic. Jeff paused and looked at the men threatening his life. Jeff matched the intensity of the gunmen with his own serenity. His explanation was composed and simple.

"That man needs help. I'm going to help him. If that's not acceptable, shoot me. Otherwise, I'm going to help the good Doc get back here so you can keep going with your fun questions." Jeff did not wait for a reply. He resumed his calm but purposeful walk to the professor.

The gunmen were enraged at Jeff's belligerence. Threats and sounds of anger emanated from them, but none took any action to stop him. Jeff's act of defiance toward the gunmen and service toward Dr. Isaacson further weakened the gunmen's control over the situation—and both groups felt and understood this. The fear of the three men remaining in the hostage line dissipated. They all felt emboldened—set free somehow.

Jeff reached Dr. Isaacson and hoisted him up onto his back and shoulder, then proceeded to carry him down the rest of the slope with caution. When Jeff reached the line of hostages, he lowered Dr. Isaacson gently into his former place. Jeff returned to his own spot—next to Jim.

"Good work, son," commended Jim warmly.

"Great," sounded the leader of the gunmen, acting to regain control that had been lost by Jeff's act. "Now, there are just a few more things we need to know from you boys." But the leader's attempt at authority did nothing to reinstate the fear of the group.

"Colton," the gunman asked, "your family has been very hard to track down. Where did you send them?"

Colton's stare showed a blank face but extreme intensity in Colton's eyes. His voice matched his eyes. "They say that there's no such thing as a dumb question, but that one was really stupid." And Colton offered nothing else but his blank stare.

The gunman felt no desire to squabble with Colton and turned his attention again to Pete. "Pete… if you lie to us, you will be killed first. So, with that reminder…" and after an intentional pause, the gunman plunged into his most critical question: "How many copies were made of *Key # 3?"*

"Do you mean the *Master Plan*?" asked Pete.

"Yes."

Pete wanted to stay alive. "Two, as far as I know."

The main gunman's eyes and weapon both moved toward Jim. "James, is this true? Did you only make two copies?"

"I am only aware of two copies—"

The gunman exploded with fury. "Don't act like you don't know for sure!"

The explosion set Jim off a bit. "I *don't* know for sure! If you want the truth, learn how to deal with the truth!"

Jim's outburst was surprising not only to the gunman, but also to the rest of the hostages. The gunman stepped forward and knocked Jim hard in the forehead with the butt of his weapon. Jim resisted the urge to strike back and just took the blow, which caused him to fall back hard, almost losing consciousness. Neither Jeff nor Colton resisted the urge. Simultaneously, both moved toward the gunman.

Instantly, the four other gunmen stepped forward and cut off Colton and Jeff with guns raised in heightened tension. Both boys came to their senses, harnessing their anger in wisdom's name. They came to a complete, abrupt stop, and then settled back into their places in the hostage line.

Jim slowly raised himself from the ground. The gunman stepped back, pointed his weapon at Jeff, and inquired, "You.... brave, brave Jeffrey..." said the gunman. "How many copies are there of *Key #3*?"

Without hesitation, Jeff answered, "My answer is the same as Mr. agent-man. I didn't make the copies, and I've only seen two copies of the Plan around." Then, after a brief pause, Jeff added, "But before you react to my answer, let me get ready." Then Jeff placed his hand over his forehead to protect it. Colton and Pete both laughed aloud. Jim and Dr. Isaacson—either out of pain or maturity—remained stoic. The gunman seemed to ignore the humor and just stared at Jeff. But his mock disdain gave way to a smile.

"You are far too bold of a comedian for your own safety, Jeffrey," said the gunman condescendingly.

The gunman was finished with interrogating Jeff and turned his attention to Colton. "Mr. Wiser... How many copies are there of *Key #3*?"

Colton answered honestly. "I made the copies. I made two additional copies. We have three copies total, including the original with the blood mark. I made the copies in Dr. Isaacson's office. You can search it all you want. I made two copies, and we have them both."

With visible satisfaction, the gunman turned to Dr. Isaacson and sought confirmation. “Is this true, Isaacson?”

“As far I know we have the original and two copies. That’s all we’ve worked with when I’ve been around.”

The gunman’s contentment carried over into a smile. He believed them. With that, he shifted his weight and began moving backward. “Gentlemen…” he announced to the others. “It’s time.”

All the hostages were puzzled. Jim sensed the meaning first. All five gunmen backed up until they were about fifteen feet away from the hostages.

“Ready!” announced the leader. Five weapons snapped up, fixed on a target in front of them. It was clear that The Thread now had all it needed from this group, and wanted them dead.

Jim began looking around, powerlessly seeking a final solution—but he could see no alternatives. They were helpless. Jim’s mind accepted the fact that he was—that instant—facing death. Perhaps they would be shot with darts that were only tranquilizers, but Jim knew that more likely than not, these darts would be lethal. It was a strange feeling.

It happened in just a fraction of a second, but the feeling came not as a panic, but more as a peace and an acceptance of the inevitable. Jim looked at the other four. He felt a well-up of admiration as he saw the peace on their faces too. Jim followed the example of Dr. Isaacson and closed his eyes in peaceful resignation. Although the peace remained, the sound still startled Jim. A succession of loud pops at close range echoed through the hillside.

CHAPTER 20

THE CABIN
8:55 A.M.

The pops were distinctive. They were the same sound as one of The Thread's newfangled dart weapons. But other than startling them, the pops did not faze any of the hostages. Rather, three of the gunmen were dazed and staggering, then falling to the ground, while the other two were coherent, but frantic and confused, erratically twisting their heads and pointing their weapons all around them, looking for the source of the sounds. Although what had happened seemed illogical, the group began to understand.

Jim's first impulse was to charge the two remaining gunmen, but then he realized he might block the line of fire of whoever was attacking his assailants. Instead, he commanded the other hostages to drop. They did so. Jim scooted toward the nearest four-wheeler that was about fifteen feet away. The others in the group followed his example, and scurried toward the best nearby shelter they could find. Dr. Isaacson was dragging himself toward one of the four-wheelers for cover when Colton and Jeff grabbed his arms and dragged him the rest of the way. They then darted on their knees for other shelter so Dr. Isaacson could rest against the little vehicle with plenty of room and protection.

The lead gunman was enraged that the hostages were scattering. He screamed in agonized frustration. But he was under attack himself and could not keep the hostages corralled.

Just as Jim reached a four-wheeler and turned to look at the two remaining gunmen, another pop sounded. Nearly simultaneous to the pop was the slapping sound the dart made as it struck the leader's face. Jim could now tell that at least one attacker was firing at the gunmen from behind the edge of the cabin. The last gunman standing now knew this too. He had taken up shelter behind the van.

On the other side of the cabin, the man who had attacked the gunmen appeared. He had run around the cabin to communicate with the group he had just rescued. He was standing behind the corner in a way that the gunman behind the van could not see him, but Jim could. The man was wearing black over his entire body—much like the gunmen, except this man had on a cloth mask that somewhat resembled a ski mask. The man was standing at ease, with the weapon in his right hand pointing to the ground. His left hand was in the air, opened up with his fingers spread out, suggesting to Jim that the man intended no harm to him or his group. Jim nodded to him. With that communication complete, the would-be rescuer reached down and pulled from a holster at his thigh a smaller weapon. He flung it in the air. It landed just a few feet from Jim.

Jim was able to retrieve the weapon and—because of the four-wheeler—remain out of the line of fire of the last gunman at the van. The gunman was totally exposed. Jim had a clear shot at him. If he bolted away from Jim's line of fire, he would expose himself to the man behind the cabin—who had already proven himself a remarkable shot.

Jim did not wait. He knew this weapon was not an ordinary firearm. He suspected it to be a smaller form of the dart guns The Thread had been using. Jim peered over the four-wheeler. His captor had not seen the transfer of the weapon, which left him completely vulnerable.

Jim took aim and fired. His dart connected, hitting the man in the chest. The gunman jerked in surprise, cognizant that the dart had come from Jim's direction. He raised his weapon and began firing rapidly toward Jim, but Jim's shelter shielded him from the darts as they pounded and ricocheted off the four-wheeler and dirt. The gunman staggered for a moment, then fell.

With that, all the gunmen were down. Nevertheless, all five men who had just been hostages remained behind cover, not daring to venture out. They were not afraid of the man who had just saved them, but they were in a state of shock and did not know what to think. Even Jim remained behind the four-wheeler.

The man appeared from around the cabin, walking toward the downed gunmen. Although the group could not see the man's face, they could see that his eyes were dark and conveyed no emotion. He was wearing a black, long-sleeve shirt and black pants. His build was thin, but athletic. He walked with a calmness that all in the group interpreted to be extraordinary confidence. He went from gunman to gunman, nudging them and confirming their status. Content, he set the group in motion, acting as its new leader.

"Quick! Gather all copies of the document—make sure we have the original. Get anything you need. We have to get out of here immediately. We will travel in the van these men brought."

Everyone went into action but Jim, who remained behind the four-wheeler.

"Wait a minute!" demanded Jim. He was not angry, just insistent. "What in the world just happened?"

"You were nearly killed by men who belong to a secret society whose members refer to themselves as The Thread."

"I know that much," responded Jim, anxious to sort things out. "But who are you?"

"My name is Alexander Markham. I am a high-ranking member of The Thread."

CHAPTER 21

THE CABIN
9:00 A.M.

Although Colton had responded immediately to Alex's instructions, he lagged a bit to listen to his responses to Jim's inquiry. But when Alex identified himself, Colton whirled around in shock. Colton was not the only one. The entire group had stopped in their tracks and was staring at Alex in disbelief.

"Then what's going on?" Jim's stern response revealed that the man's answer had done more to stir questions than to provide answers.

"I will explain in full later. For now, we must be on our way. Now, get moving, or you will be left to the mercy of The Thread!" It was urgent but not harsh and the group acted. The four other than Jim were quickly in the cabin, securing what they thought they would need. After a hesitation founded in quizzical amazement, Jim followed suit. They then returned from the cabin to the four-wheelers where most of what they would need was packed.

Alex had, in the meantime, backed the van away from the damaged four-wheeler and drove it close to both the other four-wheelers and the cabin. Colton led them in removing bags and coolers from the all-terrain vehicles and loading them in the back of the van. Although no one was moving slowly, Alex continued to urge them to go faster until they were moving at a near frantic pace. While they worked, the entire group kept glancing toward the end of the clearing, expecting vehicles to appear and charge at any moment.

The van's arrangement was somewhat like a SWAT vehicle. The rear of the van was equipped with storage compartments up high with two padded benches that lined the walls of the van. The benches could seat three people apiece, making the van essentially an eight-seater. It bore the strong smells of a new vehicle. In addition to the seating, there was a wide assortment of computer equipment splashed throughout the van, with the bulk of the electronics resting between the two front seats.

With their stuff loaded, they began to board the van and ready for departure. The boys first helped Dr. Isaacson into the van. Although he was already increasing in mobility, his knee had begun to swell. As everyone settled into a seat, Alex wiggled under the van. After a moment of effort, he emerged from under the van holding a small, blinking, electronic device. Alex then sat in the driver's seat and closed his door—everyone was in place now. Jim had watched from the passenger seat and seen what Alex had done. Assuming he understood, Jim asked, "Tracking device?"

"Yes."

"How did you know where it was?" asked Jim.

"Because I put it there," replied Alex.

For a moment, Jim stared at Alex as Alex proceeded to shut off much of the electronic circuitry on the van. For the first time, Alex offered information without prompting. "This van is equipped with a wide range of technologies. One of its features is that it is traceable by satellite. I do not want them to trace us. So, before we leave, I must shut down all the computer elements."

"What about the device you got from under the van?" pressed Jim.

"This is something we cannot turn off. We could leave it, but if we use it right, it could be our friend. That is… if it does not cause us to be killed first."

They had been fast. Just minutes earlier, the five hostages had faced their death. Now they were in a vehicle with a man they did not know who had just saved their lives. The emotions of the morning left the entire group feeling a sense of numbness. Yet, nobody was running short of adrenaline. Their relief at being alive and their adrenaline were merging to replace the numbness with a sense of euphoria. Colton knew the feeling of invincibility that had kindled inside of him was false and dangerous.

Alex pulled away from the cabin and sped for the dirt road across the clearing that would lead them away. As he drove, he tore off his mask. The group could see that Alex's hair was as dark as his eyes. His hair was short, but long enough that it looked a bit frazzled after liberation from the confines of the mask.

Jim could see a problem with Alex's efforts to avoid detection. "But surely this cabin is under aerial surveillance. That's how The Thread found us. Everything that just went on was observed by unfriendly eyes."

"True," said Alex.

"So, what will deactivating the tracking devices on the van do if we're being watched from the air?"

Before Alex could answer, Colton blurted, "What're you talking about, Jim?"

Jim turned in his seat to look at the others in the back. "Gentlemen, the most likely way The Thread could have attacked you so quickly at BYU last night is if The Thread had access to the NSA—the National Security Agency. I never dreamed that The Thread could have tapped into the NSA. I was struggling to think of what technology they had used that could have been efficient enough that they could pick up random phone calls. The NSA has the ability to monitor all electronic communication across the country."

"How can they do that?" said Pete aloud.

"They use filters," said Jim.

"Filters?" Pete was still just as confused.

"Yes, Pete. They program powerful computers to sift through all the communication across the nation and only notice certain words, phrases, or other things. For instance, if someone in America tells a friend in a phone conversation that they want to kill the President of the United States, they may soon have government agents on their doorstep to interrogate them."

"Wow," was all Pete could say in response.

"Our phone conversation must have set off alarms that were programmed into the system. They knew what phones we were using and our locations. It explains why they moved so quickly to take control of the FBI offices in Utah—when they picked up the phone call, they knew you were talking about the *Master Plan* with an FBI agent. They immediately dispatched local members of The Thread to kill you—"

"Subdue," corrected Alex. "But, yes. Your theory is correct. The Thread has tapped into the power of the NSA, and that is how we found you yesterday. And, yes, I am sure we are being watched at this moment by satellite."

"So, The Thread is watching us with satellites right now?" asked Pete, feeling exposed.

Jim looked at Alex, suggesting he wanted Alex to take the answer.

For a long moment, it seemed Alex either did not get the communication from Jim or that he preferred driving to answering the question. Finally, Alex answered. "We do have access to one satellite that is observing Utah at present. That satellite has extraordinary resolution. When Jim made his call to report the bombings, The Thread was able to use that satellite to track Jim the whole way back to the cabin."

Alex pulled the van hard onto the street and accelerated powerfully in the direction of the highway. Jim asked, "So why did The Thread send just one van with five gunmen? Why isn't this place crawling with The Thread and law enforcement?"

"The men who attacked you were not far away. They were already in the canyon and would have soon been dispatched to check out this very property. That cabin was on a short list of places at which The Thread knew you might be. The list had been very large, but The Thread eliminated most of it overnight. I am confident, though, that a large number of agents from The Thread are going to encounter us very shortly. Those five men got here so fast because they were nearby. But there is a small army now converging on us. They know we are in a van. They know where we are right now, and they will be watching us live via the satellite."

The rescuer proved prophetic. As the van neared the first bend in the mountain road, a black SUV sped around the corner at a very high speed. Alex seemed to disregard the high-speed vehicle until it was just about to pass the van. Right at the moment the two vehicles passed each other, Alex swerved left and slammed the van into the rear of the SUV. The SUV's back end collapsed and flew apart. The front half of the SUV spun wildly behind the van and came to a stop in the middle of the road. The van seemed relatively unharmed, and Alex had managed to keep the van on the road. The van's speed had reduced drastically, but Alex again accelerated hard going into the curve.

"I assume that was our friends from The Thread?" yelled Jim over the roar of the accelerating engine.

A firm but snappy nod was all Alex offered in response. The rescuer remained fixated on the road.

Jim stared at the driver for a while.

"Did you say your name was Alexander Markham?" asked the FBI agent.

"Yes. Call me Alex." And with that, Alex's body language made it clear that driving and getting to safety was more important to him now than conversation. But the others were just too curious to not inquire, although circumstances were unsettling to say the least.

"So, Alex," pressed Jim, "back at the cabin you said that you are a high-ranking member of The Thread. *Are* you a high-ranking member of The Thread, or *were* you a high-ranking member of The Thread?"

"Well, I hope they still think I am."

"So, they know someone just rescued us, but they don't know it was you?" guessed Jim.

"Yes. If they discover that I am the one who saved you, our ability to escape lessens."

"Dude, let me get this right," broke in Jeff, who was still working on getting a mental grip on their situation. "We're being watched from the sky by a group that has massive technology and control over law enforcement and media outlets?"

"Yes," confirmed Alex.

"And our rescuer is a high-ranking member of the very group that is not only trying to kill us, but is also trying to take over America."

"Yes."

"Great… sounds fun," concluded Jeff sarcastically. "Really fun… More people ought to do this. This could replace bungee jumping on the list of popular extreme sports."

Alex rounded the last curve before the straightaway leading to the highway. Coming out of the curve, to their relief, the group could see the highway in the distance. The van's speed was pushing above ninety miles per hour, and was rising steadily on the straight road. No other vehicles were in sight before the highway.

Alex offered an unsolicited announcement. "If we can get to the highway before The Thread gets to us, our chances are much better!"

But it was not to be. Three black SUVs emerged from under the overpass, having just exited the highway. The three vehicles soon closed the half-mile distance with the van. Alex slowed down, but not as much as Jim or the others would have expected. Alex was still going eighty miles per hour right up to the encounter with the three vehicles. Alex finally jammed on the brake, but only to slow and maneuver, not to stop. As Alex made his move to veer to the right, the three vehicles made a well-coordinated instant roadblock.

The sides of the road were grassy mountain meadow with trees set back a couple hundred feet. This allowed Alex room to swing well around the vehicles. But the closest vehicle was ready for this and charged right at the van as Alex attempted to get around the roadblock. He was flooring the van, hoping to beat the other vehicle. The accelerating van was bouncing through the grass, wildly tossing the entire group. Alex could not escape the SUV, which slammed hard into the back left side of the van. Pete and Jeff, who had been sitting on the starboard side of the van flew off their bench, across the back of the van, and crashed into Colton, Dr. Isaacson, and the left side of the van.

The van did a one-eighty from the violent collision, but seemed unharmed from the inside. The van was facing the vehicle that had just hit it. The other two were closing in quickly, trying to surround the van. Alex had to throw the van into reverse and jam on the accelerator. He succeeded in pulling away from the SUV enough to yank the steering wheel and turn the van away, but the SUV struck again from the rear.

Alex again pounded on the accelerator, attempting to make a run for the highway with all three SUVs now behind them. But it did not work. The other two SUVs had far more momentum, and came up from both sides before Alex could even reach ten miles per hour. The two SUVs pulled around both sides of the front, even colliding with each other. Alex crashed into the front half of both SUVs. The third SUV slammed into the rear of the van, boxing it in. Dr. Isaacson was still on his bench, but was grunting in agony from the repeated jarrings caused by the crashes.

Alex turned toward the others. “Just in case,” he said as he reached behind his seat into a compartment and began tossing guns to each person. Jim already had one, so Alex only had to produce four guns. Ignoring the men who had begun to emerge from the SUVs and surround the van, Alex gave a crash course on how to use the dart guns of The Thread.

"Your weapons hold thirty darts!" he began concisely. "The normal setting of the guns is *stun*. If you push the red lever on the back top part of the gun, the chemical in the next dart will be *lethal*—and it will kill. If you shoot to kill, you must always press that lever before every shot to kill again. The default of every dart is stun. The stun will last about one to two hours. Stun is probably enough for our needs right now, but you are free to determine what you need to do in any given situation."

The rear doors of the van both had bullet resistant glass. Once Alex finished his quick instructions, the attention of the group in the van became riveted on the surrounding enemy. Every SUV had at least two doors open. Men dressed in dark clothing—similar to Alex's clothes—were standing behind doors of vehicles in crouched positions, guns pointing toward the van. But nothing else was happening. The Thread was plainly in control and waiting for the people in the van to surrender. Alex had other plans.

Alex turned in his seat toward the group. "I am sorry. I should have told you when we left. There are restraints for you against the sides of the van. You are going to need them now." As the four people in the rear of the van looked at the sides of the van, they noticed the seat belts. All four felt foolish for not having already put them on. They quickly did so.

With everyone now armed and secured in his seat, Alex faced forward with determination. "Hold on tight."

CHAPTER 22

PARLEY'S CANYON
9:15 A.M.

Alex slammed the van into the two SUVs. At first, the van nearly came to a standstill, but it never stopped. The men behind the doors jumped out of the way reflexively. Slowly but powerfully, the van's thrust was pushing the two vehicles out of the way. By now, members of The Thread were jumping back into the vehicles. But Alex still got a good head start. The van launched away from the foray of vehicles and shot once again toward the entrance ramp of the highway—which was a couple hundred yards away.

To everyone's dismay, a string of four additional dark SUVs filed out from under the overpass. Their movements were well coordinated. All four vehicles rushed onto the entrance ramp, blocking the way. Colton assumed that Alex would burst between two of these vehicles just as he had driven through the two previous vehicles. But Alex's reaction was quite different. With the entrance ramp blocked by four SUVs, and with three more pursuing from behind the van, Alex sped under the overpass, veered left, and bolted for the entrance ramp heading east—away from Salt Lake City. Of the seven vehicles attacking the group, none were prepared to stop Alex from getting on the highway heading east.

The van was soon on the highway gaining speed. The highway remained straight for about a mile, which gave Alex time to count the vehicles rising up from the ramp. All seven dark SUVs were now on the highway and in pursuit. Alex pumped his fist in approval—he was hoping all the vehicles would follow him. A large, six-foot high cement wall divided the highway. Alex eased around the wide bend in the highway then sped for another mile. By now, Alex raced far above the normal flow of traffic and was zooming past vehicles. Then he saw what he was hoping for. About a quarter mile ahead was an opening in the cement divider for law enforcement vehicles. In an amazing driving maneuver, Alex skidded into a long, sliding turn that crossed multiple lanes of traffic and cut off cars he had just passed.

Alex pulled out of the turning skid by blasting through the opening in the cement divider. Westbound cars skidded and swerved wildly to avoid the van that appeared out of nowhere. As the black vehicles that were pursuing them neared the divider, they struggled with merging, slowing, and passing through the opening. The lead vehicle almost stopped before it was able to pass through the opening. This slowed down all the vehicles and extended Alex's lead greatly. The van was well over a mile ahead of the pursuing vehicles by the time they got up to speed.

The van also had the advantage over the other vehicles in raw power. The lead was extending. Alex expertly jockeyed his way through traffic, maintaining insane speeds—he seldom dropped below one hundred miles per hour through the canyon.

Colton was scanning the highway for new enemies—he was particularly scrutinizing the eastbound traffic and the entrance and exit ramps. But no new threat availed itself.

"How's the knee, Doc?" asked Jeff. It was an odd time to inquire.

"You know what?" said Dr. Isaacson. "It's feeling a lot better. Maybe it's just getting numb, but it doesn't feel that bad right now."

"Why haven't we seen any new friends from The Thread?" asked Jeff, turning his attention back to reality. Though Jeff asked it, the entire group was wondering the same thing.

"I don't know why," answered Alex as he continued to weave through traffic, "but I have a guess."

"What's your guess?" asked Jim.

"Have you noticed that we have not seen any law enforcement vehicles yet?" asked Alex to provoke thought.

"Yes," said Jim, "which is fascinating seeing as how The Thread has access to the FBI right now. The Thread obviously has use of a satellite, but had they used the FBI these past few minutes, we would be dealing with helicopters, airplanes, and hoards of police officers, too. We'd have been a fairly easy catch."

"Yes," said Alex, "The Thread wanted to catch you without having to deal with the mess of law enforcement. But it appears that their failure to catch us back there has made their strategy seem a bit silly. My guess is that they have now called off the dogs and are calling in the hogs."

"You people from The Thread have some thing with animals, don't you?" said Jeff. "…The Hen… the Rooster… dogs, hogs."

"He means," said Jim, "that The Thread has likely pulled back their forces and have now alerted law enforcement."

The van was consuming the curving pavement of the highway and was approaching the mouth of the canyon.

"You have about a mile and a half until we reach the mouth of the canyon," informed Jim from the passenger seat.

"Thank you," offered Alex, who had yet to show any desire to slow. Just then, they whisked past a parked highway patrol officer. The lights on the top of the car flared into life. However, by the time the state trooper could gain any speed, the van would be well over a mile ahead. But the group still felt added tension. The highway patrolman seemed as threatening to the group as did The Thread.

As the mouth of the canyon opened to view, Alex swerved toward an exit ramp. He veered around a minivan and two cars that were exiting ahead of them. Just as they descended from the highway, they could see a pack of police cars blazing toward the canyon on the eastbound lanes. Colton also glimpsed a low-flying helicopter approaching the canyon, though it was still a few miles in the distance.

"Why are we getting off the highway?" Jim asked hastily.

"I'll explain later," said Alex. There was no anger in his reply, only urgency. "But for now, everyone do exactly what I tell you. There will be no time for explanations."

And with that, Alex slowed down abruptly. He had finished passing the other three vehicles that were also exiting the highway. The ramp passed under the highway and headed south to connect to the I-215 beltway that circled toward the south and west parts of the Salt Lake valley.

"Everyone hold on tight!" warned Alex. Just as Alex was completely under the highway, he pounded the break to the floor of the van, pulled the parking brake, and yanked the steering wheel hard to the left. The van skidded into a sliding spin and ended up facing the three approaching vehicles. The van came to a full rest near the back side of the overpass—still in the shade. All three vehicles behind the van slammed on their brakes and came to an emergency stop. The first vehicle was the minivan, which came to a stop just ten feet away from the front bumper of the group's van.

"Jim!" commanded Alex. "Use your badge and authority to get the people out of the third car and to relinquish their keys to us. Everyone: load all your stuff that you absolutely need into that third car. I will handle the first two cars."

Alex scanned the group, checking to see if they were willing to comply. He seemed satisfied. He continued. "Who has the documents?"

"I do," said Colton.

"Good," said Alex. "Keep the copies and give me the original."

Something froze in Colton. It was as if time stopped. Colton was almost dizzy trying to sort out what he was feeling and thinking. He scanned the group, but nobody else seemed to notice anything wrong. Colton shook his head.

“Colton, are you okay?” asked his uncle.

Colton snapped out of it, but he could not shake the cold feeling in his chest. But he sprang into action. “No,” he said bluntly to Alex, not worrying whether he offended Alex. “I’ll hold the original.” And with that, Colton handed the two copies of the document to his uncle. Colton’s belligerence toward Alex was a bit surprising to the others in the group. Although done respectfully, the act seemed most unusual because Colton did it at such an imperative moment.

Alex seemed unruffled. “Everyone into that third car, now.” He turned to Jim. “Go, Jim. Good luck.” Alex said it with calm, but urgent, authority and the group sprang into action. Alex grabbed his large, loaded pack and the tracking device. Everyone else secured their weapons and gathered anything they needed to take with them. Jeff, Colton, and Pete all assisted Dr. Isaacson out of the rear of the van and headed back toward the third car.

CHAPTER 23

MOUTH OF PARLEY'S CANYON
9:27 A.M.

Jim ran to the third car, flashing his badge. The driver, a young woman in her twenties, opened the window as Jim approached. Her face was laden with shock.

"FBI! We need your vehicle, ma'am. Please get out of your car and hand me the keys." She obeyed right away, though she was terrified. Jim sought to reassure her. "Don't worry, ma'am, you're going to be just fine. You'll have your car back soon enough. Just wait here. There will be law enforcement vehicles here to help you out. Just tell them what happened."

She nodded as she trustingly handed Jim her keys. Her eyes watered up, and she had no idea what to do.

"Thank you, ma'am. Just sit down over there on the side of the road for a minute." She did so. He opened all the doors of the vehicle, along with the trunk. He then sat down in the passenger seat, yielding the driver spot to Alex.

Meanwhile, as Colton and the others moved away from the van, Dr. Isaacson insisted he could move on his own. Colton allowed the professor to walk on his own, but kept his hands ready to support him at a moment's notice. As Colton looked back, he was shocked to see how banged up the van actually was. As he passed, he heard what Alex was saying to the family in the minivan.

"Sir, as a matter of national security, you must deliver this envelope to FBI headquarters immediately." Alex handed the man a white, eight-by-ten envelope. The man, quite taken aback, took the envelope from Alex. "The office is located at 257 East 200 South. Do not slow down. If you catch the attention of police, keep going. They will understand when you get there. The faster you get there, the better. Your country needs you to do this."

And with that, Alex patted the side of the van. Obediently, the driver pulled around the mangled van in front of him and sped his family toward FBI headquarters in Salt Lake City. As the minivan pulled away, Alex applied the flashing tracking device to the back end. He did it smoothly, without even a clank.

Alex waved on the second sedan. The passengers in that vehicle had seen enough. They locked their doors and were content to get away from the bizarre situation.

The three roommates all understood Alex would be the driver again. When Dr. Isaacson realized that—due to the lack of room in the back seat—someone would be sitting across the three people in the back, he volunteered to be that person. He scooted himself out of the car and insisted the others sit down first. They did so after loading packs and minor miscellaneous items into the trunk. Dr. Isaacson gingerly sat across the top of the three friends, favoring his sore knee. They closed the doors.

Overhead, the sound of sirens made a steady crescendo, and then zoomed overhead. As those sirens faded off into the east, they heard more sirens approaching from the west. But no police cars were coming down the ramp or under the overpass.

With the minivan and car gone, Alex began signaling the line of built-up traffic behind them to move ahead. After playing traffic cop, he headed back to the car. All this had occurred under the overpass in a short amount of time.

Jim turned in the front seat to Dr. Isaacson. "It looks like your knee's doing much better."

"It is, thank goodness," said Dr. Isaacson. "I was afraid I'd really messed it up."

Alex put his large pack in the trunk, then handed his smaller backpack to Jim as he plopped into the driver's seat. The car's engine was already going. After a brief glance to check for oncoming cars down the ramp, Alex zoomed out from under the overpass. Jim turned to wave at the young lady whose car they had commandeered. She was sitting on the side of the road and had tears streaming down her cheeks, but somehow managed to smile at Jim.

Alex accelerated rapidly, but was careful to hold at the speed limit of the ramp. He did not want to catch the attention of any police that were all over the area by now. As Alex reached the I-215 ramps, he turned right to head north on the beltway.

"What was that all about, Mr. Markham?" asked Pete.

"You must be Peter," said Alex.

"Yes."

"Well, since we are being watched from satellite, our best hope of escape is to switch. If we switch in the open, it is obvious to The Thread what vehicle we are in. But if we switch under an overpass that has multiple vehicles underneath it, it makes it a lot harder to watch multiple vehicles with one satellite."

"And you put the tracking device on the back of the van?" asked Jeff.

"Yes," confirmed Alex. "I was hoping that trick would distract The Thread long enough for our chances to improve."

"If we're being watched, why did the police just go over the overpass?" asked Colton. "Why wouldn't they have trapped us down there? The Thread could have told them we were under that overpass."

"What you have to realize," said Alex, "is that it is The Thread, not the police, which is watching us from the satellite. They must have let the police know that we were here by some anonymous tip. But the police are not watching us with satellite surveillance. I am sure The Thread knows that we pulled a switch of some sort under that overpass back there; but The Thread has to be very cautious with how they communicate their information to law enforcement."

Alex had been on I-215 for a very short time. He exited onto Foothill Drive rather than follow the highway as it turned back west and merged with I-80. Heading north along Foothill Drive, Alex seemed to have evaded the swarms of law enforcement vehicles in the area. They heard the sound of a helicopter behind them. Jim spotted it through the rear window. It was flying low around the mouth of the canyon, heading into the canyon. Jim was grateful the helicopter had not gotten there sooner.

"Alex, the first thing we have to do is find a way to report the Salt Lake City bombing to authorities before it takes place," said Jim.

"That would not be wise," said Alex.

Jim gave Alex a look that suggested he was questioning Alex's sanity. "Why?"

"Only two people know where each bomber is hiding. If the bombing is compromised in any way, one of those two people will personally go to the bomber and inform him to go to a different location—a location that I do not know—and detonate the bomb immediately."

Colton leaned forward around the professor. "So if we report the bombings, we'll cause the bombing to happen much sooner at a different location?"

"Exactly," said Alex. He was looking vigilantly at the surroundings as he continued to press north on Foothill Drive.

"What?" said Jeff, who just now understood what had been said. "Did you say that we *shouldn't* report the bombings?"

"Yes," answered Alex.

"You mean, we may be the only ones in America who know who's behind these terrorist attacks and the assassination of the President, and that these same people are about to bomb this very city, and we can't tell anyone?"

"That is about the crux of it," said Alex without emotion.

"That's psychotic!" Jeff was agitated.

Everyone in the car was agitated too, except Alex. But with Jim's agitation came relief that he had not gotten word out to some random person at the gas station earlier that morning when he had made his call.

"So, do we just let the bombing go on today?" asked Colton.

"Absolutely not." Alex maintained a demeanor that was so calm that Colton found it annoying. Colton was surprised at the level of frustration he felt toward this mysterious rescuer. Perhaps the stresses of a crazy twenty-four hours were taking their toll.

"I take it you have a plan, then." said Jim, who did not seem as ruffled by the news or Alex's style as were Jeff and Colton.

"Not many people know where the tracking devices are on these vehicles," Alex replied. "My guess is that The Thread will not take long to notice that the weapons used back at the cabin were The Thread's own weapons, that whoever saved you knew where the tracking device was, and that I am now missing. By putting these facts together, I too will be on their hit list. My normal safe houses in Utah are not available. But I do have resources in this state that The Thread does not know about. One of those is an apartment in the heart of the city. We will go there to finalize our plans. In the meantime, we must devote our attention to getting to that apartment in safety. We'll be stopping a few blocks ahead, then make our way to the light rail train."

The road curved to the west for a short time before curving again to the north. Alex continued to remain within the flow of traffic and to drive in ways that would not draw any attention to their car.

"Well, the vehicle switch obviously worked back there," said Pete. "Why don't we just drive this car to your apartment?"

Jim knew the answer and turned and explained it to Peter and the others crammed in the back seat. "When the police get to the woman back there, they and the FBI will use traffic cameras at intersections and such to trace where we went. It will take some effort to trace this car all the way to wherever we stop, but it's only a matter of time before they track us down. We have a small window of time."

"How small?" asked Colton.

"Who knows? Perhaps a half hour to two hours," answered his uncle.

Colton directed attention back to Alex. "So, what's your plan for today's bombing?"

"Well, at the apartment we will go over all the details of what we need to do to stop today's bombing. Many things must come together. But we have a chance. The key is *The Key*. That document that you… that we have. Having that document is the key to stopping the bombing—it is our advantage. If we can stay out of the hands of The Thread and somehow get to the bomber with that key, we can stop it. Our chances are not very high, but we have a shot at it."

"So you want us to go to some apartment and hang out while we come up with a plan to intercept the bomber just before the bomb goes off?" asked Colton.

"That would be a fair summary," responded Alex with the same casualness that Colton was coming to expect.

"So, have you discovered the location of the third transaction?" asked Alex calmly.

"Yes," affirmed Jim.

"Where?" asked Alex, seeking verification.

"The Capitol Building," said Jim.

Nobody else saw it, but Colton did. For a moment, Alex's mouth parted in what seemed to be surprise. The look of surprise passed. "Very nice."

"What's wrong?" asked Colton, responding to Alex's reaction.

"Nothing," said Alex. "I am just surprised you figured it out."

Jeff spoke up. "We didn't exactly have to call in Sherlock Holmes for that one."

Alex eased the car to a stop at a red light. All in the vehicle tensed when a police car pulled up alongside the car.

Dr. Isaacson had seen it too. Dr. Isaacson slid down—as much as he could—into the tiny gap between the boys' knees and the back of the front seats. It was a feeble effort. There was not enough room to get out of sight. But it was enough; the officer never noticed. The light turned green and Alex accelerated slowly. When the police car was far enough ahead, Alex pulled in behind and maintained his slow speed. Cars filed in front of the car and moved over, thereby creating a buffer of many vehicles between the group's car and the police car.

Now that the stress of the police car had passed, Jim pressed Alex for more information. "So, if you are a high ranking member of The Thread, why are you helping us?"

Alex was silent for long enough that Jim supposed Alex might not even answer him. But when he did speak, everyone in the car listened with fascination.

"I believe in most of what The Thread is seeking to bring about—"

"Believe," asked Dr. Isaacson from the back, "or *believed*?"

"I still believe in most of what The Thread is creating."

"Wow," said Dr. Isaacson. It was not a positive response.

"But what has sickened me is the *means* The Thread has now resorted to and how far some in the top of The Thread have taken things."

"So, you're bailing because they've gone too far?" asked Colton.

"Yes."

"Why didn't you decide to bail before two major cities were bombed?" It came from Colton as a jab.

"Uh… Colton… this man just saved our life. Maybe you could show him a little gratitude," said Jeff.

"No, no… it is a fair question," said Alex. He paused. "You have to realize that leaving something like The Thread is *not* an easy thing. It is not like leaving a country club, or a poor movie. If you wish to leave The Thread once you are in it—at any level—you incur a death sentence. You had better have a way to get out of the country and exist in secret, somewhere in the world where you think nobody can find you."

It seemed as if Alex were done—that he had made his point to his own satisfaction, but he continued. "I have hated, for months now, what The Thread has been doing. But it was not until our little document came up missing yesterday that I had the courage to act."

"So your defection wasn't planned?" asked Jeff, craning his head around the professor to see Alex respond to his question.

"I wish it had been. Then I might have had a chance at surviving. But since that is not possible, I might as well do all I can to prevent some of the foolishness The Thread's deeds have come to."

"Wait a minute," said Jeff. "You mean that you not only know that what you're doing is extremely risky, but you also believe you won't survive?"

"Oh, it's not a belief. It is a certainty."

"If we can stop the bombing, perhaps you could get protection from the federal government. There's got to be a way for you to survive."

"No, there is not. There are too many members of The Thread intertwined throughout the government—including law enforcement. In fact, that is why they call it *The Thread*. As it grows, the goal is to have its members woven throughout all organizations of society."

"Wow," said Dr. Isaacson. This time his response showed fascination.

"If you wish to leave The Thread, you had better have an exit strategy," said Alex. "While The Thread would like to kill you all, if we can manage to stop the bombing, and get this document exposed, they will have little to gain from killing you. As for me, I have made a blood oath. The Thread will enforce that oath at great cost.

"You got the document from Frank Tomlinson," continued Alex. "The first clue to The Thread that something was wrong was a huge bank withdrawal he made from his account. He made it to the airport, purchased a ticket with cash, and made it onto a flight out of the country before he could be stopped."

"Where did he go?" asked Jeff.

"To Mexico. We just missed him there. But I suppose he is either dead by now or that he will be killed soon," said Alex with his emotionless way of communicating.

The road turned east again and became 400 South. Alex turned.

"Where're we heading?" asked Jim. "Trolley Square?"

"That is right," said Alex. "We will use Trolley Square—because of it being a busy, public place—to fan out to the light rail train. Trolley Square is only a couple blocks from the trains."

"But the trains have cameras on them. Surely those will be scrutinized too," said Jim. Alex passed through the last traffic light before Trolley Square, which was in full view now.

"Yes, but we will only ride them so far. Doing so will buy us more time," said Alex calmly. "Besides, we will also do a few things here at Trolley Square to change our appearance."

"Like what?" asked Jim, a bit surprised.

"You will see," It was all Alex offered before turning into the parking lot of the shopping center.

CHAPTER 24

TROLLEY SQUARE
SALT LAKE CITY
9:46 A.M.

Although the group tried very hard to not draw attention, it was impossible for them to not look somewhat like a circus act as they struggled to vacate the small sedan. But, as awkwardly as it looked, nobody was around them to enjoy the show.

The small mall was not very crowded. Finding a parking spot was easy, but there were enough vehicles that the mall would offer adequate social cover. About half the shops were open. Nobody saw any sign of either The Thread or law enforcement. The only thing that caused anyone turmoil was Alex grabbing the semi-large pack out of the trunk. Carrying around a large pack like that was not a natural thing at a shopping center.

Dr. Isaacson's first couple of steps were labored, but he adjusted to the pain and limited mobility. He still had a limp, but it was not too bad. Jeff maintained a post right next to Dr. Isaacson in case the professor needed an instant hand. Dr. Isaacson sensed Jeff's concern and gave Jeff a nod of gratitude.

Colton remembered the pictures of his uncle and himself on the news the previous night. For the first time since becoming a wanted man, Colton was now in public. The thought of law enforcement wanting him was disturbing. Colton found himself slouching a bit and ducking as he walked with the group toward the entrance to Trolley Square.

On the trip to the door, Jim was—although maintaining a casual demeanor—glancing about, surveying the situation. Colton could tell that Alex was doing the same. He could also tell that Alex was far more used to it even than his highly skilled and trained uncle was.

"Let's stagger our entrance—two groups of three," suggested Alex. Alex assumed the point position in the first group of three, which naturally formed because Alex, Pete, and Colton were already in the front. Jim had become the rearguard, walking behind Dr. Isaacson and Jeff.

The back three waited at the door. They made the appearance of conversation, but Jim kept his eyes fixed on the first three. Colton noticed that most people in the mall congregated around sources of media. Colton was confident that even though the mall would not normally be very crowded yet, the crowds were still smaller than they would have been on an average day—something attributed to the effects of the morning's terrorist attacks.

As the front group advanced around a corner, Jim urged his group forward. They came to the corner the others had just rounded. They saw Alex ahead of them, standing outside a bathroom door, but now without his large pack slung over his shoulder. Apparently he had given it to one of the younger boys to take into the bathroom. Once Alex saw the rear group round the corner, he too went in. The rear group pushed forward and eased into the bathroom.

Once in, Alex came to life. He was prepared.

"Jim, will you keep watch just outside the door," said Alex. "We will get you in a few minutes."

"I'll do it," volunteered Jeff. "I don't think my picture was plastered all over the news."

Alex looked at Jeff for a moment. He nodded approval. "Good idea."

As Jeff placed his hand on the door handle, Alex instructed: "If someone is coming, tap the door with your foot once. But still act casual."

"Got it," said Jeff, who then left the bathroom.

Alex opened his pack and allowed the contents to disengorge onto the bathroom counter. A large bundle of clothes sprawled between the two sinks. Alex used very few words. As he sorted through clothes, he scrutinized the different members of the group. "Try this," or "here," were all he would say. The others would file into stalls and come out with a new outfit. All the pants were similar—flexible waist pants that had the feel of sweats, but looked more like normal pants than they did sweats. The shirts were widely assorted—mostly earth toned in color.

Alex then pulled out a small handbag that was still in the pack. Alex produced out of the handbag cordless clippers and various bottles and tubes of chemicals and cosmetic supplies.

"James, you first," said Alex.

Alex beckoned Jim to come over near him by the counter. Jim obeyed. Alex, though gentle, was in total control as he gripped Jim's neck, pulling Jim's head over the garbage. Alex began to cut Jim's hair. It was evident that Alex had had reasonable experience trimming hair. As fast as a military barber might cut a new recruit's hair, Alex gave Jim a short, flat-top style hairdo. Jim's hair had not been long, but the change was drastic. Now, with Jim out of his professional dress clothes, and with a new hair style, even those who had been with him for the past day could not easily recognize him.

Alex then reached into the handbag and produced a small mustache. He peeled something off the back—the mustache had an adhesive on the back. "Here. Try this," ordered Alex. Alex held the mustache up to Jim's hair. "It's not a perfect match, but try it." Jim tried the mustache, pushing it even more firmly onto his upper lip than he had to. When he pulled his hands away, the transformation was complete. Jim himself could not believe he was looking at his own image in the large mirror.

Alex then gestured to Pete. “I am sorry, but your hair, as it is now, is like a beacon. Forgive me.” Pete yielded, even showing a bit of enthusiasm, obviously enjoying the disguise part of things. Alex shaved Pete’s mane of red hair without any spacer—right down to his scalp. Alex had to use great caution in shaving around Pete’s wound from the previous day, but the gash now only looked like a bad scratch—small considering how much blood it had produced at first. After the shave, Alex placed a small bandage over the wound.

But what fascinated the others even more was when he pulled out of the handbag a small wig. Holding the wig up to Pete’s head, Alex analyzed the size of the wig and cut it accordingly with a small set of scissors. One of the tubes on the counter must have been wig glue of some kind, because Alex smothered some of it on Peter’s head before pressing the wig in place. As it had been with Jim, the change was amazing, with the exception of Pete’s eyebrows, which made the new hair color look silly.

Colton could not help smiling. Pete understood why Colton was smiling. “What, Colton?” asked Pete, his excitement for his new disguise slightly deflated.

“I’m sorry, Pete,” apologized Colton. “It’s just those eyebrows. Wow!” Colton wished Jeff could be here for the entertainment.

“No worries,” said Alex to Pete. Alex applied mascara to Pete’s eyebrows. The effect was instant and sufficient. Pete’s hair and eyebrows were a near-perfect match of brown.

“That’s amazing,” said Colton genuinely. Pete’s response to Colton’s amazement showed that Pete’s enthusiasm was back.

Alex then looked at Colton. Colton’s hair was already quite short, so he wondered what Alex would do. Alex made a decision. He gestured Colton over to the garbage and proceeded to shave his hair, much like he had Pete’s. But rather than pulling out a wig, Alex instead pulled a razor out of his little bag.

“Cool,” said Colton. “I’ve never taken a Bic to my head before.”

Alex, of course, had a small container of shaving cream, which he used to smother Colton's head. Then, allowing the cream to sit for a spell, Alex surveyed Dr. Isaacson.

"For you, I think simple is the order of the day," suggested Alex. And with that, Alex plucked from the now smaller pile of clothes on the counter a hat and a pair of sunglasses.

"Thank you for your consideration," expressed Dr. Isaacson with a bow-like nod.

Colton, standing with his head plastered with shaving cream, teasingly complained, "Hey! This isn't fair!"

He looked ridiculous, and the effect was quite funny to the others, especially Pete who was, once again, entirely too enthusiastic about what was happening.

Colton was amazed at how much Alex had done to their appearance in such a short time.

"That little bag of yours is sure a lot like a magician's bag," said Colton.

"There have been quite a few times when I have needed it to do magic on my own self," said Alex.

Alex began running the razor across Colton's head. He was about half-way done with the shave when a thump on the door sent a wave of adrenaline throughout the room. Alex and Jim jammed the contents scattered across the bathroom counter into the large pack. Alex hoisted the pack and gave quick orders.

"You two," he gestured to Pete and Dr. Isaacson, "to the urinals." There were three stalls with toilets. Colton did not wait for an order. He had already occupied a stall and was closing the door to hide his sightly head. Alex occupied the next stall. Jim was loading into the third. Jim said quietly over the divider, "If he begins waiting for a toilet, I will flush, wash hands, and wait." They left one urinal open.

It seemed like they had more time than any of them would have expected. Everyone in the bathroom at their various posts began to assume that it was a false alarm. But the door opened. When they could see it wasn't Jeff, readiness engulfed the group. It was time to perform.

Two teenagers walked in. They were laughing as they entered the door, but their laughter subsided when they sensed multiple people occupied the bathroom. One of the two boys procured the open urinal. The other waited. Jim could see through the crevice in the stall divider that the one waiting was waiting for a urinal. Jim decided to remain in the stall. Dr. Isaacson sensed the situation. While the newly dark-haired Pete remained for the duration at his urinal, Dr. Isaacson moved away, allowing the automatic flusher to flush. The second boy assumed the professor's former urinal, and Dr. Isaacson then washed his hands and waited in the bathroom. He did it casually, and nothing about it looked suspicious. Both boys made their way to the sinks and washed their hands.

When the boys left the bathroom, the group went back into motion. But this time, Alex kept the pack stored in one of the stalls in case they had to hide again. He shaved the remainder of Colton's head swiftly. Colton washed and dried his head of his own accord. But as soon as Colton had his head dry, Alex applied a solution that softened the stark whiteness of the freshly shaven head, turning it a light shade of tan that was a closer match to the skin on Colton's face.

"One more," said Alex, stepping toward the door.

"Should I take his place on bathroom watch?" asked Colton, who had begun to head toward the door too.

"No," said Alex. "We'll keep his disguise simple. I'll bring him in."

Alex opened the door and motioned Jeff into the bathroom. Alex headed back to the counter where his stuff was. He had just begun to sift through the remaining things when Jeff entered the bathroom. Jeff saw Colton, Pete, and Jim and broke into loud, hysterical laughter. Colton, Pete, Dr. Isaacson, and Jim all initiated a smile at the young, light-hearted man's reaction. But the smile did not last long.

Alex's face exploded with rage. The expression on Alex Markham's face supplanted the docile, dark, calm steadiness and halted all frivolity in the others.

Alex accompanied the expression by taking quick steps toward Jeff with his finger held up and angled slightly to the side—a clear gesture that demanded instant silence and carried intense warning.

Jeff, normally not one to take notice of any control or manipulation from others, fell quiet. He felt a vibe from Alex that seemed founded on evil deeds performed in the past that had not only hardened Alex, but that had also gotten Alex used to getting his way and maintaining complete control over any situation.

Alex stopped his advance toward Jeff. With his finger still extended in warning, Alex realized that he had been too harsh in his reaction. His arm dropped and his composure returned. He glanced around the room at the shocked faces. What Alex had noticed but disregarded was the reflective step that both Jim and Colton had taken toward Jeff out of a sudden sense of protection.

"I am sorry," said Alex. "I did not want anything to attract the attention of anyone. I overreacted." Then Alex looked at Jeff. "I mean no harm to you."

"Don't worry about it, dude," said Jeff. "Just don't expect me to walk out of a room with one group of people in here, then walk back in a few minutes later to this group, and not laugh!" Like a classic Jeff statement, the comment was not out of anger, but humor.

Then something happened that was a surprise to everyone. Alex smiled.

Jeff's words and Alex's smile were like an elixir on the men gathered in the bathroom.

"Okay, let's do this," said Alex, taking control and moving things forward again. Alex looked at Jeff. "You will go with the same style as this man," Alex gestured toward Dr. Isaacson before handing to Jeff a hat and some sunglasses.

Alex reached into a side pocket on his pack and pulled out a large pouch, from which he pulled out a bunch of envelopes. Alex tossed an envelope to everyone in the group. Pete was the first to open the envelope and see the money.

"Whoa!" exclaimed Pete, much like he would have on Christmas morning when he was young. "How much is in here?"

"This is in case we get split up," said Alex. "It could come in very handy. You should each have ten thousand dollars."

Jeff whistled, Dr. Isaacson and Colton marveled, Pete could barely contain himself, and Jim had almost no reaction at all.

Alex ignored all the responses and pressed ahead, pulling a sticky-note pad out of the pile on the counter. "We need to get to that apartment. This is the address." With haste, Alex scribbled the address and apartment number on two different notes. "Memorize this address as a pair, then throw the note away."

"As pairs?" asked Jim.

"Yes. We will leave here in pairs, staggered about five minutes apart. We will make our way to the light rail train—as I mentioned earlier. James, you go with Pete. Jeff, you go with Harold—"

"Harold?" asked Jeff.

"Yes," said Alex, who looked at Dr. Isaacson. "Right?"

Dr. Isaacson looked at Jeff. "Harold is my first name."

"Oh," said Jeff, who then looked at Alex, "you mean Doc."

"Whatever," responded Alex. He was a bit bothered but shrugged off Jeff's interruption. As Jim, Colton, and Jeff noticed, this was the first time they became certain that Alex knew who they all were.

"And Colton will go with me. We will divide up the copies of *Key #3*." Alex looked at Colton. "How many copies of *Key #3* did you make? You said two, right?"

Colton did not know why, but an overwhelming impulse swept over him. He lied. "Three."

The open surprise of the others seemed to agitate Alex, who studied Colton. "You told the men from The Thread before they were about to kill you that you had only made two." The statement hung as a challenge to Colton to explain. Colton did so without hesitation.

"At Dr. Isaacson's office, I made an additional copy that I didn't let anybody know about."

"Why?" asked Alex. Things were tense again. "Why did you make a copy that you didn't let anybody know about?"

"I made three copies. But when things got dicey, I put one of the copies in a place where it was both hidden and available for quick discovery by many people at the same time. I didn't want anyone else in the group to be accountable for it, so I didn't tell them."

The surprise among the group hung in the air then gradually turned into adulation. The lie had passed suspicion. Although the dark, piercing eyes of Alex continued to stare at him, Colton breathed a sigh of relief in his heart.

CHAPTER 25

TROLLEY SQUARE
SALT LAKE CITY
9:58 A.M.

Alex had continued to stare at Colton, and Colton tried to not show any agitation.

"Colton, next to capturing and eliminating us, The Thread's greatest hope is to secure all copies of *Key #3*. We must secure that extra document. We must find a way to get it before The Thread does," Alex was adamant.

"That document is quite secure. Nobody in this group, other than me, is going to bear the burden of knowing where that last copy is," Colton replied, with plenty of determination.

"What if The Thread finds it?"

"I don't think that's going to happen."

Colton braced himself for Alex to continue to press harder, but the opposite happened. Alex softened and shrugged. "If you trust that it is secure, and that The Thread will not intercept it, then there is nothing to worry about for now. We'll talk about it later." Colton found Alex's acceptance surprising, and was delighted the issue seemed settled.

Alex resumed control of the group. "Jim, you head out with Pete. I recommend that you go straight up the block to 4th South. From there I suggest you take the light rail train to downtown, and then walk the last many blocks to the apartment. I think that would be the safest way to get to the apartment. The

Thread and local and federal law enforcement are now looking for us. Be wise and stay safe. Good luck." And with that, Alex nodded to Jim and Pete, encouraging them to leave. Jim did not wait for any further oratory or mandate. He and Pete were off. The quest for the safety of the downtown apartment had begun.

Dr. Isaacson and Jeff had left about five minutes after Jim, and about five minutes later Colton and Alex left the small shopping center. Alex had stashed the large pack in the cluttered corner of one of the shops in Trolley Square. He only had his normal backpack. Colton, too, had a backpack from the cabin slung over his shoulder. Colton had stowed his weapon in his backpack. Alex's weapon was in a very large pocket on the side of his pants. Colton reasoned that their pace was as fast as it could be without being conspicuous. But Alex was pushing hard toward the light rail trains.

When they got there, Colton and Alex crossed to the median—to where the tracks were located—headed to the passenger platform in the middle of the street, and waited. They could see no sign of the other four. Colton wondered if the others had all boarded trains there.

Colton supposed the trains were running at close intervals, because after only a couple of minutes, the Trax train zipped around the curve that was a few blocks to the east. In just another minute or so, the train had halted and the doors were opening. But just as they began to climb aboard, they both heard it: sirens. Many sirens. And the sound was quickly going from a distant whine to a swelling, dissonant orchestra.

Alex hesitated on the steps. Perhaps it was the confined nature of the train, but Alex was visibly weighing the present risk of getting on the train in light of the chorus of sirens now filling the air. The sound materialized into a trail of police cars on 4th South that sped around the same curve the train had rounded just minutes before. Nobody was behind Alex except for Colton, so Alex's delay in boarding the train was not creating any consternation from anyone; but a beeping sound warned passengers it was time for the doors to close. Alex remained perched at the top of the stairs, watching the convoy of law enforcement approach. His face remained casual, but Colton could see that Alex's grip on the railing was turning his knuckles white. The line of siren-blaring cars peeled hard into a left-hand turn—a turn that would take them to Trolley Square. With the cars committing to the turn, Alex made his decision. He leaped aboard. The beeping had now become a solid, menacing tone accompanied by a flashing light. Colton followed Alex's example by jumping in and taking a seat.

It seemed like a long time from the time the doors closed before the train moved, but Colton knew that it probably was just a perception that resulted from fears spawned by the swarming police cars. The few passengers that were on the train were awed by the wave of police cars that had now proven to be overwhelming. A couple cars were approaching from the west. The police were pouncing as if they believed they were cornering something important.

Colton relaxed back into his seat. How odd that to avoid The Thread, they had to avoid all law enforcement. He also wondered how the others in the group were doing, and if any of them had any idea how narrowly The Thread and law enforcement had missed them at Trolley Square.

Colton wanted to talk to Alex about The Thread. Colton had so many questions he was dying to ask, and had looked forward to being paired up with this enigmatic man. But though Alex had been cool as steel, he was now visibly ruffled.

The few passengers on their same car were all fixated on the television. Colton shook his head at how strange his circumstance was. Had he not found that document the day before, Colton would no doubt be spending the day in front of a television screen, learning more about another hideous terrorist attack. How odd that on such a day as this, the news reports were only of secondary interest to Colton.

For a few brief minutes, Colton tuned into the news. The news anchor gave a summary of what they knew so far. They had verified the bombs as dirty bombs. Twenty confirmed deaths in New York and over a hundred wounded. Casualties for Seattle were coming in at about half of those of New York. The thought of Americans killing Americans for power sickened Colton.

Both cities were in final stages of evacuation. Quarantine and cleanup crews from across the nation were mobilizing. The entire country was in a state of heightened security. The President had spoken to the nation from a bunker somewhere, and was to address the nation more fully that night—perhaps even from the White House. Colton shook his head at that one. What would the traitor say in his mock message? No doubt he would be playing up the threat as much as he could.

One more thing fascinated him. The anchor began describing the perpetrator of the New York bombing. "In Seattle, the bomber seems to have been pulverized in the explosion. But in New York, the terrorist, though killed, is largely intact. The front half of the van used in the attack was blasted forward. Authorities have recovered and identified the driver as one Kaleed Khavis. Identification with him shows him to be a recent immigrant from Pakistan. Authorities are now sorting through evidence to find out what terrorist organization Kaleed Khavis is a part of."

Colton gave Alex a shocked and perplexed look. Alex gave a slight nod, and said quietly, "I will explain later."

The train pressed ahead and neared downtown. As the largest buildings of Salt Lake went from looming structures in the distance to canyon-like walls through which the train now passed, Colton once again heard the distant sound of a siren. He assumed it was another vehicle bolting for Trolley Square. The sound got louder. His assumption that the siren would pass off into the distance turned now into unfounded hope. Looking back at the same time, both men could see through the rear train car an approaching police car just a block and a half behind the train.

Then growing concern in the two turned to raw anguish as the train came to a blinding halt. It was clearly an emergency stop. The few passengers in the car lurched forward, some even spilling out of their seats and into the aisle. Colton's head smacked into the bar across the back of the seat he was sitting next to. Alex's body smashed into Colton. Notwithstanding the pain and the shock of the stop, both Alex and Colton were on their feet, ready to act. Alex pulled his gun from his pocket. Colton followed suit by awkwardly pulling his from his backpack. Colton was aware of the reaction sweeping across the few passengers in the car. He could see seeds of confusion and panic, and Colton realized how much he looked like a criminal at that moment.

The abrupt stop allowed the police car to reach them in just moments. Another siren-blaring car was also approaching in the distance, but seemed far away still. Two police officers approached the rear car of the train—one car behind Alex and Colton's. They watched in heightened readiness. Colton supposed that at least one police officer would remain outside of the train, but he was wrong. They kicked the door of the rear compartment open and both officers boarded the train, searching among the passengers.

"Conceal your weapon," ordered Alex. Colton stuffed the gun into his pocket.

"I hope our disguises work," said Colton to Alex, barely loud enough to hear.

Alex's willingness to wait and find out was over the instant the second officer entered into the rear car. Colton could see that the next police car was still two blocks away. Alex lunged to the door and pressed on it. Nothing. He kicked at the door. It opened a little. The small opening gave him confidence to go at it with great force. This time, his kick drove the two halves of the door apart wide enough for them to pass through the opening.

Both men were now on a narrow cement platform that served also as a median for 400 South . They swiveled their heads, looking for danger as they moved along the narrow cement, staying close to the train. When they got to the front car, they were nearly to the intersection of Fourth South and Main Street. They bolted north across the street.

"Hide your weapon as much as you can when you run! But have it accessible!" yelled Alex in full stride. Keeping a hand on the handle of his weapon, Colton ran as hard as he could. He had to—Alex was very fast.

The police did not have to spot the two running away. Many people on the light rail train saw the two make a run for it. A chorus of informative yells, choreographed by fingers pointing at Colton and Alex, gave plenty of notice to the police officers that at least two of the people they were searching for were running around the building, heading up Main Street's sidewalk.

Just before the two men in flight rounded the corner of the tall, downtown building, both officers in the train made for the door of the rear car in which they had been conducting their search. Their exit out of the train was not as easy as their entrance, though. The door had almost closed after they had entered through it, and the first officer underestimated what it would take to pass back out the door. He got stuck on his first attempt, and the other officer smashed into him. A redoubled second effort opened the door, and both finally emerged; but precious time had been lost, and the frustrated officers knew they may have lost Alex and Colton.

Colton knew they had to do something in a hurry. They would not escape on foot by running down a street when police were quickly converging on the area. Alex was thinking the same thing, and his dead sprint slowed down enough to enable Alex's waist to swivel to assess options. There weren't many. As they pushed north, a southbound car crossed Main Street, turning left toward them, and crossed their path on the sidewalk. Both men had to slow to avoid running into the rear of the car as it finished pulling into a very small parking lot between two large buildings.

In frustration, Colton wanted to slam the car with his palm. Instead, he swerved around the car on the wide sidewalk.

This all happened quickly enough that the police had not yet rounded the corner. Then deliverance presented itself.

"You two look like you're in a hurry. Need a ride?" Although it did not look like a taxi, Colton now noticed that the car had a small cone advertisement on the top that said *Quality Taxi and Courier.* Colton smiled and stepped toward the car, already in the motion of nodding. But Alex was stiff and still on the sidewalk—hesitating much like he had when they first boarded the train.

Alex's reaction caused Colton to stop dead. The decision was in Alex's hand. In that brief moment, Alex was in turmoil. In all they had done, Alex had a calmness that was so self-assured that it seemed borderline comatose compared to how a normal person would be reacting to the pressures Alex was managing. But that calmness had evaporated when the train had stopped. Alex appeared, while he weighed the decision, as if he were closer to panic than he was to composure. In that moment, the growing sound of sirens had a clamping effect on Colton's gut. He knew law enforcement was right around the corner.

Colton pulled his eyes from Alex to look back at the driver of the taxi, but he did not swivel his head to do so—his face was still pointing toward Alex. *What was Alex's hesitation*? And then it happened. Colton saw it, and he knew he was not supposed to have seen it. It took just a moment, and Colton knew the driver had meant it only for Alex. The driver had raised his hand in the air. As Colton looked through the corner of his eyes, he saw the driver's hand swoop downward, then back upward, bending primarily at the wrist. As his hand swooped, the driver had put his pointing finger together with his thumb, with the other three fingers extended—much like an "Okay" sign. But Colton understood. The gesture was a sign. And Colton even understood the meaning of the sign. The sign looked like the motion one would make forming a stitch in sewing. It was a sign of The Thread.

CHAPTER 26

SALT LAKE CITY
10:37 A.M.

Neither Alex nor the man in the cab supposed that Colton had caught the sign. Colton's glance was now fully back on Alex. The transformation in Alex was instantaneous. Relief flooded his countenance, and he lunged toward the car, motioning for Colton to follow.

A wave of dread and awful understanding swept away any relief that came from the taxi's timely arrival. Colton sickened in his core at the realization. He now understood so many things in a tiny amount of time.

Colton knew police were coming around the corner any moment. He knew that apprehension by the police would put him into the hands of The Thread. But was apprehension by the police worse than getting in the cab and putting himself directly into the hands of The Thread? Colton also understood that Alex was not a defector from The Thread, but a special operative.

But what pushed Colton to follow Alex into the car was the certain realization that the other members of his group would be in the hands of The Thread. Without Colton and the original document, perhaps their lives would not be worth much to The Thread. The decision was clear.

Colton lunged toward the taxi's rear driver-side door, which Alex was already entering. Alex slid across the seat just in time for Colton to dive in.

A police car and the running officers rounded the corner in unison. Although the closing door of the taxi was within the vision of both the officer on foot and the two officers in the car, they did not notice it. What they did notice was the door of the high-rise on the second half of the block closing. All three pursuers supposed that closing door was from the two men they were chasing. They honed in on that door. One of the officers in the car radioed the information that two suspects had just entered a building. Much of Salt Lake's law enforcement would gather and besiege that building.

The police car zoomed past, followed by the running police officer. The second officer on foot rounded the corner and passed.

"Wow! I wonder what's going on," said the taxi driver.

Colton felt annoyed at the feigned surprise of the driver. What taxi driver would pick up two men who were running ahead of police officers? The acting was poor, too. Colton wondered if Alex and the driver thought Colton bought the charade. Colton knew so much of his ability to save the others and have any chance at later survival depended on his apparent gullibility.

"I don't know," said Colton. "It must be something serious. I can hear more sirens coming." He said it dryly. As if Colton were trying to act, but couldn't act very well. *Please let it work,* prayed Colton.

The driver deftly pulled out and turned left, crossing through the opening in the median and over the Main Street tracks. Alex and Colton looked back at the two policemen on foot. Neither noticed the taxi pulling out—or at least they paid no heed to it. Those two officers were reaching the door of the building they thought Alex and Colton had entered.

The extreme tension at the Salt Lake City headquarters for The Thread had given way to a great, collective sigh of relief. It had been too close. The Thread had underestimated the abilities of the Salt Lake Police Department. A crackerjack young technical genius with the department had pulled the information on the vehicle the group had commandeered and had traced that vehicle through traffic cameras much quicker than The Thread had estimated was possible.

That was not good. But what neither Nathan nor anyone else in The Thread had anticipated was that that same young technician would deduce the group would leave Trolley Square and head to the light rail trains.

That technician had downloaded the previous half-hour of footage from the trains and identified the face of Colton Wiser—though his appearance was significantly changed. The police then knew which train Colton was on and where that train was. Dispatch sent most of the force to go after Colton. Nathan knew that had the police searched the correct train car first, things would have gotten very ugly in a hurry.

Nathan had known the risks involved with calling in law enforcement. They were potentially a vital tool. But Nathan's underestimation of the local police had forced him and his associates into a high-tension emergency mode.

Word had just reached headquarters that the agent had successfully pulled Alex and Colton. The relief in the room was palpable. No need to undergo any major cleanup effort to get Alex and Colton out of police custody.

And now, it was time to deliver Alex and Colton to *The Nest*. The other targets had arrived with far less excitement. And although The Technicians had earlier failed to set up video surveillance in their efforts to ready *The Nest*, still The Thread would have clear audio of the targets. Better yet, the targets would be in the hands of Alex Markham.

The taxi driver was now heading south, away from downtown. But the driver immediately turned right, and headed west on Fourth South. The ridiculous acting resumed.

"Where do you gentlemen wish to go?" asked the cab driver. Colton let Alex answer.

"We need to go to somewhere near the temple block," said Alex.

"Sure," said the driver. He banked the car north on West Temple. Their taxi experience ended a few blocks later as they reached the corner of West Temple and South Temple. "Is this good enough?" asked the driver.

"This would be great, thank you," said Alex. Alex slipped money into the hands of the driver. "I trust this will cover your services?"

"You are very generous. Thank you." The men exited the taxi. Alex led the way, winding through the sidewalks of Temple Square. The path they followed was quite erratic. The two wound in and out of buildings, even passing through the waiting lobby of the temple before emerging out the north entrance of the block and crossing to the Conference Center.

While they darted around Temple Square, Colton's mind raced. Colton had been agitated at Alex, but he had by no means supposed Alex's efforts to be a ploy by The Thread. But now it made sense. The Thread, no doubt, needed someone to find out how much the little group knew and if there was any evidence the group had scattered anywhere. Colton's lie about how many copies he had made of the *Master Plan*—or *Key #3* as The Thread refer to it—was uncharacteristic. Colton could not even explain to himself the impulse at the time that led him to tell the awkward lie. But now that he understood Alex's true role in this situation, he looked back on that impulse to lie as a piece of inspiration.

Colton offered more than one silent prayer of gratitude for the inspiration that had saved his life. But he found himself also pleading for the ability to know how to get out of the trap he was now willingly walking into.

Alex led Colton to the southeast entrance of the Conference Center, down the elevators to the parking levels, then through the parking levels out the west elevators. The two then emerged from the southwest corner of the building and crossed the street, but not at a crosswalk. A quick jaunt took them to a large apartment building that overlookea most of Temple Square. They had arrived.

Colton hoped the others had beaten them there—especially considering the others would have walked the last four or five blocks, whereas the taxi ride made it so Colton and Alex had only walked the last two.

Colton found himself scanning the environment and the building vigorously. Alex was doing the same. Colton knew Alex was scanning for law enforcement. But for Colton, the scan was a frantic check to see evidence of The Thread. Surely they were swarming around this place like sharks that circle their prey before attacking. He could see three pedestrians in the area. None of them looked suspicious. But, just as he and Alex veered from the sidewalk toward the entrance to the apartment building, Colton saw something.

There was a black sport utility vehicle parked north of the Conference Center that had just come into view. Colton did not dare to give the vehicle more than just a passing glance, but that glance was sufficient.

NEST SURVEILLANCE CENTER
SALT LAKE CITY
10:45 A.M.

The man in the vest answered the phone. He knew who it was. It was Nathan calling him.

"Hello?"

"The targets are entering *The Nest*. They are yours now."

"Okay," the man in the vest was ready to end the connection.

"Keep me updated."

"Okay," and this time he did end the connection. He could hear cheering going on in the background. That was annoying. After how much the Salt Lake headquarters had repeatedly messed things up, nobody there should be celebrating. Oh well. The targets were now his. He would do better.

The room had begun to fill with smoke. The man in the vest could see he was the only one in the room who did not smoke. What a nuisance.

THE NEST
10:45 A.M.

Alex and Colton approached the apartment building from the south entrance. Colton had noticed the building was about eight stories high.

"What floor are we on?" asked Colton as the two neared the door.

"The fifth floor."

The two entered the building. Colton felt an odd feeling as he walked through the doorway. A part of him wished to turn and run, to get away from a snare that might well lead to his death. His scan for signs of The Thread continued as he walked toward the elevator with Alex. The two passed a booth with a well-dressed man behind a glass pane. As they passed the booth, the man beckoned to Alex. Alex approached the window.

"Who are you two gentlemen here to see?" inquired the man.

"I am a tenant," said Alex. "I am not here often."

"Oh, yes," the man began nodding with recognition. "You are Mr. Markham."

"Yes, that is right."

"I apologize," said the man. "I should have recognized you."

"No worries," said Alex. "I am seldom in town."

Colton wondered if this man stopped the others. Why hadn't Alex mentioned that there would be security here? Was it possible that this man was a part of The Thread?

Alex pulled away from the window and headed to the elevator doors. Colton followed. The elevator was at the bottom, waiting, so they boarded and began ascending right away.

"Is the apartment locked?" asked Colton.

"Yes, it is," answered Alex. "But the security man downstairs can unlock the apartment remotely from his booth. I suppose he will have opened the door for them if they got here before us." As he said it, Alex's face showed concern. Colton could perceive why, and had to keep his face expressionless to not acknowledge the awkwardness of the situation. There were so many inconsistencies that Colton had to feign naiveté to be persuasive.

Colton knew that everything The Thread had done since they discovered the group at the cabin was to get the group corralled at this apartment building. Why here? Colton was sure that once The Thread gathered the information they wanted, they would likely kill him and his friends. He knew the lives and welfare of the group rested on his shoulders. As Alex arrived at the door to the apartment, Colton felt as if his heart were pushing up through his throat. And in overwhelmed desperation, he felt the burden of protecting not only his group but also many other lives from the evil workings of this powerful secret combination.

At the door, there was a key slot and a keypad with numbers. Alex did not produce a key, but he did tap in six numbers on the keypad. Alex did not try to conceal the keypad as he punched in the code, and Colton took advantage of that. As Alex keyed the numbers, Colton memorized them: 847323. Colton was plenty versed texting with keypads. He was curious, and used a keypad in his mind to test his theory. Sure enough, his suspicion was correct. The basis of the code was not numbers, but letters. It was careless and would be easy to remember: THREAD.

CHAPTER 27

THE NEST
10:50 A.M.

"It's Alex and Colton... anybody here?" called Alex as the two walked in. Colton, standing tentatively in the doorway, surveyed the apartment. The apartment seemed empty. Colton saw that the first room was a modest-sized living room, divided from a kitchen by a bar with bar stools. The living room housed couches and wingback chairs that seemed nice, but old. It had the feel of an apartment in which his grandparents would be comfortable. The kitchen extended to the back of the apartment and had a sliding glass door that led to a balcony that overlooked Temple Square. Off to the left of the kitchen and dining room was a hallway that must lead to the bedrooms.

Once the door closed, the seemingly empty apartment came alive as Dr. Isaacson and Jeff emerged from the hallway and Jim and Pete arose from behind the bar that divided the living room from the kitchen.

Smiles abounded in the room. Men, who had now become a close team, exchanged handshakes and hugs, congratulating one another on their safety. Colton felt both the lonely burden of knowing they were in a trap and the joy of being back together.

Colton, as he greeted the others, kept an eye on Alex. Alex was showing more enthusiasm than he had shown to this point, expressing to the others relief that they were okay. Colton was filled with contempt, knowing Alex's spirited attitude was a complete act.

But Colton knew that he must act as well. Colton began what he hoped would be a worthy performance as he sought to blend in while racking his brain for a way to alert the others and get out of the lion's den.

"It's great to see you all," said Colton. "It's wonderful to be together." The way Colton shared it revealed he had just been through a tough situation.

Jim stepped forward, sensing something. "What happened to you guys?"

Colton told their story. The others listened with fascination. When Colton finished the telling, his uncle put his arm around Colton's shoulder.

"You've been through a lot today, Colton. Are you okay?"

Colton wanted to tell Jim everything right then. But his answer was far different than his thoughts. "Yes, I'm fine. I think I'm becoming numb to the whole thing. It's crazy to think of it as being real."

"That's a good way to describe it," said Jim, nodding his head.

"Hey, did any of you catch the news on the train?" asked Colton.

"Yah," said Jeff, who lit up at the question. "I would have thought that more people would have been killed in the bombings."

"But remember," said Dr. Isaacson, "a dirty bomb is not meant—"

"To kill," interrupted Jeff. "Yeah, I know, but it's a good thing that a huge blast in two major cities didn't kill a ton of people."

"But did you all hear that they've identified one of the *terrorists*," said Colton. As he said *terrorist*, he made quotation marks with his fingers. Then he turned to Alex. "You said on the train that you'd explain that. What's the deal with the suicide bombers? I think his name was Kal…"

"Kaleed something or other. Yes," Alex took over and began the explanation. "The Thread pulled immigrants from

Pakistan about six months ago—a group who had done some pro-democracy efforts there. They received high-paying jobs here in America and The Thread lured them into a situation that would make them appear to have been suicide terrorists. The President will soon have some made-up evidence that links these men to a major terrorist group."

"And the President will then initiate vast security control," said Dr. Isaacson, stepping forward with a cascading explanation as he looked at Alex for confirmation. "The next three bombings would then serve to cement fear and panic across America. With such leverage, the President will then tighten executive controls to the point of martial law, and enact extreme measures to remove freedom and bind Americans in the name of security—measures that are not designed to ever be loosened. Thus paving the way for the removal of Constitutional law and government and replacing it with some authoritarian rule by members of The Thread."

"That is the general idea," verified Alex with his trademark casuality.

"Now," Alex was moving into a matter of business. "I have some provisions in the kitchen. Feel free to eat whatever you can find. But first we need to make plans."

As if on cue, the entire group settled down onto the furniture in the living room. Alex leaned forward and proceeded in a concise manner.

"The bombings are scheduled for 2:00 P.M. That gives us less than three hours. As you know, the vehicle will be showing up at the Capitol Building a few minutes early. The driver will expect a key-bearer to show up at 2:00. The driver will scan the key. The key-bearer is to then leave the site. After a wait of two minutes, the driver is to scan the safe with a card. The driver thinks that he is opening the safe, but he is really detonating a bomb.

"Our advantage is that we have the key. I do not think they can get the driver to vary from previous instructions, so I think they will come up with some alternative plan. If they go ahead with the bombing, our only chance is to get to the driver before they do and secure the bomb. If they choose to not detonate the bomb at the Capitol Building, the best we can do is have you gentlemen try to expose The Thread while I go on the run. Is that clear?"

The others nodded.

"We will hold here until about forty-five minutes before the bombing, at which time we will fan out through the side streets to the periphery of the Capitol Building. From there, if we see the van, I will go and get possession of the bomb. Perhaps Jim should go with me."

"But what about the satellite surveillance?" asked Jim. "How do we get past The Thread?"

"Well, if they are expecting us," said Alex, "that will be a very difficult thing to deal with. But The Thread does not like to be near these bombs when they are about to go off. It is just not healthy. So we take a risk. If they are not ready for us, we can do this. But if they are expecting us—which is probable—we do not stand much chance at all."

And then Alex looked around at the group.

"The question is," Alex put it to a vote, "are we willing to take the risk?"

Without hesitation, the group gave unanimous affirmation. Colton was weary of pretending. But he held his peace and played the game.

NEST SURVEILLANCE CENTER
SALT LAKE CITY
11:00 A.M.

The surveillance center had been set up too quickly. But at least they bugged the apartment and tested the equipment before the group arrived. Men were in place in surrounding apartments on the same floor. The trap was complete, and the prey was contained. The words of the people in the apartment were coming through loud and clear.

THE NEST
11:00 A.M.

"I've got to hear your story, Alex," requested Jim. A chorus of affirmation from the group showed that Jim's question stemmed from collective curiosity. To Colton's relief and gratitude, Alex's response—a curt nod—indicated he was willing to play along and field the questions.

"I have been in The Thread for almost nine years. I am one of the early ones—and have done what it takes to rise to the top." Jim was not the only one who realized the dark history that must be contained in that response.

"So, how did you get in?" asked Jim.

"I was a very young politician, fresh out of college, in Cleveland, Ohio. I was trying to change the world." A thoughtful smile cut across Alex's face as he dwelt in the past for a moment and reveled. Colton could sense that Alex was not making things up here—he was genuinely telling his history. Colton considered the wisdom in Alex telling the truth—no worries about messing up with conflicting lies.

"I was frustrated with the difficulty to get anything done. Few people had a vision of what government can do. Words abounded, but action did not. Then he found me."

"Who found you?" asked Jim, who was sliding into interrogation mode.

"Judas is what we call him now."

NEST SURVEILLANCE CENTER
SALT LAKE CITY
11:05 A.M.

"What does Alex think he's doing?" yelled the man in the vest as he slammed the metal table with his palm. "Get Judas on the line. I don't care that these men will be dead before they can pass on any of this information. Alex has no business mentioning these things!"

A man sitting at the end of the same metal table dialed a number on his phone. "Sir, it's ringing," the man was holding his phone toward the man in the vest. He took the phone.

"Judas, Alex is trying to cozy up to the hostages by telling everything about us. He's even mentioned you by name." The man in the vest expected a tirade from the other end of the line. But the response from Judas was his normal, calm self.

"Alex must be persuasive. Let him persuade them with truth, and then kill them when you have what you need. Don't worry. Just do your duty and trust Alex to do his duty his own way."

The man in the suit was shocked and aggravated, but his composure hid those emotions. He consented, hung up, and tossed the phone back to the man to whom it belonged. He looked at a man standing in the corner of the room and shrugged. Shaking his head and folding his arms, he continued to listen to the audio feed coming from *The Nest.*

THE NEST
11:07 A.M.

"So, who is this Judas?" asked Jim.

"Judas is a man who everyone in The Thread fears. Only those who prove utter loyalty to him can have access to him."

"Like you and your renegade self?" asked Jeff, but with a smile.

Alex smiled, but it was a smile of resignation, not humor. "Well, Judas will now spread out his many tentacles until he can get me. Everyone close to Judas understands that if you betray the oath of The Thread, you will be hunted down and killed."

Alex's eyes were distant, indicating thoughts swirling around in his head.

"So, what is this oath you are talking about?"

"Once someone is deemed worthy, they may be invited to enter the *outer circle*. They enter the outer circle with an oath. They vow loyalty to the death," said Alex.

"The outer circle?" Jeff sought confirmation.

"Yes. That is the lowest level. From there, it is very serious business, and one must stake their life on their secret participation."

"When you say loyal and willing," inquired Colton, "what do you mean? How do you prove that?" Colton was glad to have the attention on Alex, and was fascinated with Alex's story.

After a pause, Alex answered carefully. "When your fear of the law and death is replaced by loyalty to the oath, The Thread may welcome you into the circles by invitation."

"In other words, if you're willing to break the law and kill people," restated Jim plainly enough for all to understand.

Alex showed affirmation with a shrug.

Jeff interjected. "So, are there a lot of people trying to get into The Thread?"

"Oh, no. People must not know about The Thread until they are invited in."

"So, what if they turn it down? Isn't The Thread worried that people will go and tell?" asked Jeff.

"Well, no one is to hear the title of The Thread until they accept the oath and join the outer circle. That way, anyone who knows about The Thread has already promised secrecy and knows that to violate that secrecy would lead to their death. It is quite a powerful deterrent," said Alex.

"So, why would people join a group by an oath if they don't even know the group's name?" asked Colton. "What's their motivation?"

"That's easy," said Alex. "The Thread has many resources and ways to reward. Many would do just about anything for power and treasure. People learn that you can get more power and treasure when you join forces with certain people."

"Sounds like missionary work from hell," said Jeff. But it was truthful enough to be as much of a genuine assessment as it was a joke.

"So, is there a lot of competition for the inner circles?" asked Jim.

"Yes. That is where things get dirty—in the effort to impress the folks higher up."

"With all these circles," jested Jeff, "I would think you people would have called it The *Onion* rather than The Thread." After a burst of laughter from Colton and Pete, Jeff added, "Although that wouldn't be much manlier, at least it would be more accurate."

"You say you are high ranking," said Jim. "Just how high do you rank in The Thread, Alex?"

"There are many men my equal in The Thread, but only one man is my superior."

Alex's answer had a chilling effect on the group. *And you are earning your stripes today, aren't you, Alex?* thought Colton.

CHAPTER 28

THE NEST
LATE MORNING

"So how big is this thing?" asked Jim. "How many people are in The Thread?"

"Pushing five thousand. The challenge is to be big enough to rise to power without growing so fast that betrayal becomes overly risky."

"Wow," said Pete. "So The Thread needs to grow to be able to take over the country, but as it grows, it gets vulnerable?" Before Pete finished talking, Jeff was pointing at him and mocking again. Jeff just couldn't get used to the disguise. Pete smiled as he finished his statement. Then he threw a throw pillow from the couch at his facetious roommate.

"Yes," said Alex. "We have to have enough members to manipulate every major organization and administration."

"Like the Fed, the branches of Congress, the FBI, et cetera," offered Jim.

"Not to mention the White House these past few months," threw in Dr. Isaacson. "But here's what I have a hard time understanding. How did you folks penetrate the Federal Reserve enough to say that it is saturated? The governors on that board serve for fourteen-year terms!"

"It was the bank failures and credit crunch that occurred ten years ago. You remember how much more powerful the Federal Reserve and the Treasury became then? That crisis and the ensuing federal spending explosion facilitated Judas' rise. And from there, things have continued to fall in place for him. He is the smartest man I know; and he may be the most powerful person in the world."

"So," asked Colton, "did The Thread try to recruit people who were already in public offices, or did they focus on getting members of The Thread into office?"

"Mostly the latter," said Alex. "An extraordinary amount of money and influence has been dedicated to getting our men and women into office. Our efforts were successful, too." Colton surmised that if this were true, the majority of new representatives in the past couple years were likely members of The Thread.

Colton became curious about something. "There are about five thousand members of The Thread, and there hasn't been a single significant breach or defection?"

"No breach or defection yet—at least none I am aware of. And if there had been, there would probably have been an interruption to this morning's bombings." The group thought about that for a moment before Alex added something that was moving to all but Colton. "No defections, that is, until me; and this will be felt throughout the organization."

Jeff and Pete were both smiling, and Pete was nodding his head in approval. Colton forced a smile, looking at his two roommates, trying to match their reactions.

"You really have been in on this thing from the beginning?" asked Jeff in awe.

"Pretty much."

"Why did you join?" asked Dr. Isaacson.

"I had a lot of good I wanted to accomplish. I needed power. I met Judas, became very close to him, and found in him the power I needed."

"So, how does The Thread recruit?" asked Jim. "I mean, recruiting has got to be risky. You can't ask someone to be a part of a group like this and let them say no and walk away."

"True. The Thread seeks men who place their lust to get wealth and power above any bounds or limits of morality. Men driven by moral conscience cannot be trusted."

"What?" blurted Pete. "That makes no sense."

"Sure it does," said Alex, staring now at Pete, but talking to everyone. "A man bound by morality and conscience is bound by influences that make him untrustworthy in a group like The Thread. Our unity comes from self interest that is not threatened by morality."

"How in the world do you find men like that?" asked Jim.

"That is where Judas has been a genius," said Alex. "Judas knows that the greatest loyalties come when you set people free from their greatest burdens. The greatest candidates for recruitment are men who are in major debt—especially if financial, business, political, or social failure looms over them. Men in debt are often men in desperation."

"That makes sense," said Jim. "I specialize in white-collar crimes—particularly fraud. The great majority of perpetrators of fraud are those who have dug deep financial holes and have turned to desperate, illegal means of getting out of those holes."

"Precisely," said Alex. "The Thread then comes in—if the candidate is deemed worthy—to save them from their woes."

"In exchange for their loyalty, given by an oath on their life," said Jim.

"Yes. And without them knowing it, The Thread monitors them for a time to test their loyalty. With extraordinary technology, we track them for a while—every move they make." Alex paused for a moment. "If they prove loyal past this point, they are introduced to a series of tests. Once those tests are passed, they become full-standing, fully aware, and fully initiated members."

"And if they refuse the offer of The Thread?" wondered Jim.

"They don't refuse often," said Alex. He paused for quite some time. "But if they do, their life is shortened."

"And with so many people recruited in the past ten years, how does The Thread track each new recruit, each level, and all the activities?"

"That is done through a system of what we refer to as *sponsors*."

"Sponsors?" asked Jim.

"Yes. If I invite you into The Thread, I become your sponsor. If someone invites you into the next circle, they become another sponsor. Some people in The Thread have many sponsors. We communicate through the sponsors. The sponsor who invited you into your current circle is your primary sponsor. But if someone defects, they will be killed, as will all their sponsors. If you sponsor someone who defects, your only protection would be to kill the defector before The Thread gets to you."

"No way!" said Jeff.

"Unbelievable," said Colton, shaking his head. The others reacted similarly. Colton sensed that what Alex was saying was true. But this realization made Colton aware that if Alex was being so free with information about The Thread, The Thread undoubtedly intended on killing this group before they could cause any damage at all to The Thread. Colton felt a heightened desire to corner Jim—to somehow let his uncle know what he knew.

"But The Thread's reward system, combined with so much successes in accomplishing objectives, has kept pressure to defect at a minimum."

"So The Thread is very united then?" asked Jim.

"United in secrecy… United in purpose… But it is not a brotherhood with close feelings. In fact, just as the benefits of being in The Thread have been very high, so have the risks of being a part of it. And the risk does not come from outside The Thread."

"So there have been a lot of assassinations from within the group—member killing member?" asked Jim.

"A few."

"And isn't there any sort of a punishment for that in The Thread?"

"The only punishment inside The Thread is for violating the oath. If I were to kill another member of The Thread, I put myself at risk from being killed by other members of The Thread, but that is a matter of revenge, not Thread policy."

"That is wacked," said Jeff.

"It makes things interesting," said Alex sarcastically. "But the killings within The Thread are not such a big factor as the jockeying that goes on. Thread members do so much to get the attention of higher circles. It is a very feisty group. It is tight as to its secrecy, but it is not safe or stable—at least, not like how you think of an organization being safe or stable."

"So isn't The Thread worried that just maybe someone might nark to the government?" asked Jeff.

"You make an erroneous assumption there," said Alex. "You assume the government is a threat to The Thread. And it is to a small extent. But every major federal agency has a dose of, shall we say, *threads*, strung throughout it. Even I don't have any idea which members in each government agency are members of The Thread.

"At some point in the last couple of years," continued Alex, "The Thread's success became so great that it began to steer the great armada of government agencies. When members of The Thread see that they control so much of the government, the government ceases to be such a threat. Even if someone were to report it to the government, The Thread could intercept and clean things up before any real damage occurred. Those of us who are in The Thread tend to fear each other far more than we fear the government."

CHAPTER 29

THE NEST

Colton's fascination matched his anxiety. He knew Alex would eventually go into action. Colton had to find a way to communicate with Jim soon. Was Alex alone? Were people listening to them or watching them? How cautious did he have to be in communicating what he knew to Jim?

Colton programmed his mind to be ready to reach for his own weapon should Alex produce his. And as Colton agonized, the interrogation of Alex continued.

"So there's a lot about The Thread you don't know, even though you're near the top?" asked Jim.

"That's right," said Alex. "I know much of the circle below me. Beyond the highest circle, and the next circle, I only know scattered members. Judas knows far more, but even he does not even know a majority."

"That's bizarre," said Jeff.

"You keep talking about The Thread rewarding its members with money and power," chimed in Colton for the first time in a while. "Where do they get all this money?"

"For many years, The Thread has had access to public funds. Our resources are vast."

Everyone in the group, including the professor who had separated himself and was in the other room, was marveling at how much they were learning from an actual member of The Thread. Even Colton was relishing the chance to probe the evil machinery of The Thread.

"Does The Thread communicate with some code?" asked Jim. "Or do you communicate openly?"

"Often we use codes, but we communicate openly most of the time."

Jim inquired again, "Tell us about The Thread's use of technology—how do they get it and what do they have?"

"Well, you've already experienced a great portion of the technology. We have extraordinary access to the communications monitoring power of the National Security Agency. There is almost no government power that we could not tap into right now. We are still small enough that we must be cautious. But some of our members have opened up unique technologies. We have an array of armor plated and bullet resistant vehicles—"

"The black ones," said Jeff.

"The ones in Utah right now are all black, but that is not our only color," said Alex before continuing. "We have obtained these dart guns through private connections of some members. Many came into The Thread with extraordinary resources already." Alex removed his gun from his side pocket as he commented and examined the weapon as though he were seeing it for the first time.

"So why do you use these dart guns as opposed to real guns?" asked Jim.

"More versatility and less footprint."

"What?" asked Pete.

Alex explained. "We can kill easily. But we also have the ability to subdue. And what makes these so useful is they leave a tiny little prick. The chemical used to kill breaks down inside the body and becomes hard to detect—unless a coroner has a sense of what he or she is looking for. We have killed a fair number of people with these darts that have gone down on the records as deaths of natural causes. If I were to shoot you in the scalp, for instance, and the situation looked otherwise harmless, normal investigation would be hard pressed to find evidence of foul play."

"Show me how these things work," requested Jim, pulling out his own dart gun. Alex showed Jim the storage of the darts and poison. He showed the FBI agent how the lever on the back of the gun injects poison into the next dart. He even showed Jim the flaring mechanism that Jim had discovered the previous night.

"Usually," said Alex, "the dart falls to the ground—as it did at the cabin. It seldom sticks in them. And that makes it much easier to clean up evidence of what we have done. In fact, no major law enforcement agency to date has had one of our darts on file for more than a few hours. These weapons," Alex held up the weapon as if it had extraordinary value, "have been fantastic tools for The Thread."

"What is the whole purpose of The Thread?" asked Colton. "I mean, it's obviously to take over the country, but why? Is it just to get power and control people?"

"Well, actually Colton, you are falling short. You see," corrected Alex, "the goal is to rule the world. The Thread seeks a world empire. Taking over America is the best avenue to deliver the world into their hands. This has been the aim from the beginning."

Eyes widened and eyebrows raised in reaction to this comment. Colton could see Dr. Isaacson, shaking his head in the kitchen.

Without any prompting, Alex continued to elaborate on the full weight of The Thread's goals. "And when The Thread rises to power, elections in America will cease. Government officers will be appointed, not elected. Most Americans will accept it. There will be a small portion of America that gets in the way. The Thread has already begun to remove them. That is a major project and is only in the beginning stages."

And Colton began to see that Alex's words—and the way he was saying them—were agitating Dr. Isaacson. Alex seemed thrilled. Colton supposed Alex was trying to suppress his giddiness about The Thread, but it was not working. And as Alex spoke of world domination, Colton kept post on the professor, noticing the look of disdain that matched Alex's giddiness. A look of indignation swept away Dr. Isaacson's cheery countenance. Colton wondered if his agitation was just an intellectual disgust, or if it was something much deeper.

"How in the world is that happening? This removal of those who would get in the way?" asked a fascinated, yet noticeably disturbed Jim.

"The Thread has harnessed a technology called *social network analysis*," said Alex.

Colton's face lit up, and then he caught himself. He hoped Alex had not noticed his reaction. Colton remembered the folders in the safe at the Capitol Building. The folders he had obtained from Frank Tomlinson's office were labeled *social network analysis*! The data in those files were all gibberish. But now Alex was shedding light on those files. Colton offered a silent prayer, grateful he had not said anything about those folders to Alex. Colton could see from the lack of reaction of the group that no one else remembered the title of those obscure folders. Everyone, that is, except Jeff.

Colton looked at Jeff, hoping Jeff, by some miracle, would help Colton keep those folders in the realm of secrecy. Jeff had been about to say something in excitement to Alex about them, but Jeff had first made eye contact with Colton. Colton's shake of the head was subtle, but perceived. Alex did not see it, but Jeff did. Jeff wished to ask Colton what the deal was, but could tell that the motivation for Colton's refusal to mention the files was imperative and private. And for the first time, Jeff suspected that Colton knew something that Jeff did not know.

"We have ways to identify leaders and people who are likely to be friendly to our cause. We also find out in the process people who are likely to be obstacles—especially leaders. We seek out the ones who are friendly to our cause for recruitment. At least, we are heading in that direction. And the unfriendlies are to be cleansed—a process that, as I mentioned, has begun."

"Cleansed?" Dr. Isaacson's silence was broken as he spoke up sharply from the kitchen.

Alex looked at the professor, surprised by the intensity of his voice. Alex had failed to catch Dr. Isaacson's signals of irritation and disgust. Alex stared across the apartment at Dr. Isaacson, who was eying Alex with an icy, penetrating stare. Colton saw a quick transformation in Alex. The calm, composed nice guy was bumped out of the way—much as had happened at Trolley Square with the outburst toward Jeff. Alex's surprise at the professor transitioned from defensiveness to disdain, and then offensiveness.

"Yes, Isaacson," said Alex. "That is exactly what The Thread is doing. They intend to *cleanse* all those who get in their way."

"How can you use such an innocent term for such an extraordinarily evil thing?" demanded Dr. Isaacson.

"That is what they call it, Isaacson." Although Alex had said it with his air of composure, it was clear to all in the room that an instant and deep enmity had formed between these two men. Colton looked from Dr. Isaacson to Alex. A strange thought filled Colton's mind. How crazy it was to think of the two men he was looking at. One had dedicated his life to learning and teaching freedom. The other had dedicated his life to studying and destroying freedom. Both were talented and skilled beyond Colton's awareness, but both had devoted those talents to polar ends.

And at that moment, Colton pledged in his heart—a pledge that was deep, thoughtful, emotional, and prayerful—that he would devote his own life to the cause of truth; however long or short that life was to be.

It was Dr. Isaacson's turn, and he was not going to let it pass. "You say that only a small portion of Americans will get in the way, and that your *social network analysis* can cleanse them." Alex nodded. Colton realized that Dr. Isaacson was confronting Alex as if he were indeed part of The Thread. Alex seemed to become aware that he had stepped out of character and felt the risk involved. After his nod, he sought to clarify.

"At least, that is what The Thread believes," said Alex.

"And do you still believe this?" said the professor. "You're so invested in The Thread, and you get so excited about what it's doing. You seem little concerned about how evil all this is."

Alex exploded. "Am I still with The Thread? Have I not risked everything to save you and help stop these bombings?" It was a convincing performance. Had Colton not known what he knew, he would have found Alex's defense moving. It persuaded Pete, Jeff and Jim. Colton expected this. What surprised Colton was Dr. Isaacson's response.

"I'm sorry, Alex." He said it with contrition. "You've given up everything, and I've allowed politics and emotions to get the best of me. I apologize for my ingratitude." Dr. Isaacson had turned away his personal enmity toward Alex.

But what made the greatest impression on Colton was what Dr. Isaacson did next. Although he had set aside personal animosity, the professor proceeded to move ahead on the principle at hand. And from this point forward in the argument, Dr. Isaacson's passion centered on principles, not on Alex.

"Alex, The Thread has underestimated the depth of love that Americans have for freedom. Americans struggle with understanding freedom and have allowed The Thread to drain away so much of it." They walked to the sliding glass door in the kitchen. Dr. Isaacson gestured toward the surroundings and pointed out that many flags were flying that were certainly not flying that morning.

"Alex, when America is attacked, it's like awaking a sleeping giant. The Thread has been so effective that America may be a little comatose right now. But I'm confident The Thread has not properly estimated the power and resolve of this nation to rise up and defend freedom. And God willing, America will remain the land of the free for generations yet to come, and The Thread will become only a dark and fascinating part of history from which future Americans can learn."

CHAPTER 30

NEST SURVEILLANCE CENTER
SALT LAKE CITY

Of the eight people in the monitoring room, only one of them disapproved of what Alex was revealing. The rest were actually entertained. The man in the vest never had liked Alex Markham. He had always thought Alex had far more power than he deserved. The man in the vest even thought that Alex's accomplishments were a collection of easy assignments. But he was a legend in The Thread. Still, the arrogance of a man who leads such a group into a trap and inflates them with copious amounts of secret information just prior to killing them seemed over the top.

"That fool has opened The Thread to those idiots as if he really has defected," said the man in the vest to the rest of the people in the command room. The others could easily discern his disdain for Alex—a disdain they did not share.

"You're too worried, Bradley," said the man leaning against the wall in a dark blue polo shirt and khaki pants.

"That man," said Bradley, pointing at the speakers from which the audio feed from the apartment was coming, "is revealing loads of sensitive information to knowledgeable enemies!"

"Relax," said the man in the corner again. "The situation is under control."

“We’re understaffed here, Mike,” said Bradley, his left hand resting in the pocket of his vest as he stood. “We need more resources.”

One of the technicians sitting at the metal table spoke up. “What’re you talking about? That’s Alex Markham in that apartment with them. They’re as good as dead.”

“Yeah. He’s just playing with his prey,” said another technician who was monitoring some of the technical equipment.

“He’s *what*?” asked Bradley.

“I once saw a nature show where killer whales would catch seals at the beach. Before they would kill the seals, they would take them out into the deeper water and play with them. It was quite funny. Alex here is just playing with his seals first.”

“He’d better find out in a hurry everything we need from this group and do the job. He’s being a fool,” said Bradley.

THE NEST

“Well, Professor,” said Alex smugly as the group continued to look out the window of the apartment, “I am not so sure you understand the power of The Thread.”

“Alex, I think it’s you who does not grasp the power of freedom.”

“Harold, I have studied freedom for years. I think I understand it as well as you. We just see things differently.”

“But Alex, no matter how much you’ve studied freedom, and understand it academically, freedom isn’t truly understood until it becomes a belief. Unless it’s a belief, freedom is a mystery about which we can learn so much, but never quite grasp.”

Dr. Isaacson allowed time for Alex to think and reply, but no response came. The professor added to his message. “America is a nation that has been built upon freedom—not the idea only, but the belief. The Founders trusted in freedom as a sacred thing from God. They viewed freedom as a supreme principle to which all other political and social principles must bow and yield. That trust generated the most prosperous nation in the history of the world. The Founders owned the idea of freedom—they understood it—because they believed it. Freedom—like all real truth—is understood only when both mind and heart unite in understanding and belief." As the debate progressed, the group drifted back into the living room and sat down.

"You give your own views of freedom such a religious spin. Are you suggesting that because I do not believe as you do about government that I am evil?"

"Alex, The Thread is evil to the core—lusting for power, killing humans to obtain it, destroying freedom… Yes, The Thread is definitely evil. But as far as The Thread's economic policies, I know many good people that would agree with most of them. Certainly most people would agree with at least some of their policies. Does that make them evil? No way.

"But on this I won't back down: though most are willing to get rid of some economic freedom, and some are willing to get rid of all economic freedom, I do believe departures from economic freedom are always foolish. And I do believe that if a people were completely aligned with God's will, they would enjoy total economic freedom."

"See? You make it sound like your opinions are religiously founded—as if God and everyone else must bow to your views!"

"Alex, it is God's views that I wish to bow to. Government is force. Don't you think that when humans use force they should make sure they base their force on principles of truth? So yes, I think that we'd better align ourselves with truth when it comes to government and freedom," said Dr. Isaacson.

"You assume America is still concerned with individual liberty enough to keep things as they used to be," said Alex, "but that is not what I see. I see a nation that is beginning to prefer the security of government over the vicissitudes of the free market. I see a nation that is sick of seeing the rich get richer, and the poor get poorer—and wants the government to solve that problem. I see a nation that is finally open to the idea of collectivism, central planning, and public control of property. And I think the America you see no longer exists."

"No, Alex. I think it is you whose assumptions about America are wrong."

As the two men battled, Colton indulged in a quick search through the main area of the apartment for any signs of monitoring or eavesdropping. His search yielded nothing. He had no idea what to look for. He also had to appear casual—not only because of Alex, but also because he knew The Thread may be watching him.

What Colton needed, of course, was to let Jim know what was going on. But how? Colton needed a plan. He could not just corner Jim and whisper his suspicions. The risk of a microphone picking it up was too great. He had to find out a way to do it silently, without Alex noticing.

Meanwhile, Dr. Isaacson and Alex were speaking in raised voices. Alex had let go of any pretense about the vision and mission of The Thread, and Dr. Isaacson was outraged. It was an ironic time to delve into an argument about freedom and the role of the government. But the intense argument was about to come to an abrupt end.

It was clear that neither would budge in their visions for the world. Alex waved a hand disregardingly toward Dr. Isaacson. Then he said, "You speak as if you think you are the source of all truth!"

"Thank you," Dr. Isaacson smiled.

Alex threw up his hands and let out a loud, exasperated sigh. "People like you have no vision of what society can become!"

Dr. Isaacson eyed Alex for some time. "Are you suggesting that I'm one that The Thread would cleanse?"

"Well, yes… You probably are a candidate to be identified through social network analysis and labeled for cleansing." Alex made the comment without apology.

"Wonderful organization you've helped form, Alex," said Dr. Isaacson. "If you can't persuade a man or beat him in an argument, just 'cleanse' him."

CHAPTER 31

THE NEST
EARLY AFTERNOON

Colton looked at his watch. He still didn't know how to let Jim know what was happening. His mind continued to pour over possibilities. He stood up, and almost without thinking, walked across the living room to near the door. He picked up his backpack—with no real purpose. He was half-oblivious to what was going on in the apartment now as the cogs of his mind grinded, searching for some solution. Colton sat back down in the chair, grasping his backpack. He offered yet another prayer, pleading for some inspiration about how to apprise Jim of the situation. Before he concluded the prayer, his mind recognized a hard object in his backpack—a Bible he had brought from the cabin. And at that moment, inspiration struck.

Colton had read the Bible every day for years. Although he did not have a photographic memory, he knew it well enough that he could use it now to communicate secretly with his uncle.

"Uncle Jim," Colton beckoned.

"Yah, Colton. What is it?"

"Come here. I have some things I want to show you in the scriptures. It has a lot to do with what's going on."

Jim did not seem enthusiastic, but he did oblige.

Colton tracked Alex in his peripheral vision as he began to lead his uncle into a revelation of sorts from the pages of holy writ.

Once Jim sat down, Colton flipped the Bible open to the Book of Exodus. The full title at the top of the page read: *The Second Book of Moses Called EXODUS*. Colton pointed in deliberate, slow sequence to the *al* in *called*. He then pointed to the *Ex* in *Exodus*. Colton looked up at Jim. Jim understood that Colton was giving him a secret message, and had just spelled *Alex*. Jim nodded. He was now captivated. Jim nodded a second time, encouraging Colton to continue.

Colton could sense that Alex looked at them from the kitchen. "Doesn't that sound a lot like what is happening in the country right now with The Thread?" asked Colton aloud, but the question was a cover for what Colton was communicating. To Colton's relief, Alex did not inquire as to what the two were studying.

"A bit, I guess," said Jim.

"Now, check out this one." And with that, the young man flipped to the twenty-third Psalm. Colton pointed to the word *is* in verse one before pointing to the word *still* in verse two.

Jim thought for a moment, putting the phrase together in his head: *Alex is still...* He nodded again.

Colton paused. He could not remember where to find the next word he needed. It kept fluttering next to his consciousness. He began aimlessly thumbing through pages, and then it swooped into his mind. He remembered: Luke 10. He turned there.

"Check this out," he said as he pointed to verse 42. Colton put his finger on the word *part*. Certain Jim had that word now, Colton turned back to the very beginning of the Bible.

Jim was sure he knew already what Colton was trying to say. He felt skeptical, but was interested to learn why Colton was making this claim. Colton settled into Genesis 14. He pointed to the word *of* and then to the word *the* in verse 24. Finally, he moved his finger to the previous verse, stopping with his finger on the word *thread*. The communication was complete.

Jim had been expecting this last word, but his nephew's claim had a disturbing effect on the federal agent as ne put the whole message together: *Alex is still part of The Thread.*

Jim had wondered who Alex was, and had been cautious at the very first, but had long since concluded Alex was a friend to their cause and had indeed left The Thread. Jim felt hesitant to accept Colton's claim at this point. Did Colton know for certain, or was he speculating?

Jim pulled his eyes away from the Bible and looked at Colton. "Colton, are you sure you're reading it correctly?"

"Yes," answered Colton with certitude.

"Can you back it up?" Jim's question sought verification, but did not show a lack of trust.

"Yes," answered the nephew. But as Colton looked back down to the Bible, he felt overwhelmed. His method of communicating through the words of the Bible had been effective, but not very efficient. There had to be a better way to say more in a brief time without letting Alex know, or giving away audibly that they were communicating in code.

They had both looked up at intervals. Alex seemed to have completely tuned out what they were doing. And the others in their group had neither shown a desire to join their study, nor any spark of recognition of what the two were doing.

And then the very idea of communicating through code opened Colton's mind to another idea. When Colton was young, his father had joined his brothers-in-law in obtaining a ham radio license. Colton's grandfather on his mother's side had been a ham radio guru, and his boys had inherited both the skills and a passion for communicating though short wave radio. When Colton's father had taken up the hobby, little Colton had joined him.

In fact, Colton's skills soon came to far surpass those of his father's skills with ham radio—especially with respect to Morse code. Colton had become fluent with Morse code as a young man—spending hours and hours communicating with it over the radio. He still had the language ingrained in his mind. He knew that Jim—like all his uncles—was fantastic with Morse code, too. That realization filled him with such excitement that his dramatic effort to seem casual yielded to such a thrilling rush that Colton could not help grinning from ear to ear.

He took his pencil in hand and—acting as if he were underscoring words in the scriptures—began to place dots and dashes between lines of scripture.

Colton had quickly etched out the following sequence:

... .- .-- | -.-. .- -... | -.. .-. .. ...- . .-. | --. .. ...- . | .- .-.. . -..- | ... . -.-. .-. . - | ... .. --. -. | ..--.. | | - .... | .. ... | .- | - .-. .- .--. | ..--.. | | .. | - .... .. -. -.- | .- .-.. . -..- | .-- .. .-.. .-.. | - .-. -.-- | - --- | --. . - | .. -. ..-. --- | - .... . -. | -.- .. .-.. .-.. | ..--.. |

Jim had the code translated by the time Colton finished writing it: *Saw cab driver give Alex distinct sign. This is a trap. I suppose Alex will try to get info then kill.*

Jim took the pencil from Alex and wrote the following sequence:

.... --- .-- | -.-. . .-. - .- .. -. | | -- ..- ... - | -... . | -.-. . .-. - .- .. -. | ..--.. |

Colton likewise interpreted it quickly: *How certain? Must be certain.*

And Colton said aloud, "I'm positive I'm interpreting it correctly." The problem was, Alex heard, and took interest.

"What's going on?" inquired Alex.

"Colton here's showing me some scriptures in the Bible that all this has him thinking about. Like this one." Then, with smooth covertness, Jim turned away from the page on which they were communicating and turned to Galatians, chapter five, and read a first verse aloud: "'Stand fast therefore in the liberty wherewith Christ hath made us free, and be not entangled again with the yoke of bondage.' I was telling Colton that this is talking about sin, be he says it has a lot to do with the country and The Thread."

Alex did not seem too interested in the scripture. He simply asked, "Are all of you religious?"

"We are," said Jim.

"We have tried, as I mentioned earlier, to put at least one member of The Thread in every major organization—more if we could in some situations. But our effort to get into the leadership of some churches has been most difficult."

"I can't believe The Thread has gone after churches!" exclaimed Pete.

Alex looked at Pete emotionlessly. "Oh yes. We have been well aware that some of the greatest obstacles to the new order will be from churches. I think we—they… The Thread—have been foolish to proceed without more fully infiltrating them."

And with that, Alex seemed to lose interest in the whole religion topic. Neither Colton nor Jim made any efforts to rekindle Alex's interest or include him in any further discussion. It was not time for a missionary moment. Rather, Jim returned to the scriptures and fired a coded message back to Colton: *Third Copy of Plan real?*

Colton responded in code: *No. Not true. Lie.*

Nice work. Saved us with lie, returned Jim in code. Colton took the pencil and Bible back from Jim and began to etch more coded message: *Not much time. Alex dangerous. Cameras? Bugs? Plan?*

Jim did not respond to Colton. He nodded, thought for a moment, and then excused himself. "That was fascinating, Colton. Nice work in the scriptures. I have got to go to the bathroom." Then Jim called to Alex, "Alex, mind if I use the bathroom in the hall?"

"Go ahead. Make yourself at home."

Before going to the bathroom, Jim thought of everything he had gotten from Alex. He grabbed his money envelope, pocketed it, and left the room. On his way to the bathroom, Jim made a silent visit to the other two bedrooms as well.

Because of Jim's training, he made efficient work of things. He identified one bug in each of the two bedrooms. He also found one bug in the bathroom under the faucet. The discoveries were disturbing. Although Jim trusted his nephew, he had hoped Colton was mistaken. Now he knew Colton was right, which meant they were in far greater peril than Jim had supposed.

He felt like a fool—especially after having taken on the responsibility for the protection of the group. But Jim refused to beat himself up with guilt. He would need all his focus placed on extricating the group from a difficult situation.

Before he left the bathroom, Jim removed the money from his envelope. Sure enough, Jim found a tiny tracking device on three out of the 100 bills in the envelope. Jim placed those three bills together at the front of the envelope, and put the envelope back into his pocket. Jim turned on the faucet for audio cover for what he was doing.

Next, Jim inspected his dart weapon. He continued to work as silently as he could. He found no signs of any tracking devices on the weapon. Jim decided to take his chances, and put the weapon back into his pocket. Satisfied his search was complete, Jim flushed the toilet then moved for the door. But he stopped before opening it. He remembered that the entire group was wearing outfits and disguises provided by The Thread. Jim made a hasty, but thorough inspection of his clothes.

Placed in the drawstring hole on the front waistline was a tiny tracking device—just like the ones on the money. Jim pried the device out of the clothing with his fingernail. It was not too difficult, and he made quick work of it. He placed the tiny device in the money envelope and put the money envelope back into his pocket.

Jim was now on a mission. He had to be sly as well as bold. Jim walked through the kitchen and opened the sliding glass door before stepping out onto the balcony.

"What are you doing?" called Alex from the living room. He got out of his chair and headed to the rear door to join Jim and investigate.

"I am just thinking about how we're going to stop this thing," said Jim. Alex was now standing in the doorway, looking at Jim with an air of authority and confrontation.

"Jim, your face has been all over the news. I don't think you should be out there. Besides, we have a plan. Stop worrying."

But for the first time since they had been to the apartment, Jim could sense some concern on the part of Alex. Jim realized he must not alarm him, and had to let Alex lead out for the time being. Jim finished a scan of the surrounding urban landscape. He scanned Temple Square, the Conference Center across the street, and glanced toward the direction of the Capitol Building. Before his scan was complete, Jim saw the same black SUV Colton had seen upon arriving to the apartment. Satisfied with the information he gathered, Jim reentered the apartment.

"You're right, Alex. I'm sorry. I'm just getting a little antsy to stop the bombing," said Jim.

"No worries," shrugged Alex, looking more relieved than he realized.

Jim returned to the main area of the apartment. Taking inventory, he realized everyone in the group likely had three tracking devices in their money envelopes, and one on their pants. The apartment seemed to have at least one bug per room, but no video cameras that he could see. Jim determined to risk the camera issue as he formulated his plan. If there were cameras, Jim realized his efforts would lead to disaster.

Jim knew that he must assume the greatest possible forces of The Thread were around them. Jim also surmised that if he could spot one vehicle belonging to The Thread on one side of the apartment complex, there were likely others surrounding the building at various locations.

Having completed his brief survey of risks and obstacles, Jim sat down and formulated a plan. Colton had done well passing the baton to Jim. Jim understood the success of the group now depended on his ability to generate a plan that would help them not only accomplish some miraculous escape, but to also prevent a disastrous terrorist attack that could step America ever closer to destruction.

For some reason, though, Jim did not have any fear. He simply went to work—and the ideas began to flow.

CHAPTER 32

THE NEST
EARLY AFTERNOON

Jim looked at his watch again. He knew Alex would not waste much time before seeking the information he needed and finishing his job. As he worked, Jim had to exercise major caution to not tip Alex off.

"Alex, do you have some blank paper here in the apartment?" requested Jim.

"I do, in the first bedroom on the left. It is an office. Just grab some paper out of the printer."

"Thank you." Jim already knew about the paper because of his quick tour of the apartment. In a moment, Jim had returned with the paper—about ten or so sheets. Jim situated himself on the couch and went to work. He was already finished writing a full page worth of information and was working well into his second before his work drew the curiosity of Alex. Alex did not sit down with Jim, but he did walk over to him.

"What are you working on?" Alex tried to not sound too interested or concerned.

"We need to somehow get word to the FBI. So I'm preparing briefings that can say a lot for us in a short amount of time." Jim then reached out and handed to Alex the first page he had completed. "Do you want to peruse it, and see if it says it well enough?"

"No thanks, I've got my mind on other things. You do that." And with that, Jim's cover of writing a couple of pages hid his real project. He added a bit more to the second page of his "report" and then began to work on the important page.

Knowing that he would have to do some major things without making any noise, Jim began to write instructions to the others. He wrote as fast as he could without losing legibility. He also wrote in large print, knowing that multiple people would have to read the instructions at the same time.

Next, Jim took out his dart gun and began to fiddle with it. He opened the compartment that housed the darts, and then closed it. He opened the compartment that revealed the small tank of lethal poison, and then closed it. He set the safety, and then released it. He wanted to get Alex used to seeing him fidget with the weapon.

After a while of fidgeting, Jim opened the dart compartment for what had to be the third or fourth time. But this time, Jim nudged a couple of darts out of their compartment. As Jim saw the darts loosen and begin to fall out, he lowered the weapon toward his lap. The darts fell without catching the attention of anyone else—most importantly, Alex.

Jim—knowing he had to be cautious while handling these darts—carefully pushed one of the two darts back into its slot. He took the second dart and nudged it into his pocket. He then closed the latch to the dart compartment, and resumed his fiddling with the weapon for another thirty seconds or so. Then, feigning antsiness, Jim arose and began pacing the apartment. His behavior was quite natural, seeing as how the time to act would be approaching soon for the group. But his pacing was a strategic way of keeping a post on Alex without having to sit there and stare at him. Jim's pathway of pacing ranged from the front door of the apartment all the way back to the sliding door. And with that, he was ready for Alex to make his move.

Jim did not have to wait long. Colton had seen Jim writing, and then tinkering with his dart gun. The circumstance prevented Jim from communicating the plan with Colton, but

Colton knew Jim had a plan. More importantly, Colton trusted his uncle. All Colton could do was wait on Alex and Jim to act. And then it happened. Alex attempted to be smooth, but it was evident that he had determined to act now.

"Colton?" said Alex as he went to sit near Colton. Jim, watching Alex, shortened his pacing to just the front living room. Jim was watchful to make sure Alex did not make any sudden moves. But Alex was first after information, and Jim knew this. So did Colton, and Colton played his part well.

"Yes," said Colton, looking at Alex, ready for conversation.

"We have got to go and do this in just a short time. We may have to split up. If most of us are caught by The Thread, they will confiscate our copies of *Key #3*. We have very little proof beyond our own words that The Thread even exists, let alone what all they have done."

"Yes?" said Colton, indicating he was listening and expecting Alex to proceed.

"Every member of this group would benefit from knowing where that last copy of *Key #3* is." Although Alex failed to sound genuine, the point was a good one. But Colton was ready to play the game.

"I understand that, Alex. But knowing the location of that third copy is a burden I don't want to put on anyone else," said Colton.

"Why?" said Alex. His patience was gone.

"Because these people will do anything to find out where it is." Colton upped the intensity of his voice to match Alex's. Alex shook his head, his breathing reflecting a burgeoning rage.

"Let's say Pete is the last one of us alive," Colton said. "And let's say they capture him. If he knows where the last copy is, they'll find that out. These people follow no code of decent human behavior. They will do whatever it takes to get the information out of him. That's a burden I don't want Pete or anyone else to have to deal with."

"Well, if Pete doesn't know where it is, they are going to do those same things to him to make sure he doesn't know!" said Alex. "So what advantage is it to not tell?"

"I just won't. ...I've made up my mind."

Jim was impressed with the persuasiveness of Colton's retort. Colton had based his posture on stubbornness, and not logic. By now, the argument had caught the attention of Jeff, Dr. Isaacson, and Pete—all of whom were standing in the kitchen. All three stayed out of the debate, but it had their full attention. Why was Alex so persistent? And why was Colton being stubborn? It seemed like a minor point to them considering what they were all about to try to do as a team.

"Colton, you are being a fool!"

"That document will find its way into the public where I left it! It's going to be hard for The Thread to find it before someone else does. Just leave it alone. Let's just forget about it and move on. I'm not going to tell anyone in this group where it is!" It was now obvious that Colton would not yield. Jim knew that this moment may well be the trigger that launches the assassination of the entire group. The time to act was now. Jim was now about ten feet away, close to the front door of the apartment.

Jim leaned over the wingback chair next to the door and lifted a small pillow. Jim fidgeted with the pillow, but focused on not drawing Alex's attention—as if he were playing with it out of nervousness. Jim walked over and sat in the chair next to Alex, sitting as close to Alex as he could get.

Alex was in action. He had entered a state of heightened alertness. Jim could sense this. Alex was ready, and his weapon was available in the open pocket of his pants. Jim's approach peaked Alex's curiosity. Alex looked away from Colton to survey why Jim had come and sat down near him.

Jim acted expertly, leaning over Alex, but staring at Colton, leaning toward his nephew. "Colton, I think Alex is right. You make a good point that us knowing where this last copy of yours is would be a burden. But everything we know about The Thread is a burden to us! And I think we should all share this burden together. I'm siding with Alex on this. We all need to know where that copy of *Key #3* is."

Alex, seeming relieved, smiled and turned to Colton. Perhaps he would succeed after all in his effort to get the information he desired. "Colton, your uncle is right."

Jim's intervention succeeded. Alex did not see Jim reach into his own pocket, ready the dart in his left hand, and situate the pillow in his right hand. Nor did Alex sense Jim reaching around his neck with the dart in his left hand, while the pillow in Jim's right hand rose toward Alex's head.

Jim stabbed Alex near the left front of Alex's neck. Jim wanted to get as close to the carotid artery as he could. The sedative would then have a quick trip to the brain. He did well. At the same instant Jim stabbed Alex, Jim also lunged upward and forward, thrusting the pillow against Alex's mouth and nose. Jim held the pillow in place by holding the pillow and Alex's head against his own chest. To Jim's relief, the dart did snap, but the snap was not loud.

The struggle did not last long—maybe two or three seconds—before Alex's body went limp. Alex thrashed, but could not break from Jim's grip before he went unconscious.

To cover the noise, Jim yelled, "Colton, think about this! You are being too stubborn!"

Jim had executed the attack flawlessly. But the silent, visually-raucous outburst caught the attention of the others in the kitchen, who rushed into the living room. Jim was ready for this too. He let go of the dart he was still pressing into Alex's neck. Colton was frantically gesturing to them to be silent and stay calm—but it had to be all body language. Before Jeff, Dr. Isaacson, or Pete came into the living room, Jim was holding up a sign—one of the papers he had borrowed from Alex. The paper had large, block letters that read: *SILENCE!!!*

"What's going on?" Pete did not understand in time. Jim prayed that it would not give them away. He knew the best way to deal with it was by being casual in his voice and response.

"Colton's being stubborn. Alex wants Colton to tell us all where the last copy of the document is, and I agree. Come on Colton, don't be stupid, and don't waste our time. Just tell us." Shock and confusion dominated the facial expression of the other three, but they now would trust Jim and obey his mandate to be silent.

"Jim, I don't feel right about this! I wish you understood. I'm not saying where that other copy is!" Colton did well continuing the verbal drama that mismatched what was happening in the room.

Jim eased Alex's limp body onto the couch. This freed Jim up enough to reach into his pocket and remove a detailed page of instructions and information for the other three. They began poring over the contents of the page, which reminded them to be silent and instructed them not to read the paper aloud or discuss its contents. They read about how Alex was still a part of The Thread and that he had trapped them. They now understood that the apartment was bugged.

As the three continued reading, Jim motioned for Colton to stand still. Jim removed the tracking device from Colton's waistband. Jim rubbed his fingers together in the money symbol and mouthed a request to Colton. Colton pulled out his money packet from his backpack and handed it to Jim. Jim opened it and put the tracking device from Colton's waistband into it. Jim then placed Colton's money packet on the couch and his own money packet on an empty chair.

Jim searched Alex's clothing for a tracking device, but could find none, then gestured to Colton to help him remove Alex from the apartment. Jim opened the apartment door silently and walked back to the couch where Colton was standing by Alex. Colton wanted to ask Jim why they did not just leave Alex and bolt. But he acted on trust, lifting Alex from the legs while Jim lifted him from his armpits.

Jim knew this might be the most vulnerable part of his plan. As they neared the front door, Jim turned and said, "Colton, I think you're wrong. But if you think you're right, maybe you'd better follow Alex and try to talk him out of it. I suggest you just tell us all." The other three remained confused.

Colton and Jim got Alex into the hallway. Jim made it clear to the other three to stay put, and not follow them. It was difficult to not make noise while carrying the man. To Jim's relief, the hallway was empty—a sign that this just might work. Jim closed the door of the apartment most of the way and scanned the hallway. He was planning on using another apartment, hoping it would be empty—or at least not have people from The Thread in it.

At this point, Jim was not afraid of sedating innocent people to get the job done. But he saw something providential. About three doors down the hall on the opposite side was a room labeled as a janitorial supply closet. Jim led Colton to it, and tried opening it. It was unlocked and unoccupied. Jim and Colton eased Alex onto the cement floor of the utility room. Jim then unrolled an industrial paper towel roll, which he spread over Alex to hide him. Colton could see what Jim was doing and helped his uncle. In just a few moments, they had Alex's unconscious body well concealed. Before leaving, Jim produced his weapon, removed another dart, and stabbed the sedated Alex.

"Sorry, Alex," said Jim to the listless body. "We need you to rest for as long as possible."

"Jim," whispered Colton, "why didn't you just leave him in the room?"

"Because we need The Thread to be as confused as possible. If they don't find Alex, they'll be more distracted. I want them to think he might be with us. It may not work, but I think our chances are much better with them not knowing where Alex is."

As Jim and Colton reentered the apartment, Dr. Isaacson greeted them with a smile and shook his head. The communication from the professor was one of silent admiration and understanding. Pete, on the other hand, was in a mild state of panic. But he somehow kept his composure enough to not make any sound. The group kept gesturing to him reminders to stay calm and be quiet. Jeff was annoyed that Alex had duped him, and that so much important stuff had been going on without him being aware of any of it.

Jim knew that if there were cameras too, they would already have seen members of The Thread storming the apartment. For this, he was relieved.

Jim's written instructions had told the other three to stay quiet and to place their money packets on the couch and chairs and stand next to those packets. The three had done that. Jim removed the tracking device from their waistbands. He placed everyone's tracking device in their own respective money packets on the couch. He then bunched all the packets together into his hands and walked toward the apartment door. It was time to flee.

Jim gave the group a look of confidence and nodded. They understood what that meant. They all—including Pete—mustered the courage to make a run for it. Jim turned and ran down the hallway, the others following right behind him.

As he shot down the hallway, Jim shifted all the money packets into his left hand and pushed his right hand into his pocket to grasp the handle of the dart gun. He knew the dart gun would be more useful now than his regular gun. He ran down the hallway with his hand in his pocket, ready to respond at a moment's notice. The others followed him. As he arrived to the stairway, he could see it had a swinging door with no latch. He lowered his shoulder, keeping his hand to his weapon.

Jim's readiness paid off. The opening door startled a man standing at the top of the stairs. Jim raised and fired his weapon immediately. He fired even before he was sure the man was a threat—a benefit from having the tranquilizer option. The dart hit the man squarely in the chest.

The man was unprepared. He began—while he was yet conscious for a moment—to do two things at once: He reached for his weapon in his pocket and for some communication device on his hip. Before he could aim, Jim kicked the man, sending him flying down the stairs.

Jim collected the communication device from the landing below and checked if the man was conscious. He was not. Jim ignored the man's dart gun other than sliding it under the man's sedated body. The group heard voices coming from the communication device—though they were not loud. Jim looked at it. The volume was turned down most of the way. He turned it off before pocketing it and led the group down two more flights of stairs.

NEST SURVEILLANCE CENTER
SALT LAKE CITY
EARLY AFTERNOON

"Something's wrong," said one of the technicians at the metal table.

"What do you mean?" asked Bradley.

"You can hear what's happening. They're having this argument, and then Alex gets weird. It sounds like he communicated to this Colton dude that he wants to talk to him privately. And he did it in a way that we couldn't hear."

"Perhaps our friend has decided to more than pretend to defect," Bradley suggested.

"Just relax," said Mike. "Let Alex do his thing. He knows what he's doing." The conversation in the room prevented the eavesdroppers from noticing the subtle patter of steps that receded into the distance.

Then the communication device on Bradley's hip beeped. He held it up and pressed a button. "This is Bradley."

"What's going on?" demanded a harsh voice.

"What do you mean?" Bradley was equally gruff.

"Why are they out of the apartment?" said the angry voice. "What just happened?"

"What are you talking about?" asked an incredulous Bradley.

"Every tracking device we have on these people just left that apartment and is now in the stairway!" The man talking was now in a state of panic. That the group could leave the apartment without the surveillance group even knowing was disturbing. His panic set off a wave of dismay in the small room. Even Bradley lost it.

"Where've they gone?" asked the frazzled Bradley.

"They headed north down the hallway. We think they're in the stairway."

Mike stepped forward, pulled out his communication device, and tried to signal the man who had been in the stairway. Nothing. "No response from Jason!"

Meanwhile, Bradley had sent out a signal that hit all communication devices of agents at *The Nest*. Within seconds, the doors to the two apartments flanking the group's apartment burst open. Some men ran into the empty apartment to sweep it, but most men ran for the stairs.

Simultaneously, seven agents filed out of an apartment on the main floor near the small lobby. A few others merged out of an office in the basement parking lot. All these agents were in emergency mode and had their weapons ready.

In the surveying room, many blocks away, Bradley began to relax a little. The escape would be a futile attempt, and they would capture and eliminate the group in just minutes. Alex's agonizing game would be over. Then something happened that robbed him of all comfort. It was the obnoxious noise now coming from the speakers.

"What in the world is that?" yelled a startled technician.

Bradley's face reddened. His fists clenched. He felt like he was about to explode. "That…" said the enraged leader, "… is a fire alarm."

CHAPTER 33

THE NEST
EARLY AFTERNOON

Colton estimated that people had emerged out of half of the apartments. But that was enough to cause more than twenty people to fill the third floor hallway. Though most people were not in a panic, the bulk of them were taking the fire alarm seriously. Colton realized that many of these people had no doubt been watching news reports for hours about the New York and Seattle bombings, and were a little sensitive regarding emergencies.

The people who were now evacuating ranged widely in age. There were a couple of young families. There were also a few elderly people shuffling toward the stairs. Some were middle-aged.

Colton counted his uncle as brilliant for pulling the fire alarm. But what his uncle did next caused Colton to smile in admiration. Jim turned into a helpful usher, reassuring, comforting and encouraging people. But what amazed Colton is what Jim did while he was doing this. Most people exited their apartments carrying a few critical belongings. Jim was placing packets of money with people's stuff—dropping a packet in a bag here, placing a packet between some photo albums there—so artfully that they failed to notice his strategic sowing of money packets.

Finishing the task, Jim let the evacuees clear out of the hallway and into the stairway for a few moments—ensuring some distance between themselves and the people who were now transporting the tracking devices. After a time, Jim motioned for the others to follow. With that, the group plunged into the veritable river of people charging down the stairs from every floor.

NEST SURVEILLANCE CENTER
SALT LAKE CITY
EARLY AFTERNOON

Bradley knew they had a communication problem. The people who could track the hostages were at headquarters in Salt Lake. But his own team had the direct line of communication with the forces at the *Nest*. The small, harmless group had somehow escaped from the fifth floor—the floor where the bulk of his men at the *Nest* were waiting. Bradley had to wait for updates from headquarters on where the targets were. He then had to communicate that information to his men in *The Nest*. The whole thing was proving to be an inefficient nightmare.

"Sir," sounded Bradley's communication device.

"Go ahead," said the project commander.

"The apartment's empty. There's no one here!"

That was a disturbing piece of news. "No sign of Alex?" asked Bradley.

"None, sir," came the reply.

Bradley looked at the man who had been in the corner. "Well, Mike? What do you think? What's happened to our little hero?" Bradley was not only asking for Mike's opinion of what happened, but also jabbing Mike for trusting Alex so much.

Mike was bothered. "You don't think he's behind this group escaping, do you?"

"How else do you explain it?" roared an agitated Bradley. "Our man gets quiet, leaves the apartment, and this group takes off too."

"Look, Bradley," Mike spoke with great force, "you may not know Alex Markham, but I do. If there's anyone loyal to The Thread, it's him. I suggest you stop assuming and focus on apprehending these men. We'll find Alex. But don't give up on him. This isn't over!"

Before Bradley could respond to Mike, the technician communicating with the trackers at headquarters sounded out information. "Sir, the entire group is now in the stairwell. They seem to have been on the second floor."

"Okay," Bradley was speaking mostly to Mike, but also to everyone in the room. "They have to get out on either the first floor or the basement. Let's be ready for them." Then Bradley sent out a communication to all agents at the apartment. "They are on the stairs. Be prepared for them. Have your weapons ready but concealed." The Thread was desperate, but still did not want to overdo the scene.

"Sir," said the technician, "three tracking devices are now entering the main floor. But they are splitting up! Two more individuals are heading down to the parking garage!"

"Three targets just entered the main floor!" communicated Bradley to all forces at the *Nest*. "Two more are heading down to the parking garage! They've split up! Close in! GET THEM NOW!" ordered Bradley.

Then, speaking to everyone in the room, Bradley wondered aloud, "What in the world is their plan? Why are they splitting up?"

No one had an answer. For a moment, the room fell silent—a silence which was awkward and annoying. After a moment, the speaker coming from communications at the *Nest* blurted, "This is the first floor. Where are they? We see no signs of them! Are you sure they've left the stairs?"

"Confirm with headquarters!" growled Bradley to the technician. The relay method was inefficient. They could not afford the time it was taking to get the information they needed.

"Sir, they've left the building through the front door! The two who headed to the basement seem to be in the basement, splitting up," informed the middleman.

Before Bradley could respond or send a message to the *Nest*, his phone rang. It was the commander at the Salt Lake headquarters. Before answering the phone, Bradley barked at the men at the *Nest*.

"Three of them have left the building out the front door. You missed them! All agents outside the *Nest*, seal in the evacuees and find our targets. Basement people, you have two down there, and they seem to have split up."

By now, the phone was on its fifth ring. Bradley answered calmly, which took extreme effort. "Hello, Nathan."

"So, do you know what's going on?" Nathan was much too calm in Bradley's estimation.

"Yes. Three of them have just left through the front door, and two of them are split up in the parking garage," answered Bradley, somewhat frantic now.

"Sir," blurted the communication device in Bradley's left hand. "This is Stan in the parking garage. We've been checking out everyone that's come through those doors. We see no sign of them. Are you sure two of them came down here?"

It was a question that Bradley and Nathan both heard. With the phone in one hand, and the local communication device in the other, Bradley looked at the technician who had been speaking with the techs at headquarters. The technician blurted a quick question, then spoke to answer Bradley's demanding glare.

"One of the two in the basement's now leaving the building. Based on the speed, it's gotta be in a car."

"Stan, one is driving out right now!" said Bradley with the communication device.

"Sir, the vehicle driving out right now is driven by a very old woman," said Stan.

Bradley was dumbfounded. Then he heard Nathan's voice, loud enough to hear it though the cell phone was about a foot from his ear. "Do you get it yet?"

And then things began to click in Bradley's mind. But Nathan did not wait. The commander tonelessly informed Bradley of what must have happened.

The area commander was at the Salt Lake headquarters, standing behind the technicians tracking the targets. He understood, and he spoke to Bradley condescendingly. "They've removed their tracking devices and have placed them on people evacuating the building. They've distracted us." It made sense to Bradley now. He stood, staring at nothing. He hated himself for not noticing this sooner. Then he set aside any pretense of knowing what to do.

"What should we do?" asked Bradley. He was now as calm as Nathan.

Nathan was just about to suggest they post people back at all exit ports of the building and wait, but a report from the parking garage at the *Nest* interrupted him. The report was a frantic one, announcing an attack in the parking garage.

As they had neared the door into the garage, Jim held his weapon in the air, indicating the others should ready their weapons. Many people wanted to get to their vehicles and remove them from the building in case this was an actual emergency. The mass of people plugging ahead focused so much on getting out to cars and driving off that nobody saw the guns.

Jim crouched low in the crowd as he entered the garage. He could spot three members of The Thread. They were standing aside from the fountain of humans that was pouring out the door into the parking garage. The three were scrutinizing faces. Their weapons were out, but lowered, ready. In a moment, Jim caught sight of a fourth member of The Thread near the exit from the basement garage. The fourth was identifiable because of the communication device he had up to his mouth. All this recognition happened in just a moment. That moment was just enough advantage.

Jim opened fire with his dart gun, firing two quick shots that both hit their targets. Jeff stepped forward, luckily aiming at the one Jim had not yet targeted. Jeff fired three rapid shots. The first was wide, but the second two both connected with the third man. In the franticness of the attack, all three members of The Thread failed to radio for assistance before they slipped into unconsciousness.

But the fourth man, who was farthest away, scurried behind the shelter of a car at the sound of the pops. Screams and startled yells burst from the people who were coming from the stairs or scattered throughout the garage. The ensuing panic proved to be a boon for the group.

Jim moved forward into the garage—to get out of the open and away from the vulnerability of the stairs. Jim knew the fourth man was now radioing that they were under attack in the basement. Their time was precious.

Jim removed his badge with his left hand as he kept moving. He was watching the area of the garage where the fourth agent of The Thread had taken refuge. A lady was just a short distance ahead, fumbling with her keys, trying to get into her car. The vehicle was a large luxury sedan with tinted windows. Jim approached her.

"Ma'am, I'm agent James Berry, with the FBI," he spoke with a mixture of authority and reassurance as he made his badge plain for her to see. "We need your vehicle."

Much to Colton's surprise, the lady obliged. She stepped aside, holding the keys out for Jim to use. Jim thanked her, taking the keys. Although he looked familiar, she would not remember for many minutes that she had seen him on the news. Jim closed the door, started the engine, and moved to join the steady stream of vehicles filing out of the garage.

Colton was in the front with Jim. There was still no sign of the fourth member of The Thread. Jim was relieved that vehicles were still free to leave the building. Jim supposed that luxury would not last long.

"Everybody lie low," ordered Jim. He merged into the line of cars, waving thanks to the vehicle that let him enter. Colton, in the passenger seat, was ducking. Jim rolled down the passenger window using the driver-side controls. He held his dart gun low and out of sight, but ready. He edged ahead to where he had last seen the member of The Thread.

As Jim drove past the gap in cars where the man had hidden, he saw that the man was still there. The man proved to be a poor sentry. He did not even notice Jim behind the wheel as Jim passed out of sight and on toward the exit. He even thought that the man looked outright traumatized. He rolled the window back up.

Letting go of the weapon, Jim tried something audacious. Just pulling into the line of vehicles a little ways behind their vehicle was a dark blue minivan. He grasped The Thread's communication device out of his pocket and pressed the button.

"They're in the blue minivan!" Jim had said it hastily and in a muffled way—he had thrown his voice a bit. This was the decisive moment. The tension in the car was extreme.

Jim pulled out of the building. Colton saw three dark SUVs parked in the street just outside of the outdoor parking lot for the apartment building. The vehicles made their move from the street. One black vehicle was close to the exit from the garage, but evacuees from the building were swarming around it and obstructing its access to the parking garage exit.

Jim's diversion worked. He slipped right past the black vehicles and headed for the street. The entire group could not resist lifting their heads enough to look back and see the dark vehicles surround and trap the blue minivan. Jim prayed that the occupants of that vehicle would be safe. But he did not wait around to make sure. He pulled onto 100 North and headed west, away from the apartment and away from downtown. Jim pulled out the communication device and turned it up. An entire array of voices filled the channel as The Thread came to discover—with great rage—that the targets had slipped out of their hands.

When they were out of sight and Jim was certain The Thread had had ample time to realize the minivan was a false lead, Jim pressed the button on the communication device.

"You will not succeed! Not today, not ever!" And with that outburst, the device went silent for a moment. Jim did not wait for a response. He rolled Colton's window down and threw the device out the passenger window, right in front of Colton's face.

"Wouldn't that've been a handy tool to keep?" asked Colton.

"It could be a wonderful tool, Colton," agreed his uncle. "But it could also be a tracking device. We can't take the risk."

CHAPTER 34

SALT LAKE CITY
EARLY AFTERNOON

When the blue minivan proved to be a false alarm, Bradley ordered a withdrawal of most forces from the *Nest*. The Thread removed the three unconscious members in the parking garage as they vacated the building. Within minutes, the apartment building went from a center of total control for The Thread to a failed fiasco. And in the haste to try to catch the targets and then evacuate from the premises, nobody from The Thread bothered to check the small janitorial closet on the fifth floor.

Bradley was en route to Thread headquarters. They had lost the *Nest*—a complete disaster. A couple of members of The Thread, posing as employees, were still there to do some quick, expert editing of the security camera footage.

Nathan had ordered an emergency council at headquarters, and had invited all members of the top two circles—which would form a council of five.

Bradley was irate that his mission had been a failure. But most of the high-ranking members of The Thread in this office had failed in some way within the past day. Bradley entered the smaller side room and assumed his place at the small table. Nobody in the room was in the mood to greet Bradley. They jumped right into business.

"The *Nest* failed. It's now crawling with law enforcement," said Nathan as the leader of the group. "Is there anything we've left there that must be cleaned up? Any trail of evidence?"

"Yes," said Bradley to explain what everyone already knew. "We have a man in the stairway the targets sedated. We vacated and did not know he was still there until it was too late. He was left behind."

"Right. There are cameras in the stairway, are there not?" asked Nathan.

"Yes. The *Nest* has cameras in the stairway and the elevators. The incident should be on tape. We also have cameras in the basement-parking garage. But since we pulled those men out, we need to edit those tapes."

"Why didn't you use those cameras when they escaped?" pressed Nathan.

"It happened too fast," Bradley did not say it defensively, just matter-of-factly.

"So we do two things," said Nathan. "First, we get those tapes, edit out anything that might point to us, and then make sure the police get footage of the targets shooting our man in the stairway. Second, it has to be a murder."

It took a few moments for that order to sink into the group. But the others could see what Nathan was suggesting. The case against the targets would be far more powerful to the police and public if The Thread could offer footage of the group killing a man while they were on the run from the law. Simply sedating a man would not be so incriminating.

"I hate the idea of killing our own, Nathan," said one of the men at the table. "That could have some bad effects among us."

"Well, we're going to have to deal with that," said Nathan, brushing aside the comment with his hand. "It's happening even as we speak."

THE NEST
EARLY AFTERNOON

Jordan Nielson climbed the last few steps before coming to the unconscious body. Two fire fighters and one policeman were hovering around the unconscious figure, preparing the man to be transported to the hospital. With the arrival of a fourth man, the group was now large enough to put the man on the stretcher that was at his side. One of the fire fighters signaled to Jordan to jump in and help.

Jordan Nielson stared for a moment at his unconscious comrade. Jordan was one of only three members of The Thread who had been born and raised in Utah. Jordan was gaining respect in The Thread because of his willingness to do whatever evil they asked of him.

When The Thread selected Salt Lake City as a site of one of the bombings, The Thread sent a few more agents to the state. But with the debacle of the loss of the third key, The Thread's massive influx of power into Utah had been fascinating for Jordan to watch. This was a great chance for him to gain recognition.

Jordan did not take long to accomplish his assignment. As he crouched down near the man's feet to support the transport, Jordan removed the dart from his pocket. Jordan stabbed the man as he grabbed the legs. The dart was lethal.

As they rolled the man onto the stretcher, the weapon Jim had stuffed underneath him was exposed. Jordan pulled out a plastic evidence bag from his pocket.

"I'll take care of that," he said to the other three. "I wonder if this weapon belonged to this man, or the one who hurt him?" said Jordan aloud. It was an innuendo. No one, not even the other police officer, took notice that it was not time to be removing evidence from a crime scene.

And with that, Jordan Nielson's evil mission was accomplished. The man in the security room was deleting certain footage from earlier in the day and putting together a nice video for law enforcement of James Berry evidently killing an innocent civilian. Soon, the group wanted for questioning would be wanted for murder.

THREAD HEADQUARTERS
SALT LAKE CITY
EARLY AFTERNOON

Nathan's announcement that he had ordered the death of a fellow member of The Thread had a visible effect on the group. But these were not sentimental men, and the meeting pressed on.

"So where's Alex?" asked one of the men around the table who had not said anything to this point. "Did he just disappear?"

Bradley spoke up. "That's where it gets a little strange. Alex was pressing the Wiser kid for information on where the last copy of *Key #3* was. It seemed like he would get that information. The FBI agent even pushed Wiser to say it. But then it seemed as if Alex motioned for Wiser to follow him. Things went quiet. A minute later, they were all gone. The rest is history. If anyone can explain what Alex was doing, I'm all ears."

"So, has Alex betrayed us?" said another man around the table who spoke for the first time.

"No way," said the final man to speak in the group. This man had short, blonde hair and was wearing a brown sport coat—he looked very over-dressed for this group. "Anyone who even entertains the possibility that Alex Markham would defect from The Thread doesn't know a thing about Alex Markham. That man would never betray The Thread. He's as loyal as Judas himself."

"Then how do you explain any of this?" said Bradley.

"I can't. But I'm certain there's an explanation. And anyone who counts out Alex Markham is wrong and will be making a terrible mistake," said the man. "Either Alex has *Key*

#3 or he'll get it. I bet he had to act on something before he could communicate with us. I say we trust Alex."

"What is the deal with all this Alex admiration?" wondered Bradley aloud. "The man has either failed miserably, betrayed us, or has left us hanging." Bradley's contempt for Alex Markham was plain to the group. Bradley set aside the emotion that had begun to well up regarding Alex and returned to a more business-like mode. "All of our forces at the *Nest* claim they saw no sign of Alex with the group. The video footage from both the stairway and parking garage confirms this. Their group had five people in it, not six. Alex did not leave the building with them. If he left it, he was separate."

Nathan was satisfied that everyone understood the key points of information, and it was time to make some conclusions and plans.

"Okay, we don't know what happened with Alex. But I agree with Dave here. We must trust Alex. We go with the planned site. We guard it. If Alex shows up with the key… great. If he doesn't, we go to plan B. With plan B, as we've discussed, we have an agent go into the bomb vehicle, sedate the driver, and scan the bomb. Of course, we need the driver to be in the vehicle so that this bombing matches the same pattern as the others."

"So, whoever volunteers for this job is going to die when they scan that bomb. Who's gonna volunteer to commit suicide?" challenged Bradley.

"Very few of us know that the bomb goes off right as it's scanned," said Nathan. "We have plenty among us who'd perform this mission. We tell them they'll have two minutes to get away from the bomb before detonation. I'm sure we'll have no problem finding a volunteer."

"Hold on," said Bradley. "This entire operation is botched. I think we're fools to continue. Why don't we scrap this bombing and focus our resources on tracking down this group and all the evidence we've spilled?"

"I suggested that to Judas. That's not an option. He's dead set on this bombing happening. He wants this. So we proceed," said Nathan.

"But if we focus on catching these guys…" persisted Bradley.

"There will be no more discussion on that." Nathan's tone was threatening, and Bradley backed down.

"So, we guard the site and hope mystery-man Alex shows up," said a frustrated Bradley. "If he does, we let him present the key, and we all drive away with Alex before the bomb detonates. If Alex *doesn't* show, we have some gullible agent go into the van, sedate the driver, and kill himself by detonating the bomb while we drive off for safety. And if the targets try to intervene, we first kill them and then go to plan B."

Nathan shrugged. "That's the gist of it. We'll come up with some excuse of why we have to leave when our guy goes in to detonate the bomb. Maybe we'll leave them an empty vehicle with the keys to make them feel better. Shall we proceed?" All the men around the small table either concurred or had no protest. "Good. I'll let Judas know what we're going to do."

CHAPTER 35

DOWNTOWN SALT LAKE CITY
1:19 P.M.

Jim drove around the periphery of Salt Lake City before returning to downtown. He chose to ease into an underground parking lot of a hotel in the middle of downtown. The group secured their belongings and abandoned the car. Jim led them about a block and a half to a sports grill that would normally have been very busy.

The restaurant was not crowded—the lunch rush had passed, and no doubt many people were at home and watching the news. The group settled into a booth. Jim ordered some fries, which arrived very quickly. The group devoured the food, having eaten only light snacks for the past few hours.

There, surrounded by a few groups of people, they found enough isolation and privacy to make their final plans as a group. Jeff began laughing. As the others looked at him to see why he was laughing, Jeff pointed at Pete. Jeff still had not gotten over the costume. Pete smirked at Jeff and then turned away from him. Jim took the lead of the council.

"Okay, we don't have much time. In less than an hour, we'll have either succeeded or failed. May God help us," said Jim. "We have two major things we have to accomplish. We have to stop this bombing. That's our first priority. Our second objective is to reveal The Thread to the world. And that's an objective we must accomplish whether we succeed at our first goal or not."

"I think we have to split up from here if we want to guarantee that we get the word out about The Thread," said Dr. Isaacson.

"I agree," said Jim, nodding at Dr. Isaacson. Then Jim scanned the four other faces. "I think we should have Jeff wait somewhere near the headquarters of Channel Two. They're less than two blocks from here. When the time of the bombing comes, Jeff makes an attempt to get in and inform them of what's going on."

"That's risky, Jim," warned Dr. Isaacson. Jim was about to acknowledge that it was risky, but Jeff spoke before Jim could.

"I'll do it," Jeff said it with finality. Everyone was looking at him. Both Dr. Isaacson and Jim found in Jeff's countenance a clear communication of confidence and decisiveness. Jeff would do the job.

"God be with you, son," said Dr. Isaacson. "You must expect that The Thread will guard all the major network news outlets."

"I'm sure. I'll be fine," said Jeff, with a confident casualness that was almost too casual.

"Professor?" resumed Jim.

"Yes, Jim?"

"You and Pete must find some way to inform as much of the public as we can about The Thread," said Jim.

"I agree," said Dr. Isaacson.

"But I don't think you should target a media outlet. The Thread may put most of their eggs in that basket. We have to find another way," said Jim.

"I can do it by mass email," said Dr. Isaacson. "The trick will be to find somewhere where I can get online without catching the attention of The Thread."

"Good," said Jim. "And remember that you must not send out any communications about The Thread until the time of the bombing. We have to assume that they do have the resources now to analyze all electronic communications. If you send anything too early, it could mess up our chances of stopping the bombing."

"Right," said Dr. Isaacson.

"Perhaps you can get to the library," suggested Jim.

"Too open and obvious," said Dr. Isaacson. "We may be better off finding a friendly office somewhere."

"That could be risky too. Beware of stirring much suspicion," said Jim.

"I agree," was all the professor said.

"Then that leaves Colton and me to stop the bombing," announced Jim. That announcement had an impact on Colton. But the thrill was not without a healthy dose of anxiety. Jim looked intently at his nephew. Colton nodded firmly at his uncle, and that was the end of that. Jim lifted his stare from Colton and resumed looking at the entire group. "Colton and I will head to the Capitol Building and hope for a miracle." They seemed finished with the planning. Jim's countenance changed.

The professor was shaking his head. "Jim, forgive my negativity, but I don't see how we can stop this bombing. If The Thread goes through with it after our escape—which is questionable—they're not likely to do it at the same location. And if they do, you can bet that they'll have a ridiculous level of security in place."

"I know, professor. But you know that we've got to try," said Jim.

"I do," acknowledged Dr. Isaacson.

"All right, then. May God bless us, gentlemen," said Jim. But it was evident that he had more to say. He leaned forward and spoke with controlled emotion. "We've all grown up and learned to love freedom. We've all been to fireworks shows and parades and sung songs celebrating freedom. We've appreciated and celebrated the men and women of the armed forces for defending our freedom. But now—" Jim paused to harness his emotions again. "But now, we have an overwhelming job to do, and the freedom of so many may depend on it. If we fail, imagine what could happen to our nation." Jim was going to continue, but, shaking his head, found himself unable to at the moment. The professor jumped in.

"Boys, remember that it is the God of Heaven who's given you your freedom. Remember how He feels about this nation and its Constitution and freedom. Remember that He cares about your mission. And, above all, allow Him to be with you." It was what Jim wanted to get across. Rather than saying more, Jim nodded to Dr. Isaacson gratefully. And then the moment of action had arrived.

"Okay, men, we have less than forty minutes." As Jim said this, he focused his gaze on a booth a little ways down along the same wall in the restaurant. Jim arose out of his seat at the edge of the booth, walked a few feet, and squatted before the group in the booth he had been looking at. Colton could see Jim pull out his badge and show it to the group as he talked to them. As Jim put his badge back into his coat pocket, Colton noticed that the group was all teenagers. Colton judged them to either be seniors in high school or first year college students.

The men gave each other curious looks of confusion—nobody being able to explain what Jim must be doing. Then something amazing happened. The young people around the table in the booth tore little slips of paper and wrote on them; then they reached toward Jim, handing him the little slips of paper along with their phones. The group greeted Jim upon his return with looks demanding an explanation of what just went on.

"That is one good, trusting group of kids," said Jim, letting the curiosity hang in the air for a moment.

"What just happened?" Colton asked for the rest of the group.

"I told them who I was, and that something critical was about to occur, and I needed their cell phones for a few hours. I promised them that they'll get them back if they inquire to the FBI office, and that they'd get a small reward. I asked them to write down their phone numbers, so we can call each other. I also told them not to say anything about this for at least an hour, after which they can tell anyone they wish. I told them to stay away from downtown and watch the news later, but to stay silent about the issue for at least an hour. And they agreed."

"You mean, you flashed your badge and they all just gave up their phones like sheep?" asked Jeff.

"Well, one of them refused, but he at least agreed to stay quiet for a full hour. I trust him." And with that, Jim pressed ahead. "Now, if any of us are caught by The Thread, they have the technology to call the other phones and track down where everyone else is through triangulation. So, I suggest you record the other phone numbers in the address book of your phone under some code name you'll recognize but The Thread couldn't pick out." Jim looked everyone in the eyes to make sure all understood. Satisfied, he moved on.

"Don't say anything that gives out our names or anything that openly refers to The Thread or the bombing. The Thread's monitoring may pick up those things."

Jim placed the phone number that went with his new phone on the table for the others to see. He then passed out the other three phones—one to Colton, one to Dr. Isaacson and Pete, and one to Jeff. Jim then passed out the phone numbers, placing them in front of the matching phone, turned for the rest of the group to see. Everyone understood and began entering in phone numbers.

"Colton, you and I will take the *Master Plan* original. Give the copies to Jeff and Dr. Isaacson," said Jim. Then, speaking to everyone: "Be ready at all times to use your weapons." And then Jim shared another idea. "I'm going to try, before the bombing, to see if I can't use the FBI to go after The Thread."

"Jim, that's risky to try before the bombing is scheduled," said Dr. Isaacson.

"I know, but I have a plan that just might work. Anyway, let's go do this."

And with that, the group got out of the booth, exchanged handshakes, half hugs and well wishes, and left the restaurant.

DOWNTOWN SALT LAKE CITY
1:41 P.M.

Jeff left the group and moseyed a block south. From the corner, he could see the building housing his target media outlet across the street. He crossed the street and entered into the building that was a half a block north of the news station. He found a somewhat-isolated chair in the corner of the lobby of that building and sat down. He was watchful, but cautious enough to maintain a casual appearance. And there he waited. Jeff's mind was reeling, wondering if he would ever see Colton again.

FINANCIAL BROKERAGE OFFICE
DOWNTOWN SALT LAKE CITY
1:43 P.M.

Unlike Jeff, Dr. Isaacson did not know where he would end up. The professor wandered, looking for possibilities among the different buildings and offices of downtown Salt Lake City. Pete was following Dr. Isaacson like a loyal lamb. Dr. Isaacson had a slight hobble, but by now it was not very noticeable. Finally, after wandering first to the east, and then to the south, the professor saw an office that seemed like it might work.

Dr. Isaacson turned into the office, walked through the lobby, wound through a series of corridors, and then entered into what appeared to be a branch of an investment company. The professor surveyed the scene, and then walked past the receptionist. Dr. Isaacson's gait was so determined and sure that the receptionist assumed he knew where he was going and what he was doing. The only communication Dr. Isaacson got from the receptionist was a kind smile before she went back to work on a computer.

Dr. Isaacson slowed his pace, studying the various offices he was now passing. Near the latter part of the hallway was a worker whose desk was in the hallway. The professor assumed she must be a secretary of sorts for someone who was in a nearby office. Dr. Isaacson approached the lady.

"Pardon me..." the lady looked up at Dr. Isaacson for the first time. "I have a very strange request."

"Well, this is a strange day. What is it?" She was polite, but came across very professional and confident. The professor was close enough to hear the sound coming from the lady's computer—it was the news.

"I need to scan a document and send it out in an email. And I'll need the use of a computer for about an hour. Is that possible?"

The lady stared at Dr. Isaacson for a while, and then looked at Pete for a moment before returning her gaze to the professor. Despite her delay in responding, her demeanor was not rude; but she was curious and cautious. She finally answered.

"This office right here," she was pointing straight ahead, "is used by three different people, and none of them are in today. I'm sure you could use the computer in there."

"Thank you," said Dr. Isaacson. "I know this is a strange request. Thank you so much."

"What is it for?" asked the lady.

Dr. Isaacson did not know how to respond to the question. And then Dr. Isaacson's odd sense of humor led him to act on a wild impulse. Leaning in close to the woman and speaking in a secretive, quiet voice, the professor revealed, "I need the computer because we're trying to stop an evil organization from taking over America and destroying our freedom."

Dr. Isaacson leaned back, away from the lady. After a long, awkward pause during which she had no response other than the incredulous look on her face, Dr. Isaacson leaned back toward her and added, “They call themselves… *The Thread*.” The professor said the last two words dramatically. He did not notice that Pete, too, was gawking at him in disbelief.

The lady’s hands came up, fingers pointing upward and outward. “Look, you came in here and asked if you could use a computer. I thought I had a right to ask. But if you can’t tell me what you’re doing, at least you could have the dignity to just tell me it’s private. Okay?”

Dr. Isaacson smiled a big, genuine smile for a while, and then said, “I’ll tell you later why I used the computer. You’ll be glad you were kind enough to let me.” Dr. Isaacson’s kindness was disarming.

“The computer’s in there,” she said, waving at the office, “and it has a photo scanner, too.” And then she resumed watching the news on her computer. With a shocked Pete following, the professor ducked into the office and went to work.

DOWNTOWN SALT LAKE CITY
1:39 P.M.

Colton and Jim left the restaurant and began to wind northward through the parks and shops just south of Temple Square. Jim pulled out his newly acquired phone and dialed a 1-800 number and put the phone to his ear.

“Yes, would you please forward me to the Denver branch office for the Federal Bureau of Investigation? …Thank you.”

After another pause and about forty feet of walking, Jim spoke again. “Yes, I need to speak with Thomas Oliver. It’s urgent. …thank you.”

And after another delay—this one shorter, Jim was speaking with Thomas Oliver.

“Tom!”

Colton could hear the voice loud enough to know that Tom did not recognize Jim.

"This is J-I-M, B-E-R-R-Y," spelled Jim without any humor in his voice, "and don't say my name back to me," requested the FBI agent to his friend.

"Man! What's going on? You're a wanted man. The straightest arrow I know, and you've pushed your way to the top of the wanted lists! On a day of a national security disaster, no less!"

Jim ignored this. "Look, Tom, I need your help right now! I've got to be cautious and concise, so listen carefully." Jim plugged along, exercising caution to not use words or word patterns that would trip any electronic filters. "The episodes in the two cities that happened this morning…"

"Yes…" said Tom to show he was listening.

"Those episodes were perpetrated by Americans."

The silence was awkward. Tom prodded, "Go on."

"The man who leads the country, many in congress, many in the Fed and other organizations are part of a secret society called The T-H-R-E-A-D." Jim worried about stringing together the words *secret* and *society.*

Jim could tell that Tom was now taking notes, so he plugged ahead. "Tom, you used to work for a powerful listening agency. This group is using that listening agency's technology and at least one orbiting man-made object in space to do their thing. I'm in Salt Lake right now. This group is planning on another episode here in just a few minutes. They're also responsible for terminating the life of the former head of this country. I need you to use your connections with that powerful listening agency to try to stop this group. Do you understand?"

"Do you have to be so vague?" asked Tom.

"I do, Tom. I learned yesterday just how powerful these guys are and how sensitive their phone filters are. Do you understand what I said?" inquired Jim once again.

"So, you think that these people, whoever they are, have penetrated the power of the—"

"The powerful listening agency you worked for for many years, yes," interrupted Jim, making sure computers would have a tough time picking up the conversation.

"And you want me to ferret them out?" asked Tom.

"I do. And it has to be fast," said Jim.

After a brief pause, Tom replied, "I'll see what I can do, friend. I just hope I don't lose my job over this."

"You might. But it would be worth it," said Jim, with some humor this time.

"Should I call you back at this number?"

"Yes. Thanks, Tom."

Jim hung up the phone and continued pushing north with Colton.

CHAPTER 36

FBI FIELD OFFICE
DENVER, COLORADO
1:44 P.M.

Tom Oliver stared at his phone for a time in deep thought. Jim Berry was one of the greatest friends and best people Tom had ever known. The waves of reports and alerts the past twenty-four hours that had painted Jim to be a fugitive had rocked Tom. To have his old friend call and make such extreme claims was having a major mental and emotional effect on the old agent. Tom shook his head.

Tom could not bring himself during the past twenty-four hours to believe the reports that were coming in regarding Jim. He knew Jim Berry, and the reports flew in the face of everything Tom knew about the man. It was like hearing that the wonderful couple down the street is getting a divorce. It just didn't make sense. And so, Tom had tremendous hope that the outrageous claims his old friend had just made on the telephone were true.

Taking a deep breath, and mustering enough courage to do something that could get him into loads of trouble for aiding and abetting a fugitive and renegade agent, Tom Oliver went to battle. He dialed a familiar phone number at his former work place: the National Security Agency.

"National Security Agency, how may I direct your call?"

"The Director's office, please," said Tom.

"One moment."

After a brief moment of silence: "Office of the director, this is Jillian speaking."

"The Director, please."

"I am sorry, but the Director is not available at the—"

"This is a national security issue. I must speak with the Director, now please."

"Who is this?" requested Jillian.

"I am Tom Oliver, with the FBI. I'm a former employee there. This is an issue of critical national security."

"Look, Mr. Oliver. With all due respect, on a day when America is attacked like we've been today, *everything* is an issue of national security. There's no way you are going to talk to the Director today. Now, if you'll leave me your contact inf—"

"If you don't put me in contact with the Director, you'll have a third bombing on your hands." Tom said it without rage, but he now had Jillian's attention. There was silence. Then Jillian again spoke, her voice much different now.

"If I put you through, and your business is not as important as you suggest, the Director will not be a happy man."

"I am sure you're right," said Tom, who was now finished with all posturing and pretense in this little conversation. Tom's silence let Jillian know he expected to be connected and would wait until it happened.

"One moment please," and then there was a click. After about thirty seconds, a deep voice answered.

"Director."

"Sir," Tom plunged right in, "my name is Tom Oliver. I'm with the FBI in Denver and I worked for twelve years there at the NSA until three years ago."

"So what do you need?" The Director asked in annoyance, suggesting Tom get right to the point and stop wasting the man's time.

"I have a friend who's in trouble in Salt Lake City—an FBI agent. He just informed me that a powerful secret society has infiltrated the NSA and is using your technologies and one of your satellites to do its work. He informed me that this same group is behind the assassination of our former president and is responsible for today's bombings. He claims that another bombing is about to occur in Salt Lake City. He requested that I do all I can to cut off this group's access to NSA power."

There was silence. Tom had been concise, and had offered the Director a lot to swallow in one quick barrage.

"Let me make sure I understand your claim, Mr. Oliver. You're suggesting that I have some secret group using my complex to perpetuate today's bombing?"

"Yes, Mr. Director… that's what I was informed, sir."

"And you say this group is responsible for the death of the President?"

"Yes, sir."

"This sounds ludicrous," said the Director.

"Yes sir, it does… and I believe it."

"You do, do you?" The Director did not.

"I do, sir. I suppose our conversation has tripped the filters this group is using in your own facility there. I suggest that you sweep all access points to eavesdropping and filtering technology. I'd guess there's some nice, hidden room there where some very bad people are doing some very bad things to this nation."

"Is that what you would do, then?" The tone communicated cynicism. The Director was not used to others telling him what he should do. But Tom was not in the mood to play power politics. And then Tom said something that affected the Director enough to prompt action.

"Sir, these are bold claims and requests. But I've communicated to you critical information for national security. I've recorded this conversation, and can prove forever after that I informed you clearly of what's going on within your own facility. I suggest that if you act on this information and find that it's bogus, you can have me fired and prosecuted over the inconvenience I caused you on such a critical day. But if you fail to respond, you'll not be judged kindly by this nation."

After more silence, the Director went into action.

"Look, I'll follow your recommendation. If your claims are false, you *will* be held accountable."

Tom breathed a sigh of relief.

FORT MEADE, MARYLAND
3:48 P.M. EASTERN (1:48 MOUNTAIN)

The Director of the National Security Agency turned the phone call back to Jillian to get Tom's contact information. After the exchange of information, Tom informed Jillian that he would be standing by, and then Tom hung up to wait for an update.

The director paged two men in nearby offices. They rushed into the Director's office, sensing urgency.

"Gentlemen, I just got a very disturbing phone call. An FBI agent has made a wild claim that a secret group is operating within this facility and NSA power is being used for evil purposes, including today's bombings. If this is true, another bombing is to occur in Salt Lake City in a very short time. Dan, I want all exits sealed for the time being. Nobody leaves this complex without my specific authorization. Joseph, I want the full, available security detail to sweep the entire complex, focusing on access ports to filtering and satellite technology. If this alert is correct, these folks will be hostile. Conduct the sweep with weapons locked and loaded. I want the sweep done now—we don't have much time. Go."

And without any reaction, the two men went to task, organizing the security sweep and sealing the building.

DOWNTOWN SALT LAKE CITY
1:48 P.M.

Colton and Jim wound their way through Temple Square. Colton marveled at the fact that this was the second time in just a couple of hours that he was winding covertly through these sacred grounds. What a crazy day! They emerged out of Temple Square at the Main Street junction, just north of the reflection pool. Crossing North Temple and heading north, up the east side of Main Street, the two cautious men pushed toward the Capitol Building. What both men could not have known was that the vehicle they were seeking at the Capitol Building was a vehicle they were in the process of passing.

Just pulling up alongside the west curb on Main Street, just north of Temple Square, was an armored carrier, driven by a kind, young man from Pakistan. The man had been in America for nearly six months now. But the man had no idea that his cargo was a bomb laced with radioactive material. Nor did the young man have any clue that two of his great friends and associates who emigrated at the same time as he did were now dead—killed earlier in the day as they loyally followed instructions that were nearly identical to his own.

FORT MEADE, MARYLAND
3:52 P.M. EASTERN (1:52 MOUNTAIN)

In the dark *War Room* of The Thread at NSA headquarters, a very busy technician was about to respond to an alarm that had been sounding for more than five minutes on his computer signifying a high percentage filter had been tripped. The filter had indeed caught the conversation between Tom Oliver and the Director of the NSA. But it was too late for the technician and his associates from The Thread in the *War Room*.

This particular security detail had twelve men. Two other details of ten men each were combing the main building. Similar groups were scouring all buildings in the NSA complex. They had searched four rooms. This was the fifth. They did not knock. As they burst through the door, the reaction from within the room was so wild that it was clear to the men of the security detail that this was not a normal, innocent operation going on inside this room.

Dart weapons were drawn and members of The Thread began popping the doorway with sedative darts. Three members of the security detail had already entered the room. Those three received multiple darts each from the weapons of The Thread. But, before they were unconscious, all three returned fire, shooting their weapons wildly toward the source of the popping sounds. The men outside the door were on their radios, reporting the incident and calling for the other two security details to come and assist.

One of the two men, the one named Joseph, burst into the Director's office.

"Sir, we've found it. Our men have the subjects trapped in a room, but they've opened fire and have taken out a few of our men. They're in the main wing, on the second floor."

And with that announcement, the Director smiled out of shock that the reports were true. The Director's first impulse was to call the White House and inform the President of the situation—which would be normal protocol at such a time. But he opted instead to first call Tom Oliver back and give him a brief update.

The director ordered a secretary to get Tom on the phone. Moments later, Tom Oliver was on the line.

"Tom here."

"Mr. Oliver, this is the Director of the NSA."

"Yes, sir."

"Thank you for taking a risk for your friend. Your man was right. We've disrupted some covert, illegal action. There's a standoff right now within our complex. We don't have the perps yet, but that's only a matter of time. I'm confident to say that whatever they were tracking, whatever they were listening to, they won't be doing any more."

"Thank you for the update, sir." Tom Oliver felt a surge of relief and excitement. Jim Berry was the most impressive agent he had ever met as far as sheer goodness goes. That goodness led Tom to be willing to take a risk for Jim. And the risk had paid off.

But they had so much to do in emergency fashion. And both men knew it.

"Mr. Oliver, can you get your agent friend who reported this to you on the line?"

"Yes, sir. Give me just a moment." Then, as Tom worked his phone to make the connection, he informed the Director, "Let me remind you that Jim suggested earlier that this group is somehow involved in the assassination of the President a few months ago and that they're responsible for the bombings this morning."

"Whether it's true or not, that's almost unbelievable."

And then both men heard the line to Jim begin to ring.

CHAPTER 37

NEAR UTAH STATE CAPITOL BUILDING
1:55 P.M.

Colton and Jim had zigzagged through side streets and alleys on the way to the Capitol Building. Their movements were slow, calculated, and methodical, knowing that The Thread was likely expecting them to show up to the bombsite. The two arrived at the houses just south of the Capitol Building. They could see no trucks or vans that might signify the bomb. Nor could the two men see any of the telltale dark vehicles of The Thread.

Feeling conspicuous, the two men looked for shelter from whence they could watch the Capitol Complex without being seen. Colton was all nerves because the two men had no idea what they were going to do to stop The Thread from detonating the bomb.

Colton spotted a hedge near the sidewalk that would offer a good vantage point. A large tree offered a cloaking canopy to shelter them from any aerial view. The two men settled down on the grass and took up watch. They were now within five minutes of the scheduled bombing. But there was no sign yet of the bomb or The Thread.

"So, do you think they might have cancelled the Salt Lake bombing?" asked Colton.

"I hope so. But I fear that rather than cancelling the bombing, they'd just change the location," answered Jim.

Jim's phone rang. He could see it was from Denver.

"This is Jim."

"Jim, this is Tom."

"Any luck?" asked Jim.

"Tons, Jim," said Tom. "In fact, I have the Director of the National Security Agency on the line with us." The Director joined the conversation.

"Jim, this is Director Thompson of the National Security Agency. The group that was pestering you is now under siege here. They won't be listening to you or watching you any more. What can you tell me?"

For the first time in a long time, Jim felt free to speak at will over the phone about The Thread. "Sir, we're hiding across the street from the Utah State Capitol Building. The third and final bombing of the day is scheduled here in about five minutes. We see no signs of it, though. Maybe they've relocated it due to interruptions to their plans. I'm with my nephew, who found one of their documents yesterday and got this whole thing rolling. We have three others throughout the city who are ready to get the word out about this group through media. This group's plans involve changing the time and location of the bombing if media or law enforcement discovers their intentions. For that reason, we're waiting until the time of the bombing before we blast the world with news and evidence. That's where we stand right now."

"So, you say that this group plans to bomb the Utah State Capitol Building in less than five minutes, and you're there right now?"

"Yes," confirmed Jim.

"Who are these people, Mr. Berry?"

"They're a secret, powerful society that calls itself *The Thread*. They've placed many members in Congress, the Federal Reserve, and were behind the assassination of the President a few months ago. Sir, we suspect that our current President is counted as one of their members."

That piece of information sent the phone line into silence for a spell.

"Tom mentioned that. Mr. Berry, you do realize the weight of that accusation?" asked a sober Director.

"Of course I do, Mr. Thompson," said Jim.

"I almost called him before I called you, Mr. Berry," said the Director.

"Well, we probably still would have been okay, Director Thompson, but it's a very good thing that you didn't. I think we will be a whole lot more successful if we were to do all we can to first stop these people before we start communicating with top leaders of The Thread and put them in charge of our efforts to catch them."

"Good call, Mr. Berry," said the Director as he chuckled. "But you do realize that if you're wrong about the President, this could get real ugly?"

"I realize that," said Jim, "but that's a risk we have to take."

After a brief pause, the Director spoke again, "Mr. Berry, it's about time for the bombing. Still no signs of it happening, I take it?"

"Nothing," said Jim.

"Okay, James, the power of the NSA has been used against you. I'm now going to turn that power over to your side. We're going to get a fix on the area and let you know everything we can see," said the Director.

Jim smiled and spoke with gratitude. "That sounds wonderful, Mr. Thompson."

"Is there anything else we could do for you right now?" inquired the Director in closing the conversation.

"Yes," said Jim. "there is, I feel like a fugitive right now. A member of The Thread is running the regional FBI office and has turned the resources of the office in Salt Lake to stopping us. Some high-ranking member of the FBI sent this agent. No doubt that high official is part of The Thread, too. I need you to get the FBI and police departments off our backs and onto our side."

It was a far bigger request than the Director was expecting at the end of the conversation; but the Director obligingly said, "We'll see what we can do with that, too."

"Thank you."

"No problem. Nice work, James, and God bless. We'll keep the line with Tom open to us. If you have any updates, just call him again."

"Good luck, Jim," sounded Tom, making clear he was still on the line.

"Thanks, Tom, for everything."

Jim turned to Colton. "Nothing? No signs?"

"Nothing." Colton was not sure whether he wanted to be frustrated or elated that there were no signs of the bombing. But his gut was moving in the direction of frustration.

"I feel like something's wrong," said Colton.

"I wonder what the deal is with The Thread," said Jim. "I'm going to get a hold of the others."

DOWNTOWN SALT LAKE CITY
2:04 P.M.

Jeff had seen the time of the bombing arrive and pass. His heart was pounding. It was now four minutes past the hour on his watch. Jeff knew it would be time to act any moment now. He had not heard from Jim, and that made him nervous. But then his phone rang. He could see it was coming from the phone Jim had taken.

"Hello?" Jeff spoke with a hushed voice in the corner of the lobby.

"Jeff, the phones are safe now. You can talk about The Thread," said Jim.

"How?" asked Jeff.

"We got in contact with the Director of the Agency The Thread was using to track us down over the phones and from the satellite—"

"The NSA?" asked Jeff.

"Yes. Now, have you made any attempts at getting your document into media yet?"

"No. I've been mustering the courage, and was about to give it a shot."

"Wait for a few minutes, Jeff. We may soon have the police on our side. Wait till you hear from me, okay?"

Jeff was willing to go for it now, but was still welcome to the idea of waiting. "Sounds great to me."

"Jeff, if you don't hear from Colton or me in the next half hour, just go for it. Okay?" instructed Jim.

"Got it."

FINANCIAL BROKERAGE OFFICE
DOWNTOWN SALT LAKE CITY
2:05 P.M.

Dr. Isaacson had scanned the document and saved it onto the computer in the empty office. He had then created a new email account online. He attached the saved electronic copy of the *Master Plan*. He then wrote a brief bit of information in the email to explain the nature of the attachment. Dr. Isaacson typed in a couple of addresses of key people that he knew from memory. And with that, he was ready, with a moment's notice, to get evidence of The Thread out to a few other computers with just the click of a button.

But Dr. Isaacson readied himself to inform more than just a few. Dr. Isaacson accessed the address book for his personal email. He knew that was risky. But he deemed it worth the risk. He loaded more than sixty email addresses into the 'send to' box. Finally, Dr. Isaacson took advantage of remaining time to create a message that was loaded with more and more detail about The Thread.

Dr. Isaacson had been waiting for Jim, ready at any moment to send the message. Pete was content to watch the professor work. The phone rang.

"Hello?" said Dr. Isaacson with more cheer than the situation called for.

"Dr. Isaacson, this is Jim," said the FBI agent.

"Has it happened? Anything happened with the bomb?"

"Nothing yet. I'm thinking they either cancelled it or changed locations."

"That could be good or it could be very bad," said Dr. Isaacson.

"That's right," said Jim. "Are you ready?"

"I am," said Dr. Isaacson.

"Send it." With Jim's command, Dr. Isaacson pressed the button that sent the message out to computers across the world. And with that simple click, the professor accomplished a major part of the group's mission.

"It's done," said Dr. Isaacson, smiling with relief.

"Great. Now, the NSA is on our side at this point. The Thread has been ferreted out there, and we can use the phones openly."

"How did that happen?" asked a shocked professor.

"I'll explain that later. But we're trying to get the police on our side now, too. That shouldn't take too long. But my advice for you is to just stay put and stay safe."

"Thanks for the update, Jim. Good job." And then Dr. Isaacson realized that the relief he felt for having accomplished his mission was not a relief that Jim or Colton could yet feel. "You men be careful."

"Plan on it. Talk to you later."

TEMPLE SQUARE
2:08 P.M.

Nathan was sitting in the passenger seat of a black SUV. Directly in front of his SUV was an armored carrier. There were three other dark SUVs within two hundred feet. The vehicles—parked on both sides of Main Street, just north of Temple Square—formed somewhat of a semi-circle around the armored carrier. The occupants of the dark vehicles didn't like being there. Nathan had just hung up the phone.

"That man is obsessed with this bombing going through. I think he's crazy. Judas claims that the folks at headquarters can clean up as much of the mess as possible. But he insists we proceed with the bombing. He thinks we'd be surrendering by not going through with it. He won't yield."

"He's being a fool. Too much has gone wrong today," said Bradley, speaking from the back seat of the same vehicle.

Nathan spoke into his communication device. "Folks, Judas says we stay put and guard the package. Let me remind you that our enemy does *not* know where the bomb site is. But watch out and report anything suspicious. Hopefully Alex shows fast, or we just get this thing done and get out of here." Then, after a pause, Nathan resumed talking into the device.

"Again, we wait for Alex. If he doesn't show within ten minutes, we go with *plan B*." Nathan looked at the other man in the back seat. It was a young member of The Thread—relatively new to the organization. "Are you ready for *plan B*?" All Nathan got was a confident looking nod.

FBI FIELD HEADQUARTERS
SALT LAKE CITY
2:09 P.M.

The phone rang at FBI headquarters in Salt Lake City. A secretary answered it.

"Federal Bureau of Investigation, how may I help you?"

"I need the agent-in-charge, please. I believe that is Mark Jensen," requested the man on the phone.

"We have someone else here that's been the agent-in-charge for the last twenty-four hours or so: Agent Williams from Denver. Would you like to speak to him?" asked the secretary.

"No thank you. I need Mr. Jensen, please."

"May I ask who's calling?"

"Yes. Tell him this is Sam Russell, the Deputy Director of the Federal Bureau of Investigation."

"Oh!" this response took the secretary completely off guard. "I'll get Mr. Jensen right away, sir."

"Thank you."

After a short pause, Mark Jensen answered the phone with all the deference and respect people show when addressing the leader of their organization.

"Mr. Deputy Director, this is Agent Jensen."

"Agent Jensen, you should have your weapon in hand as I speak to you," warned the Deputy Director. The words filled agent Jensen with curiosity as he withdrew his weapon from its holster.

"What's going on, sir?" inquired agent Jensen.

"Your Special Agent… I understand he is from Denver?"

"Yes. He was announced by the Executive Director of Field Operations."

"Good. I was wondering about that. Now listen, he's part of a secret society that has in essence run your office the past twenty-four hours. You're to apprehend Mr. Williams, stop hunting down Agent James Berry and his group, and instead do all you can to assist them." Agent Mark Jensen felt light-headed. He was looking around the office in a state of shock. He could see no signs of the special agent who had flown in the day before.

"Agent Jensen?" The Deputy Director's inquiry snapped him out of his shock.

"Yes, sir?"

"Your first priority is to arrest this man who I understand calls himself Special Agent Williams, and take your office back over. Is this clear?"

"Yes, sir. I can see no sign of him in the office right now. I don't remember seeing him for about five or ten minutes now. But we'll do it. I'll call this number with any updates."

"Thank you, Agent Jensen. I would appreciate that. Your city is at risk of being the third bomb site today. The man running your office is part of the group that may be responsible for the bombs. When you can guarantee that you have full control of your office, let me know. We'll then go to work to stop these people."

This was too much information to take in and process all at once for a rational mind. Mark Jensen simply said he'd do it and said goodbye before hanging up the phone and getting to work. But Special Agent Williams, who had controlled and micromanaged nearly every detail the past twenty-four hours, had abandoned ship and was nowhere to be found.

CHAPTER 38

JUST SOUTH OF THE STATE CAPITOL BUILDING, SALT LAKE CITY 2:09 P.M.

Colton and Jim were still keeping watch at the Capitol Building. In just one minute, ten minutes would have passed since the time scheduled for the bombing.

"Alex told us it would happen in front of the Capitol Building at 2:00 P.M. Do you think he was telling the truth about that?"

"No way to tell with Alex," said Jim. He was amidst a break in phone calls and was watching with Colton. "I hope they've called this whole thing off. That would be wonderful news."

"That would be," said Colton. But he did not believe it at all. It was obvious that nothing was happening at the Capitol Building at this time—at least, not yet. The most probable explanation was that The Thread had cancelled the bombing. But a swelling anxiety was rising within Colton. Something was not right. He could *feel* it. While Jim seemed relieved and cheerier with every passing minute, Colton was becoming so anxious that he could hardly stand himself. He was full of adrenaline, and could not explain why.

While still glancing around at intervals, Colton removed the *Master Plan*—or as The Thread called it, *Key #3*—from his backpack. He turned the document over, staring at the blood mark on the back. Colton ran his finger over the paper, nearly touching the bloodstain before shuddering and pulling his hand back. Colton turned the document over so it was face up. He stared at the site of the third transaction of the first day. He could see again that it did indeed say that the bombing would be in *SLC* at the *C.B*.

And then the wheels began turning. Colton remembered that *Alex* had asked the *group* if they knew where the bombing was. Alex had confirmed the group's guess that the bombing would be at the Capitol Building, but Alex had not come out and said earlier that this is where it would be.

Colton's heart began to race even faster. *What if there was a different 'C. B.' in Salt Lake City?* He thought. *What if Alex had lied about the site? Although most of what Alex had told us was proving to be true, what if this little fact was a lie?* But the Capitol Building made so much sense. Frank Tomlinson worked there, and he had been the key-bearer for The Thread. But what if that was wrong, and Alex let them believe it? The idea was too heavy for Colton to set aside. In his mind, Colton began poring over all the possibilities that *C. B.* could stand for.

Colton kept repeating those two letters in his mind, searching for an alternative explanation. His thinking got so intense that he began thinking aloud.

"What did you say?" asked Jim.

Colton shook his head, "Nothing. Sorry."

And he kept thinking aloud to himself. "Cash Bank… Credit… Church… Church building?" It didn't seem to be a good match at all, but his heart lit on fire with the possibility. Perhaps it was because he was just up the road from Temple Square. The thought so dominated Colton's mind that he did not even notice that he had stood up and blown his cover.

"Get down!" commanded Jim. But Colton paid no heed. Rather, Colton further blew his cover by racing out from the bushes. Jim called out after Colton, telling him to pull back. Colton ignored Jim and sprinted along the sidewalk toward Main Street, which was just a short distance away. Jim broke out from the bushes and chased after Colton with a strange mixture of annoyance and trusting curiosity.

Colton paused at the corner of Main Street, looking down the hill toward Temple Square. He could not see over the hill's rim, so he advanced further down the hill, following the Main Street sidewalk along the east side of the street. Colton had now thrown all caution to the wind and was trotting, scanning the scene down the street. And then he stopped cold.

Down at the bottom of the hill—alongside the Conference Center, near the intersection of Main Street and North Temple was a swarm of dark vehicles. And in the midst of those dark vehicles was an armored carrier. Colton glanced down at his watch—eleven minutes past the scheduled time of the bombing. Colton's heart exploded with adrenaline. He acted on his first impulse, and launched into a full run toward the vehicles below.

Jim had almost reached Colton before he had taken off again. In frustration, Jim yelled Colton's name. Jim had focused so much on Colton and his strange behavior that he had not looked down the hill at what Colton had seen and had been reacting to. When Jim's gaze rose and took in the whole scene for the first time, his heart sank.

"Colton!" called Jim again. The second call was even louder, and stemmed from great concern.

Jim's voice rocked Colton to his senses. For the second time in just a few seconds, Colton stopped cold. Jim caught up.

"They're late—the time's passed! What are they doing?" asked Colton, who had had a moment longer to consider what was going on. The two men stood on the sidewalk, breathing heavily, trying to figure out what was going on. "Why are they parked around the bomb?" asked Colton. "That doesn't make sense."

"You're right!" said a perplexed Jim.

"There's no way they are planning on being there when this bomb goes off," said Colton. "What are they doing?"

"They're guarding the site," said Jim, thinking aloud. "But why?"

And then it came to Colton. His head cocked to the side, and a smile of sorts pulled over his lips. It was the kind of smile people get when they remember something important that had been eluding them.

"I know what they're waiting for…" said Colton with a very distant expression.

Jim began to ask Colton what he meant, but he never had the chance to. Colton cut Jim off. "I need your badge!"

"You what?"

"I need your badge! Now, Jim!" Colton was pleading and it was obvious he did not have time to explain. Jim pulled his badge from his pocket and trustingly handed the badge to his nephew.

Colton burst into a full sprint, racing west across Main Street, dashing through traffic.

Jim called after Colton, but it was to no avail. It was evident to Jim that Colton was not going to slow down. Jim began to run after him, but did not even make it a stride or two into the street before he stopped. He merely watched Colton. To Jim's relief, Colton veered West on the street above the Conference Center. He was not running to the bomb. *What in the world was Colton doing? And why did he need the badge?*

About a minute later, Jim would figure it out.

Colton did not break stride until he reached his destination. He shot along the north side of the Conference Center, heading west on the sidewalk at full speed. He rounded the corner of the Conference Center and angled toward the apartment building that The Thread had referred to as *the Nest*. It was now in full view.

The authorities had not yet permitted the residents to enter their apartments—which was evidenced by the crowd still gathered outside the building. Colton could see three police vehicles and one fire truck that were still on the scene.

Colton chose the north entrance of the building. As he neared the crowd and broke through it—still nearly at full speed—a police officer tried to flag him down. The officer had seen him racing toward the building, but had assumed that Colton would stop at the edge of the crowd. When it was unmistakable he was not going to stop, the officer closed in, waving his arms.

Colton responded by maintaining a high speed, but pulled Jim's badge out of his pocket, displaying it toward the police officer as he approached and ran past.

"FBI! Emergency—no time!"

With reluctance, the police officer allowed Colton to proceed. To assuage his reluctant conscience, he got on his radio and reported that a very young FBI agent had just rushed into the building.

Colton chose the elevator. There were three police officers in the lobby, but none of them tried to stop the urgent, young man. The elevator was sitting at the main floor. The doors opened immediately. When the elevator delivered Colton to the fifth floor, he lunged across the hallway and down a few doors.

The sound of approaching sirens filled the air. Colton's heart tightened even more. Had his dramatic entrance tripped a massive police response? If so, it did not matter. He would have to use his badge, break through, whatever. He had a job to do and he was going to do it.

Colton flung open the door to the little janitor supply closet. There, on the ground—just as they had left things—was a sedated Alex Markham, hidden with paper towels.

Colton quickly swept the towels off the sleeping man. He closed the door. In less than two minutes, he emerged from the small room. This time, however, he bore the clothing of Alex Markham.

To Colton's relief, the sirens had approached and moved past. Although that brought a measure of relief, he wondered what could have stimulated another large police response in the area. He was sick of the incessant repetition of sirens.

Colton still needed something else. He capped off the costume by racing into the apartment they had been in earlier. He went straight for Alex's backpack. He found what he wanted, and pocketed the mask that Alex had worn earlier in the day when he had first encountered the group.

It had now been six minutes since Colton left his post at the Capitol Building. He hoped he was not too late.

Colton's departure from the building caused much less curiosity than his arrival had. Without difficulty, he cut through the crowd and once again opened into a full sprint, charging around the south side of the Conference Center this time. As Colton pushed around to the front of the building—on the sidewalk along North Temple—the vehicles merged into his view. The sound of sirens still dominated the audio scene. The emergency vehicles were settling not very far away. But that didn't matter right now to Colton.

Colton donned the mask. He knew Alex would likely never have worn the mask in public, but Colton had to take that risk. As Colton closed in on the vehicles, a steady, background prayer settled behind his consciousness. If ever Colton needed the hand of Divine Providence in his life, it was now.

CHAPTER 39

TEMPLE SQUARE
2:16 P.M.

It was not until Colton was long out of sight that Jim pieced together what Colton might be attempting. Jim was again full of admiration for the courage of his nephew. But he also realized the chances of pulling off something of this sort were not great. He knew he may well be witnessing the end of Colton's young life.

Then Jim heard the sirens. They seemed to approach from multiple directions.

"Oh no…" moaned Jim. "I must not have been clear that we didn't want any police on site yet," thought the FBI agent aloud. "How do they know we're here?"

Jim dialed the phone as fast as he could. Tom answered a moment before the Director of the National Security Agency. As the two men answered, the first approaching police car sped around the corner. It had come from the west on North Temple. The racing vehicle did not stop, though. It went right past The Thread's vehicles, racing northward on Main Street.

Much of Jim's panic changed to curiosity. He addressed both men while two more vehicles raced around the corner and up Main Street. Jim was relieved to see that The Thread had stayed put despite the scare from the police vehicles.

"Gentlemen!" addressed Jim to his fellow federal agents.

"Jim, we have a problem!" said the Director of the NSA, somewhat cutting off Jim. "In notifying the police department to stop searching for you, there was a miscommunication. It somehow leaked that the Capitol Building may be bombed. I guess the police department is sending its full force there, to the Capitol Building, right now. We're trying to call them off—but I can hear from the sirens and see on the screen here that we must be too late."

"Well, let them be for the moment. I'm no longer at the Capitol, and neither is The Thread. I know where the bomb is. We're at the corner of Main Street and North Temple, just two blocks south of the Capitol Building. But do *not* send the police here at this time! That could be disastrous! The Thread seems to be staying put, content to let the police pass."

"What's happening, and what do we do from here?" asked the Director of the NSA.

"My nephew is going to try to pull this thing off," said Jim, and he explained what he suspected Colton was trying to do.

"Okay Jim. We had a satellite fix on the Capitol Building. We have now shifted it to the location you just mentioned. We see at that intersection a few black vehicles—"

"That's The Thread!" said Jim.

"Jim, we have four satellite angles on the site now. Stay on the line with us and let us know what's happening from your perspective. We're in the process of accessing full federal resources to stop this thing. We have the Air Force involved, but it's hard to do a whole lot more without notifying the President. But we'll do what we can."

TEMPLE SQUARE
2:18 P.M.

The sound of approaching sirens had been like a ratchet on the hearts of the men in the dark vehicles. Fear had swept through the group. Every driver in the group started the engine of his SUV, despite Nathan's order to stay put.

"Let me make this very clear. Nobody budges until I give the word." Everyone knew that when Nathan talked like that, you listened.

But, to everyone's surprise—even to Nathan—the first police car had rounded the corner and gone right past the group of dark vehicles. When the next two cars did the same, the group relaxed immensely—although they were far from feeling comfortable. Fear remained.

"Boss, it's been ten minutes," informed a man in another vehicle who was antsy to get out of the area and be done with this mission.

"Actually," said Nathan into the communication device after a glance at his watch, "it's just pushing past nine minutes. We will not proceed with *plan B* until *I* give the word." And with that, the awkward anticipation of the group entered another brief spell of radio silence.

After more than five more long minutes, the silence broke with a loud announcement.

"I see Alex!" yelled one of the men through the communication system.

Nathan did not yet see Alex. Like most when they heard the announcement, he began whipping his head around, searching the scene. Then he saw him. Running toward the bomb, wearing his dark clothing, was Alex Markham.

"I can't *wait* to hear his story… that man is amazing," said one of the men.

"Why is he wearing a mask?" asked someone else through the communication devices.

"I am sure he has a reason," came the response from yet another vehicle.

Alex began waving the *Key* in the air triumphantly. Relief spread over the men in the vehicles.

"He's got *Key #3,*" barked another man. "Looks like we're in good shape."

Nathan fired off a quick phone call. After a moment, he said, "Judas, this is Nathan. Alex just showed up. He's got the *Third Key.*" He nodded briefly in response to something Judas had said in return. "Yes… you certainly did," said Nathan before closing the connection.

"Jim, we can see a man running along the sidewalk, approaching the vehicles from the west!" said the Director of the NSA over the phone. It was the first thing anyone had said over the connection in some time.

"What's he wearing?" asked Jim.

"Dark clothes... Probably black," said the Director.

"That's gotta be Colton, my nephew," said an exhilarated Jim. His knew his assumption must be right.

Colton was still wearing the mask. He ran right to the passenger door of the armored vehicle. Colton opened the door and climbed in, closing the door behind him. The Pakistani man who sat in the driver's seat had seen Alex approaching for some time. Colton's wearing the mask created extraordinary tension with the driver. Colton could sense the man's sudden fear. He had already been nervous that nobody seemed to be showing up. The driver was afraid he had somehow failed to follow instructions. And now, the mask annulled any relief he would have felt at having the *Key* finally arrive.

"I'm sorry to make you nervous. I had to wear this mask." The comment did nothing to set the driver at ease. Colton did not know what to say, so he thrust the document into the hands of the driver. The driver, with shaking hands, turned the document over and scanned the blood mark with a hand-held scanner. The device beeped, notifying the driver that the document was legitimate. The driver's next instructions were to scan the "safe." Colton knew the time to act was now. The driver nodded as if to communicate that Colton had done his job and was more than welcome to get out of the vehicle and leave. But Colton did not leave. Instead, Colton said something very strange.

"My friend, I'm sorry about what I'm about to do, but I hope that we both live to see our families again." And with that comment, Colton pulled his dart gun and shot the driver.

Nathan had as good a vantage point as anyone. He saw Alex shoot the driver.

"What's he doing?" shouted Nathan to the others in his own vehicle. The radio sounded.

"He shot the driver! Something must have gone wrong!"

"Stay calm!" said Nathan into the radio, trying to keep people's reaction to the new, strange event from cluttering the communications. "The driver must have refused to cooperate. Maybe the scan was wrong, who knows. Let's wait to find out." But there was little need to wait. Alex was now in the driver's seat of the vehicle, having removed the unconscious driver. He had a phone to his ear.

One of the dark vehicles edged away from the sidewalk, preparing to speed away. The driver of that vehicle assumed that Alex was perhaps about to scan the bomb himself. Nathan understood this.

"Hold your ground!" roared Nathan into the others. "We'll leave when *I* give the order!" The skittish vehicle jerked to a halt and remained in place. Nathan's threat had been sufficient.

Jim had caught a glimpse of Colton approaching the vehicle. The Director had informed him that Colton had, indeed, gotten into the armored carrier. Jim could see no visible reaction from the dark SUVs. The Director confirmed that he could see no reaction from the vehicles from his vantage point in the air, either. This gave Jim great hope.

And then his phone beeped. Another call was coming in. He could see that it was from Colton's phone. "I am getting a call from Colton right now!" announced Jim before connecting with the line coming in from Colton.

"Colton!"

"Jim! I've got the bomb!"

"I know. Great job!"

"Jim, I'm making a break for it! Can you get these guys off my back?"

"I'll see what I can do. Go for it!"

Jim switched lines back to Tom and the Director. "Colton has possession of the bomb! He's going to make a break for it. But we've got to get The Thread now!"

"We're on it, Jim!" said the Director. And, though the line was still open, the Director broke away for a while, issuing orders and setting in motion the machinery of federal and local resources to clamp down on The Thread.

Colton closed the line on the phone. He knew his chance to make a break for it would soon pass. He made a quick assessment of the driving panel and features of the vehicle. The vehicle seemed normal enough, and the keys were still in the ignition. Colton turned the key, glanced in the mirrors and over his shoulder. The way was clear. He pulled out hard, away from the curb, and burst through the intersection, turning right on North Temple.

Colton felt extraordinary trepidation at the thought of driving with a bomb on board. But he also knew that if he were too cautious, The Thread could catch him and close him in. He erred on the side of recklessness. It paid off. He got a good jump ahead. In just moments, the dark SUVs followed in a frantic pursuit.

As soon as Alex pulled away with the vehicle, Nathan shouted aloud to himself, "This is not right!"

Nathan sounded into the communication system. "Something's wrong! Don't let him go! Stop him!" And for the first time since he had seen Alex running toward the vehicle, Nathan thought that maybe this was not Alex after all. *The mask… Why would Alex wear his mask*? But it was too late now to ask that question. Nathan's fists clenched in rage as he realized what a fool he had just been.

The Director of the National Security Administration had fine-tuned his communication lines with local Salt Lake City law enforcement. Less than thirty seconds after Colton had bolted west, away from Temple Square, the swarms of sirens—now a familiar sound to the group—started up again. The sirens approached from the Capitol Building three blocks north of Jim.

Within a minute of Colton pulling away, the streaming pack of law enforcement vehicles filed past Jim. He smiled. It was a smile of nervous hope. It would not take long for the police to overtake the dark vehicles that were now chasing Colton. And then it hit Jim just how critical his young nephew's predicament was for not only this city, but also the nation. Jim prayed for his nephew. He wished he could do more. And as he thought on the courage and brilliance Colton had just displayed, Jim—standing on the side of Main Street with police cars zooming past—could not hold back the tears. And then a mixture of peace, hope, and relief settled over Jim. It was so strong and overwhelming that Jim abandoned all inhibitions. There, standing in public on a street corner, Jim openly wept.

As Jeff waited, police cars came near and stopped at the entrance to the building next door—the building housing the news agency he was to penetrate with the document. This development was unnerving to Jeff.

Jeff's phone rang again. As before, he knew the caller was Jim.

"Hello?"

"Jeff."

"Yes. Is it time?" asked Jeff, ready for action.

"It is, Jeff. Proceed to the main entrance of the news station. Are there any police in the area?"

"Yeah. They just showed up within the last minute or so."

"Good. More should be showing up, too. They are expecting you and will protect you. Show them the document, but keep it with you and explain it to the highest ranking news personnel you can talk to. With the police escort, you should get the attention of the top brass in the building. Tell them everything you know about The Thread—as if you're the only avenue through which the world will learn about their plan."

"Got it," said Jeff. "What's going on?"

"I'll explain later. It's wonderful though, so far. Keep Colton in your prayers."

"What's up?"

"I said I'll tell you later. I gotta go now. But Jeff, remember that your life is still in great danger. Be careful, and God bless you, son."

"Thanks, Jim." And with that, Jeff closed the connection. He was anxious to know what was happening with Colton, but he transferred his nerves for Colton into focus for what he was about to do.

Within just a few seconds, Jeff had emerged from his temporary sanctuary and approached his target building. Officers spotted him and approached him long before he got to the building. Jeff tensed.

"Are you Jeff Palmer?" asked the lead officer. Jeff took courage, trusting the law enforcement corps that now surrounded him.

"I am. I understand you're on my side now."

"We are. We hear you have a vital document for national security, you will not relinquish it, and you need an escort into the news station here."

"That's right," said Jeff.

And then the group of officers, keeping Jeff in their center, entered the building. Jeff passed through the lobby, requested to speak to the highest people in the news agency. After a wait of a minute and a half, Jeff was speaking with the right people. Within ten minutes, the news team interrupted the regular programming for a breaking news update.

Something Jeff could not have known, and what he would never find out, is that two men who had subtly passed out of the building while Jeff was explaining his story and describing the document were agents of The Thread. They had chosen to leave quietly rather than fight futilely.

The Thread was still cautious—not yet pulling in front of Colton nor trying to stop him. They had followed closely, pulled up along side him, and were trying to communicate with him. Colton had wisely kept the mask on, and that had spread just enough doubt in the pursuing members of The Thread to buy him time.

And then Colton did something brilliant. A dark SUV pulled up along side him, holding the same constant speed. Colton could sense the occupants in the vehicle were very uncertain about who he was and what they should do. Colton, still wearing Alex's mask, looked directly at the passengers of the dark vehicle, lifted his hand, put his thumb and forefinger together, and made the swooping, sewing sign of The Thread.

CHAPTER 40

"It is Alex!" announced the driver of the vehicle next to the armored carrier. "He just gave the sign!" A wave of relief again flooded over the members of The Thread.

Nathan heard the message and didn't know what to think. Nathan had apprised everyone of his conclusion that it was not Alex. The others were slow to accept that. This group had such homage for Alex Markham, and it bothered Nathan. Their overblown loyalty could cost the entire operation.

But he had given the sign. There was no doubting that it was, indeed, Alex. And then Nathan heard the first intimations of sirens.

At the same moment that peace had settled over Jim, a similar peace settled over Colton. He could hear the sirens approaching from behind him. That had been fast. How wonderful those sirens sounded—a sound that had filled him with trepidation many times that day.

And then something happened that touched Colton deeply. Although it had begun earlier in the day, Colton realized that something new and special was occurring. It was the flags. People had been putting up flags throughout the day here and there. But the situation had so consumed Colton that he had not *really* noticed.

But now, it was impossible to *not* notice. It seemed as if every flag that people could get their hands on was either on display or was in the process of going up. As Colton passed a neighborhood, he saw young boys in scout uniforms placing flags with white poles into people's lawns. He saw many people in front of shops and restaurants, in the process of hanging flags. Most businesses had flags on their façade, or had people out hanging a flag.

The explosion of flags came from a reaction to the terrorist attacks of the morning. A half hour earlier, a blast of text messages had swept the nation. There were many messages, but they all had the same theme. The most common message was this:

Does that Star Spangled Banner yet wave, o'er the Land of the Free and the Home of the Brave? Raise the Flag!!!

America responded. Colton took notice, and it gave him courage.

And there, on North Temple, heading west, surrounded by men who had taken an oath to destroy liberty, driving a vehicle loaded with a bomb and radioactive material, alone except for the unconscious man laying on the floor of the vehicle, Colton Wiser began to sing. He started out timid and quiet, but by halfway through the first verse, Colton was belting out the National Anthem.

Colton had grown up with a hymnal that listed the first, second, and fourth verses of the song. It did not include the third verse. And although most Americans were not familiar with anything beyond the first verse, Colton had memorized and grown to love all three verses in the hymnal. So, to manage his nerves, he sang all three verses with increasing intensity.

Oh say, can you see, by the dawn's early light,
What so proudly we hailed at the twilight's last
gleaming?
Whose broad stripes and bright stars, through the
perilous fight,
O'er the ramparts we watched, were so gallantly
streaming?
And the rocket's red glare, the bombs bursting in air,
Gave proof thru the night that our flag was still there.

Oh say, does that star-spangled banner yet wave
O'er the land of the free and the home of the brave?

On the shore, dimly seen thru the mists of the deep,
Where the foe's haughty host in dread silence reposes,
What is that which the breeze, o'er the towering steep,
As it fitfully blows, half conceals, half discloses?
Now it catches the gleam of the morning's first beam,
In full glory reflected, now shines on the stream;
'Tis the star-spangled banner! Oh, long may it wave
O'er the land of the free and the home of the brave!

At this point, tears were freely flowing, being absorbed into the cloth mask. Colton did not care, and his voice was unaffected as he sang the final verse.

Oh, thus be it ever when free-men shall stand
Between their loved homes and the war's desolation!
Blest with vict'ry and peace, may the heav'n-rescued land
Praise the Pow'r that hath made and preserved us a nation!
Then conquer we must, when our cause it is just,
And this be our motto: "In God is our trust!"
And the star-spangled banner in triumph shall wave
O'er the land of the free and the home of the brave!

By now, the sirens were upon the dark vehicles and the armored carrier Colton was driving. The Thread had still not made any move to stop Colton—a blessed result of Colton's wearing the mask and showing the sign.

Then something wonderful happened. Colton passed through the intersection of North Temple and Redwood Road. The light was red. As he approached, he slowed. But seeing a break in the traffic, Colton burst through the intersection without ever going slower than thirty miles per hour. Colton then looked in his mirrors on the side of the armored carrier. To his joy, the dark vehicles turned hard to the left—fleeing the police and abandoning Colton and the bomb in the hopes that it was, indeed Alex. And then Colton's deep emotions of patriotism transitioned into deep feelings and emotions of gratitude. For the first time in his life, Colton discovered in completeness what it means to pour out your heart in prayer and thanksgiving.

The pack of dark vehicles raced south before splitting up and trying to evade the tsunami of law enforcement vehicles that followed them. Their maneuvers were expert and might have eluded the police had it not been for the multiple satellites of the National Security Agency that were tracking every move each SUV made. One of the satellites, ironically, was the very satellite The Thread had been using less than an hour earlier to facilitate their evil plan. The men in the dark vehicles never had a chance.

Colton's goal was to get the bomb as far from population as he could. As he neared the merge of North Temple with Interstate 80, a pack of police cars that had not broken off to chase the dark vehicles of The Thread came up behind Colton. One of the police cars came up alongside Colton. Colton thought it was now safe to unveil his face. He removed the mask—hoping the cop would see it as a gesture of goodwill.

The police officer was alone in the vehicle. He signaled with exaggerated hand and lip movements for Colton to pull over. But Colton did not want to bring the bomb to a stop anywhere near people. Were anything to go wrong—whether through an accident or some unexpected intervention by The Thread—Colton wanted to be far from where the bomb could do any real harm. So rather than pulling over in obedience to the young officer, Colton shook his head at the officer and pulled out his phone again. He dialed Jim's number. Jim answered.

"Jim! The Thread's gone! They turned away about a mile behind me now!"

"Wonderful!" The relief in Jim's voice was easy to detect. "The NSA tells me you're approaching Interstate 80."

"I'm there now," said Colton. "And I need you to do something for me."

"What do you need?"

"I need you to tell the police I'm heading out west. I won't stop until I get far away from people. The police are free to escort me, but I will *not* stop this vehicle." Colton's request made a lot of sense.

"No problem, Colton," said Jim. "That's a great idea."

"Yah," agreed Colton. "The officer next to me is telling me to pull over. But you get the message to them that I refuse. They can have this thing when I get it away from this place."

"I'll take care of it. Talk to you in a minute."

"Thanks, Jim."

Within a minute, Colton was blazing west on Interstate 80 at about 80 miles per hour. Colton's fear of the bomb and its stability restrained him from going faster. The police car that had urged Colton to pull over had since pulled in front of Colton along with two other police cars. Two more were behind Colton. The five cars kept their lights blazing and sirens sounding. They were in escort mode. The phone rang. It was Jim.

"Thanks, Uncle. They're escorting me. Any suggestions where I should take this thing?"

"I'll tell you what, Colton," said Jim, "I'll have the folks at the National Security Agency work with the police department to plot a course and lead you from here."

"Great. Thanks, Uncle Jim."

"Colton."

"Yes?"

"You did it. You really did it. And I'm proud of you."

Colton smiled. "We all did it."

The police cars escorted Colton off the highway at Rowley Junction of the Skull Valley exit. Colton had been on the highway heading west for about a half-hour. The escort group originally had the three cars in front and two cars behind Colton. But different agencies had responded enough that the escort now included about twenty law enforcement vehicles. Also approaching the scene were multiple government agencies and special task forces—such as bomb squads and hazardous materials specialists. Two military helicopters hovered and multiple jets circled in the air above Colton.

As the montage exited the highway, they eased onto Amax Road and followed it, heading parallel to the highway for a short distance before veering north, away from the highway. Colton followed the three police cars, leading the other vehicles over railroad tracks. After a brief jaunt north, the three police cars led Colton to turn off Amax Road onto a road that headed east—back toward the Great Salt Lake.

But they only traveled about a quarter mile away from Amax Road before the lead police car came to a stop. From this vantage point, Colton could see a steady stream of vehicles getting off the highway and following the entourage to where Colton had stopped and where multiple vehicles were coming to rest.

Colton took a great breath and exhaled a huge sigh of relief. He closed his eyes and spent a moment alone unwinding before he opened his door. The police force now knew that Colton was not an enemy, but they were taking no chances. Colton was on wanted lists just an hour earlier, and there would be no mistakes made now in trusting Colton before things settled down and were sorted out. The cars stopping in the radius around the armored carrier had doors open, with police officers behind those doors with guns pulled—pointed at Colton.

This did not bother Colton. He understood they had to be cautious. He was not afraid. Colton climbed down to the ground. He put his hands in the air and walked toward the nearest line of police vehicles. Officers emerged and formed a smaller circle around Colton—but still kept some distance. Colton was now standing in the center of about thirty police officers—all standing about forty feet away from him.

"Keep your hands in the air and get down to your knees," ordered one of the police officers.

Colton obliged without hesitation. With his hands in the air, he yielded to the police force. A sense of relief overcame Colton. They had done it. Against amazing odds, they had secured the bomb and had most likely already begun to notify the world about The Thread. Colton, on his knees, submitted to the crowd of law enforcement, filled with peace and satisfaction. And now he could rest. Colton wearily closed his eyes for a moment.

But what Colton could not have been aware of was the awful fact that one of the police officers was Jordan Nielson. The Thread had given this young and audacious member a new assignment. Colton's little group had to be eliminated before they could explain what they knew. And Jordan was in a perfect position to go after Colton. He realized that he was giving himself up to law enforcement by doing this assignment, but Jordan trusted in the power of The Thread to release him from the hands of the government.

Jordan knew it was not Alex driving the armored vehicle, because he had seen Colton in the room at the Nest in Alex's clothes, and it was he who had seen Colton remove the mask. Jordan had tried to get Colton to pull over back in Salt Lake City. But Colton had refused. It would have been so much easier to deal with Colton and possibly to set off the bomb. They had told Jordan that he had two minutes to swipe the scanner then get away. But Colton's refusal to yield made things more complicated. But no matter… Jordan would come through.

And with that determination, the diabolical young officer pulled the trigger of his weapon. The bullet raced toward the young man who had his arms in the air and his eyes closed. The bullet struck Colton in the head.

EPILOGUE

Colton's eyes were open for a long time before he became even slightly aware of his surroundings. The grogginess was too thick to overcome. By the time Colton could make sense of anything, he realized that his parents were standing over him, looking down at him. His mother was crying. His father was smiling.

"What's going on?" asked Colton. His throat was so dry and sore that it came out raspy.

"What do you remember?" asked his mother. It was difficult for Colton to think. How long had he been out of things?

"The last thing I remember is that I'd parked the bomb, and had just gotten out of it. Did it go off?" Colton tensed in the bed as he asked the question.

"No, no, son," his father reassured, putting a hand on Colton's chest to calm him. "The bomb was secured. You did wonderful." There was a sense of pride and a touch of tender emotion in the voice of Colton's father.

"Then what happened?" asked Colton.

"Hold on, son," said Colton's father. Colton's father then walked out of the room. He returned a few moments later with his brother-in law.

"Jim!" said Colton as he saw his uncle.

Jim walked up to the side of the bed and took Colton's hand, shaking it in a firm grasp. "Great job, young man. It's great to have you back."

"Will someone tell me what happened?" asked Colton, who was as filled with peace as he was curiosity.

"Colton," began Jim, "one of the police officers that escorted you was a member of The Thread. His name is Jordan Nielson. He shot you in the back of the head. The bullet passed through your skull and just barely missed your brain. We have had quite a scare because the bullet did bruise your brain and cause it to swell a little. Having your head shaved by Alex earlier that morning was a tremendous blessing. It made it much easier to get working on your head right away. You have been in a medically induced coma for the past two weeks."

"Wow!" said Colton. The news was unfathomable to him.

"Once we got the bomb from them—once *you* got the bomb from them," said Jim, "they launched an effort to find and kill all five of us who were in the group. We knew enough to pull them down. They went after us, hoping to kill us before we could tell our story. That's why they sent Nielson after you."

"So, if the cop who did this to me was part of The Thread, why didn't he detonate the bomb?"

"I don't know," said Jim. "With all the police there, he had a choice to try to kill you or try to detonate the bomb. He went with killing you. I'm guessing that blowing up a bomb out there would not have had much effect on people. I assume his first priority was to kill you because of what you knew. But we don't know for sure."

"Is everyone else okay?" asked Colton, suddenly filled with concern.

"They're fine," said Jim, "except Jeff. He's still sarcastic."

Colton laughed, and it hurt a little. Jim could see the pain in Colton as he laughed and made a mental note to go easy on any humor. But the news that everyone had made it, safely, was wondrous to the young man in the bed.

"My boss at the FBI, in coordination with the Director of the National Security Agency and the Deputy Director of the FBI, quickly got Dr. Isaacson, Pete, Jeff, and me safely stowed away in different places. We were placed under the care of veteran agents—the theory being that The Thread's secret agents would tend to be new in most organizations."

"And what about the thug who shot me?" asked Colton.

"Well, he made a run for the bomb after he shot you. The good news is that the rest of the police officers went ballistic on that man and had him subdued before he could get to the bomb. Authorities placed him in federal custody. The bad news is that The Thread got to him and he is now at large again."

Colton tensed—not out of fear, but anger. Colton noticed that Jim was furious, too.

"But they didn't get Alex in time," said Jim. "Ironically, they went after Nielson before they went after Alex. So, after The Thread got to Nielson, the authorities transported Alex to a secret location. We still have him."

"So has word about The Thread gotten out?" asked Colton.

"Oh boy has word gotten out," said Jim with gladness. "By that night, the President was fielding some tough questions. He will soon be arraigned, I'm sure. The evidence is mounting. The dragnet to catch The Thread is going to soon cover Congress and many federal agencies. It has all just begun, but a lot of good things are happening in a hurry."

"That's wonderful!"

"Well, it's not all wonderful," said Jim with somberness.

"What?" asked Colton, matching Jim's sudden shift in mood.

"The Thread hastened and detonated the remaining two bombs—the Chicago bomb and the Los Angeles bomb—that same night. They detonated the bombs in different locations than the original plan called for, and they were obviously a day early. But they did succeed in four of the five bombs. The last two didn't kill many people, but they did have an effect."

"You mean," inquired Colton, "even after we stopped them in Salt Lake, and their plot and plans were made public, they still kept after the bombings? That's crazy! There's no way they could have brought about their regime change that they were after. It was fruitless!"

"That's just it, Colton. Those last two bombings are a sign that though The Thread was foiled, they will not be giving up any time soon."

"Those last bombings were acts of defiance. They were declarations of war!"

"You're exactly right," said Jim. "And that war is the most important one America now faces. Hopefully The Thread disintegrates. But all indications show a withdrawal and an effort to regroup."

"Then we have to go after them!"

"We?" asked Jim.

"America, I mean," said Colton.

"Well, this is not the time to talk to you about it, but I'm going to run it by you anyway."

"Run what by me?" Colton was curious now.

"The Director of the FBI has put me in charge of a task force to go after The Thread on a national level. We'll be working in conjunction with all the major law enforcement, intelligence, and homeland security agencies. I requested that you be on that team if you wish to be. The Director agreed that your performance a couple weeks ago was effectively a high quality job application. They said they will see to your being hired if you want the job."

"You've got to be kidding, Uncle Jim."

"No, I have no desire to make you laugh any more. I can tell it hurts you," said Jim.

Colton was quiet for some time.

"That would be amazing. And looking back at how much the hand of the Lord was with us that day, we're dealing with things the Lord is concerned about. …But I don't know, Uncle Jim."

"You don't need to decide now, Colton. Just think about it."

"I'm not even married. I want to get married and move on with my life."

"You're a good man, Colton. You'll make a great husband and father," complimented Jim sincerely.

"I just don't know."

"Well, think about it. There's no rush and no time limit."

They were both silent for a while. Colton's parents were watching the two talk. Although they had been close over the years, there was now a deep bond between the uncle and the nephew.

"After I've had some time with my family, I want to see the others. Can I see Jeff and Pete—and Dr. Isaacson?"

"Sure, Colton. I bet they can be here sometime in the next couple of hours."

"Great. Are they safe to come? How risky are our lives regarding The Thread?"

"Oh, I think the benefit they would get from killing us is minimal now. Everything we knew about their plan, with a few exceptions, is analyzed every day on every major news network."

"Good. I want to see everyone," said Colton again. "I'd like that very much."

Two weeks later, Jim answered his telephone.

"Hello?"

"Jim?"

"Colton! How are you feeling?"

"Great, they had me jogging today. I'm going home in the next couple of days."

"That's what I heard. That's great!"

"It is. I can't wait to get out. I'm going crazy."

"I bet," said Jim. "So what's up?"

"I'm calling about your offer to join your team—to go after The Thread."

"Yeah?"

"Is the offer still good?"

Jim smiled. “It is, Colton. It’s always good if you want it.”

Colton was silent for a while. Just as Jim thought maybe the connection might have been broken, Colton broke the silence.

“I’m in.”

THE THREAD LECTURES

LECTURE 1: INTRODUCTION TO ECONOMIC FREEDOM

The largest auditorium on the campus of Brigham Young University was filled to capacity, and the anticipatory buzz of conversation ebbed and flowed. It was time. The door near the front opened. Dr. Harold Isaacson walked to the podium, attached a microphone to his lapel, and smiled at the gathered crowd.

He began by taking a dollar bill out of his wallet and holding it up high.

"There are federal agents whose job is to identify counterfeit bills, trace them back to whoever made them, and prosecute the perpetrators. Those agents have to be expert at identifying fake bills. Many people would think that those agents are so good at identifying counterfeit bills because of the time they spend studying them. But that is not the case. Certainly those agents spend a lot of time looking at them because of their job. But when they develop their ability to identify fake bills, they do not spend most of their time studying *counterfeits*. Rather, they spend most of their time studying *real* bills. Why?

"Being an expert on yesterday's imitation may not help you notice tomorrow's replication. But those who understand and recognize the *real* bill have the power to identify any counterfeit."

"To 'take over' America and destroy the Constitution, you would have to destroy freedom. To do this, you must first understand what freedom means. What makes The Thread so threatening is the fact that they do understand freedom. Their plan was successful right up until the attacks. This group has pulled off changes in our nation that would have been politically impossible just fifteen years ago. In this course, we will look at many of those changes.

"But though we will look at what The Thread has done, our primary focus in these lectures will not be on The Thread. Rather, my purpose is to teach you *economic freedom*—the real bill. Armed with that knowledge, you will then have the power to grasp not only the efforts of The Thread, but also similar efforts from anyone else trying to destroy freedom. Our founders established a system of economic freedom. The Thread has sought to destroy that system.

"I am indebted to the administrators of Brigham Young University for permitting this lecture series. These concepts are now at the forefront of the minds of every freedom-loving human.

"I will teach these lectures as if you had no background in economics. These lectures cover the following topics:

Lecture 1: Introduction to Economic Freedom
Lecture 2: Freedom versus Equality
Lecture 3: Natural Rights
Lecture 4: Thread Objective— Neutralize Traditional Institutions
Lecture 5: Thread Objective— Continue to Concentrate Power to the Center
Lecture 6: Free Trade and Protectionism
Lecture 7: Focused Benefits and Generalized Costs
Lecture 8: Licensing and Regulation
Lecture 9: Income Mobility and Unions
Lecture 10: Price Controls

"I am an economics instructor. Most of our topics in this lecture series will heavily involve economics. But we will also delve into philosophy, government, and other subjects to broaden our understanding of economic freedom.

"When I teach economics, I teach economics. I do not teach my world view without indicating that I am veering into personal beliefs. I will handle this course differently. Let me warn you now that this course is a split between objective facts and my view on things. I will not disclaim my opinion during this course. I will base much of what I teach on belief. So let me attach to this series of lectures, from the beginning, one big *in my opinion*.

"And with that as an introduction, let us briefly discuss The Thread's main target: economic freedom. Economic freedom, in its nutshell, is the condition where government uses power and force solely to enable people to live the Golden Rule. When government fails to protect the Golden Rule, or uses force to enable people to break the Golden Rule, economic freedom is perverted, abused, or destroyed.

"I hate to lose. But I can handle a loss if my opponent played by the rules and the rules are fair. But I hurt the economic freedom of others when I use government power to bend the rules in my favor in such a way that destroys the Golden Rule. I have done to others that which I know would not be just were they to do it to me. The Golden Rule is at the heart of economic freedom.

"J. Reuben Clark said that economic freedom is 'the right of every citizen to pursue that particular vocational activity which he wishes to follow, unregimented, untrammeled, uncontrolled, subject to the right of every other citizen to have the same privilege. This means each citizen must yield something from his full liberty for the benefit of others, so that he and they may live together without anyone unduly infringing upon the rights of another, each enjoying the resulting right to free enterprise.'

"We cannot overstate the fundamental importance of economic freedom. It is the basis of all freedoms. Without it, all other liberties collapse from the weight of tyranny. Human nature leads us to constantly press against the economic freedom of others. We must therefore understand it and preserve it for ourselves and our posterity, for it is precious and fragile.

"I close this lecture with the words of David O. McKay: 'The fostering of full economic freedom lies at the base of our liberties. Only in perpetuating economic freedom can our social, political, and religious liberties be preserved.'"

LECTURE 2: EQUALITY VERSUS FREEDOM

"Freedom is the supreme principle of all human interaction. If you lived on an island, alone, your choices would not affect others at all. When you live and interact with people and your choices affect them for good or for bad, your use of agency becomes an issue of *freedom*. Freedom is a social concept.

"Freedom is the most important of all social principles, and we must hold it higher than all social principles—including equality.

"Now, let me distinguish something. When we talk about freedom and equality today, we are not talking about freedom and equality before the *law*. Freedom and equality are equal partners when it comes to law. God created all men equal, and the preservation of that equality—equality before the law—is a key role of government. Rather, today we talk about freedom and equality regarding *stuff*—property. In other words, we compare economic freedom versus economic equality.

"Two of the greatest competing principles of social interaction are *freedom* and *equality*. They work closely together; but the reason I say they are competing is because *whichever one you think is more important will determine much about how you view the world*. So much is determined by whether you feel freedom is more important than equality, or whether you feel equality is more important than freedom.

"Freedom is God-given and human removed. It seems clear to me that governments which remove freedom in favor of having more *equality* end up losing their equality along with their freedom. Governments that maintain *freedom* as a supreme economic principle end up with a lot of economic equality—comparatively—to go along with their freedom.

"Let me help you see how this affects the real world. Where there is freedom, there will be those with a lot, and those with not so much. Here's the question: Do you find disparity among incomes offensive? Most good people value equality. But are we willing to sacrifice economic freedom to bring about equality?

"In other words, would you rather take away people's freedom by taking their money and giving it to others who are less fortunate, so as to bring about equality? Or is it so important to you that people are free to choose what they will do with their own property that you are willing to sacrifice a little equality to maintain that freedom?

"It's the Robin Hood issue. Those who are for *equality* at the expense of freedom are willing to *take* money and property from the wealthy. That's the key word: *take*. It's not about people *giving*. In any system, charity and alms are keys to a happy and prosperous society.

"But this is a question of government and freedom. Does the *government* have the right and moral obligation to *take* wealth from people and redistribute it? Your answer to that question will reveal much about how you see the world. The answer for you personally depends on whether freedom is, in your mind and heart, more important than all other social virtues—including equality."

"So, why do you put freedom above equality?" asked a student.

"Well," began Dr. Isaacson introspectively, "when you get to the bottom of it, my opinion stems from what happened in the pre-mortal world." The professor's response surprised many people. Their readiness to learn empowered Dr. Isaacson to be bold.

"We know in the grand council in heaven the Father presented a plan. Satan presented an alternate approach. How did Satan's approach differ?"

Many hands shot up. Dr. Isaacson chose one. "Satan wanted to remove our agency by forcing us to do good and return to Heavenly Father. Satan said he would save everyone."

"I don't know how much he intended to force us to do *good*," said Dr. Isaacson, "but he certainly was seeking to destroy our agency, wasn't he?" Then he concluded.

"Think about those two approaches. One plan was based on *freedom* and *choice* and *individuality*, with no guarantee of equality. The other plan was sold under the banner of *equality*—all would be saved. But to ensure equality, that second approach would remove freedom. One plan held up freedom, the other equality as its foundation. One of these plans is good, perfect, and righteous. The other is foolish, impossible, and seductively evil.

"These contrasting ideas spawned the war in heaven spoken of in the twelfth chapter of Revelation. I believe the same battle of ideas plays out now. I believe Satan is constantly attacking freedom. He will use any good virtue—including economic equality—to topple economic freedom. He does not care about equality. He only uses equality to persuade good, reasonable people to let go of their freedom. I believe the battle for *agency* is over, and the war has now transferred to the fight to maintain *freedom* so that agency can be used to the fullest for God's children."

A student ventured with a final question. "Do you believe that Satan has an influence in countries letting go of economic freedom in the name of economic equality?"

"I do."

LECTURE 3: NATURAL RIGHTS

"The Founders built this nation on the concept of natural rights. The principle of natural rights can be a little tricky to understand at first. But, once you grasp it, it can dramatically affect your understanding of the role of government.

"To understand natural rights, imagine that there's no government. We all live as separate individuals. And let's say someone kills your child because of your child's hair color. Would you say that what they did was wrong? Of course you would.

"So, even if there is no government, and no laws, there is still right and wrong. There is still fairness and justice. In other words, we still have natural rights. You see, natural rights are God-given and inherent; mankind and governments don't create them. And though governments cannot create them, the entire role of government is to protect them.

"Many of you are already familiar with the concept of natural rights. It was well known among the Founders, and one of the greatest articulations we have of natural rights is the Declaration of Independence.

"'We hold these Truths to be self-evident, that all Men are created equal, that they are endowed by their Creator with certain Unalienable Rights, that among these are Life, Liberty, and the Pursuit of Happiness.' *Unalienable* Rights are *natural* rights. Life, liberty, and the pursuit of happiness are three of them. The next sentence in the Declaration states that 'to secure these rights governments are instituted among men, deriving their just powers from the consent of the governed.'

"Jefferson lists life, liberty, and the pursuit of happiness as natural rights. Please note that the Founders often used *happiness* and *property* interchangeably. We were born with our *natural right*s. Humans form governments to 'secure,' or protect, those rights. The Founders declared that when governments fail to protect natural rights, those governments must be changed or overthrown. This was their justification for rebellion. They argued that the colonial-style government of Great Britain was not honoring the natural rights of the colonists, and was therefore to be overthrown.

"In his landmark essay, *The Proper Role of Government*, Ezra Taft Benson—who you remember was also the Secretary of Agriculture for eight years—taught about natural rights clearly and powerfully. He explained that without a government, we would all be obligated to defend our own natural rights if we wished to be free. We would have to play the role of law-enforcement officer, judge, jury, and executioner. But defending our own natural rights costs time and effort. So, to make life better for everyone, we hire a sheriff to defend our natural rights, and government is born.

"So, we all have a right to protect our own natural rights. But it is much easier to hire a government to do it for us rather than to have all of us do it ourselves, separately.

"Government is instituted solely to protect our natural rights. It can only do what the people would have the right to do themselves if there were no government. It eases the cost—in wonderful ways—of enforcing our own natural rights. The authority of government is the sum of the natural rights of the people. *But the government cannot take upon itself powers or rights that are not part of the natural rights of the people.*"

The murmur across the auditorium informed Dr. Isaacson he had better try the point again.

"Think of it this way. If you were to take all the natural rights of the people and bundle them up, that bundle entails the power and duty of the government. If the government fails to protect that bundle of rights, it falls short of its duty. But if the government exercises authority *beyond* what that bundle offers it, it is going too far.

"This is why we identify Hitler as evil. He *was* the German government. Now, just as individuals cannot randomly take life, governments cannot randomly take life either. Hitler was unjust because he used the power of government not to protect natural rights, but rather to violate them. His actions constituted great evil and his overthrow was just.

"Now, we are good at sensing injustice when it comes to the right to life," Dr. Isaacson paused. "Well, I guess with abortion we have now become callous to the protection of life, too. But generally we have a consensus that governments cannot arbitrarily kill. We sense this because individually we don't have the right to do so. But what we have let go of the past century—and this leads us back to The Thread and their plan—is the natural right to *property*.

"Let's go back to the scenario where we have no government. Imagine that Farmer Rich has a lot of cows and a small family. Pretend that Farmer Poor has only one cow and a huge family. Would it be okay for Farmer Rich to donate some of his cows to Farmer Poor?"

A student responded. "Sure. The cows are his. Farmer Rich can do whatever he wants with his own cows."

"I agree," said Dr. Isaacson. "But let's say that *you* notice the unfair situation and go to Farmer Rich's hut and *take* five of his cows. Then you go and give them to Farmer Poor as a gift from society. What do you think?"

"No way. That would be stealing," concluded the same student without hesitating.

"But the situation is obviously not fair!" countered Dr. Isaacson. "You might have taken Farmer Rich's cows, but you used them to do good and make things more equal."

Waves of understanding swept the auditorium. But the student did not yet see where the professor was leading him, and felt a little defensive.

"If Farmer Rich wants to give his own cows to Farmer Poor, he can! But I can't just go and take his stuff and give it to someone else!"

"So, if *people* cannot remove your property and give it to another, does the *government* have the right to do so?" That was the golden question.

Dr. Isaacson continued. "When governments fail to protect natural rights by abolishing the right of individuals to own and control property, they go beyond the bounds of their responsibilities. Such is the case with socialism. Socialists argue that although *individuals* should not plunder and take from some to give to others, the collective power of the people—the government—*does* have the power to do so.

"Socialism is a system of legalized plunder where the government wields tremendous power through the redistribution of wealth. In such a system, governments perceive economic freedom as a great nuisance, not as a natural and God-given right as the Founders understood it to be. Socialists often hide their plunder under the guise of good intentions, but the core evil is in the violation of the natural right of property—which socialism disregards and destroys. The natural right of private property is another way of stating economic freedom." Dr. Isaacson held up some scriptures.

"When the children of Israel wanted to have a king like everyone else, the Lord gave them a sobering warning about the future consequences of their present preference. Study that admonition in Samuel 8, verses five to 22. You will see that the Lord's warning centered on the fact that a king would destroy economic freedom. He would go after their property. And that warning is fundamental because the role of government is to protect the right to property, not destroy it. The act of government unjustly destroying private property rights is evil, and will always bring undue burdens upon the people." The professor set the scriptures back down.

"Up until 100 years ago, America, by and large, honored the right to property as an unalienable right. But now, we think that the government can control and distribute private property as it wishes simply because it is the government. Our government is exercising powers that are unjust. The result is that with many things people used to take responsibility for, they now look to the federal government; and the effect on individuals and families has been devastating.

"Remember that every one of the economic objectives of The Thread is designed to remove economic freedom. That means The Thread is riding on the wave of socialism generated in the past. The Thread is dependent on Americans being dependent. To do that, the government must govern as if property is not a natural right and that they can redistribute property at their discretion. Recently, The Thread has pushed for anything that accelerates the destruction of private property and places it into the hands of the federal government. In the name of compassion and equality, our government has become the greatest thief most Americans have to deal with. And that is exactly what The Thread has exploited on their road to power."

LECTURE 4: THREAD OBJECTIVE— NEUTRALIZE TRADITIONAL INSTITUTIONS

"The first stated objective in the *Master Plan* of The Thread is to *Neutralize Traditional Institutions*."

"Traditional institutions are organizations that have been around for a long time and *that serve to strengthen* ***individuals***—to help people become more self-reliant and reach their potential. *The most important traditional institution is the* ***family***. After the family, I believe the award goes to churches, then community groups. There are many others, but I think you get the gist now of what they are. When individuals cannot care for themselves, traditional institutions fill that role.

"Why would The Thread have an interest in destroying the family?

"The answer is simple: a free society is built on strong families. Families and churches help us to be free by teaching us how to take care of ourselves and interact with others in appropriate ways. Remember, freedom is a social concept. It is in the family that we learn how to manage freedom.

"A free society requires people to be self-reliant and good. Bad people don't stay free very long—they can't handle freedom. And people who need others to care for them are dependent, and are not fully free. Families and churches help nurture people to be able to handle freedom. Good, self-reliant people tend toward freedom.

"Now, The Thread understands that if families, churches, and other traditional institutions are weakened, individuals will be less self-reliant and less free. They will be dependent on others and will be more willing to turn to the government for care. Governments that wish to grow in power tend to take over choices and responsibilities that individuals could and should handle themselves. Governments that seek for more power often get it by weakening or destroying (or in a word: *neutralizing*) traditional institutions.

"Society's greatest problems stem from the breakdown of the family: poverty, crime, abuse, and many others. The Thread has pushed for policies that weaken families. Remember, this is their first stated objective.

"Marriage is the foundation of family, and is ordained of God. The primary attack on family is always an assault on marriage. There are many ways to weaken marriage. These attacks may come by redefinitions of marriage, removing protections to marriage, or by subsidizing the alternatives to marriage and the ideal family. The more the government is willing to step in and provide for families, the less costly it is for fathers to leave the home. After all, why do we need fathers when the government will do just fine providing for families in their absence?

"And I suppose this would explain the dramatic increases in the welfare state the past three years—policy changes we know The Thread helped enact. These increases in government welfare ignored all past evidence and experience. It would also explain major efforts in the past two years to scale back tax breaks and benefits that have always gone to married people—including benefits to married people with children.

"I suppose recent efforts to create socialized child care may well have The Thread written all over them. That policy will effectively make the decision to leave home and go to work a much less costly choice for parents. And while that seems like a great help to many good people, the results may well be yet another wave of families weakening and government stepping in to fill the role of parents."

Dr. Isaacson acknowledged a raised hand. "All those policies don't exactly sound evil to me. Helping single parents?

I don't think most people would agree with the spin you put on that as being an evil policy."

"Well," said Dr. Isaacson, "all those policies do sound good. And they are sold as policies that help the less fortunate and make things fairer. But in the end, those policies will have a negative effect on the family and an overall negative effect on society. All the good intentions in the world cannot make up for a price tag like that."

The professor called on another student raising her hand. "What's so evil about a government taking on responsibility for its people? It seems to me that that's why we have governments."

In response, Dr. Isaacson proclaimed: "Government has some very important roles to play in our lives. But *not in the realm of personal, economic choices.*

"So often, when people get power, they restrict people's freedom under the assumption that they can provide for those people better than those people can provide for themselves. They essentially say to the people, 'I am going to restrict and limit you, because *I* can take care of you better than *you* can take care of you. *I* know what is best for you. *I* will meet your needs. Just give me enough of your freedom to take care of you.' It is a nasty side of human nature that tells ourselves that we can do more good for people by controlling them than they can do for themselves if left alone. That side of human nature comes out in so many misguided government policies that *seem* good, but end up doing more harm than good.

"Governments that take away economic freedom act like parents over those they are to serve—foolish parents at that. The art of parenting is to know when to grant each increase of freedom to children. But a parent that withholds freedom from a child, when the child could and should manage it, is a parent that is not properly training that child in self-reliance. The overall cost of *governments* caring for people who are capable but dependent always outweighs the costs and problems that arise when you let the people care for themselves.

"Now, I know some of you think I am unjustly attacking welfare. Welfare *is* critical for a society," clarified Dr. Isaacson. "But welfare is not a function of the *federal government*. There is no constitutional authorization for using public funds for welfare. James Madison—the Father of the Constitution—refused to support the use of government revenues for purposes of benevolence. Horrible effects follow government efforts to administer welfare and redistribute wealth. *Welfare is the role of traditional institutions*: first the family, and then churches and community groups. These institutions have plenty of power, potential, and effectiveness to take care of society's welfare needs.

"The portion of the federal budget that America dedicates to wealth redistribution is staggering: over two-thirds of the federal budget goes to entitlements. And I know that all the problems those programs are designed to solve are legitimate problems. But the grand question is this: Whose *responsibility* is it to solve those problems?"

Dr. Isaacson allowed a time of silence before continuing. "What we have developed is an attitude of socialism, and our freedom is at stake. When problems occur now, Americans cast their eyes at the federal government and abdicate their personal and family responsibilities to America's central government. America has held the federal government accountable for every natural disaster in the past many years.

"In the eighteen hundreds, multiple presidents refused to spend federal money on regional disasters, stating that the Constitution gives them no authorization to use federal funds for public charity. If the federal government is going to acquire tremendous amounts of money, of course the American people will expect to see that money used for good. But in the process, freedom suffers more and more from the centralizing of power and the abandonment of individual responsibility.

"Expansive governments love to do good by creating entitlements. But here's the problem: removing entitlements and government programs that serve people is like removing cancer without anesthetic. The procedure may be right, but very few patients and doctors would be willing to go through the trauma.

"You see, the problem with entitlements and income redistribution is that whoever you spend money on becomes dependent—less free. But that dependency creates security for that program. In fact, the dependency created by government welfare actually tends to *create* poverty.

"Back in 1996, major reforms trimmed back welfare dramatically. Many people warned that poverty would explode if you were to remove welfare from the people. But what happened was this: as welfare rolls dropped, *poverty dropped as well*. The increase in work that pulling back welfare caused also led to a drop in poverty. Work, not welfare, is the cure for poverty."

"So, do you want us to just let people fail?" asked a student.

"Nobody likes it when people fail," said Dr. Isaacson, "but again, the very way you ask that question, you place the solution to the problem on the government. That is not a role of government. At least, not if we wish to be free. When the government becomes a rescuer of individual economic circumstances, the effects on freedom are devastating. To protect our freedom, the Constitution delineates certain roles for the federal government. The Tenth Amendment even states that the items not given directly to the federal government in the Constitution are to be left to the states, or the people. And nowhere in the Constitution does the federal government find commission for plundering the rewards or bearing the burdens of individual economic choices."

LECTURE 5: THREAD OBJECTIVE— CONTINUE TO CONCENTRATE POWER TO THE CENTER

"The second stated objective of The Thread is to '*Continue to Concentrate Power to the Center*.' The Thread has sought to make the federal government as powerful as possible. As an organization, The Thread assumed that the more power they could amass to the federal government the easier it would be to destroy freedom and constitutional government when they made their move.

"The greatest expansions to America's federal government have occurred on the back of some form of calamity, disaster, or crisis. Let me repeat that. The greatest expansions to America's federal government have occurred on the back of some form of calamity, disaster, or crisis.

"The Thread hoped that the panic created by these multiple attacks—and the threat of more attacks—would allow them to step in, pose as our saviors, remove our freedom, and rule over us.

"During crisis, humans grow weary of dealing with the burdens of freedom. Amid such desperation, we tend to turn to the government for salvation.

"Many tyrants blame these crises on freedom and free markets. Ironically, the cause of most of these crises is the very government we turn to to save us. The Thread has learned this lesson from history.

"For much of America's past, the federal government was small. The great transformation from a small federal government to a large federal government happened during the Great Depression. Before the Depression, the federal government spent what amounted to about four percent of everything that was spent in America—or, in other words, four percent of the GDP (the Gross Domestic Product). By the end of the Great Depression, federal spending exploded to about twelve percent—it essentially tripled. And that is just *federal* spending—that does not include state and local expenditures.

"The irony is that the Depression was caused by foolish government responses to normal economic patterns. The Depression's length and extent was due to our own federal government."

"How did the government cause the Depression?" asked a skeptical student.

"Simply put, the government raised interest rates during a recession, causing the money supply to contract dramatically. At the same time, the government enacted massive trade restrictions and business limitations. All combined, two different administrations so mismanaged the money supply and fiscal policies that the federal government turned an otherwise brief, hard economic cycle into a long, drawn-out tragedy.

"There is one major difference between the Depression and what we face. America's leaders during the Depression took advantage of desperation to reform government. But The Thread has sought to *create* desperation to enable them to increase the power of the federal government and destroy the Constitution.

"Let's shift gears a bit and look at how and why the Constitution limits the power of the federal government.

"America is a collection of states. Those states have separate governments. If I want to take over America, the more power the states have compared to the federal government, the harder it will be for me to succeed. If the federal government pretty much has all the power—which has become the case—then taking over the whole nation is much easier. It's easier to topple one big government than fifty smaller governments. Let me show this visually."

Dr. Isaacson had a few blankets spread out in front of the podium. Atop the blankets were a series of containers. A large, center bin (that would hold about twenty five gallons) was surrounded by six five-gallon buckets. All the containers were filled with water. Closer to the podium was an empty bin, which was even larger than the center bin.

Dr. Isaacson walked to the front row. "I need volunteers!" Multiple hands were up and he selected six students. He directed each of them to take a spot at one of the five-gallon buckets. He handed each of the students a small microphone, which they clipped onto their shirts. He then handed each participant a spoon. Dr. Isaacson positioned himself in the open space between the center bin that was full of water and the large, empty bin that was close to the podium. Everything was ready.

"We're going to play a game," said Dr. Isaacson.

"Goody," said one of the less-shy students. "I love water games!"

"All right! It's you six against me. The rules are simple. Using your spoons and the water in your buckets, your goal is to keep the center bin full. My goal is to empty the bin."

"How do we know who wins?" asked one of them.

"You'll know," said Dr. Isaacson. Just as students were straining to get a better view of the action, the professor pulled out a remote control from his pocket and clicked a button. An image appeared on the screen that showed the group in the front very clearly from a camera mounted overhead. In the corner of the image was a timer that showed three minutes.

"When I say 'go,' we have three minutes to compete. Afterwards we'll check the water level of the central bin."

A big grin from Dr. Isaacson announced to the students it was time.

"Okay, is everybody ready?" Dr. Isaacson leaned toward the bin dramatically. The other six also leaned in. "On your mark!" said Dr. Isaacson. "Get set! Go!"

Dr. Isaacson leaned further toward the bin, but did nothing. He pulled back to observe. He was chuckling. The six students were motoring their spoons as fast as they could. The water in the bin and all their buckets was sloshing from being disturbed. Yet, the water level—which had already been close to the top—did not seem to be increasing.

"What're you doing?" One of the participants had noticed the professor's lack of effort.

"I'm giving you all a head start." The professor laughed.

It had been about two minutes of full action from the students with no action from Dr. Isaacson. Finally, a small difference was perceptible in the students' buckets, and the center bin did seem a mite fuller.

It was time for the professor to join in. He brandished a pitcher he had been hiding. Dr. Isaacson leaned in and took a giant draught of water. He turned behind him and flung the water into the large, empty bin. He repeated the motion.

"Hey!" The competitive student sensed injustice. His spoon continued to fly during his protest. "That's not fair!" But the student got no empathy from the professor, only more laughter. Dr. Isaacson was now moving with fast, powerful dips. After just about a minute, the water in the bin was almost gone.

A student turned his aim and started flinging the water from his spoon at Dr. Isaacson.

"Ha Ha!" said Dr. Isaacson. "You're bitter because I made you look like sissies." The irony is that the student who had cried foul really was bitter. Most of the students in the auditorium knew it had been a lesson, and were curious to see how it would tie in.

Dr. Isaacson, instead of avoiding the competitive student's response, decided to confront it head on. "Don't be sad. The six of you had little chance considering my athletic prowess."

The student lightened up a lot and mustered a partial smile.

"So, Dr. Isaacson," asked one of the students. "Is this a sample of your family night activities? You set up some losing situation for your little children and then dominate them?"

Dr. Isaacson laughed. "Actually, my children are much better at this than you are. We do this particular activity all the time."

"You do?" asked the competitive one. He was serious. There was a pause as everyone realized he meant it. Laughter rumbled throughout the auditorium.

"Okay, okay." Dr. Isaacson tried to cut the laughter short to rescue the student. The student realized now how gullible he had been, and he had the good nature to smile and start cupping water in his hands and fling it at the scoffers around him.

As the tumult subsided, Dr. Isaacson taught. "Who remembers the second objective of The Thread and the topic of this lecture?"

A student nearby in the crowd blurted the answer, "Continue to centralize power."

"Yes. Now, the water here represents freedom. The center bin—the large bin—represents America as a whole." To make sure they understood, he scooped some water with his hand and flicked it a few times toward the six young students, saying, "Freedom, freedom, freedom." He then knocked on the side of the large, central bin. "America. Got it?" Dr. Isaacson continued.

"Good. Your spoons represent the power of the state and local governments. My pitcher," he held it up as he explained, "represents the power of the federal government.

"The Founders protected America by spreading out the power. Most are good at identifying how the Founders *horizontally* divided the federal government into three separate branches that check and balance each other. But another safeguard they put into the Constitution that people don't seem to be aware of is the *vertical* separation of powers—dividing power between the federal, state, and local governments. We call this division of power *federalism*. We have now lost most of the federalism the Founders put in place."

"*Lost* federalism?" asked a student.

"Yes," verified Dr. Isaacson. "We are now living in a country that is much like the way we set up this activity. At

America's founding, the Constitution provided the states with a lot of power. That state and local power was an effective check on tyranny. However, in order to be more efficient, or for whatever other reasons, we have chipped at the power of the states and have altered the Constitution until state power is now insignificant compared to the power of the federal government. To use our analogy here, the federal government has now got a large pitcher while the states have small spoons."

"Wait a minute!" said a student. "You said that the Constitution has been *altered* in a way that gets rid of state power. How?"

"Good question," said Dr. Isaacson. "It was through the Seventeenth Amendment. Most Americans aren't familiar with the Seventeenth Amendment. Through it, the Progressives changed the way we elect the Senate. You see, the federal Senate was originally elected by the *state* governments, whereas they are now elected by the *people* of each state in popular elections."

The professor could see from facial expressions that many did not understand what he had just said.

"How many senators does each state have?"

"Two," answered a student.

"And how are they elected?" asked Dr. Isaacson.

"They are elected every six years, by the people."

"Yes!" said Dr. Isaacson. "But that is not how the Constitution had it originally. That is how we do things since the Seventeenth Amendment. Originally, the *government of the state of Utah* chose the senators that were to represent Utah in the federal Senate. State legislators would gather and vote for the two people to represent the *state* of Utah in the federal Senate."

"That's foolish," said a student. "The people didn't have a direct say in who their senators were. Electing them directly is smarter."

"Well," said Dr. Isaacson, "the Founders never intended the senate to represent the people."

"That's crazy," said another. "That's what the government's for—to represent the people."

Dr. Isaacson persisted. "Here's what the Founders were thinking. They knew that the government must represent the needs of the people, so they created the House of Representatives. The *people* would vote for them, and they would represent the people all across the nation. However, the Founders knew that to protect freedom, the power of the states must check the power of the central government. To do this, the Founders created the senate to represent the *states*.

"The Founders knew that democracy was important, so they created elections by the people. They also saw pure democracy as being another form of tyranny. The majority would tend to trounce on the minority, and freedom is easily lost when the mass population makes every decision.

"How would the performance of federal senators be different if they were to represent the state *governments* as opposed to the *people* of each state?"

One of the students in the front with a microphone showed her understanding. "Senators would make sure the states were defended—especially their own state—so that they could get reelected."

"Great," said Dr. Isaacson. "The House of Representatives and the Senate would check and balance each other. The Senate would protect the interest of state governments and the House of Representatives would protect the interests of the people of the nation. As a result, the people and the states would be protected by two competing branches of Congress."

"But now, that competition is removed," said a student.

"Yes. We now, in essence, have *two* Houses of Representatives, we just call one the Senate, and it has two representatives for every state. The result is ever-increasing federal power and ever-diminishing state power."

A student made a great inquiry. "I don't see why having the people vote for senators doesn't do just as well at protecting the states as having the state governments vote for senators."

"Wonderful point," said Dr. Isaacson. "What you have to understand is that governments derive and exercise their power by serving the interests of their citizens. When the federal government bypasses state governments and directly serves the interests of the people in the states, the power of state governments diminish and the power of the federal government increases. Without states checking the federal government, people in the nation are more vulnerable to tyranny. By protecting the interests of state governments, the Founders were protecting the interests of the people by using the states to limit the power of the federal government.

"Now, the Tenth Amendment leaves to the states all things not specifically delineated in the Constitution. But with the Seventeenth Amendment in place, the tenth Amendment is essentially meaningless. The federal government now controls a vast array of local issues. And that is a problem. You see, Salt Lake City knows what Salt Lake City needs far better than Washington, D.C. knows what Salt Lake City needs.

"Listen to what Thomas Jefferson said about this." The professor clicked his remote, and the screen switched from showing the group up front to showing a slide with a quote on it. Dr. Isaacson read it to the students. "'It is by dividing and subdividing these republics from the great national one down through all its subordinations, until it ends in the administration of every man's farm by himself; by placing under every one what his own eye may superintend, that all will be done for the best.'"

Dr. Isaacson paused to ensure the students were paying full attention. "Listen carefully to how he concludes: *"'What has destroyed liberty and the rights of man in every government which has ever existed under the sun? The generalizing and concentrating all cares and powers into one body.*'"

Dr. Isaacson again paused. "No wonder, then, that The Thread has made it a priority to concentrate 'all cares and powers into one body.' Even prophets have talked about how important federalism is. President Benson was a major advocate of state rights and federalism. He said, "*It is a firm principle that the smallest or lowest level that can possibly undertake the task is the one that should do so.*'"

A student attempted the tie-in. "So what we need to do is to get the pitcher out of the hands of the federal government and replace it with a spoon, right?"

"No," said Dr. Isaacson, "we did that and it failed. The Articles of Confederation was the form of government we tried after we declared independence from England. In the Articles of Confederation, the states had tremendous power. They were separate governments coming together for a common purpose. The federal government was too weak, though. The states were too powerful compared to the federal government.

"In 1787—eleven years after declaring independence and four years after the treaty with England had been signed—the states sent delegates to amend the Articles of Confederation and tackle the problem of a central government that was too weak. They ended up scrapping the Articles and writing the Constitution instead. What they created—and I believe it is inspired—is a system that struck a balance between the power of the state and the federal governments. Or, in one word: federalism."

The student tried again, "So the federal had a pitcher, but the states had pretty large containers, too."

"You could say that," allowed Dr. Isaacson. "In fact, let's try it."

Dr. Isaacson was ready for this. He walked to the podium and got six large cups. He passed them out to the students, who were still at their posts near the five-gallon buckets. Dr. Isaacson, with the help of the students, topped off the five-gallon buckets and refilled the center bin. He beckoned, and some assistants helped him haul in three more five-gallon buckets for each of the six students. They all now had four buckets of water. He then urged them to get ready with their glasses while he got ready with the pitcher.

Dr. Isaacson again pulled out the remote, set the screen to project the competition, and readied the six to begin. On cue, the students began shoveling water into the center bin with their large cups while Dr. Isaacson hefted water with his pitcher. After three minutes, the professor announced the time was up. The water in the center bin was just slightly lower than when they had begun. Dr. Isaacson was out of breath.

"Well done, States!" cheered the exhausted professor. "Your efforts to preserve freedom have counteracted the efforts of a tyrant!" Applause rang out through the auditorium. It was applause not only for the six participants, but also for the concepts they now understood. Dr. Isaacson excused the six to return to their seats. After the applause subsided, Dr. Isaacson moved into his final point of the lecture.

"No doubt The Thread has been as successful as they have in part due to the Seventeenth Amendment. But something else that has concentrated power to the federal government is the Sixteenth Amendment. You see, the Sixteenth Amendment opened up income tax as we know it today. Prior to the Sixteenth Amendment, the Constitution essentially restricted taxing individual incomes.

"The Progressives pushed for the removal of those restrictions so the federal government could raise funds more easily and get more done. They made the change so the federal government could do more good. But the more good it could do, the more evil it could do as well. From that time, income taxes have expanded. The faucets from the people's wallets to the federal government opened up. Money poured into America's central government. With that money, the federal government began to expand the 'good' it did across the nation. And that set the stage for an ever increasing federal government. At first the increases were constitutional, then questionable, and now blatant actions way beyond anything authorized by the Constitution.

"A major use of federal money is the grant system. You will probably find a grant writer at every major local organization. Much of the funds for law enforcement, education, community programs, etc. are covered by grants from the federal government.

"Now, a lot of great things are done with grant money. But the government doesn't just hand out money to various groups and say, 'Good luck, enjoy the funds.' They pretty much say, 'If you take our money, you will play our music.' What ends up happening then—and The Thread needs this—is the federal government wields massive power to manage and control much of what happens in local communities across the nation. If local communities do not meet the requirements set by the federal government, the federal government can cut funding. People yield local wisdom to national requirements. The result is further breakdown in federalism, even more centralization of power, and a central government far more dominant than the Founders ever would have tolerated. As a result, our precious Constitution has become weak enough for The Thread to amass tremendous power to the federal government."

LECTURE 6: FREE TRADE AND PROTECTIONISM

"Although 'protecting American jobs' has been a popular political mantra long before The Thread even came about, all known members of The Thread who have been in public policy positions have been big advocates of 'protecting jobs.' Our recently impeached President fits squarely into this category. The act of using government power to *protect* jobs is referred to as *protectionism.* Protectionism is antithetical to free trade and economic freedom.

"To understand why free trade is important, we'll start at the beginning. The essence of economic freedom is the power to freely buy, produce, or sell. The driving force behind these actions is voluntary exchange.

"Something beautiful happens when people voluntarily exchange: both parties tend to be better off as a result of the exchange. Let me use a simple scenario to illustrate this point. Let's say you go to the store and choose to buy a candy bar for a dollar. What do you value more: the candy bar or your dollar? Obviously you value the candy bar more than your dollar or you would not have purchased it. What does the store value more: your dollar or the candy bar they sold you? Surely the store values your dollar more than the candy bar, or the grocer would not have made the exchange. Both of you are better off because of the trade.

"That is the nature of economic freedom. When we are free to pursue our own interests, our honest pursuit of self interest serves to better not only our own situation but also society.

"Many people hesitate to embrace economic freedom because they are afraid of greed. But this leads us to one of the great beauties of freedom. It is a paradox. Though undesirable, greed is a natural human condition. Where humans are, there greed will be also. However, the best way to manage greed is by letting people be economically free.

"If you want to make money in a free, capitalistic society, you have to serve people. To succeed, you must provide things for people that they value more than their money. That process channels your self-interest into things that better others' lives. Hence, economic freedom channels people's greed toward serving and bettering society in ways that cannot be matched by any system where freedom is removed in an effort to better society.

"The tendency to remove economic freedom in an effort to combat greed is the essence of socialism and communism. But socialism and communism fail to consider fundamental human realities. People operate by incentives. If you want to get the best from society, we must align incentives with society's good. The best way to do that is to let the people be free.

"Do you think greed disappears if governments destroy your ability to pursue economic freedom? Greed is still present even in communist and socialist societies, but freedom can no longer channel human greed toward the service of neighbors and the betterment of society; and the results are ugly. Poverty, corruption, and privilege by connection rage when societies smother freedom.

"And what about those whose greed is rewarded? What about those who seek riches and obtain them? Most people who become wealthy in a free society have offered far more to society in the form of total benefit and living standard than society has offered them in the form of money. Consider vaccines, technological advances, and so on."

A student near the back raised his hand. "So this idea about economic freedom for individuals blessing society is basically Adam Smith's invisible hand idea, right?"

"It is," said the professor. "You must have had some economics." The professor went on to explain.

"A man named Adam Smith—the Father of Economics—said that when there is freedom, society as a whole is benefited by an invisible hand as people seek their own individual interests. That invisible hand guides a free system to do things in the best, most efficient way.

"Now, in their speeches, leaders of The Thread have spoken about 'protecting American jobs.' Why would The Thread worry about protecting American jobs? That seems like a good thing, doesn't it? But what they really mean by 'protecting jobs' is limiting or destroying economic freedom.

"When people and companies are economically free, they can buy or sell with whomever they wish—whether the buyer or seller lives in Nebraska or Japan. And you should now understand clearly that when two parties voluntarily exchange, they both tend to be better off as a result of the exchange."

"So, Professor," asked a student near the front, "you are suggesting that we should freely and openly trade with everyone?"

"Not everyone. There may be a few exceptions where economic sanctions may be appropriate. But for any country qualified to trade with America—which would be most countries—free and open trade should be the norm."

"Completely free?" asked the same student.

"Completely free," confirmed the professor. The student pounced.

"But that only works in theory. In reality other countries will *not* engage in free trade. Take one of our best trading partners: Japan. They block so much of our stuff with heavy tariffs and fees while pumping product after product into America. If other countries won't play fair by freely allowing our products into *their* country, you can't expect America to be free on our end with *their* stuff. The trade has to be fair."

"Please understand," said the professor, "that one of the sneakiest terms politicians use is the term *fair trade*. Beware of that. That politician is trying to placate free market people while destroying economic freedom. And they do it for votes." After the warning, the professor proceeded with his point. "If Japan blocks American products by putting high tariffs and fees on American products, who does that hurt the most?"

"Us," the student stated it as if it were obvious. "We can't sell our stuff to them like we should be able to. It's not fair."

"Wrong. If Japan blocks American products, we will take a hit. But by far, the brunt of that policy will be borne by Japan. More alternatives for consumers mean lower prices and a higher standard of living. Blocking other nation's products lowers alternatives and raises prices, thereby lowering standard of living. Trade restrictions are like grudges: they feel like they are getting back at the other fellow, but they really do the most damage to ourselves. So, if Japan hurts Japan by blocking American products, do you think we should hurt ourselves by blocking Japanese products? If we match other nations' policies that go against economic freedom, we only match their foolishness."

"But," protested the same student, "what if every country in the world put tariffs on American products. Wouldn't we be bad off?"

"Well," said the professor, "that would indeed be unfortunate for America. But what would be far worse for America is if we retaliated by blocking everyone else. Even if every country in the world abandoned economic freedom, we as a nation would *still* be better off to open our economic borders to allow people to freely exchange with each other."

A student stood up. "You make politicians sound sinister when they talk about protecting American jobs. But you know what? We all know that unless the government steps in, corporations are going to send good, American jobs into third world countries. *We* lose good jobs while the people in those countries get totally exploited."

"Thank you. I could not have asked for a better transition into our next concept! In the year 1900, forty percent of America's workforce was farmers. But now, less than two percent are. Is that bad?"

The student sat down and shrugged in response to the professor's question.

"Well, those farmers who make up two percent of our workforce today are far more productive than the forty percent were back in 1900. And the same thing applies to manufacturing jobs. For many years now, the number of manufacturing jobs in America has dropped steadily. But our manufacturing output has grown. You see, in a flexible economy, the economy shifts toward better and better uses of its resources." The professor paused.

"To try to hold our economy in a way that keeps everyone who is working in farming or manufacturing in those respective fields would shackle and damage our economy. In America, newer and more valued jobs—such as jobs dealing with new technologies and services—will eventually replace the jobs that go overseas. Had the government 'protected' farming from market forces, we would have a lot more farmers today and they and the rest of us would all be worse off."

The confused expressions provided feedback to the professor. He thought for a moment. "Okay… try this analogy. Suppose the human body were to shut off its own waste system, so the materials the body would have gotten rid of will now stay inside the body. This would lead to the sickening and eventual death of the body. An economy is essentially a living thing. It needs flexibility to adapt and grow. An economy, if left free, will naturally take on new jobs and functions and cast off certain functions in a way that brings about peak efficiency and prosperity. This process is painful when it's your job that disappears. But people have the power to adapt, and entire societies benefit long-term when economies are flexible and free."

The professor continued. "And about those exploited workers in third world countries: if someone *voluntarily* takes a job, we can assume that that job is currently that worker's best alternative. The fact that some people take tough jobs tells you how restricted their alternatives are. I don't think they would consider it very charitable of us to go in and take away what is currently their best alternative. What they need is not for us to restrict trade and remove their best alternatives. What they need is more alternatives. Then, employers would have to compete for the best workers. And that competition—born from alternatives—would improve their situation.

"That brings us to a critical point. Economic freedom is the great cultivator and fertilizer of alternatives. Alternatives provide the upward thrust of our standard of living."

A student raised her hand. "Would you say that the role of the government is to create as many alternatives for the people as it can?"

"Be careful," said the professor. "When it comes to the economy, the government is *not* responsible for creating the alternatives. Governments often try and always fall short. The primary economic role of government is to cultivate a free environment where the rule of law is established and people can freely exchange with one another.

"Remember, *freedom* is the great cultivator and fertilizer of alternatives. With less freedom there are fewer alternatives in people's lives, thereby reducing their standard of living. Governments should espouse and maintain policies that allow people to voluntarily exchange in an environment of freedom, so long as their actions do not infringe on the natural rights of others. Alternatives and prosperity are natural results of free environments. Keeping people economically free is the primary economic goal of governments.

"To prosper as we should, we as a nation must now reverse the trade restrictions that are beginning to wreak terrible economic damage on this nation."

LECTURE 7: FOCUSED BENEFITS AND GENERALIZED COSTS

"This lecture is a continuation of our lecture on free trade and protectionism. In fact, it is within the concept of focused benefits and generalized costs that we begin to grasp how protectionism destroys economic freedom.

"Friedrich Hayek was once asked by Walter Williams what he would do to keep America free. His answer was that we should not allow congress to pass laws unless those laws benefit everyone in general. In other words, when you pass a law that is only beneficial to a small segment of society, freedom suffers.

"Once governments begin to let go of economic freedom, those governments tend to use their power to award benefits to small groups of citizens. This gifting of benefits to small groups is a burden on society. One little group gets the benefit, and the entire nation bears the cost. But group after group gets focused benefits, and the spread out costs add up. Government power increases while economic freedom decreases by degrees in the process.

"In the months since the bombings, we tried to discover which government actions in the past five to ten years were perpetrated by The Thread. This lecture stems from that analysis. Sadly, America has used focused benefits and generalized costs so extensively the past one hundred years that The Thread simply blended right in. This tragedy will not end until America wakes up to what is happening and how it threatens economic freedom.

"Focused benefits with generalized costs are a two-edged sword against freedom—they open up programs that create votes for leaders while creating dependency for the recipients of the program. Both effects increase the power of government over citizens.

"People don't easily let go of programs that are to their personal advantage. Like a person addicted to drugs, we become economically addicted to government's gifts that benefit ourselves. Although we may not like all the pork and spending coming from Washington, we all tend to line up with our own hands stretched out, begging for our fair share.

"Think of it this way. Let's pretend I am a political leader. Your little group has a lot of power and money. You give me money, and I pass laws or policies that benefit your little group—sort of a quid pro quo special favor. The people in America pay for it, but they let it happen because the burden is so spread out that they don't notice or don't care enough to resist.

"This happens all through our government. Let me begin with the example of sugar. For many, many years now, Americans have paid about three times the world price for sugar. Three times the world price! And most Americans have had no clue that they were paying so much for sugar. How can that happen? It's because of focused benefits and generalized costs.

"Here's how it works: there are a few thousand jobs in the sugar industry in America—most of them in Florida. For various reasons, America's sugar industry failed to produce sugar as efficiently as the world's sugar industry. So, rather than respond with more efficiency, the sugar industry approached law makers and persuaded them to block foreign sugar.

"By putting tariffs on cheap sugar from Mexico and other places, we have raised the price of foreign sugar to match the price of the inefficiently produced American sugar. This way, the American sugar industry is *protected* from competition and goes on inefficiently."

A student raised her hand. "Why does the government do this if it's so dumb?"

"Well," said Dr. Isaacson, "I'm sure the sugar industry pumps plenty of money into Washington. As a result, Washington maintains the tariffs on Mexican sugar." Hands shot up across the auditorium.

"But what if America's sugar is a better quality than foreign sugar?" asked a student.

"It isn't," was all Dr. Isaacson said before selecting another hand.

"Doesn't this protect good American jobs?"

"Nope," said Dr. Isaacson without hesitation.

"How can you claim that?" asked the same student.

"Well, think it through," said Dr. Isaacson. "Who buys sugar?"

"Everyone in America," said the student loudly.

"Right. And the average American home back in 2007 paid approximately twenty-one additional dollars each year for the extra cost in sugar."

A subtle rumble of person-to person communication came and went as Dr. Isaacson let the statistic settle in. He continued.

"So we all pay a price. But *individuals* are not the only ones who purchase sugar in America. The candy industry, the soft drink industry, and many more. All these industries use sugar as a major material for production. If the cost of sugar is illegitimately high, they have to pay more for their supplies. The result is less money to grow and pay employees. The price paid by society far outweighs the benefits channeled into the sugar industry. *The result of saving a few jobs through government protection will always be a loss of more jobs throughout the economy than were saved.*

"Such protectionism is a foolish practice that politicians sell with emotional power and feigned compassion. Those politicians act like their protectionism saves people's jobs by restricting greedy executives that would send those jobs away from America. But economists have concluded that for every job saved by protectionism, three jobs will be lost. Keeping things free and preserving those three unnoticed jobs does very little to bring in votes for politicians.

"And again," said Dr. Isaacson, "it all begins when governments allow themselves to grant government money or power to the benefit of specific groups in ways that do not bless the people generally. The beneficiaries of these policies are motivated to pour money into Congress because they receive extraordinary remuneration from these policies. Getting rid of such programs may be great for the body as a whole, but the pain and screaming from the beneficiaries make surgery unlikely. As I mentioned in a previous lecture, it's better to suffer and die slowly than to endure the intense pain of surgery, so it seems."

The professor clicked the front bank of lights off as a quote filled the screen.

"Okay. Here is a quote you might be interested in. I don't think we really know who said it for sure. It has passed around the internet for many years. Many speakers attribute it to Alexander Frazer Tytler. As far as I know, we haven't been able to verify that. Regardless of who said it, it contains a profound message.

"'A democracy cannot exist as a permanent form of government. It can only exist until the voters discover that they can vote themselves largesse from the public treasury.'

"Largess," interrupted Dr. Isaacson, "means money, funds, treasure, gifts, that sort of thing. In this case, it means public, government-controlled money. A democracy is in danger when the people realize they can vote money back to themselves. I continue: 'From that moment on, the majority always votes for the candidates promising the most benefits from the public treasury with the result that a democracy always collapses over loose fiscal policy, always followed by a dictatorship.' To clarify—fiscal policy means taxing and spending. Loose fiscal policy means lots of careless spending.

"Here is a second quote, often connected with the previous one. 'Great nations rise and fall. The people go from bondage to spiritual truth, to great courage, from courage to liberty, from liberty to abundance, from abundance to selfishness, from selfishness to complacency, from complacency to apathy, from apathy to dependence, from dependence back again to bondage.'

"This is what is happening in America. We send enormous amounts of money to the federal government. Special interests clamor for that money. They pay politicians. Government leaders dole out the money to whatever sources will help them as leaders increase in power. The people bear the burden, and we lose freedom. Meanwhile, the leaders of our government and their preferred special interests benefit at our expense. And since The Thread has infiltrated government, the engines of such spending have gone into overdrive."

"So what programs do we cut?" asked a student from the wings of the auditorium. "There are so many government programs now. Which ones do we cut?"

Dr. Isaacson's answer was instant. "I would begin with the programs that do not benefit society as a whole. If we design a law to benefit someone, it must benefit everyone. That would have a profound effect on freedom. No more bailing out certain corporations, or subsidizing individuals or industries. We must eliminate focused benefits that dump costs among the people. We gripe about interest groups, but they are a natural result of a system of generalized costs and focused benefits. Where there is money to hand out, there will be hands out for the money.

"In summary, focused benefits and the redistribution of wealth is a powerful monster that feeds off people's self-interest, devours freedom, and leaves dependency in its wake. These programs persist because funds that flow from special interests shout so loudly in the ears of politicians that they cannot hear the groans from the masses that bear the costs."

LECTURE 8: LICENSING AND REGULATION

"Many people believe business leaders are pro-freedom because those business leaders are reaping the rewards of capitalism. In reality, the business and corporate world is not as interested in freedom as it is in its own gain. This leads us into the heart of today's lecture.

"Businesses and industries fight hard for profits. That is a wonderful fight, and it does much to raise our standard of living. Competition brings better service, quality, and lower prices to customers over time. While competition blesses society, industries are not so fond of it. Like us, businesses and corporations want the most benefit from the least effort. Competing takes effort. Hence, the self interest of industries leads them to try to restrict and eliminate competition.

"When someone finds something people really value and they begin making money on it, others will want to join the party so they can also profit. These new entrants often take market share and pull down profits of existing firms. Existing firms and participants, therefore, don't like competition.

"Now, as long as businesses are beating their competition by winning the customers' business, the competition will benefit society. But what happens is that industries try to eliminate entrants into their industries through *tapping into government power.*

"Here's how it happens. An industry usually cannot convince the government to pass a law allowing 'only one company in this industry per city.' But what industries get governments to do all the time is to pass laws making it necessary to have a license to join an industry. And then they make it as costly as they can to obtain that license.

"Most industries do this in some form or another. Some industries may have a legitimate safety-based reason. I think the best example of that is the medical field. We want to know that the man about to perform surgery on our brain is qualified. So we don't mind the licensing issue for doctors, and we pay the price accordingly. But even there, some of the motivation for medical licensing is based on blocking entrants rather than ensuring the safety of patients and the qualifications of doctors. Most industries rationalize their licensing procedures with the government under the auspices of safety and public well-being. There are ways to ensure safety that do not block entrants.

"If you wish to drive a cab in New York City, you must procure a license that does very little to make the people more safe. But to get that license, you must pay well over a half a million dollars! Current cab drivers have gotten their hands into city laws requiring new entrants to pay an enormous sum of money if they wish to participate. By so doing, many would-be-entrants cannot play the game. They must find a less-appealing method of providing. Meanwhile, customers pay more for cabs. Current cab drivers and politicians benefit, would-be cab drivers and customers lose. It is an unethical, private exchange at the public's expense."

The auditorium had been buzzing from the moment Dr. Isaacson had mentioned the cost of a New York City taxi cab license.

"I'm going to talk about licensing's twin sister: regulation. There is a massive revolving door between industry leaders and the government administrators who regulate those industries. In other words, the people who run the regulated industry and the people who run the regulating government agency are often the same people. Can you see a problem with that?"

"In all fairness, Dr. Isaacson," said a student, "those people are often the most knowledgeable and highly qualified people to do both."

"Yes. Fair enough. There is nothing necessarily wrong with the employment arrangement there. The issue is simply the fact that the regulated industry is not so much being regulated as much as it is doing the regulation—through the government—against entrants into their industry. A good example here is the TSA—the Transportation Safety Administration. The government designed it to regulate the railroad industry—to keep it safe! Well, as always seems to occur, the TSA administrators intertwined with leaders in the railroad industry. They effectively made things for new entrants into the industry extremely difficult. But, eventually a new competitor comes along: trucks. You can imagine what response the TSA had toward a new, competing industry."

Dr. Isaacson paused and scanned the auditorium. "It's not that hard to predict now, is it? The TSA tried to restrict the activity of the new trucking industry. But, in time, the market helped truckers win, so the TSA broadened its protective cloak and began protecting the trucking industry as well.

"Go and search government licensing policies and laws. You will have an eye-opening experience as you see how many industries seek to tap into government power, under the banner of safety, to increase their profits.

"The most common and entrenched monopolies in America tend to be monopolies created and supported by government power. What governments seek to accomplish through licensing could be done better in the market through registration, certification, or mere market forces. For industries where safety is critical, private certification firms would naturally arise and provide reviewing, rating, screening, comparing, and other services. But the private firms would be much less susceptible to corruption because they do not have the power to enforce government monopolies like government regulators can.

"Now, to conclude, we know The Thread has been around for ten years, but their influence in government policy has been a phenomenon of the last five years. Can you guess what has happened in regards to licensing policies throughout the nation these last few years?" Dr. Isaacson waited, allowing time for personal conclusions.

"Through grants and legislation, the ratchet of licensing has gone from mildly oppressive to extreme in the last three years. What Americans could do freely just a few years ago now takes excessive money and hoopla with government agencies. The Thread has affected these changes in preparation for taking us over the edge of totalitarianism. I only hope that America has the political and moral courage to break these chains and restore economic freedom."

LECTURE 9: INCOME MOBILITY AND UNIONS

"We will discuss two topics today. These two topics are quite separate. First, we will talk about income disparity in economically free societies, then we will talk about The Thread's push for unionization."

Dr. Isaacson projected a slide. "This chart compares the world's most economically free nations with the most prosperous. As you see, the correlation is remarkable. The world's most economically free societies are the world's most prosperous societies. The implications are crucial. The amazing thing is how many nations continue to pull away from economic freedom—including the United States—despite the clear relationship between economic freedom and prosperity.

"But critics often point out that in prosperous, economically free nations, there is a large gap in income. Some people earn so much more than everyone else. Many find this offensive.

"Politicians are eager to pontificate about the gap in incomes as if it is a static thing. They portray America as a land that has a rich class that rules the nation from generation to generation. They also want us to believe that America has a poor class that goes on in grinding poverty from generation to generation. They wish to show that this is a land of inequality, and that things unjustly stay as they are. In other words, they hope to paint a picture of an America that has very little to no income mobility.

"All such talk is designed toward one purpose: the removal of economic freedom and the expansion of government power. Politicians who intend to preserve economic freedom do not play the inequality power card. But for those politicians who do, there is always a problem in your life, and the government will solve it for you.

"But what is left out of the equation is this: *when governments destroy economic freedom to bring about economic equality, the ordinary person will be economically worse off.*

"The best way to see this is to look at those countries that have tried to level the playing field—countries that have sacrificed economic freedom to have more economic equality. Those societies became very *unequal*. Those citizens with government connections become the elite class. Everyone else experience what Americans would consider poverty, or near-poverty conditions. The outcome is always predictable. The result is that the average person is far worse off in economically restrained systems than they are in systems of economic freedom. Those nations sought for equality at the expense of freedom, and ended up unfree *and* unequal."

A student could see a hole in Dr. Isaacson's logic. "How can you say there isn't a big problem with inequality in America? I mean, hasn't America led the world in the gap between the rich and the poor?"

"What America has," said Dr. Isaacson, "is a great income disparity—or a large gap in incomes. What we don't have is a rich and poor *class*."

"How can you say that?" asked a student.

"Listen to the facts about America's income mobility. When most people set out for college, or begin a trade, they don't have much wealth at all. Let's say they get married. They usually start with very little means. As the years go by, most people accumulate wealth. They don't live like their parents *do*, but they are likely to soon live better than their parents *did*. By the time they retire, they are part of—on average—the wealthiest class of citizens in the nation, and even the history of the world."

He continued with his point. "We tend to grow in wealth as we age in America. The wealthy are not a set class that transfers wealth from generation to generation. The bulk of America's wealthy did not inherit their wealth. Most of the wealthy have *earned* their wealth during their lifetime. Likewise, the poor in America are not really a class that transfers poverty from one generation to the next. The closest thing we have in America to that is the transfer of broken families from one generation to the next—and that will effectually pass on poverty. The great irony here is that the bulk of the truly poor *class* in America has been created, arguably, by welfare. It is apparent that government-based welfare does less to attack poverty and more to create it.

"Many people bemoan that the rich keep getting richer while the poor keep getting poorer. Well, the first half is true. The rich do become richer. But the poor don't become poorer in America. The gap between the rich and the poor tends to widen over time. But it's not because the poor are getting poorer. Rather, it's because the rich are increasing in wealth at higher rates than the poor are. But that inequality is a problem that only consecration can solve. Any other attempt—such as using the government to forcefully level the playing field—will have disastrous consequences that are worse than the inequality that you are trying to fix.

"Let me point out some other fascinating facts about America's wealth and income mobility. If you look at America during a twenty-five year period, you'd learn some eye-opening things about incomes in a free land. For example, you'd see that *more than half* of Americans who start in the *bottom* twenty percentile of income at the beginning of the twenty-five years would make it to the *richest* twenty percentile sometime during those years. And that is remarkable. Not many Americans who start in the top twenty-percent of income will stay there for the entire time. Americans move up and down in their incomes, but generally up. The Americans who stay in the bottom twenty percentile the whole twenty-five year period make up about one percent of America—hardly a group large enough to consider a major class. Take away government welfare and it would be interesting to see what would happen to that one percent.

"And let me just conclude the discussion on income disparity with this warning: Politicians who seek to use economic equality as political bait often will likewise appeal to the worst sides of human nature. They will use enmity, hatred, and jealousy to garnish political power. For such politicians, mantras about greed, oppression from the rich, and disparity become fuel for their missiles targeted at gaining power and destroying economic freedom."

A student toward the front stood up, hand raised high in the air. Dr. Isaacson acknowledged her. "Throughout these lectures, you've warned us about inequality. You've talked about the Constitution and the Founding Fathers. But what if their way isn't the best way to do things? What if modern times and a maturing country could and should have their government do more for the people? What if the Constitution—at least the way they formed it—no longer meets our needs? What if the federal government *should* do more than the Constitution prescribes?"

"Well," said Dr. Isaacson, "you have boiled the issue down to the crux of the matter. I say we make a decision as a nation. Either the Founders' inspiration on economic freedom is still right, and the document they created is still inspired and best in its approach to government, or it is not. Either we espouse the Constitution, or we forsake it for socialism of some form. But if we choose socialism, we must let go of the Constitution. The two are not compatible. And if we take on socialism, we should write a Declaration of *Dependence* announcing to the world that America is now abandoning the foundation of economic freedom and self reliance upheld by the Constitution.

"But I, for one, believe with all my heart that the Constitution is *still* inspired and holds the keys to our continued freedom. You ask if the Constitutional approach is not fit for our modern times. The Constitution is designed to meet the needs of a changing world. But I do not buy for a second the notion that *freedom*, as the Founders set up in the Constitution, is not sufficient for today's needs. I cannot accept that. I am saddened that socialism and other philosophies have chipped away at the

Constitution. We must uphold the Constitution, for it is now in great danger.

"And with that, let us discuss our second topic: unions.

"The Thread's plan included a push for as much unionization as possible. Are unions evil? In economically free societies, there is nothing wrong with people uniting based on common causes and interests. Why would The Thread push for heavy unionizations?

"The answer is simple. When *governments* combine with unions and use laws to give undue power to unions, the government gains a dominant economic grip over the nation's private economic resources.

"An example of such laws is when government mandates that businesses cannot replace workers who are on strike. The First Presidency even released a public statement many years ago decrying such laws as immoral.

"So, if unions form, and people exert their united influence toward bargaining power, nothing is wrong. But, when governments pass laws that enable those unions to operate in ways that violate the economic freedom of others, injustice festers and prosperity suffers. So, unions are certainly not inherently evil. The problem is that unions turn to politicians and offer political benefits in exchange for greater power.

"The Thread has helped create a few recent laws that give phenomenal power to unions. Such laws, if not repealed, will devastate America's economy in the years to come because we will be far too rigid to adjust to economic needs.

"Let me give you an example. Voting on whether to unionize or not, within a company, used to be by private ballot. But the law now requires that companies file ballots and later give them to the union. Hence, new unions always know which employees voted for and which employees voted against the union.

"Another example is the one I mentioned earlier about not allowing companies to replace workers who are on strike. Such laws give extraordinary power to unions—power that markets would never grant and that will serve to abuse far more people in our nation than those laws could begin to help. And there are other laws. Go and learn about them.

"Now, although the concept of unions—without government force—is not *evil* in the least, massive unionization of our economy would be a very *foolish* thing. Here's another example of when unions can be foolish. Many years ago, the coal workers' union colluded and formed, essentially, an industry-wide, national union. In other words, if you worked in West Virginia for a coal mine, you were part of the same union as someone working in an Ohio coal mine. This meant that companies could not fire workers who demanded more pay from their current workforce and replace them with experienced coal miners from another mine because all those workers were part of the same union.

"This united effort of the workers successfully drove up wages. That sounds wonderful until you see the outcome. Union influence drove up the price of coal until it was sufficiently higher than the price of other sources of fuel that the coal industry as a whole plummeted. People chose other fuel alternatives. A huge portion of those workers being protected by their union were now unemployed. Through high wages, unions forced the coal companies into inefficiencies that killed much of the industry. So, the workers those unions represented were given artificially high wages in the short term, and a loss of their jobs in the long term. But the brunt of the damage was on consumers. Their standard of living lowered because prices rose. And we are *all* consumers.

"A more recent example is America's automobile industry. The heavy unionization they experienced made it difficult for companies to compete in the world markets—and an entire national industry struggled because of it.

"In the short term, unions can do a lot of good for union members. Again, I have nothing against combining forces with people who have similar interests. But, in the long term, unions may not benefit employees as much as we might think. Society as a whole would have benefited more from the open competition of unrestrained economic freedom than it did from the efforts of the unions intermingling with government."

LECTURE 10: PRICE CONTROLS

"The concept of price is at the heart of economic freedom. Price is sacred because it touches that holy realm of human existence that we call moral agency.

"People use choices to maximize their happiness. We base our choices on knowledge. The better our knowledge, the more capable we are of making choices that bring happiness. And prices provide the knowledge we need to make economic choices. Price is therefore fundamental to our pursuit of happiness.

"Prices are the sum of human wisdom and circumstances. When societies are economically free, prices work miracles and coordinate human choice and activity toward the best, most efficient ways.

"If I am a farmer, and wish to provide for my family, prices tell me what to produce. Prices punish inefficiency and waste and reward production. They are the fairest judge and smartest consultant. Prices provide information to everyone in the market so they can make the best decision as individuals based on the wants and needs of all of society.

"When governments mess with prices, they pit their limited, vain minds against the omniscience of the masses. No committee or bureaucracy, regardless of how intelligent its members are, can compete with the genius of the collective people.

"In an effort to destroy economic freedom, The Thread has sought to bring about as many government price controls as they could enact.

"One example is the oil industry. The lines at gasoline stations are the result of price caps on petroleum.

"Another example is controlling rent. Few cities used rent controls before The Thread infiltrated the government. But beginning two years ago, the federal government began offering grants to those cities which 'promoted fairness in housing' through ensuring 'affordable' rents for low-income families. City after city has abandoned wisdom and economic freedom by implementing destructive rent controls just so they can claim the federal grant funds.

"Rent controls put a cap on how much landlords can charge for rent. That might sound good to those of you in apartments, but think it through. If the city comes in and sets a price cap that is lower than what the current market price is, what do you see happening?"

A student answered. "People pay less money for their apartment, and landlords get less filthy profits."

The professor warned, "Be careful. If someone wants to destroy economic freedom, one of the most important things they have to do is convince society that profits are evil—and that pursuing higher profits is a wicked motive. Once people believe that, it becomes very easy to remove their economic freedom. But know this: although it does bring out the full range in human motivations and behaviors, the pursuit of profit has done far more good for mankind than the benevolent efforts of governments. Profits reflect work, creativity, efficiency, and production. If you make profit evil, you then make many good things evil.

"If less profit in the hands of landlords was the only result of rent controls, then rent controls might increase our standard of living and could be a great thing. But the effect rolls on far beyond that first result.

"Rent controls sound as if they support the poor; and politicians who oppose them come off sounding heartless. But let's analyze what rent controls really do.

"Let's pretend you and two roommates shared a three bedroom apartment for $1,200 per month. And let's say Provo

City ordered rent controls that lowered your rent to *$600*. At first this sounds good. But apartments down the street—much larger and much nicer—that used to be $2,000 are now just *$1,200*. Can you see you now have an alternative? You can stay where you are and save $200 per person each month, or you can have a much nicer place for the same price you have been paying in the past.

"Can you see that some may stay and save money, but many will also wish to improve their situation by moving to a nicer place? What you're going to have is a massive swelling in the desire among the people for larger and nicer housing. The family renting a small apartment will want the now-affordable large apartment. People will want and pursue housing that was previously not even an option.

"Now, all this wanting is exciting. It may seem like life is improving because everyone can now afford better housing. But it is as substantial as cotton candy. It is a facade. You see, there is still the same limited number of housing units as before. There is still the same scarcity. But *before, price did the rationing*. If many people wanted to be in a certain apartment, the price of that apartment would rise until just the right amount of people still valued the apartment. Free markets ration through price. Price rises or falls until buyers and sellers agree, and the resource is used to the maximum.

"But if you mess with price, it fails to ration properly. And here is the kicker: because there is still a scarcity, you still have to ration the apartments somehow. Over time, price is by far the most consistent, fair, and efficient method of rationing for most things.

"If you don't let price ration things, the most common form of rationing is through waiting lists. You can also ration through the lottery method. And what often happens in these situations is nepotism—those with connections get benefits. But choosing anything other than price is usually going to be wasteful and—ironically—less fair than price.

"When you force prices below what the market is willing to pay (price caps), you get shortages. When governments keep prices low, more people want something. But that something remains scarce. Waiting lists develop, and people undergo the frustrations of wanting something that seems affordable, only to have it rationed out by some other frustrating method.

"Now, let me give you an actual scenario. In Sweden, many years ago, they initiated government mandated rent controls. These rent controls were something like what The Thread has recently pushed through in America. Can you predict what happened?

"If you guessed waiting lists, you guessed correctly. Sweden's demand for larger and better housing skyrocketed. Waiting lists formed. Sweden tried to alleviate the waiting list problem by building more housing. In fact, they began a building project that set up Sweden as the greatest housing constructor in the world. But, even with the phenomenal growth rate of new housing over the next couple of years, the waiting lists grew faster than the housing availability did!"

A student asked, "So, if you want the nicer housing, you pay for it by waiting, right?"

"Good question," said Dr. Isaacson, "but no, that is only a part of it. The costs of rent control go far beyond waiting lists. We've been talking about how rent controls affect renters. But what about how rent controls affect those who invest and manage housing: the landlords.

"Landlords work in a competitive market too. They have to compete well to earn a living. Now, if the government comes in and pushes rents below market value, what is going to happen to the value of rental property? How motivated will landlords be to maintain their apartments and serve the needs of customers from whom they cannot profit? If you remove the profit incentive, so much collapses.

"Many of you have had a difficult time getting your landlords to respond this year, haven't you?" Sounds of collective assent filled the auditorium. "Can you now see why? When governments control rent, they destroy landlords' motivation to maintain property. Slums are not a market result. Slums are often a government assistance result. 'Affordable housing' often means *deteriorating* housing. One communist economist stated that if you wish to destroy a city, you can either bomb it, or you can initiate rent controls. If you bomb it, you destroy it suddenly, but it will rebuild quickly—perhaps to a better state than it was before the bombing. But if you initiate rent controls, the destruction is slow, but lingers as long as the controls.

"If you wish to delve deeper into the Sweden housing issue and rent controls, I recommend Thomas Sowell's *Basic Economics*.

"Another form of price control that America has used for a long time is subsidies. With subsidies, governments intentionally manipulate prices to bring about more or less of something than what the market would naturally produce. Subsidies create inefficiencies. Also, people who receive subsidies often become dependent upon them. Our government has been subsidizing agriculture for a long time. When Ezra Taft Benson was Secretary of Agriculture, he tried to get rid of much of the subsidy system. He met great opposition. In response, he said, 'No true American wants to be subsidized.' He took a lot of grief for that, but I agree. He was right economically, and therefore right with freedom.

"Another foolish price control that recently passed is the restriction on how much money pharmaceutical companies can charge for pills. The government now forces companies to set prices based on production cost plus a set percentage of profit. Now, I understand that high pharmaceutical prices trouble many people. However, controlling the price of medicine is going save a few dollars for people now, but is going to kill millions of people down the road.

"Think of it like the famous story of the artist. An artist painted in about an hour a portrait of a tourist in New York City. The painting was completed, and the man—pleased with the result—asked how much his portrait would cost. The artist responded that the price would be a hundred dollars. Wanting to barter, the man said to the artist, 'That's a lot of money for just one hour of your time.' To which the artist responded, 'Oh, you are mistaken. This painting has taken twenty-eight years to develop.' The artist was not charging for his effort on that single painting. He had developed his skills over a lifetime. If the artist could only charge an amount based on physical effort and one hour of labor, how motivated would he be to develop his talent?

"When you buy a pill at the pharmacy, you are paying not only for the physical production of the pill, but you are also paying for the research and development that went into that pill. And that price enables the company to continue to research and develop new drugs that will benefit the next generation. If you cut off the price, you cut off the future drugs. Is that a fair exchange?

"Many countries have long placed restrictions on pharmaceutical prices. Obviously their citizens have paid less for drugs since those countries instituted those price caps. But those countries have not produced many new drugs.

"America for a long time has led the world in the production of new medicines. This production comes down to one thing: economic freedom.

"Now, let's talk about minimum wage. You may not think of minimum wages as a price control, but that is exactly what it is. You see, employment is a voluntary exchange. Employers and employees come together—one offering services while the other offers money and benefits. If workers and employers are economically free, the two parties set the price of the exchange. But when government steps into the private exchange and mandates minimum wages, we have a price control.

"When there is a minimum wage, the two parties may not be free to agree on a wage because the government may force the wage to be higher than what they would have agreed to. They are not economically free. This may sound good for the poor, but don't be fooled.

"*Minimum wages are destructive to the poor—especially the poorest and least skilled.*" This claim sent a buzz throughout the auditorium. Dr. Isaacson confronted it. "First of all, let's say Experienced Emily earns fifteen dollars an hour as a security guard, and has a degree and five years of experience. Now, let's say that New Nathan joins the company. He is still going to school. He is just learning the ropes. He is hired at the minimum wage—which, let's say, is nine dollars. Now, pretend the government increases the minimum wage to fifteen dollars an hour. Both Emily and Nathan should be paid fifteen dollars an hour, right?"

"No way," said a student. "Emily is worth more as an employee."

"Right," agreed Dr. Isaacson, "so what is she going to do about the situation?"

"They will either increase her wage a similar percentage, or she's going to go work somewhere that pays people what they're worth."

"Now," Dr. Isaacson built off the student's comment, "that is exactly what is going to occur everywhere. In the very short term, some people will earn more with a minimum wage. But wages will ripple up, nullifying the benefit to the lowest wage earners.

"But that only explains why minimum wages won't do much good over time. It does not explain how minimum wages do harm to the poor," said Dr. Isaacson, as if pulling out a trump card and making ready to reveal it.

"Consider this: let's say that Bob owns a small business. Now, let's say that Doug is an untrained, high school drop-out who has been living on the street. Doug the drop-out turns his life around, gets married, has a child, and now longs to provide for his little family. He has no education and no skills. He looks at the job possibilities and remembers an acquaintance—Bob the businessman. Let's say that Doug, with hard work, can offer Bob about *seven* dollars worth of production per hour in Bob's business. Now, if the minimum wage were *nine* dollars an hour, is it worth it for Bob to hire Doug?"

A quiet murmur of the word *no* rumbled throughout the auditorium.

"Why not?" asked Dr. Isaacson before calling on a student.

"Well, if Bob hires Doug at nine dollars an hour, and Doug produces seven dollars of stuff an hour, Bob loses money. There's no way he is going to hire him," answered the student.

"That's right," said Dr. Isaacson. "So, Bob would be willing to hire Doug at a wage that benefits *both* parties. But Bob is not willing to hire Doug when the government *compels* Bob to pay Doug a wage that is higher than what Doug can produce for him. So, you now should be able to tell me what happens to the poorest, most unskilled workers when the minimum wage goes up."

A student answered. "They won't get jobs."

"Correct. They won't get jobs. Politicians market minimum wages with the sheep's clothing of being a boon to the poor. But minimum wage is a bane to the unskilled poor. There is always a spike in unemployment among unskilled workers whenever minimum wages go up. Such increases are like wolves. Minimum wages even have racial implications as well, since those hardest hit by minimum wages tend to be young, unskilled black workers. These are workers whose best avenue out of poverty may well be skills learned from working on the job. There are many who cannot get jobs but would gladly work at wages below the minimum wage. They could gain skills, begin earning money, and move up the income scale over time. But the government, in feigned compassion, forces wages beyond the capacity of the unskilled.

"So, what would you rather face if you were a low skilled worker: a job starting at six dollars an hour, or a minimum wage job that offers nine dollars an hour at which nobody is willing to hire you? Low wage or no wage: which is a better option? Letting people choose is the best long-term elixir for poverty.

"We had the biggest minimum wage increase in history just two years ago; and that rise in minimum wage was passed with a built-in yearly index to help the minimum wage keep pace with inflation. The problems created by a minimum wage will be with us every year. The Congressional leaders we know were in The Thread were major proponents of this legislation.

"And limiting how *little* you are allowed to accept or pay in jobs is not the only hot topic that affects economic freedom when it comes to wages. Economic freedom is also assaulted when the government limits how *much* you are allowed to accept or pay."

"Executive wage caps," said a student.

"Yes," nodded Dr. Isaacson.

"Don't tell me you're for CEOs earning bazillions more than other employees in a company," said another student.

"Well," defended Dr. Isaacson, "income disparity within a company can be terribly foolish, but what I am certain of is that the government has no right telling people at what price they can voluntarily exchange. People are offended by high executive salaries, especially when those executives fail or are bought out of their contracts. But if a company believes that hiring one person over another as the CEO can have an impact of multiple billions of dollars to the corporation, can you blame that corporation for offering multiple millions of dollars to attract that person? And if a high-paid CEO proves likely to lose *billions* of dollars, does it not seem in that corporation's best interest to buy that CEO out of his or her contract for *millions* of dollars?

"If you limit executive salaries, won't corporations find other means of compensation to attract the best executives? If a corporation hires a CEO who turns out to be a disaster, don't you think the market will do well to address the issue? Economic freedom calls for companies to be free to choose how much they will pay *all* their employees.

"Remember: there is a difference between actions that are *wrong* and actions that are *foolish*. We should punish wrongness according to the law. But market justice deals with economically *foolish* behavior with far more effectiveness than government justice can."

The auditorium was quiet. The professor made a final transition. "The last price control we discuss today is one that was once very unpopular, but after some close calls, it has now become quite fashionable in America—largely due to the workings of The Thread in the last few years. I am alluding to universal medicine.

"Now, the system our nation has worked out these last few years, culminating in the most recent version of this past year, is not a completely universalized medical system, but it is nearly so. It is essentially the same thing.

"Let's talk briefly about universal medicine. Government-run health care systems are, in reality, massive price controls. In short, universalized medicine will bring with it the same old problems associated with all price caps: waiting lists, deterioration of assets, lack of proper investment, and disappointment from the masses who expected the golden egg. You cannot get something for nothing, not even in health care.

"If the government pushes to run things with as much quality and efficiency as the market, you end up with a full-blown monopoly. Because of a lack of market competition, prices will balloon and the public will bear enormous tax burdens. If the government chooses to cut costs, then quality, availability, and so much more go out the window. And beware of any government program that garners popular support because most people coming in anticipate getting more out of the program than what they put in. There is no free lunch. Either those people will be disappointed with the service or they will find the price tag much higher than they anticipated.

"Unfortunately, universal health care is here. And now that we have socialized medicine, I suppose we will not do away with it until the inefficiencies that come from a lack of freedom wear us down as a people.

"And although The Thread—who did so much to push these things through—has been discovered, I suppose that mustering the political will to renew economic freedom in our nation is going to be a tough, long battle. If only we understood these things as a people before we found ourselves in such a situation. May God bless America to arise from the dust and shake off these oppressive chains and to 'stand fast in the liberty wherewith we have been made free.'"

ABOUT THE AUTHOR

Donny Anderson is a religious educator and teaches in northern Utah. He and his wife, Mollie, and their five children live in Millville, Utah. Donny earned a Bachelor's Degree in Business at Brigham Young University and a Masters in Social Science with an emphasis in Public Administration from Utah State University.

Donny loves to teach. He is currently working on a three-novel series he hopes will capture the full splendor of the Law of Consecration, and will compare capitalism, communism, and the Law of Consecration in action. The first volume, *One: Division of the Indivisible* will be released in 2011.

IF YOU WANT TO KNOW MORE ABOUT THIS BOOK VISIT...

The author's website at **donaldbanderson.com**
This book's website at **hangingbythethread.com**
Donny's blog at **donaldbanderson.blogspot.com**
The publisher's website at **granitebooks.com**